THE TAKING MEN

*

'Nobody but a fool,' said the elder Miss Delaine, 'would think a girl of nineteen with no experience of *any* kind, brought up as a lady, could keep a village shop.'

But Priscilla wasn't a fool, and she *did* think that she could. It had been left to her by her sensible Border Scottish aunt Jane. One thing her aunt had determined on above all else: the Maitland family would never get the shop. The Maitlands, descendants of the old border reivers, the Taking Men as they were called, inheritors of the old instincts but devious in the new commercial ways.

And when Priscilla impulsively decided to defy her aunts and leave their home for the strange world of the little village, she began to realise the awful difficulties that lay ahead of her and knew that she would be very dependent on the help and goodwill of the villagers. And the first person to help her, dour and uncompromising though he was, was a Maitland. And a Maitland never helped anyone without wanting something in return.

Also in Arrow Books by Anne Hepple

Evening at the Farm
The House of Gow
The Old Woman Speaks

Anne Hepple

The Taking Men

ARROW BOOKS

ARROW BOOKS LTD
3 Fitzroy Square, London W1

AN IMPRINT OF THE  HUTCHINSON GROUP

London Melbourne Sydney Auckland
Wellington Johannesburg Cape Town
and agencies throughout the world

✳

First published by
George G. Harrap & Co. Ltd 1940
Arrow edition 1965
This new edition 1972

*Made and printed in Great Britain
by The Anchor Press Ltd.,
Tiptree, Essex*
ISBN 0 09 906310 7

1

The Aunts

'A shop!' exclaimed the tall Miss Delaine.

'A shop!' echoed the stout Miss Delaine.

Then they both said:

'Don't be ridiculous, Priscilla!'

'But I like shops,' said Priscilla meekly; then she sighed, 'I expect it's the Purdie in me.'

This was the reproach with which all her sins had been met since she was five.

'Don't be impertinent, Priscilla,' said both her aunts together.

'And it's my shop; the lawyer says so,' Priscilla persisted.

'Then you will sell it,' said Aunt Maud (the tall one), 'and bank the proceeds. It will be a nice marriage portion for you.'

'But Aunt Purdie says I can only have it if I keep it. I know it sounds nonsense, but sense often does, and it's true. I can only *have* the shop if I *keep* the shop. Sell the things in it myself and run it. My aunt says so, in her letter.'

'One does not like to speak ill of the dead,' said Aunt Flora, 'but, besides being an ignorant, vulgar country woman with neither refinement nor education, your aunt seems to have been quite mad.'

'Totally incomprehensible,' said Aunt Maud. 'Her mind must have been afflicted towards the end.'

'The lawyer doesn't seem to think so,' said Priscilla, 'and he seems a very serious man.'

'Nobody but a fool,' said the elder Miss Delaine, 'would think a young girl of nineteen with no experience of *any* kind, brought up as a lady, could keep a village shop. The thing's absurd—too utterly fantastic for discussion. I will not listen to another word on the subject.'

She took up her knitting and began to knit with a vigorous clicking.

'If I'm old enough to be married I'm old enough to keep a shop—and you wanted me to marry old Mr Porter,' said Priscilla mildly.

'That is quite beside the question. Old Mr Porter, as you call him, is barely forty-two years old. It would have been a very advantageous match, with good settlements. To compare it with this wild-cat scheme is simply childish, undignified nonsense,' said Aunt Flora.

'But I like a shop better than I like Mr Porter,' said Priscilla.

At this shocking and irreverent announcement both aunts laid down their work and gazed at their niece as if they thought she had completely taken leave of her wits. They often gazed at Priscilla like that. She had a habit of coming out with simple statements that made them wonder if she was quite—well, quite . . . They left it at that.

The remark was, however, altogether too much for Aunt Maud, who had declared she did not want to hear another word on the subject. She opened her mouth for a lecture, when Priscilla, seeing what was coming, hastily forestalled her.

'You said I was to read you the letters,' she reminded her. 'Do you not want to hear them now?'

They were both dying to hear the letters that had come for Priscilla by the afternoon post. They could scarcely believe what she had said about their contents, and had immediately wanted to see them, but Priscilla didn't want them to read her aunt's smudged epistle. It had been written on her deathbed, and was sacred to Priscilla. She could not bear its rather wandering and sometimes ill-spelled contents, its Scotticisms and turns of dialect, to be exposed to their scorn. Besides, there were some home truths about the aunts in it that would not dispose them to view its propositions favourably, so she had said she would rather read the letters out to them, as her aunt's, at least, had been meant for her alone, and she had written it when she was dying.

To this they would not demur. They were, after all, two gentlewomen, and had always taught Priscilla that to read letters not meant for oneself was beneath contempt.

'Yes, you had better read them,' said Aunt Maud, grimly reserving her lecture for another time. 'Then we shall at least know exactly what it is all about.'

Priscilla slowly lifted the large business-looking envelope that had come by the last post, and had opened up, so she felt, a new world for her.

Priscilla's father had married beneath him, the daughter of a small Scots farmer—I mean, the farm was small, not the farmer, who was a huge, independent Borderer—much to the chagrin of his two elder sisters, who were poor, proud, and excessively genteel. Both her parents had died when their small daughter, named Janet Purdie, after her mother's sister, was still a child. This aunt, who kept a little village shop, had actually wanted to adopt the small Janet, but the Misses Delaine, appalled at such a fate for the only scion of the house of Delaine, had quickly circumvented her, and had borne off the howling Janet, who was contrary enough to prefer her fat, comfortable Aunt Purdie to the dignified ladies who descended upon her and took her away, yelling at the top of her lungs, to their ancient town house in Baxton, where they renamed her Priscilla, after their own mother, dropped the vulgar Purdie altogether, and did their best to bring her up a little lady. The Purdie strain was vigorously quelled, but in spite of all their efforts Priscilla would never completely be a little lady. She kept on showing signs of the Purdie blood with which they reproached her. She said she *liked* to be a Purdie. Neither would she, in spite of all their prayers, *look* like a tall, fair, willowy Delaine with the pinched mouth, high forehead, delicately hooked nose, and long, thin feet of that aristocratic family.

She was short and thin, but sturdy, and stood upright as a juniper-bush, on small square feet; her nose was as delicately tip-tilted as theirs were hooked, and her wide, enchanting mouth was gallant and unafraid. Her straight black hair was dragged back from her forehead, cut round by the ears, and held in place by a ribbon tied in an upright bow at the top of her head, which gave her the air of a plover with its crest raised. Her young cheek-bones stood out too plainly, and her face was so white at the moment that no one could have called her pretty. The only gifts she had from the Delaine side of her house were her clear blue eyes and the long,

11

slender hands with which she was now smoothing out two letters, one clean, typewritten, and business-like, on thick office paper, the other smudged and blotted, on cheap paper from a threepenny pad, so thin and hairy that the pen had frequently jabbed right through it, or trailed inky hairs across the script.

She sheltered the latter as much as she could behind the lawyer's sheet, and when she came to read it missed out what she called to herself 'the worst bits.'

The lawyer's epistle was brief, and merely stated his regret at having to inform Miss Janet Delaine of her aunt's death. She was, he said, the sole legatee of her aunt's estate, which consisted of a house, shop, outhouses, garden, and field in the village of Crumstane. There were also various livestock and the sum of two hundred pounds, duty free. They were left to her, however, under certain conditions, which she would find stated in the enclosed letter, which the late Miss Purdie had asked them to send, with the news of her decease, after her funeral.

They enclosed a ten-pound note, as directed by Miss Purdie, for travelling expenses, and asked her to come at once, or as soon as she conveniently could, to hear the will and consult with them, as there was no one to look after the house or the livestock, pending her decision.

That was at least pretty much what it meant within the legal phraseology.

'And now we will hear the conditions,' said Aunt Maud, picking up the knitting she had dropped when Priscilla began to read.

Priscilla shivered a little, partly because it was cold on that March afternoon in the bleak drawing-room with its blacked-out fire, and partly from apprehension of what her aunts would say on hearing certain parts of the scrawled sheets.

However, there was nothing for it but a brave front, so she plunged in.

My dear Niece and Namesake, Janet,

Thank you for writing to me at last. Fifteen years is a long time to wait for an answer to one's letters, written with heart-scaldings many a time, but I have my suspicion your fine lady aunts never gave them to you.

The first volley came pat as she expected: 'So you have been writing to your aunt behind our backs.' Aunt Maud's voice was cold and grim with displeasure.

'Yes, I did; but only once, Aunt Maud, and it was for your sakes as well as mine. I know you can't afford to keep me now you've lost that money, though it's so kind of you to want to, and you wouldn't let me apply for a job—a post, I mean—in Baxton, so I wrote and asked my Aunt Purdie if she knew of anything for me in Crumstane or the towns near it, but I never got an answer—at least, this is the answer—and now she is dead.'

'I consider . . .' began Aunt Maud, and then stopped. 'Well, go on,' she added. 'We can go into that later on. Read your letter.'

Priscilla went on:

After a year I hardened my heart, but now I'm on my death-bed, and you have written to me at last. I remembered you as a little lass and the love I bore you, and have made up my mind to let bygones be bygones and help you the only way that's left to me now. My lassie, I was gey and sorry when I got your letter, poor bairn, asking for a job. I aye thought those two *ladies* [read Priscilla, as a hasty substitute for 'impitent huzzies'] were rolling in money and would leave you their fortunes or I'd have had my say about you, but what's done's done. So I got Mr Elder here, the lawyer, and changed my will. Aye, I thought you'd be well off, and never jaloused my shop and bits of savings would be worth anything to you, but from your letter you sound a Purdie at heart, and Purdies were never afraid of working hard to make an honest living, so I'm leaving the house and shop on two conditions, and they are that you come here and run the shop and take the name of Purdie. It's no more than I did masel at your age, and you'll soon get into the way o' things if you're wullin to work and learn.

Then there's the powny and Barkis, the dog, and Meggy, the cat, and the rest of the beasties, they're not to be sent to strange places at their time o' life, so you'll make a home for them here. You can do as you like about the fowls and the pig and such-like. Molly, the cow I'm giving to Christy, for she's been a good friend to me, and you maun give her the pig if a pig's too much for you. She'll let you have the drop milk and cream and butter you need and a bit o' bacon. Christy has the key, and kens everything, and she'll see you through.

Now, my dear lassie, if you canna see your way to keep the shop and live here you must content yourself with my bits o' savings, and the shop and house will go to my nevvy, Murdo MacPherson, not that he needs them, but he'll see that that auld deevil Maitland doesn't buy them up, as he's tried this many a long year for

13

sheer greed and envy. Aye, he's tried to buy me oot, and then to ruin me, and he's just waitin' till the breath's out of my body to buy everything up, but I'll circumvent him yet, and mind you this: no *Maitland* is ever to touch my property or shop. I put my trust in you for that if you accept my offer. A Purdie never betrayed a trust put on them by the livin', let alone the dead, so I die with faith in you.

Have naught to do with Maitland. The Maitlands are all Taking Men—aye, the blood of the auld raiders and reivers is in every one o' them. That's the auld name—Taking Men. Besides, that auld Maitland's a Pharisee and sinner, and a mealy-mouthed hypocrite and as cunning as a weasel, so be on your guard. The Lord forgi'e me, but even on my death-bed I canna stomach forgivin' a Maitland.

I hope you are a good Christian lassie, you'll sit under the Revd. Lamont, a good man, though a bit hazy about preachin' the Word.

He's made me say I forgi'e the auld rogue, but it wisna' frae the heart, the Lord'll mebbee un'erstan'.

Now, my dear bairn, if you want to be a leddy and a Delaine you'll be better where ye are, even if it means skimpin' and savin', which I never could abide; the Purdies ha 'e aye workit hard and lived weel with aye a bite and a sup for a freen or a neighbour.

But if you're a Purdie at heart you trust your auld aunty and come and carry on. You'll make enough to keep you and a bit ower and above, if you're no afraid of work and a plain way o' livin'.

And now, my luve, I'm tired and ready to go. I'll die happy thinking another Janet Purdie—and, eh! you were a darlin' bairn—and my ain niece will carry on and live in the auld hoose that has sheltered Purdies for generations. The auld signboard will do.

My respects to your Aunts Delaine. There's no luve lost between us, but I believe them to be upright women, poor things, and bear them no grudge. Now my eyes grow dim, and I must make ready to appear before my Maker, though what He'll say about me and Auld Maitland I do not know.

Fare you weel, and God bless and keep you.

Your affectionate aunt,

JANET PURDIE.

There was silence for a few moments as Priscilla stopped with a slight choke in her voice. Two tears ran down her cheeks and blotted still more the ill-written, scrawled epistle, but she hastily wiped them away.

'I certainly bear her no grudge either,' said Aunt Maud at last.

'Nor do I,' said Aunt Flora. 'Poor woman, I expect she had a hard life.'

'Struggling with a village shop,' said Aunt Maud.

'But she liked it,' said Priscilla, swallowing the lump in her throat and preparing for battle, 'and I think I'd like it too.'

'Fiddlesticks!' said Miss Flora, recovering her equilibrium.

'Now, Priscilla,' said Aunt Maud, 'let us have no more of this. Two hundred pounds will be a nice little nest-egg for you, but the conditions on which you inherit the property are quite impossible. You will write to this Mr Elder, the lawyer, to-night and say so. It would not be fair to keep him waiting. If you post it by to-night's post he will receive it tomorrow.'

There was a silence for a few moments, and then Priscilla broke out, the tears standing in her eyes:

'But I don't want to refuse, Aunt Maud. I ought to be earning my own living and not living on you. It's not fair to you. I'm young and strong, and I ought to be helping *you* now, not you keeping me when you have so little.'

'Much you'll help us,' said Miss Flora drily, 'losing your two hundred pounds and running into debt. You silly child, how could you keep a shop? You know nothing of buying and selling. You know nothing of getting in stocks or pricing what you have to sell. You're a complete ignoramous about trade in any form, as all the Delaines are. How could you possibly keep a shop? The idea is not only absurd and ridiculous, but monstrous!'

'I don't suppose you could even add up a bill or give correct change,' said Aunt Maud.

'Oh, yes, I could,' said Priscilla. 'I was good at all that sort of arithmetic at school, and I could learn all the rest. Oh, Aunt, do let me try!'

'It's not a case of trying,' said Aunt Flora. 'It's a case of take it or leave it.'

Miss Delaine rose.

'It's time we dressed for dinner,' she said. 'Now understand, Priscilla, there can be no more discussion or talk about it. It is the well-meant but insane idea of an uneducated and ignorant old woman, made when doubtless she was mentally deranged by her last illness. For you even to think of considering it shows how ignorant, young, and wrong-headed you are. I forbid you to mention it again. Your stubborn folly is really beyond all words—almost beyond forgiveness when one remembers what we have done for you. You will go now and change for dinner, and after dinner you will write your

letter of refusal and post it in time for the last collection. Do you understand me?'

'Yes, Aunt, but . . .'

'That's enough. I will not listen to any more of your nonsensical suggestions. The subject is closed, and you will do as you are told. You are Priscilla Delaine, and Priscilla Delaine you will remain. Janet Purdie indeed!'

Priscilla made no reply. She knew it was quite hopeless. With tears running down her face she followed her aunts from the room and went up to change her dress for dinner.

But once in the room she stood still till she heard their bedroom doors close, and then she sped downstairs.

2

The Desperate Adventuress

Her flying feet took her to the library, where she desperately turned over some old almanacs and guides till she came on a large ABC time-table. It was out of date, but the main trains, she knew, were seldom altered, and the first change on the way to Crumstane would be York.

She had decided to act on her own initiative and go and see the lawyer. It was no use trying to talk to the aunts any more: they would never allow her to leave the house on what they would consider a wild-goose chase.

Not that she meant to run away exactly, but she would spend her ten pounds on going to see into things for herself —to see the lawyer and talk to him, to see Crumstane and Christy and the shop. She might even get a glimpse of the arch-enemy, Old Maitland? Wasn't there a Border ballad about Old Maitland? She must look it up, but later on. She had no time just now. If she was to go it must be at once. As her aunt had said, it was not fair to keep the lawyer and that Murdo—whatever his name was—and the livestock waiting.

Not tonight, of course, but—she rustled through the leaves of the time-table—by the first train tomorrow.

York! She ran her fingers up the column. The first train from Baxton to York left at seven-thirty in the morning. Another hunt for the York-Newcastle trains and then among the branch lines for Lammerton, where Mr Elder lived, convinced her that if the trains were still running the same she could if she wished get to Crumstane that evening. She could arrive at Lammeton by four o'clock. She would have time to go and see Mr Elder and then decide about going on. There were evidently no trains to Crumstane itself, but there would be a bus in all probability.

She shut the book quickly after having made a hurried list

of trains she ought to catch, and flew softly upstairs again
and changed into the only evening frock she had, a black
velvet, home-made, but not unbecoming. Since her aunts lost
their money she had made most of her own clothes and
altered and refurbished theirs, and had even boldly suggested
serving her time and becoming a dressmaker. Needless to say,
she had at once been quashed. No Miss Delaine had ever been
a dressmaker—or anything, indeed, but a young lady, who duly
came out and got married.

'But how do I come out when we've no money?' Priscilla
had asked.

'We shall manage something for you,' said Aunt Maud,
'coming out' was as out of date as the aunts themselves.

'So I'll never get out,' Priscilla had remarked then, like the
lark in the cage.

'You will, in due course, marry, we hope,' said Aunt
Flora.

And then Mr Porter had appeared, but Priscilla hadn't
liked Mr Porter, nor his house, nor his money, nor his short,
fat legs, nor anything that was his, much to the aunts' dis-
appointment. It would, as Aunt Flora had sighed, have been
such a satisfactory solution of the problem—the problem of
keeping three people on an income barely sufficient for two
in a house big enough for forty and with two servants, because
the Misses Delaine simply could not imagine life without at
least a cook and a parlour-maid. So they skimped on food
and they skimped on coals and skimped on wages and on everything possible to keep up appearances.

The large icy dining-room was lighted by two candles in
large silver candlesticks, and warmed, though you wouldn't
have noticed, by a tiny oil stove set in the huge fireplace. The
table was laden with priceless old silver and crystal, but little
else, for the dinner consisted of grey-looking hash with a frill
of cold fat round the edge, watery potatoes, and a too-hard
jelly, made out of a fourpenny packet from the grocer.

'If only they'd let me be the cook,' thought Priscilla,
shivering with cold. 'I know I could do better than this, and,
besides, I'd get warmed at the kitchen range and keep a kit-
ten to play with. I'm not aristocratic enough to be a parlour-
maid, but I just know I could cook.'

The Misses Delaine, dressed in old brocade dresses and

18

wearing their jewels, were politely conversing on non-committal, subjects till Taylor, the parlour-maid, who was also the table-maid, should leave the room.

Janet knew the letter would come up again then, and was just wondering what excuses she could make about it, when Taylor saved her by announcing that the Misses Carlyle were in the drawing-room. After a gossip they would probably start a game of bridge, and then she'd be safe. They'd be too much engrossed in their game to remember her unless she brought herself and her letter to their notice.

She joined them for a few minutes, saw the cards come out, and slipped away.

She sped up to the attic, got a suitcase that she could carry, and, safely in her room again, packed it, and then sat down and wrote a letter to her aunts, saying she was sorry, but she felt she must go and see the lawyer for herself, as her Aunt Purdie had evidently meant her to, when she sent the ten pounds for travelling expenses. She expected to be back the next day, but would wire and write from Lammerton or Crumstane.

She hoped they would forgive her for going without asking permission, but she felt they would not listen to her, and she did want to know more about her inheritance before refusing it for ever. It was, she felt, only fair to Aunt Purdie to find out more about it, but she loved her Aunt Maud and Aunt Flora, and was sorry to vex them, and again begged their forgiveness.

She wrote as gently and kindly as she could, because she really was fond of them in spite of their overbearing ways.

She was wakened about six with the pattering of rain on her window, and looked out to find not rain but grey sleet sliding down her window-pane. It was a dismal outlook for travelling, especially as she had no waterproof and always borrowed a mackintosh cape and umbrella of her aunt's when necessity took her out in the rain, which she could not do that morning.

She dared not go down to the kitchen to make herself a cup of tea or even get a piece of bread and butter, as she was not sure when Cook and Taylor got up, and she wanted to be off without their seeing her. Once away she would be safe till nine o'clock, when she usually had breakfast. She

might not even be missed till eleven, when her aunts had theirs. They lay long in the mornings to save the fire, which was not lit in the drawing-room till eleven.

It was a long walk to the station, and there was not much chance of picking up a taxi at that time in the morning, so she dressed herself quickly, fastened her suitcase, put her letter on the dressing-table, and slipped quietly downstairs. At the bottom she stood listening, but everything was still; then on tiptoe she crossed the hall and let herself out. If the servants noticed the unlocked door they would blame her Aunt Maud, who always locked up last thing at night, before she went to bed and after she'd given Pilot, the pom, a walk to the corner of the street.

Outside it was bitterly cold and the sleet was falling heavily, but once in the open her spirits rose. She loved adventures, but so far had only read about them. Here, at last, she was off on an adventure of her own.

Her coat was thin and let in the cold; her shoes were thin and let in the wet; but she was too excited to feel either. With ten pounds in her pocket and her suitcase in her hand she felt like Christopher Columbus and Sir John Franklin rolled into one.

'It's cold enough for the Arctic regions and the North-west Passage anyhow,' she exclaimed to herself, trying to see if her nose was as red as it felt.

Then somewhere in the distance a train blew off steam, and, feeling perfectly sure it was hers and she would miss it, she began to run, the heavy suitcase clumping against her wet knees.

But she had twenty minutes to wait in the cold and dreary station. She sat on the edge of a seat, too afraid of missing the train to go into a waiting-room, dreading every moment that her aunts would by some magical ill-fortune arrive and stop her.

But nothing happened, and at seven-thirty she stood, still terrified of seeing her aunts, watching the station slowly slip past as she glided into the unknown future.

Then and then only did she feel safe. She was off!

She slipped into a corner seat; a few minutes later breakfast was served.

'I'll eat everything you've got,' she said to the attendant.

'Porridge, fish, hot coffee, bacon and eggs.' She was on the top of the world.

But after that things began to go wrong. The sleet swept over the passing fields, growing whiter as they ran north. She was late at York, and had to run for her train. She missed lunch between the two, and was turned out at Newcastle before tea was served, and there was none on the slow train she just managed to catch, as they were now running differently from the time-table. Instead of four, it was seven o'clock when she found herself at Lammerton, shivering in the sleety snow that was now falling more heavily, her feet in their thin shoes and ankle-deep in icy slush, her thin coat wet through, her fingers in her soaking gloves, clutching the heavy suit-case.

What was she to do? It was no use looking for Mr Elder at his office now. It would be shut long ago, and she did not know his home address.

She had never in her life stayed in a hotel, and she was too shy to venture into one. Besides, what did one do about tips, and who did one tip? She felt that, rather than face the awful question of who, where, and what to tip, she would walk the streets all night.

She was hungry, forlorn, wet, cold, and miserable. She had asked a porter if there was a bus that night to Crumstane, but he didn't seem to know where Crumstane was. He had told her to go to the bus station, but she had lost the way and couldn't find any bus station.

As she stood there, lost in dejection, she saw a small bus coming up the street towards her. It was almost past her when she noticed a small bill pasted on the window—CRUM-STANE.

Instantly she took to her heels, down the middle of the street, splashing through the muddy slush, dragging her heavy suitcase as best she could, in full chase after the rocking bus. It had almost disappeared when it stopped to pick up a passenger; panting and gasping, she arrived just as the girl was about to ring the bell. She grabbed the suitcase and helped Priscilla inside. There was one empty seat left at the back of the bus, and she sank into it, her heart beating wildly, her hat knocked to the back of her head, her stockings and coat covered with mud.

21

It was full of country folk, who looked curiously at her, and then continued the hearty talk which was being bandied from side to side of the steaming, smoky interior. Dogs lay on the floor, stout women held large market baskets on their knees, men in wet raincoats and muddy leggings puffed at their pipes. Priscilla felt like a small, wet, sooty town sparrow among a flock of country ducks.

'That was a near thing,' said the girl. 'Where to?'

'Crumstane,' said Priscilla, not very sure now if she should not have stayed in Lammerton, where there would at least have been somewhere to spend the night.

The girl gave her a ticket; then inquired, 'Where shall I set ye doon?'

Priscilla wondered. The only place she knew of was her late aunt's shop and house, and they would be shut up—and she had no key.

'Do you know Miss Purdie's shop?' she asked.

'Janet Purdie? Aye, but she'd deid, and it's shut. There's naebody there.'

'Is there an inn?' asked Priscilla in desperation. An inn at least would not be so bad as a hotel.

The girl hesitated.

'No what you'd call an inn,' she said—'just Dickie Bird's.'

'Dickey birds!' thought Priscilla. 'What a queer name for an inn!'

She paused for so long that one or two people near her stopped their conversation and stared.

Priscilla was thinking of Christy. Christy had the key, and her aunt had said Christy would help her—but who was Christy? What was her other name?

For the first time she began to regret her hurried rush away, to wonder if her aunts were right after all and she had been a silly fool.

She decided that she had, but she was in for it now. There was no going back—not even to Lammerton.

'I suppose,' she said shyly, and feeling very silly, 'you don't know anyone of the name of Christy?'

'Christy what?'

'I'm afraid I don't know her other name.'

Never had Priscilla felt such a complete nincompoop. The girl stared at her.

'You see, I was to make inquiries at Mr Elder's, the lawyer's office at Lammerton, but I missed my train, and it was closed,' she went on lamely.

'It'll be Christy Teugh she's wantin',' said a man with a collie between his knees. 'She lives just ayont the shop.'

'Are you going to Crumstane?' Priscilla turned with relief to ask him.

'Nay,' he said. 'My place is a mile farther on.' He looked up the bus and then called, 'Ye'll be getting down at Crumstane, Bessie? Here's a bit lass wantin' Christy Teugh.'

'Aye,' called a woman from the front seats. 'I'll put her right. Christy may be doon at the Haughs, but her mither'll be in.'

They turned away and carried on their conversations, filled with curiosity about Priscilla, but their Northern politeness forbidding them to ask questions.

At her side a tall man was sitting reading a paper. He had given a half-turn towards her when she asked for Christy, but the farmer had spoken first, and he had turned back to his paper. All she could see of him was that he had red hair and was exceptionally tall.

The bus rattled along through sleet, mist and darkness, and Priscilla, heated momentarily by her run, now began to shake with cold. There was an icy draught from the door, and she could scarcely keep her teeth from chattering.

Suddenly the man with the red hair rose.

'You will be more out of the draught in my seat,' he said briefly. He spoke with a Northern accent, but quite differently from the others, whom Priscilla could scarcely understand.

She glanced up, but his face was in the shadow. She could only see the light gleaming on his bare red head.

'Oh, thank you,' she said shyly. 'Thank you very much.'

He said nothing more; just waited till she had taken his seat, then sat down in hers and continued his reading.

It was now getting on for nine o'clock, and Priscilla was growing more and more anxious. Country people went early to bed. Suppose Christy and her mother were in bed and the house shut up? Suppose, even if she had the temerity to rouse them, they would not give her the key? Suppose they shut the door in her face, What was she to do alone in the middle of

a strange country, in total darkness amid a storm of sleet and snow—she could see by the moving lights of the bus that snow was lying in the hedgerows.

It was not so cold in the corner protected by the tall form of her neighbour, but her involuntary trembling was now as much from fear and apprehension as cold.

Suddenly the farmer with the collie leaned forward and spoke.

'This is Crumstane we're coming to,' he said.

Priscilla tried to look out, but there was not a light to be seen; just flakes of sleet or snow gleaming as they slanted through the light of the bus, which at that moment stopped with a grinding of gears.

Priscilla and her suitcase were willingly helped out by the few people who now crowded to the door and began to descend and disappear. She was too engrossed trying to see some sign of lights in the village to notice anyone till a woman touched her on the arm.

'Christy's is just a step,' she said. 'I'll tak ye to the gate.'

She led the way through what appeared to Priscilla to be a pitch-dark, uninhabited region, till she saw the faint square of a lighted window and beside her the fainter glimmer of a white gate, where they stopped.

'There ye are,' said the woman. 'Ye'll be all right now,' and she hurried off with her two baskets of parcels weighing her down on either side. Priscilla entered the gate, put down her suitcase at the door, and knocked.

There was no answer, and she knocked again. Then she heard a shuffling noise, and after some time the door opened, and an old, old woman appeared, wrapped in a shawl and with a white cap, with a goffered frill round it, on her head.

'Is Miss Teugh in?' asked Priscilla.

'No, she's doon at the Haughs.'

Priscilla hesitated.

'I was wondering,' she faltered, 'if I might have the key of Miss Purdie's house?'

'And who may you be?'

'I'm Miss Purdie's niece. I was to call at the lawyer's, Mr Elder, and get a note for Christy. My aunt wrote and told me Christy would help me. Do you think she will be long?'

'Aye! Belle's expecting her third. Christy'll mebbe no be

back or the morn's morn, but if you're Janet Purdie's niece Christy was expecting you'd be comin'. I daursay I can find the key.'

She came back with it in a few minutes.

'Hae ye ony credentials?' she asked.

Priscilla handed her the two letters. The old woman had a candle in her hand, and she glanced at them.

'Weel, I warrant it's all right,' she said, 'but Christy'll be in a gey state when she hears o' ye gaun into an empty hoose and no so much as a spunk o' fire. Hae ye a box o' matches?'

'No,' said Priscilla. 'If you could lend me one . . .'

She took the proffered matches, and the old body, offering many apologies that she wasn't able to offer help as her fire was out, and she had 'the rheumatics', and had been in bed when Priscilla knocked, shut the door and went shuffling off.

Priscilla found her way to the gate, and then remembered she hadn't asked the way to her aunt's house. She felt she could not disturb the old woman again, yet what was she to do?

She lifted her suitcase, and stood looking up and down. Then with infinite relief, she heard footsteps approaching, and the next moment a man's tall figure came through the sleet that still fell persistently.

'Please,' she said, 'could you tell me where Miss Purdie's house is?'

'Yes,' he said, so briefly she was afraid he was annoyed at having to turn back and help her. At the same moment she realised to whom she had spoken. It was the man with the red hair.

3

The Man with Red Hair

Without another word he took her suitcase and strode on, his long legs covering the ground so quickly she had almost to trot to keep up with him.

In a moment or two they reached a gate, which he opened, standing aside for her to enter. Her eyes were more used to the darkness now, and she could just make out a snowy path between low hedges of some sort. She went quickly up it and came to a door under a porch, overgrown with some creeper. Everything was completely dark.

'There is no one in the house,' said the man behind her. His voice sounded distant and disapproving.

'No,' she answered timidly. The forthright Priscilla, cold, hungry, frightened, and nigh to tears, was thoroughly intimidated by the cold, disapproving, stand-offish voice.

'But I have the key,' she added forlornly.

It was a huge monster of a key. Holding it in both hands, she fumbled for the keyhole. He waited a while, then took it from her, inserted it in the lock as though he had cat's eyes, and turned it. The door opened on a black gulf.

'Thank you very much,' said Priscilla, trying to be impressive and very independent. 'I shall manage now quite well. Good night!'

In reply, if one could call it a reply, he struck a match and walked in. They were in a wide passage with doors to right and left and a narrow staircase at one end which took up half the hall or passage. He seemed to know his way, and, opening the second door on the right, went in, followed by Priscilla.

His match went out, and he struck another and lit a lamp hanging over the table. It was far above Priscilla's head, but almost on a level with his. As he lit it the light suddenly fell

on his upturned face, and she saw it for the first time. It immediately made her think of pirates and sea-hawks, it was so lean and brown and hard. A bold nose, close, thin-lipped mouth, firm chin, and small, keen, reddish-brown eyes. The red hair rose up in a crest from the seamed forehead. He might have been anything from twenty-five to thirty-five in years; the thick hair was young, but lines spread out in a fan from the corners of his eyes and were dinted deep at the sides of his mouth. His skin glistened ruddy and wet from sleet and snow, and now they were indoors she smelled the smell of wet leather and straw and horses, as if he had just come from the stables.

He glanced down at her, but with no warmth of interest or smile, a cold, distant glance.

'As if he were a hawk, looking at a wet, yellow chicken,' thought Priscilla. 'A hawk that wouldn't deign to kill a chicken —thank goodness!'

'Where is Christy?' he demanded shortly.

'She can't come. She's at the Hoffs.'

'The Haughs,' he contradicted her.

'The Hau-aughs,' she repeated as raucously as she could, but no smile was forthcoming.

'Then what are you going to do?'

'This is my house,' she replied, getting up a little spirit. 'I am going to stay here. Thank you for helping me. I shall be all right now.'

'Who are you?'

'I'm Priscilla Janet Purdie Delaine, but I'm going to call myself Janet Purdie here.'

'You are Janet Purdie's niece?'

'Yes, I am.'

He stood looking down at her, frowning with his eyebrows drawn together.

'You cannot stay here alone.'

'Why not? It's my house. The shop is mine too.'

'Have you nowehere you can go for the night? The Murdo MacPhersons are connections of yours, aren't they?'

'I don't know the MacPhersons. I'm going to stay here. This is my home now.'

He made no answer to this. He strode over to the fireplace,

27

poked among the ashes, then went out and returned with an armful of paper and firewood and a pail of coals.

In two minutes he had the fire blazing up the chimney; then he took the kettle which was hanging on a hook across the fire, went out, and returned with it filled. In his other hand was a basketful of chips, which he threw on the fire. Then he lifted a canister from the mantelpiece, looked into it, and set it on the table.

'Tea,' he said.

He went out through another door, and returned with a huge ham under his arm.

'Ham,' he said. Then he strode towards the door.

'I'll be back in ten minutes with bread and milk,' he announced, and the door closed behind him.

Priscilla gazed at the closed door, expressed her mixed feelings by saying 'Christopher Columbus!' and then started to take off her soaked outdoor things.

She had just pulled off her shoes when the front door opened, and a knock came at the kitchen door.

'Come in,' she called.

Through the door came a large Airedale on a string, followed by the man with red hair. He had a variety of parcels and a cat under his arm. From pockets he took two kittens.

'I've brought Barkis and Maggie and her family,' he said coldly. 'They belong here, and will be company. Better speak to Barkis while I'm here.' He bent and spoke to the dog, his whole expression changing as he did so, and Priscilla put out her hand to pat the dog's head.

With a lightning movement he seized her fingers in his own hard grip, a grip which she felt was somehow very reassuring, though it was quite impersonal.

'Don't pat dogs till they've had a look at you and taken you in,' he said. 'And Barkis doesn't like being touched by strangers, but he'll look after you.'

He released her hand, and strode to the door.

'Good night!' he said, without a backward glance.

'Good-bye,' said Priscilla firmly. She promptly locked the door as loudly as she could. 'I hope he hears it,' she said to herself. He had really done nothing to annoy her—in fact, he

28

had helped her since she set eyes on him—but she did not feel in the least grateful; she felt nothing but resentment.

On the table were a loaf, eggs, milk, and a round of farm-house butter. The cat and kittens had settled on the hearth-rug. Barkis sat on his tail and looked at her.

She went and drew the curtains. As she did so a lovely feeling warmed her all through. She had come home! This was her own house, and she was drawing her very own curtains. Give them up to some Murdo MacPherson? Not she! Let Old Maitland take them from her? Not on your life! A tiny sip of ownership had settled everything. She would no longer be Priscilla Delaine, she would be plain Janet Purdie and keep the village shop. The idea of Priscilla Delaine selling cheese, bootlaces, and paraffin oil in a village shop was simply silly, but Janet Purdie just fitted in.

There was no one to explain this to, so she explained it to Barkis and Maggie and the two kittens.

'This is my house, and my shop's somewhere about, though I haven't seen it yet, and you are my dog and my cat and my kittens, and now we'll have a house-warming and a feast to celebrate.'

She got into dry things, opened a drawer in a chest against the wall, and discovered towels, tablecloths, and an out-size apron, which she tied round her slim form, tucking in the folds.

In the scullery she discovered pans; she sliced off a piece of ham, boiled it a little, and gave it to Barkis with bread soaked in the brew. Maggie got warm bread and milk, and then looked after the kittens herself, but first the kittens were each sprinkled with water and given a name—'Polly' and 'Flinders,' as they seemed to like to 'sit among the cinders warming their pretty little toes.' Then she spread a cloth and cooked her own meal; her country blood had come out, and instinctively she fed the animals first. She wondered about the other livestock, but had no means of finding them.

She disovered that she was starving of hunger, a fact she'd forgotten among her earlier miseries, so she fried ham and eggs and made tea, pulled the table near the hearth, and sat down to enjoy her first meal in the warm, friendly kitchen. It was while she was eating her third slice of bread, thickly

spread with delicious country butter, and polishing off her second egg that she suddenly found that her mind's eye was gazing at a hard, thin, rain-wet face with a crest of red hair and gimlet eyes.

She quickly blacked it out. 'I think that's *the most* disagreeable person I ever met,' she said to Barkis, who blinked his eyes at her, but said nothing.

After that announcement she felt better, and, having finished her meal, she lit a candle and set out on a tour of inspection, followed by Barkis, who kept watch on every movement.

On the ground floor she found four rooms, the kitchen and scullery, a large sitting-room that looked as if it was kept for show, and a smaller parlour with a cheap, brass bed and a chest of drawers with a crochet cover and looking-glass crowded in among a set of lovely old chairs, a long inlaid mahogany table, and a corner cupboard full of china. Upstairs there were four bedrooms opening off a square landing with a window in it. They were all chilly, clean, and unused-looking, except that one of them had piles of cardboard boxes and balls of string lying on the floor.

'Overflow of stock,' remarked Priscilla. 'Now, where is that shop?'

She had seen no sign of a shop so far.

Carrying her candle, she descended the stairs, and discovered a locked door with glass panels curtained with red twill behind a long settle that stood out from the hearth. At the side of the wall a key was hanging on a brass hook. She took it and unlocked the door into a dark cavern, whence came a smell of leather, cheese, coffee, and apples.

She stepped in and promptly fell flat, the candle rolling away and going out. She had not noticed a step down into the shop.

She picked herself up, rubbed her knees, relit the candle, and returned for another survey.

Never had she seen such an untidy conglomeration of stuff. Shelves were stuffed full of ravelled wool, half-opened drawers revealed a mixter-maxter of everything from slate pencils to coffee, the counter was crowded with sweetie jars, a large mouldy cheese, sandshoes, bunches of candles, and

half-empty trays of damp, melting toffee. Dust lay thick over everything.

'Goodness!' exclaimed Priscilla. 'Did Aunt Purdie keep her shop like that?'

It was bitterly cold, and she hastily shut the door. As she did so a loud clang made her start. It was the grandfather clock in the passage. It struck twelve.

' "Now the day is over",' quoted Priscilla, suddenly realising that it had been a very long day and that she was dead tired.

She shivered at the thought of the icy bedrooms upstairs, and still more at the thought of the parlour bedroom, where she guessed her aunt had lain ill and died.

On the long settle was a thick padded rug. She put on her grey woollen dressing-gown, turned down the lamp, put some coal on the fire, and, curling up under the rug on the long settle, was fast asleep in two ticks of old grandfather clock.

4

Auld Maitland

Before turning in she had made up her mind to go into Lammerton by the first bus to see Mr Elder and get things settled. Until she had seen him she would still feel a bit of an interloper, in spite of her assurances to Barkis.

She slept late, and had a fearsome struggle to make herself a cup of tea. She had never lighted a fire, and, thinking coals would take too long to burn up, she heated the kettle over some sticks, but the tea was half warm, with bits of dry leaves floating on top. She made up her mind that one thing she must have was an oil stove of sorts to boil hasty kettles.

She arrived at Mr Elder's office at eleven, and was at once shown into his private room.

To her amazement he was quite a young man. She had expected something wizened, with a white beard.

'Oh,' she said involuntarily, 'are you Mr. Elder?'

'I'm Mr. Elder the younger,' he said, and they both laughed.

'Did you write to me?'

'I did.'

'Well, you sounded Mr Elder the elder—in fact, the eldest.'

She felt at home with Mr Elder.

After these preliminaries she plunged into her story and told him everything about her aunts, the journey, the arrival, but very little about the man with the red hair. Just a casual mention that he'd shown her the way.

'And what about the livestock?'

'I've got a dog, a cat, and two kittens. Is there any more?'

'Lord, yes, hens and ducks and geese and turkeys and ponies and pigs and cows and everything that walks on four legs—or two.'

Then he read the will to her, which was in essentials a repetition of her aunt's letter.

'Would you advise me to accept?' she asked, trying to be very impartial and remembering the aunts.

Mr Elder conscientiously went into all the difficulties, and as conscientiously into the advantages. It was quite a good little property, he said, in first-class order—in fact, he had had a splendid offer for it already if she could have sold it, and the cottage contained a number of fairly valuable antiques.

However, in the end it was Priscilla herself who must decide.

'I've decided,' said Priscilla. 'Nothing would induce me to give it up.'

'Well, I see no reason why you shouldn't get in an experienced person to help you run the shop till you get into the way of it. I've been through such books as Miss Purdie kept, and it was certainly quite a paying little concern, though, of course, it must have suffered considerably through being neglected during her long illness, and it has been closed for some time.'

But nothing could daunt Priscilla. She meant to carry out her aunt's wishes, and finally signed some papers with a flourish of relief.

'It's mine now, isn't it?' she asked.

'Yes, it's your now, and I wish you the very best of luck. You must have a glass of wine, and we'll drink to your success.'

After the glass of sherry and a biscuit which revived her considerably she asked if she might write a letter in his office, as the post would leave Lammerton earlier than she could catch one at Crumstane.

She had sent a telegram that morning to tell her aunts of her safe arrival, and now she had the more difficult task of writing to tell them she had gone against their wishes and accepted the whole of her inheritance, conditions and all. She explained that, having accepted these responsibilities, she could not return, as there was no one to look after the place, and asked if she might have her things sent on. She would come and see them as soon as she could, and hoped they would come and visit her as soon as she had got the house in order.

All this mixed with her love, her gratitude for all they had

done, and her thanks made a long and slightly incoherent letter, and it was after one when she left the office.

She had a hasty cup of coffee, went to buy an oil stove, but was persuaded to take one of the new gas ones with gas container, and was given an estimate of what it would cost to install lights on the same system, so that she had barely time to make a few more purchases before the bus left.

She arrived home about five, tired, cold, and hungry and rather dreading the problem of lighting the fire.

'I wish I'd looked and seen how that man did it,' she said to herself, as she opened the gate.

To her amazement she caught a glint of firelight from the window as she passed it in the garden.

She opened the door with her key, to find a huge fire blazing on the kitchen hearth, the kettle boiling, the table set, and hot home-made scones on a girdle, swinging by the side of the fire.

As she stood gazing a tall, gaunt woman with a weather-beaten face came rushing out of the back kitchen, wiping her hands on a striped woollen apron pinned round her flat body. She stopped and held up her hands when she saw Priscilla.

'Mercy me! You're nobbut a bairn!'

'You're Christy,' said Priscilla.

'Deed am I, and eh me! I'm that put aboot to think of you coming here to a dead hoose with no as much as a spunk of fire to welcome ye. What for did ye no let me know ye were comin'? But you're cauld as clay'—seizing Priscilla's hands—'sit ye doon and get your tea.'

She ran for the teapot, and was going to pour out and wait on Priscilla when she stopped her.

'You've only put out one cup.'

Christy hesitated.

'Eh, it's no for the likes o' me to sit doon . . .' she began, when Priscilla interrupted her.

'Oh, Christy,' she said, 'I've been dying to see you. There's to be none of that nonsense between you and me. Get another cup while I put this cold ham on a plate and make the mustard. I had no lunch, so we're going to have a high tea, and if you've had yours you'll just have to have another.'

Christy needed no second bidding. She was as eager to talk

34

to Priscilla—whom she would insist on calling Janet—as
Priscilla was to talk to her. After the first moment there was
no shyness between them. Christy poured out, and Priscilla
served the ham in silence; then they started off.

'I'll tell you first how I happened to arrive as I did last night,'
said Priscilla, 'and then you tell me about my aunt and everything.'

Then she began, and while Christy put in her North
Country 'Hechs!' and 'Hochs!' she told the whole story of
getting the letter, of her aunts' refusal even to consider the
question of her accepting her Aunt Purdie's offer, right
through till she arrived in the darkness and sleet at Crumstane.

'A man showed me the house,' she finished up, and left it
at that.

'Keep us and save me!' exclaimed Christy. 'They'd never
have stopped ye frae comin' and takin' your ain hoose and
runnin' your ain shop!'

'Yes. You see . . .' But she realised it was no use trying to
explain the Misses Delaine's point of view about a village
shop to Christy, who would simply be bewildered.

'Such a good settin'-doon!' she exclaimed. 'My certes, they
maun be a couple o' poor daft creatures, but there's no
accoontin' for leddies—of course, you're a leddy-lass yoursel', but ye seem to have sense.'

'But I know nothing about running a shop, Christy. Do
you?'

'No me. Your auntie aye ran the shop hersel', but you'll
soon get into the way o't,' she went on cheerfully. 'You're a
Purdie, and the Purdies were aye doing folk.'

This rather took Priscilla aback. She had made up her mind
that Christy knew all about the shop.

'The lawyer said I might get some experienced person to
help me at first,' she said.

'Na! Na!' said Christy. 'You dinna want other folk to ken
your business. You just open the shop. The folks is sayin'
ye'll be losin' all the trade if you don't open at once. Ye see,
that Auld Maitland is sending his vans regular from Lammerton.'

'Who *is* Old Maitland?' asked Priscilla.

'Eh, that auld deevil! He's a Crumstane man, worse luck!

Yer Aunt Janet was gey and kind to him, but she should never have let a Maitland into the shop. Ye see, Auld Maitland, as we call him, started what he calls a general store in Lammerton. He's done very well there, but no content with that he's tried to buy up all the little village shops round about and either run them himsel' or shut them up and send his vans round. He tried to buy your aunt's house and shop when she had had a bad time and was hard pressed for money, and when she wouldn't sell he tried every devilment to get her out.

'It began with her breaking her leg, falling off the stepladder, and he sent his nevvy, who was serving his time in the Lammerton store then, to help her.

'She didn't know then what devils they were, and was glad to have some one who knew the business to keep things going for her. But the trade went back and back, and she got into debt, and of course the nevvy, Redd Maitland, knew all about it; that's why his uncle sent him to help Janet—to nose into her affairs. In gratitude she bought most of her stock from Auld Maitland, who deals wholesale as well, supplying small shops. Young Redd had aye said it would be all right lettin' things run up a bit with his uncle. Then when her nevvy, Murdo MacPherson, got into trouble she mortgaged the hoose to pay his debts and get him started again—that's another story I maun tell ye—and of course Auld Maitland was there ready to take out a mortgage.

'Well, he let things go on till they were at their worst. Then he put the screw on, insisted on having his debts paid at once, and, when Janet couldn't pay him, tried to get the house and shop. Eh, but it was an awful time. Mony's the time we've sat and grat together thinkin' the place would have to go, but we warstled through. Folks liked Janet and wouldn't buy from his vans, though he tried to get her customers by underselling her. Then young Murdo got on his feet breeding pigs— you see, he crossed Large Whites—eh, but you wouldn't understand all that, but he took prizes everywhere, and now he's the biggest pig-breeder in the countryside. Well, he helped his aunt—as well he might—and between them, though it was a hard struggle for him too, then, they kept the place from getting into Auld Maitland's clutches.

'But he swore to her he'd get it yet; that's why she was

36

leaving it to Murdo. She knew Murdo would see he never got it.

'Then your letter came, and that's why she wanted you to come yourself. You see, the Clock House has belonged to Purdies for generations, and she wanted a Purdie to have it. Aye, blood's thicker than water.'

'But her nephew Murdo would be a Purdie too—I mean, as much as me. My name was really Delaine.'

'No, he'd never change his name. He's as proud o' being a MacPherson as she was of being a Purdie.'

Priscilla's eyes were here opened. She had thought only old aristocratic families like the Delaines were proud of their names. She hadn't before come up against the pride of Borderers and Scots in their ancient patronymics.

'Well, she was right. I am proud of being a Purdie, and I *am* Janet Purdie though I have Priscilla and Delaine tacked on to each end. But, of course, I'm a Purdie now. The lawyer is seeing about that, and I'll keep "Janet Purdie, General Dealer" on the sign above my shop. But what is the Clock House?'

Christy opened her eyes.

'Why, this is the Clock House. Have you not seen the old clock over the yard gate? Ye see, the Clock House was an inn in coaching days, and then it went down when steam came in, and your grandfather started the shop. It was left to Janet when she was seventeen years auld.'

By this time tea was long over, and Christy rose to go. She had to go to the Haughs, she said, where her sister, Mrs Martin, was lying ill. She was terribly sorry she could not spend all her time with Priscilla, but she would come in in the mornings and 'redd up' and start the fires, and in the evening when she could. Her sister had got someone to stay with her at night, but Christy had to be there through the day.

When she was gone Priscilla suddenly remembered that she had never asked her who the man with the red hair was. She must do so tomorrow.

She was too tired to do anything more that night. She found Christy had lighted the fire and prepared a bed for her upstairs, so she went early to bed.

Since Christy had arranged to come in in the mornings

before leaving for the Haughs, when she came downstairs next morning, she found the fire lighted, the place swept and dusted, and her breakfast set.

'And now we'll survey our domain,' she said to Barkis, who was beginning to adopt her as his mistress.

First she went all over the house, which was crammed with the accumulations of generations. She knew something about antiques from her aunts, whose house was full of them, and was able on a rough-and-ready way to spot the valuables from the rubbish. Her aunt Purdie had seemed to have no idea; valuable Chelsea, Staffordshire, and Worcester ware stood cheek by jowl with hideous vases bought at fairs or sixpenny stores. A lovely old Nuremburg jug was filled with newspaper spills and stood on a rickety fretwork atrocity with bits of looking-glass pasted into it. Crowded in among brass beds, Japanese tables, painted drain-pipes, and ugly 'three-piece sets' in imitation leather, there was enough fine old furniture to more than furnish the house. Every cupboard and chest of drawers was packed full of stuff. At the top of the house was a large attic at which Priscilla took one look and shut the door. It looked as if it would take a month to clear it out!

'I've work for months just going over things and clearing out rubbish,' said Priscilla. 'It makes me wish I didn't need to open the shop for weeks and weeks, but could start straight off and make the house lovely.' She was itching to begin and full of plans, but everything must wait on the shop. The shop had been closed too long—several weeks, she gathered—and she must get it put in order and opened before anything else.

Through the back door was a large cobbled square, which had evidently been the inn-yard. In it were stables and outbuildings, all in good repair, but mostly empty. The pony, Ginger, was in his stall, and his cart and an old governess-cart next door. There was stabling, she thought, for a dozen horses. She saw that the house had originally been much bigger, but the larger part had been cut off. The empty rooms were dusty and cobwebbed and had sacks of meal and piles of turnips and potatoes in them.

She found the old clock over the closed gates. The poultry runs were outside the yard, and a hedge and wire-netting

divided it from the large garden running down to the Kelpie burn, which flowed through the property. There was a plank bridge across it from the garden leading into her field, a large grassy pasture.

While the buildings were sound, there was a neglected air about everything.

It all looked too much for Priscilla to take in. Christy had the cow and the pig—'Thank goodness!' she thought—and was feeding the poultry and the ducks that swam about the burn at the bottom of their run. She also brought in and bedded the pony at night, and let him out into the field in the morning, so that was off her shoulders.

She hoped Mrs Martin would soon be well, when Christy was to come for the whole day, but Christy would need to be paid, and the money would have to come from the shop and the poultry—mostly from the shop.

She went indoors to have another look at the shop.

Never had she seen such a dismaying sight!

The shop itself and a storeroom through it were evidently a part of the old house. There was a fireplace in each, and corniced ceilings and cupboards let in to the walls. Shelves and nests of drawers and a counter had been put in by some joiner and painted an ox-blood red, and the shelves, as she had seen on her first look round, were overflowing with dusty, muddled stock.

Having taken it all in, she decided that she must at once have a sale, burn the rubbish, redecorate and paint the shop and storeroom, and start afresh.

The only thing was she did not know where to begin; all was in such confusion. She supposed her aunt had just tried to carry on when she was ill, until she had to go to bed. Christy had said a young girl had come in for a week, but had been so useless Miss Purdie had sent her packing.

Anyhow, she must begin somewhere. She brought a broom and dusting-cloths, and spent the day getting rid of some of the dirt and dust.

She was standing on a step-ladder after tea, turning over piles of loose stationery, when a knock came at the shop door.

'Goodness!' she exclaimed to herself. 'If that's a customer what am I to do?'

Wildly trying to smooth her hair and remove some of the dust from her face and hands, as she unpinned her aunt's large apron she opened the door.

An elderly, patriarchal-looking man was standing there, with a white beard and expressionless, wet brown eyes.

'Miss Delaine?' he asked.

'Yes,' said Priscilla, then corrected herself, 'but I'm Janet Purdie now.'

'My name's Maitland,' he said. 'Ye'll mebbe hae heard o' Auld Maitland? A'body kens Auld Maitland.'

'Oh,' said Priscilla, completely taken aback.

Her hand had dropped from the door. He walked calmly in, and sat down on the only chair in the place.

5

Priscilla's Troubles Begin

Priscilla, too bewildered to gather up her forces and deal with this unexpected invasion by the enemy, stood staring for a moment; then she shut the door against the icy wind blowing in, and came forward.

'I stand enough on my feet,' he remarked. 'When I can sit I sit.'

'Yes,' said Priscilla stiffly. 'Did you want anything? The shop is not open yet.'

He laughed a short laugh and looked round.

'Not much of a stock,' he said.

'The shop has been closed for some time because of my aunt's illness.'

'I ken, I ken,' he said. 'No, I've no come to buy anything in your bit shoppie—just to hev a talk wi' you. You're vaira young to think of rinnin' a shop. Had ony experience?'

'No. And I don't think there is anything to talk over, and I'm very busy.'

'No experience, eh? I thought as much. Well, I'm an auld haund, and though your aunty and me didna' aye hit it off'— he closed an eyelid at Priscilla, who stared back in astonishment, not being used to being winked at—'that's no to say you and me couldna' be on a friendly footing and help yin anither—all in a way o' business, of course, all a matter o' business.'

Utterly astonished at the old man's audacity, his 'nerve', as she called it, Priscilla remained dumb, and he went on:

'Aye, Auld Maitland's no sic a bad chap. Though your aunty and me couldna' 'gree, I'm willin' to let bygones by bygones and gi'e you a hand, but ye needna' feel you're acceptin' a favour; ye can help me a bit in return.'

'I don't think there is any way I can help you,' said Pris-

cilla at last, 'and if you will excuse me saying so, I do not want any help from you, Mr Maitland.'

'Now nae! Now nae! Dinna be in sic a hurry to refuse. You havena' heard yet what I want to say.'

He looked so patriarchal and benevolent sitting leaning towards her with both hands folded over the knob of his stick, his white beard spread on his chest, that Priscilla was nonplussed. She did not like to be rude to an old man.

'But I don't think it's any use . . .' she began.

'Never refuse an offer before you've heard it, my lassie; that's no way to run a business. Now listen to my proaposeetion. I supply goods to a' the little shops in the district except Crumstane, and I'd like to supply you. Ye'll no hae made ony arrangements yet?'

'No.'

Priscilla was wishing he would go away, but how did one get rid of an old man who just planted himself on a chair and sat and sat?

'Then we'll come to my bargain. Tit for tat ye ken—giff-gaff makes good freens.'

Priscilla was silent. She didn't understand what 'giff-gaff' was, but wasn't going to ask, as it might keep him longer to explain.

'If you deal with me for stores—to begin with, mind ye. If ye can do better elsewhere you're welcome to; I only ask a trial—I'll lend you a lass that kens all the ins and oots of the trade—she and her mither ran a village shop theirsel's afore she came to me—for a week or two, just to get you into the wey o' things. Ye'll pey her her fares and gie her a bite at mealtimes, but that's a' it'll cost you. Ye'll take all your stock from me for, say, the first month or six weeks, or as long or short as ye like—all I ask is a trial. Ye see, business has to be sought; it doesn't come o' itsel'; that's why I'm here. I aye veesit new customers mysel'—the personal equation, ye ken, the personal equation.'

Having made his proposition, he sat with his hands on his stick looking straight in front of him, as if he had said his say and was no longer particularly interested.

'Aye, aye,' he remarked slowly to himself, 'the place has got into an awfu' state—customers gone and all. It'll take a bit o' working up.'

If anyone else had made this offer Priscilla in her innocence would have seized upon it at once. Christy evidently knew nothing about the shop, and she had absolutely relied on Christy, thinking her aunt had meant in her letter that she would help her with the shop. A girl for a week or two who had the whole thing at her finger-ends would have been a god-send, and there was no reason why she should not buy her stock, at first, at least, from the local purveyor, until she had had time to look round.

But from Auld Maitland—not on your life! She wondered how he had the cool impudence to suggest it. He must think she knew nothing about the way he had treated her aunt.

She stood staring at him, but he never turned his head. He put his fingers in his pocket and took out a little tortoise-shell box from which he took a pinch of snuff and sniffed it up first one nostril and then the other. Then he snapped the lid and put it in his pocket again.

'Well,' he said, 'I'll need to be gettin' on. When would ye like Mysie? She's a nice lassie, is Mysie.' His gentle, assured voice might have been that of a grandfather talking of his favourite granddaughter.

Priscilla took a deep breath.

'Thank you, Mr Maitland,' she said, 'but I am making my own arrangements, and as my aunt and you were not on friendly terms I could not accept any favours from you.'

He glanced at her, and she saw a swift flash pass and immediately go out of his expressionless eyes.

'Weel, weel,' he said calmly, 'think it over. Never make up your mind in a hurry.' He rose slowly and looked all round the shop very deliberately. 'And never make an enemy o' a freen; it's bad for business'—he shook his head—'verra bad.'

He paused to let this sink in. Then as he approached the door he turned again.

'I'm an auld man, and you're a young lass,' he said. 'It doesna' come well frae the young tae scoff at an offer o' kindness frae the auld. Though me and your aunt had oor bits o' differences, we were auld acquaint, and my offer was weel meant; I was willin' to let bygones be bygones. Good night to ye.'

He spoke with such gentle reproach that Priscilla immediately felt guilty and uncomfortable.

'I didn't scoff . . .' she began, when he held up his hand to stop her.

'Think it ower, think it ower,' he said. 'Ye'll find a good freen in Auld Maitland.'

Then he went out and shut the door.

Priscilla immediately ran and bolted it, as if she were afraid he'd come back. She heard the car rattle off, and then closed the shutters and went back to the kitchen.

'Well!' she exclaimed, standing gazing at the fire. 'Well!' Then after a moment's pause, 'I'm sure he's an old humbug, but I hate having even to *seem* to hurt an old man, even if he is an old humbug. I'll tell Christy about him. But accept his offer when he hurt my Aunt Purdie—no, indeed!'

The next few days were busy ones for Priscilla, but that would not have mattered if only she had not felt herself getting deeper and deeper into difficulties.

She wished from the bottom of her heart she could have accepted Old Maitland's offer—that it had been anyone else who had made it.

Christy's horror when told of Old Maitland's visit and proposition was if anything deeper than her own, but she had no useful suggestion to make. Christy was a master-hand at work, and could do anything in house, field, or garden, but when it came to the shop she confessed absolute ignorance. Aunt Purdie had seen to all that.

Priscilla had wondered if there was any other experienced person she could get, but Christy shook her head. Not in Crumstane certainly. Besides, an experienced woman for a village shop would be hard to come by; an experienced assistant would need a big wage, and there would probably not be anyone willing to come for only a week or two.

Priscilla saw all that for herself. She had only her two hundred pounds, growing less daily, to fall back on. Christy would need a decent wage when she came all day, though she would accept nothing at the moment; the shop had to be redecorated and stocked; and she had herself to keep besides the livestock, which were expected to pay for themselves, of course, but Priscilla was too ignorant of everything to have gone into that yet. She had enough to think of at the moment with the shop.

If only she could get some one to go over the stock with

44

her and tell her all the prices! Some things were, of course, marked; a few she found out by asking Christy the usual prices for such things, but there was heaps of stuff for which she had no idea what to charge. She thought now any other kind of shop would have been easier, any shop that sold one kind of goods only, but her aunt seemed to have sold anything and everything.

Besides all this, there was the sale. She had put a placard in the window saying the shop would open on the following Tuesday with a sale; it was now Thursday, and not only did she not know the proper prices, but she had no idea what reductions to make.

She knew no one from whom to ask advice except Old Maitland. She saw how cunning his proposition had been. He had guessed exactly what her need would be. In her dilemma she sometimes even wondered if he *had* wanted to let bygones be bygones and give her a helping hand, but there was her aunt's letter saying plainly no Maitland must have anything to do with her shop.

She worked hard all this time, forgetting her meals and almost worrying herself sick, so that she grew still thinner, and her little wedge-shaped face under the severely brushed black hair with its incongruous childish bow at the top grew whiter and more transparent than ever.

She dusted and sorted, piled the scattered stock into heaps, tidied up drawers and shelves, emptied out the barrel of rotten apples, but left the new one standing for Christy's attention, as she could find no way to break into it. She prayed for Mrs Martin to recover so that she could at least have Christy's help all day, and grew more and more despondent.

On Thursday evening she was sitting exhausted in the shop, so deep in despair that she had to keep wiping the tears away. It had been a dreadful day—the blackest yet.

Christy had not turned up at all, as Belle had had 'a bad turn', the poultry had not been fed, and she had run out of meal. The pony had refused to come in, and after chasing him all round the field she had had to get a strange boy to help her; she'd given him a shilling, and then worried herself into a state of misery in case it wasn't enough. As a matter of fact, he'd nearly dropped flat with surprise at get-

45

ting anything at all. Neighbours helped one another over such matters at Crumstane as a matter of course, and enjoyed it. He'd been astonished into dumbness, and didn't dare tell his mother, in case she whacked him and sent him back with it.

She had left the glass-panelled door open, and returned to discover the kittens playing with the pile of wools she had just tidied up, and they were ravelled all over the place. She was so annoyed at the little imps that she closed the inner door opened the outside one, and after a heated chase drove them out into the rain as a punishment, and started on her work in the shop.

In a few minutes she heard them mewing at the front door, and went to let them in. They were already soaked with the rain, and dashed past her looking like two bottle-brushes with their wet fur all in points.

To her surprise a large trunk was standing on the step, which she immediately recognised as her own. The carrier must have left it when she was chasing the kittens and so had not heard his knock.

Her heart lightened. She would hear from her aunts at last! She could not move the trunk, so left it where it was, and hurriedly looked in the letter-box for a letter—she had watched for the postman every day—wearying to hear from them.

There was no letter; just a postcard. She could not read it in the dim passage, and took it into the shop and read it under the lamp, thinking it would be the notice from the railway people.

She read it twice before she grasped its meaning.

The trunk, as requested, has been forwarded to the address given; no acknowledgment required.

That was all. It wasn't even signed, though she recognised her Aunt Maud's handwriting.

'No acknowledgment required.' That meant they didn't want her to write again. Stupefied, she read it over and over again. So they weren't going to forgive her! They had cast her off. Suddenly the tears choked her. After all, they were all she had, now Aunt Purdie was dead, and the world seemed lonely without them.

Contents

1	The Aunts	9
2	The Desperate Adventuress	17
3	The Man with Red Hair	26
4	Auld Maitland	32
5	Priscilla's Troubles Begin	41
6	Strangers Yet	48
7	Redd Maitland	55
8	The Sale	61
9	Dr John	69
10	The Stable	77
11	'Hast Thou Found Me, O Mine Enemy?'	86
12	The Mackintosh	94
13	Getting in the Stores	101
14	Maudie Jones	108
15	Auld Maitland Again	117
16	The New Van	123
17	The Powny	132
18	Mysie Cree	140
19	The Owl's Nest	147
20	The Quarrel	156
21	Right of Way	163
22	Priscilla Waters the Mare	171
23	The Lantern	181
24	Lindy	192
25	Miss Prudence Steps in	203
26	The Aunts Once More	214
27	The Taj Mahal	221
28	The Pigeon-hide	229
29	Scenes	239
30	The Taking Men	250

At the back of her mind, in the last dreary days, as she had struggled with the shop, had always been the slightly comforting though unacknowledged thought that they were there to creep back to if utterly defeated. It was undoubtedly lonely being among complete strangers, and her heart had warmed towards them. She had longed for a letter; she had longed to sit down and write to them and tell them all her news.

Now she felt utterly cast off. She could never go back. They were done with her; they wouldn't forgive her. She turned the card over in her fingers. It was addressed to 'Miss Janet Purdie'! A stranger—some one they did not know. They did not want any letters from Janet Purdie, or to hear how she was getting on. They didn't want to know anything about such a person.

She sat down and gave way to tears. All her bravery was gone for the moment; this cruel blow had come when she was feeling most defeated and weary. For a moment she hated the shop and the house, the ducks and the hens and the pony, Crumstane and everything it stood for.

She just let the black waves roll over her, and, laying her arm across the counter, she sobbed and sobbed. Once begun she could not stop. It was all too much for her.

6

Strangers Yet

She had forgotten that she had unbolted the outer door of
the shop to shoo the kittens out into the ran as a well-
deserved punishment, so she was startled out of her wits when
the bell suddenly tinkled, and, looking up, she saw the door
being slowly pushed open.

'It's that Old Maitland,' was her first resentful thought, as
she started up with wet eyes, red nose, and ruffled hair, vainly
trying to scrub the signs of tears from her face, but only
making it worse, as she'd hastily picked up a duster, thick with
dust, instead of her handkerchief, and was leaving muddy
marks all over her face.

But the tall figure stooping to enter the doorway was not
Old Maitland—it was the man with the red hair.

As he came forward, his lean hawk face in the shadows
above the lamplight, his rough homespun coat beaded with
rain, his breeches and leggings splashed with mud, bringing
in the smell of cold hillsides and peat-reek mixed with the
slight odour of horses, there was something so hard and
primitive about him that it seemed to strike against her softness and helplessness with the force of a blow.

The icy rain blew in with him into the stuffy warmth of
the shop, heated by a paraffin stove, making the whole con-
trast more apparent.

As he turned and shut the door she noticed that he carried
a horse's shining bit and some pieces of leather harness in one
hand. —

'I've come . . .' he began shortly, without even a 'Good
evening' as he took the floor in a stride, then he suddenly
stopped. 'What is the matter?' he asked.

'Nothing,' she answered sullenly, trying to pull herself

48

together, furious at being caught all 'woolly and wobbly', as she said to herself, against his straight, indifferent hardness.

'Why are you crying?'

'I'm not crying. I have a cold. Can I serve you with anything?'

She tried to be dignified and put on her best saleswoman's manner. It was not exactly a success, with her smudged face and the awry ribbon on top of her head.

She detested him; he made her furious, but for all that she was glad it was he and no one else who had walked into her shop and found her crying. He would never tell or go discussing it; of that she was profoundly aware.

'I came to see if you could sell me some waxed thread,' he said, answering her question as if she was a *real* shopkeeper in a *real* shop. She almost liked him at that moment, only she hadn't a notion what waxed thread was, or if there was any in the place. Still, she kept her end up.

'I'm not sure if we have any in stock at the moment,' she announced, after one wild glance round for inspiration.

Not a smile crossed his face.

'It used to be kept in the third drawer to the left, second shelf,' he said.

She went to the drawer and pulled it out, trying secretly to blow her pink nose as she did so; the tears seemed still to be going down that way. All she could see were some hanks of thread. She took one out.

'Black,' he said. 'And a packet of strong needles. They are below the thread.'

All the paper she could see were some little sweetie bags with puzzles for children on the back. She put his purchases in one, wildly wondering what to charge.

'That will be threepence, won't it?' he said carelessly, looking at her puzzled face. 'Twopence for the thread and a penny for the needles.'

He took an old leather purse from his breeches pocket and counted out the coppers.

'Thank you. That is quite correct.'

'Good night.' He turned away and strode towards the door. His hand was on it, when he hesitated, turned round, and looked at her. Her eyes had again filled with tears.

He left the door and came back.

'Can I help you in any way?' he asked. His tone was not impatient, but it was quite detached.

'No, thank you.'

'Are you still quite alone here?'

'No—yes—I mean, I have Miss Teugh when she can come, but her sister is ill.'

She pronounced it 'Tuff.'

'Christy cannot help you with the shop. Do you know anything about keeping a shop?'

If his voice had been more sympathetic everything would have rushed out, she was so distracted with worry, but there was something so detached about him and his questions that she resented them both. She resented too the relief she felt at speaking to *anyone* about the shop and her worries, in spite of the fact that she felt sure he did not want to have anything to do with her.

'I expect he's afraid I'll become a nuisance,' she thought to herself. 'Perhaps he's afraid I'll fall in love with him.' She glanced up at the lean, weatherbeaten face with the hot-coloured, yet cold, orange-brown eyes and fiery hair. 'Well, nobody would call him handsome,' she thought, 'and as for falling in love, it would be easier to fall in love with a red eagle.'

She wanted to say haughtily that it was none of his business and she knew all about keeping a shop, but his cold force-fulness compelled the truth out of her.

'No,' she said, after a long silence.

'Then—what are you doing here?'

'My aunt left me the shop. She said I was to keep it my-self or I couldn't have it. I *must* learn how to keep it. I *will* learn—if only Christy could have helped me a little at first!'

He glanced round at the untidy piles of stuff, the ravelled wools, the rows of shelves with their mixter-maxter of goods.

'What is bothering you particularly?' There was, if any-thing, a slightly kinder note in his voice.

'I want to have a sale, and I don't know the prices of half the things. I don't know what they cost, what is the price they are sold at, or what to reduce them to, or what it would be fair to ask for damaged goods—like this!'

She picked up the first thing that came to hand, a little

50

wooden box of slate pencils with the lid crushed and one pencil broken.

'A penny the box was the price, but they are very little used now. Give the broken ones away to children at the sale, and keep half a dozen of the best in case you are asked for one occasionally.'

He glanced at a pile of faded writing pads, standing next to them on the counter.

'Those used to be a shilling; price them sixpence and fourpence.'

'Oh,' she said, 'thank you. I wonder how you remember.'

She thought he must have bought things in the shop and remembered the prices.

'I served my time in a store.'

'Oh, then you could help me!' It was out before she had time to think.

'Well,' he hesitated, looked rather curiously at her for a moment, and then asked, 'You want your stock taken?'

'Oh, I didn't mean,' she began hastily to apologise, 'I didn't mean—I expect you are too busy . . .'

'Get a sheet of paper,' he interrupted. 'No, take an exercise book; there are plenty of them.'

'But . . .'

She got no further. He had crosssed the floor in two strides, pushed aside her step-ladder, and taken an exercise book from a pile on the top shelf. With a pencil he swiftly drew some columns and marked them 'Cost Price,' 'Selling Price,' 'Sale,' talking quickly as he did so.

'This isn't really taking stock. I'm just helping you out. Afterwards if you go over the items yourself and add up the sale prices you'll have a rough idea of the present value of your stock. You could also find out what it should have been and what it originally cost—very roughly, of course—by adding up the different columns. Do you understand?'

'Yes, I'm good at arithmetic.'

Then, swiftly but thoroughly, he went over her stock, going methodically along the shelves, through the drawers, and along her piled counter. Once she asked him if he was sure he had time, that she wasn't keeping him from his own work.

'Yes, you are,' he said frankly, and with that detached air of his, 'but I'll manage. Don't waste time.'

She wasted no more. He went over article by article, even to the little cards hung about with flasks of aspirin, corn cures, iodine, packets of dye, and washing blues.

He opened the barrel and they found it full of apples. They looked in the storeroom and found a few boxes of dry goods, but the storeroom had been mostly used for unpacking boxes.

At last they had finished. An hour or two had passed so swiftly that Priscilla had scarcely noticed them. Now she saw that it was after nine o'clock. She hesitated, and then asked him if he would have a cup of coffee.

'No, thank you,' he said briefly. 'I must be going.' He was rolling up some of the ravelled wool which had been left to the last, and she thought how incongruous he looked with his height and in his rough coat, breeches, and strong boots rolling up wools, but his long fingers were deft and sure. He twisted up the last hank and laid it on the others.

'You'll manage your sale now. Go on a rough estimate of half-prices; most of it isn't worth more, but reduce further if things don't sell. Clear it all out, burn the rubbish, then freshen the place with distemper and paint—Christy can do all that—and start afresh . . .' He paused. 'You'll need another lesson on buying in . . .' He paused again, and she thought he was going to offer to come back and give her the much needed lesson and help, but after a moment he turned away.

'Good night,' he said, and, picking up his harness and the bit, he strode to the door.

'Good night,' she said, 'and thank you again.'

He opened the door and was just going out when he turned and looked at her standing there, frowning and puzzled, her questioning eyes on him.

'Go and wash your face and have your supper and go to bed,' he said, as if he was speaking to a child. 'You'll manage all right. Good luck!' Another slight pause. Then:

'Good-bye,' he said, and went out and strode off into the night and the rain.

'Good . . . bye,' feebly echoed Priscilla.

'He doesn't like me,' she said to herself, rather slowly. 'I

52

wonder why he helped me. . . . I suppose he looks on me as a drowning sparrow he just poked out of the water with his foot in passing. I'm grateful to him, but I dislike his beastly superiority and aloofness. I didn't ask him to help me.'

She felt lonely again when she went into the kitchen for a cup of coffee. The fire had gone out, and the place was in darkness. She stood leaning on the table, remembering her aunts. They might have written a little note, they might have left a way open. . . .

She was roused by the back door opening, and Christy blowing in.

'Good gyte, lassie! Are ye all in the dark?'

In five minutes she had the lamps lit and a fire roaring up the chimney. She saw that Priscilla had been crying, but had noticed her despondency that last few days, and said nothing. 'A guid greet will do her good,' she said to herself. 'It empties the heart.'

She had brought in fresh cream and country butter and two chicken livers from the Haughs, whence she never came empty-handed. In a few minutes they were seated before steaming and scalding tea. Christy would have nothing to do with coffee. Priscilla drank a cup and felt better at once, and by the time the meal was finished she felt more happy. Outside the window—they never drew the curtains, for it looked on to the garden and the river—the stars were shining. The rain had stopped.

One particular star seemed to be twinkling at her personally from over the apple-tree. She forgot the aunts for the moment, and remembered the shop with a sudden glow. She knew something about prices now; she could go straight on tomorrow really preparing for her sale.

'I feel better,' she said, smiling across the table to Christy.

'That's right, and I've a bit o' good news. Ma sister Phemie —her that's mairrit tae the gamekeeper at Blackhall—has come to bide a bit with Belle, so I can bide at hame noo and come in as you want me. Ma mither's as blythe as a bird. She doesna' like being left ower long, but here I can rin oot and in and see to ye baith.'

'Oh, I am glad!' said Priscilla. 'And I've good news too. That man who showed me the house the night I arrived came into the shop and he stayed and helped me after he'd bought what he wanted. He knew all the prices and everything. I wonder who he can be? We were so busy I never had a chance to ask him.'

'He helped you with the shop?'

Christy was staring at her in amazement.

'Yes. He's a very tall, lean man with red hair that goes up in a crest and . . .'

'Lassie!' exclaimed Christy, jumping to her feet. 'Ye don't tell me ye let that villain go all over your shop! Yer aunt would turn in her grave if she heard ye!'

'What!' exclaimed Priscilla, overcome in her turn by surprise at Christy's vehemence. 'Why? Who is he?'

'Whae is he? Whae is he? I'll tell ye whae *he* is. That's Redd Maitland. Aye, *Redd Maitland,* Auld Maitland's nevvy, the same as worrumed himself in before. Wae's me! Wae's me! The deil's gone ower Jock Wabster!'

7

Redd Maitland

Priscilla, as dismayed as Christy herself, stared back at her with her mouth open. She had no idea why the deil should have 'gone ower Jock Wabster,' but she was getting used to Christy's extraordinary expressions. Anyhow, the name Maitland was enough.

'Redd Maitland,' she repeated, in such horrified tones it might have been the devil himself she was speaking of. Then she recovered herself a little.

'Oh, no,' she said. 'It couldn't be. He wasn't a bit like a Maitland.' She had a picture in her mind of the Maitlands as being little tubby men, with dark moustaches or grey beards, wearing broadcloth or with white aprons tied round their stomachs.

'No, I grant ye that. The Maitlands are all wee men. Redd's a Badenoch on the mother's side. The Craigowry Badenochs are a' red-heided giants and daft aboot horses.'

'But—I thought he kept a shop. I'm sure this wasn't a Maitland, Christy. He was a farmer.'

'It was Redd Maitland, I tell ye. Can ye no take a tellin'? And now you've let him in the deil hissel' kens what mischief he'll make. Eh, lassie, could ye no have mair sense than that?'

'But I didn't know. Are you sure, Christy?'

But her voice faltered; she was remembering how much he seemed to know about the shop.

'Sure? Aye, I'm sure, worse luck! They're as cunnin' as adders, every man Jack o' them.'

'But he looked like a farmer, and he was carrying some harness.'

'Like enough. Ye see, he fell oot wi' the auld man. He was an orphan laddie, and his uncle, Auld Maitland, brought him up, and put him in the business to serve his time. The auld man has no son of his ain, and Redd was to heir everything.

'Your aunt and Auld Maitland were friendly enough then, and when she broke her leg she was glad enough when he sent Redd over to look after the shop for her. Then all the mischief began. He found out how hard pressed she was, what with getting Murdo out of trouble and one thing and another, got her into big debts for stock from his uncle—well, I've told ye all that. The upshot was all the misery and poverty she was in for years. He was just a lad at the time, but tarred with the same brush as all the Maitlands.'

'But you said he quarrelled with the old man.'

'Aye, but that was later on. They were hand in glove then, but Redd was aye a thrawn deil, and he must have done something that angered the auld man, for they had an awfu' set-to, and Redd flung himself oot o' the hoose and went and hired himself to a farmer. But he was aye set on horses, and started horse-copin' on his ain, and now he has the Mill House and rents the Long Haugh from Martin for his horses, but it's a hard struggle, and I misdoot me but what he'd like fine to get back to the cushie place he had with his uncle, but the auld man got another nevvy in his place; *his* mother was a Turner—they're as cunnin' as the Maitland's themselves, and they say he has worked hissel' in so well with his uncle that now *he's* to heir the whole rik-ma-tik. Aye, Redd's a fool as well as a rogue.'

'Do they call him Red because he has red hair?' asked Priscilla inconsequently.

'No exactly; it's *Redd*—two d's. All the Craigowry Badenochs are red-heided, and there's aye been a Redd Badenoch, and so his mither—his father was killed in an accident before he was born—called him Redd Badenoch Maitland.'

'But, Christy, if he has quarrelled with his uncle he wouldn't want to help him to get the shop or to put me out.'

'Never you trust a Maitland. He may be wantin' to get in again with the auld man; now he's older he'll understand better what he's lost. It's a sair struggle he has to make a livin', and he couldn't find a better way to get in wi' the auld rogue than to go claipsin' about your affairs and helpin' him to find oot all he can. Na, na, Redd diddled your auntie, and he'll do the same wi' you if you're no' carefu'.'

'No, he won't—as if I'd have anything to do with a Maitland after what my Aunt Purdie said! I just hate them all.'

She was filled with resentment against the man with the red hair. He had sneaked in to betray her, well aware that she did not know him. Of course, that was all an excuse about thread and needles. What a fool she had been! What could a man want with needles and thread? He had been laughing at her all the time.

No wonder he had never mentioned his name. He knew she would have turned him out if he had as much as whispered the word 'Maitland'!

'He won't deceive me!' She turned on Christy now. 'I detested him from the moment I saw him. I must have guessed deep down that he was an enemy. It was just because I was desperate I let him help me. You should have warned me about him. How was I to know a Maitland looked like that? Anyhow I hate red hair!'

'Now nae! Now nae!' said Christy soothingly, for Priscilla had jumped up, and with her crest of ribbon and the black hair rising up behind its confines looked like an angry little hawk about to pounce. 'Now nae! Now nae! Dinna put yoursel' aboot like that. There's no that muckle ill done. I was just warning you about him. You're that innocent I sair misdoot me if you can take care of yourself.'

'I'm not innocent!' This was adding insult to injury. 'And I know quite well how to take care of myself. In lots of things'—she remembered the respectable wooing of poor Mr Porter—'I'm not so innocent as you are!'

Christy actually had the audacity to laugh; not merely to laugh, but to go into rumbles of amusement that kept breaking out in spite of herself, while she cleared away and washed up.

Priscilla heard her with indignation from the shop, where she had marched off, determined to bring in the exercise book and cast it into the flames to show what she thought of Redd Maitland.

But wiser counsels prevailed. After all, where would she be if she burned it? Back into the slough from which she'd just been dragged. She pushed it into a drawer, put out the

57

light, and went back to show Christy how very old and dignified she could be, in defiance of those irrepressible rumbles.

'There's nothing to laugh at, Christy.'

'Deed no!' said Christy. 'If I was you, Preescilla, I'd burn
that book ye spoke of and change all the prices; that would
put a spoke in their wheels, the deevils!'

At this simple method of circumventing the devil Priscilla
could not forbear to smile.

'But Christy, you can't just change prices and make them
what you like.'

'What for no? Wha kens but what he told ye all the wrong
ones anyhow.'

'Oh, no,' said Priscilla at once. 'He didn't do that.'

'And how are ye to ken? Ye said ye knew nothing about
them.'

'I don't know *how* I know, Christy. Don't be tiresome. I
just know that I know he didn't do that.'

'Well, mebbe you're right. I'm no' sayin' he did. I'm just
sayin' *never trust a Maitland.*'

'I detest and loathe every Maitland,' retorted Priscilla, 'and
I'm sick and tired of talking about them.'

'You're fair done up,' said Christy. 'Away to your bed.
There's the clock chappin' ten. I'll be in afore six and bring
ye a cup o' tea, and ye'll lie and have your breakfast in your
bed.'

'I will not, then,' said Priscilla. 'I hate getting breakfast in
bed. I'll get up at seven.'

'Eh, but ye're a thrawn lassie.' Christy was smiling as she
pinned on her shawl. 'As like your aunty as two pins.'

As she went off Priscilla heard more rumbling of secret
amusement.

'Don't you giggle at me,' she shouted, as she looked back
down the stair. 'I won't have it.'

'Wha's gigglin'?' said Christy solemnly, and, going off, she
locked the back door after her. She always locked Priscilla in
so that she need not disturb her in the early morning.

It was long before Priscilla went to sleep. She knew that
Christy had been more alarmed over Redd's visit than over
Old Maitland's, though she had fulminated enough about him
too, but she could not think why.

'After all,' she said to herself, 'the old man might do me

58

harm in all kinds of ways, but his nephew couldn't. What is all the fuss about? Anyhow, if I couldn't make the shop pay and got into debt I'd do something, but I'd never, never sell it to Old Maitland, so what am I frightened of?'

But she was frightened. She felt herself very young and ignorant to be pitted against a clever and cunning old businessman who really must want to get her into his clutches and then get her shop.

Then, just before she fell asleep, a lean face with a red crest of hair came before her eyes.

'I didn't like him,' she said to herself, 'but I do wish I could have trusted him. He did look as if you could trust him, though he was so hard and cold and stand-offish. I suppose that's why he doesn't like me either; we are enemies. I suppose he thinks I'm a soft silly. Well, I'll show him!'

That Old Maitland, for reasons of his own, wanted to get a finger into her pie she had more proof the next day.

Christy was out to bring in the pony and her cow, which fed in Priscilla's field, when a soft tap came at the door.

She opened it to find a girl with a slight deformity of her shoulders standing there: a shabbily dressed girl of about thirty she seemed, very plain, with a pale but freckled face and big, shy grey eyes.

'I'm Mysie Cree,' she said. 'Mr Maitland sent me over to see if I could be of any help to you.'

'Oh,' said Priscilla, taken by surprise. 'Will you . . .' And then she stopped.

It was a bitter day, and the girl looked cold, and with her natural kindness Priscilla had been going to ask her in. Now she faltered. The girl's deformity made her sorry for her, but she'd come from Old Maitland.

'I think there is some mistake,' she went on quickly. 'I told Mr Maitland I did not need anyone. I'm so sorry you have troubled to come.'

The girl looked even more embarrassed.

'He said I was to say he'd want nothing in return for lending me for a day or two. It's the quiet season, and we're no very busy in the shop.'

'It's very kind of Mr Maitland,' said Priscilla, 'but I can manage quite well. Thank you very much, though, for coming to offer to help me.'

59

Still the girl hesitated. She looked a little frightened, Priscilla thought.

'I'd like to help you,' she said. 'I wouldn't want anything. It would be a change from the shop.'

Priscilla looked straight at the girl.

'I'm sorry,' she repeated. 'But the truth is I don't want to accept any favours from Mr Maitland.'

'No,' the girl said uncertainly; then added after a moment, 'Well, I'll be gettin' along.'

Christy had said she would have tea with her mother that day, so it was some time later when she came in.

'So you had Mysie Cree here,' she said.

'Yes, I nearly asked her in to tea, and then I thought I'd better not because Old Maitland sent her—but I was sorry for her.'

'Aye. I met her, and took her in-bye for a cup. Poor lass, she had a longish wait for the bus, but dinna you put your self aboot, she knew fine why you didn't ask her in. She hates Auld Maitland, but is feared of losing her job. Mealy-mouthed old hypocrite, he pretended to her he was sorry for you, and said you wouldn't be long in comin' a cropper unless somebody gave you a helping hand. She's a nice lass, Mysie; it's a peety she's under his thumb.'

The subject of Mysie and her mother's shop, which now belonged to Old Maitland, kept Christy's tongue going for the rest of the evening, but Priscilla only heard bits of the tale, as she was very busy making final preparations for her sale, coming and going in the shop, while Christy, equally busy, chattered on.

8

The Sale

Priscilla was standing in her shop having a last look round before she unlocked the door for her sale.

Everything was ready. She and Christy had brought in two or three tables from the rooms and displayed the best goods and biggest bargains on them. Priscilla was terribly proud of her tickets. She was good at printing and fancy penmanship, and she and Christy considered them works of art.

Christy had on an enormous snow-white cooking apron, and her reddish-brown hair was scraped into a bun at the back. Priscilla wore one of the neat blue coat-overalls she had worn at her domestic science classes at school. Her black hair was scraped back as severely as Christy's own, and she was trying hard to look large and capable, but her inches and the blue ribbon tied in a bow at the top of her head to keep her hair back rather gave the show away, not to speak of her curved humorous mouth and her nose. Priscilla's nose simply would not look sedate and capable. It was the perky species—there's nothing to be done with them.

'Oh, Christy,' she said nervously, 'what shall I do if nobody comes to my sale?'

'*They'll* come,' replied Christy serenely. 'Curiosity killed the cat.'

Priscilla got what comfort she could from this dark allusion because Christy seemed to think it ought to cheer her up.

'Well, here goes!' Priscilla unlocked the shop with a flourish.

There was a long silence, and then the bell rang, and in walked Bessie, the blacksmith's wife, with a large basket.

'I was the first to speak to you at Crumstane,' she announced, 'so I thought I'd be your first customer. Eh, but I'm glad shop's open again.' Bessie had come from Yorkshire long ago and still missed out her 'the's.' 'Shop's been a real miss.'

Christy had absolutely refused to sell anything or come out into the open. 'No me,' she'd said. 'I'll bide ahint the door and keep an eye on the folkses, and mebbe roll up a parcel if so be I'm needed.' No sooner, however, did she see her old friend Bessie than she rushed out of her hiding-place, and the two were deep in village gossip, the shop forgotten.

It didn't matter, however. Bessie was only the first. It wasn't often Crumstane had anything so exciting as a sale. Aunt Purdie had never had sales, and this was what sportsmen call a double event. There was the sale, and there was Priscilla.

Priscilla had never been out in the village or seen anyone in the few days she'd been there. She'd been too busy, and meantime gossip had spread, not unassisted, perhaps, by Christy, who loved a good mixture of gossip and mystery.

They were all dying to see the new Janet Purdie, 'Auld Janetie's niece, an English lass frae the sooth,' the tales ran. 'They tell me she's a leddy, brought up in a castle and never soiled a finger in her life, waited on hand and fut, and might ha'e mairrit a millionaire.'

Naturally every one wanted to see this rare bird among them.

'And she's selling all her aunt's good stuff for *nothing*. Christy'—they pronounced it *Crystie*—'Christy Teugh's in a fair takin' the way she's lettin' it go for an auld sang, but she kens naught aboot the business. She didn't even ken the price o' sugar or a loaf o' bread!'

Christy as a publicity agent was indeed worth her weight in gold. Who could forego a chance like that?

Soon the little place was crowded. Christy was in her element, though not as a saleswoman. Alas! She couldn't sell for talking, inquiring about this one's Kirsty, and the other's Jamesie, and 'Hoo did the weddin' go off?' and 'You don't tell me it's yersel', Mistress Broon. I haven't seen ye in Crumstane sin' Michaelmas, and hoo's a' wi ye?' It was as good as the Annual Fair to Christy.

But it didn't matter; every one was good-natured, and nobody in a hurry, and they bought. They bought everything, slate pencils and sandshoes—in March!—caster oil and blue paper bags full of damp sugar, corn cures and leather laces, bottles of coffee and sauce, yards of butter-muslin and rolls of linoleum.

No doubt many of the things were great bargains—Priscilla, in her anxiety to clear the dusty, muddled shelves, had rather underdone than overdone the prices—but heaps of stuff were just rubbish. However, once people have found bargains are going they are apt to think everything a bargain.

Then, Christy was a favourite in the village, and they liked Priscilla at once. Perhaps it was her shyness and modesty, and her anxiety to help them, but just as probably it was her nose. Priscilla's nose accounted for a lot in Priscilla's life, or that cheeky bow of ribbon above the small, anxious face.

Anyhow, they took to her. She wasn't 'proud'. She answered questions as frankly as they were put to her, and wasn't above asking them herself.

'But what will you do with all that sugar?' she asked the joiner's wife. 'It's damp.'

'Bless your heart! If you'd six bairns you'd know what to do with a stone of damp sugar at that price,' returned Mrs MacNab cheerfully.

Another thing they liked was her way of talking. It amused them hugely; a South-country accent always did amuse Crumstane, but they liked it.

'I dae like to hear ye speak,' one woman said. 'It's like a doo cooin'.'

Priscilla thought it was one of the nicest compliments she had ever had—not that she'd had many. Compliments had not come her way, except from Mr Porter, and Mr Porter would have blacked out any compliment just by being Mr Porter.

By eleven she was dead tired, and very glad to see the shop begin to empty as housewives hastened off to prepare midday dinners for husbands and school children. By then the shop looked as if a cyclone had passed through it. The tables were bare, the apple barrel was empty, the floor trampled and muddy, but Priscilla's spirits, in spite of her weariness, were soaring high.

She was just about to rush into the kitchen for a cup of coffee when the door opened and two elderly ladies dressed in homespun suits and thick shoes came in.

'Good morning,' said the stout, short one. 'I hope you are having a good sale.'

She spoke with a strong Scottish accent, but with a beautifully refined and educated voice.

'Good morning,' said Priscilla shyly. 'Yes, thank you very much, I am having a good sale. Every one is so kind.'

A pair of sharp, humorous brown eyes looked at her, taking her all in as she stood behind the counter looking very young and slightly flustered.

'We knew your aunt very well—a great friend of ours—and we know who you are—Miss Delaine, isn't it? But I expect you are wondering who we are.'

'Yes,' said Priscilla, as she paused. 'I was Priscilla Janet Purdie Delaine, but I'm Janet Purdie now because my aunt wanted me to be, only it's difficult getting out of the Priscilla.'

'I shouldn't try. Keep the firm "Janet Purdie"—I'm sure that's all your aunt wished—and stick to your own pretty name of Priscilla. We are two of the Misses Selby of the Hall. This is Tibbie, and I'm Prudence. We want you to come and have lunch with us on Sunday after church, if you can manage. We'll drive you up. Would you like to come?'

'Yes, thank you,' said Priscilla. 'I should like to come very much.'

'That's settled, then. We should have called before, but we thought you would be too busy to be bothered with callers, so we're killing two birds with one stone—paying you a call and attending your sale. Now, have you got that list, Tibbie?'

Christy had evidently been keeping a look-out from behind the red curtain of the glass-panelled door, for she now appeared with an extra chair, as there was only one in the shop.

'Keep us and save us, Christy!' exclaimed Miss Tibbie. 'Where did you get that apron?'

'Well, ye see, Miss Tibbie, I thocht I'd better look clean if I couldn't look bonnie. I hed the stuff laid away for some good strong shifts, so I took it along to Ann Pinn, and she got twa out o' the five yards.'

She had dusted the chairs as she spoke, and now they both sat down and brought out their list, which was a lengthy one and included some items that Priscilla hadn't got.

'Never mind, child,' said Miss Prudence, when she saw

64

Priscilla looking worried. 'This is just a sale, but we always dealt with your aunt, and we mean to deal with you, so when you are ordering your stock be sure to get . . .' And she gave Priscilla a list of things including the kinds of tea they liked, how much sugar of various kinds they were likely to use a month, and various other details, all of the greatest practical help to Priscilla.

'I know lots about the shop,' said Miss Prudence, 'and who your aunt dealt with and so on, so if you think I can help you any time just take a walk up to the Hall. 'Deed, I'd like fine to keep a shop myself. I've aye thought I could make it pay.'

'I've no doubt ye think ye could make anything pay, Prudence,' said Miss Tibbie, 'except, of course, the garden.'

Priscilla found out afterwards that the 'leddies at the Ha',' as they were always called, were hard up and tried to make the garden pay by selling vegetables and fruit.

Christy evidently thought it was time she put a word in.

'Teenie says she can't stand that heathen broon sugar ye like, Miss Tibbie. She says it'll no melt i' the cup like Christian sugar.'

'Teenie'll no be asked what she likes,' retorted Miss Tibbie. 'What's good enough for the parlour is good enough for the kitchen.'

At that moment the shop door opened, and an ancient-looking, elderly man with a fringe of whisker under his chin put his head in at the door. He was wearing a pair of patched, stained corduroy trousers, but above them was very smart in an old green coat with silver buttons and a tall hat that looked as if it had been brushed the wrong way round.

'Time's up!' he roared into the shop.

'And who do you think ye are, Andra MacPherson,' said Miss Tibbie, 'to tell your betters when their time's up—no to speak o' your manners?'

'Wha said twal o' the clock, then?' asked Andra, touching his hat. 'No me.'

'Well, I dare say we'd better go now.'

With renewed invitations to come and see them they went off to an ancient carriage, waiting at the door, followed by Andra with his arms full of parcels.

'Hech!' exclaimed Christy, as soon as they'd disappeared. 'You're *made*.'

Priscilla looked at her questioningly.

'D'ye no ken whae *they* were? The leddies at the Ha'. You're a' right now.'

'But I thought you said they were so poor.' Christy had told her something about the Selby fortunes.

'Aye, they've no much to come and go on, but if the leddies take ye up everybody'll follow suit.'

'But you never said anything of that before.'

'No me! Miss Prudence is that thrawn, and she cast oot wi' your aunty over Redd Maitland. That's when your aunty went over to the Haughs and told my good-brother, Donal Martin, that if he let the Long Haugh to Redd Maitland she'd never speak to him again. Miss Prudence cam here and told your aunt she was acting in an unchristian speerit, and your aunty said she'd been taught to beware of the devil and all his works—eh, what a set-to they had!

'Then Miss Prudence wanted Murdo MacPherson—he's kin to their Andra, the gairdner—to get the shop, and they'd another set-to about that. So I didn't know how she'd take it, you comin' here. She said it was a daft-like thing to put a niminy-piminy young leddie frae the toon in a country village shop, and that it would never do. Miss Prudence rules the roost up at the Ha'—though Miss Tibbie comes a good second. Howsomedever, it's all right. She's taken to you.'

Christy seemed to think that now all Priscilla's troubles were over, but Priscilla had too much sense and independence to take that for granted. She wasn't going to rely on the ladies at the Hall for the success of her shop; she was going to depend on herself. 'If it's a shop, where people get what they want, and where they like the shopkeeper, they'll come to it,' she thought to herself. 'If the village doesn't like me, and it's a poor shop, they will buy from the vans.' There was a good strain of practical common sense in Priscilla, in spite of her nose!

By the end of the afternoon the shop was pretty well cleared out of the better stock, and Priscilla was dead beat. Christy, however, was as lively as a cricket, and after she'd fed the fowls, bedded the pony, and gone over and milked her own cow she came back and helped Priscilla to fill up the

66

tables and turn all the remainder of the stock out of the drawers and upper shelves and put it where it could be seen.

By this time Priscilla was beginning to grasp what a busy life her aunt had led. Not only had she kept the shop, but with Christy's help she had managed a cow and a pig, sold the milk 'at the door,' as they called it, sent eggs and poultry to the weekly market at Lammerton, getting up early and driving in herself with her produce, and opening her shop later on market-days. Christy had been sending some in by the carrier, but she said that ran away with all the profits, which in any case were much less, and wanted to start the stall in the butter-market again.

Priscilla baulked at at he stall in the butter-market, but Christy said she could do that herself, as it was only a matter of poultry and eggs and 'clish-clashing wi' the toonsfolk.'

Priscilla was sure Christy would be a past-master at the clish-clashing. It turned out that she could sell her own butter too, now she had a cow. So they arranged that Christy should take the pony and trap into Lammerton on market-days.

Priscilla was going to learn to drive too, as the pony and the old tub might prove useful to get about in, seeing she had no bicycle and had never learned to ride one. The aunts had not approved of bicycles, and, indeed, there had been little use for them in Baxton.

They were discussing all this with Christy mounted on the step-ladder, when suddenly the step she was standing on gave way and she crashed to the floor.

Priscilla, terrified when she saw her ashen face, rushed for the brandy, and helped her into a chair, when they discovered that the only real damage was a dislocated thumb, which was giving her great pain.

Priscilla was distracted.

'Where can we get a doctor?' she asked, holding Christy's hand and looking with dismay at the strange angle the thumb had taken.

'Eh! eh!' lamented Christy now. 'What a peety we've cast oot wi' Redd Maitland! He's the only man in Crumstane that can set a bone. They doctors is nae use wi' bones. They ken naught aboot bones.'

'Nonsense!' exclaimed Priscilla. 'Where is the doctor? I'll

get him. A man who isn't a doctor—a horse-breeder—can't possibly know anything about bones.'

Christy was between two fires. Doctors knew nothing about bones, but Redd Maitland should never darken their door, though Redd was the man for the job.

Priscilla took matters into her own hands at last and rushed off to the blacksmith's to consult Bessie, who also recommended Redd, but told her she had seen the doctor's car going up to the Hall. Miss Leslie, she heard, had had another of her fainting turns.

There was no telephone in the village—nothing to do but go herself. However, she learned that the Hall was not very far, and she rushed off, hoping to meet the doctor's car.

She did not hear Bessie call out, 'Redd Maitland's up there too. I saw him go by. He's far better at the bones than any doctor.'

9

Dr John

The Hall gates were within a quarter of a mile of the village, but the avenue seemed very long to Priscilla, especially as it was uphill, so she was glad to see a car approaching her. She guessed that it was the doctor's, and held up her hand.

It stopped, and a young man's face appeared at the open window.

'Are you the doctor?'

He jumped out and lifted his hat, showing a thick crop of brown hair. 'I'm Dr John Field. Can I help you?'

'Oh, yes. Could you please come at once? Christy Tuff has dislocated her thumb.'

'Teugh,' said a voice from the farther seat in the car.

Priscilla looked in. It was Redd Maitland.

He was gazing straight before him as if he did not know of her existence.

The doctor opened the door at the back.

'Get in,' he said briefly. 'I'll run you along.'

'Oh, no,' said Priscilla at once. Then she began to stammer as she saw his surprised stare, but she was not going to ride in the same car as Redd Maitland.

'I mean, I like to walk—thank you very much.'

'You mean you like to run?' asked Dr John, with an engaging grin. 'You were running when I saw you.'

'I don't wish to go in the car . . .' began Priscilla stiffly. She had turned away after the first glance and kept her eyes off Redd Maitland.

'Hullo, Maitland, what are you up to?' The doctor's voice interrupted her.

'Thanks, John. I think I'll walk. I can take a cut across the fields. Come over when you are ready.'

Redd Maitland was already out of the car, striding off into the undergrowth.

'Bless my soul!' said Dr John, turning a puzzled but laughing look at Priscilla. 'What's the matter with my car? Or is it me? Or the germs? Or . . .'

'Oh, no,' said Priscilla, distressed, and as red as a tomato. 'It's just—I thought I'd better walk.'

'Two minds with but one single thought—to get rid of me,' said Dr John.

'He's not a *bit* like a doctor,' thought Priscilla, rather resentfully. She thought doctors should all fit her idea of a doctor—a sort of serious sawbones with lantern jaws. This was a broad young man of medium height, with a face she liked in spite of herself, a blunt, open face with humorous blue eyes and a tiny, narrow, straight moustache, brown like his hair.

All the same, doctors should be doctors, not young men with rather taking faces. She tried to look very stiff, and might have managed if it hadn't been for that nose—and, of course, the mouth beneath it, which *would* go up at the corners. As she stood hesitating he went round to the door which Redd Maitland had left open.

'Come along, jump in,' he said. 'You look tired, and Christy will be in pain with that thumb. Where is she?'

'She's in my shop.'

'Oh, you are Miss—Purdie, is it?'

'Yes,' said Priscilla.

'Ah! I think I see the light; the ancient Purdie-Maitland vendetta. "A curse on both your houses!" and all that sort of thing. . . . Tell me what happened. It would take something to dislocate Christy's thumb.'

'She fell off the step-ladder.' Priscilla was recovering herself. She wasn't afraid of this young man: he hadn't red hair—she hated red hair. 'And what's more,' she went on, in the forthright way that was natural to her when she wasn't quelled by men with red hair and stony faces, 'you'll have to be very *tactful*. Christy thinks doctors know *nothing* about bones.'

'I know. Any shepherd can put us in our places. I bet you five bob she wanted you to go for Redd Maitland.'

'No—she doesn't like Redd Maitland. You owe me five shillings.'

He put his hand in his pocket.

'Oh, no,' she said, her cheeks red again and speaking quickly. 'That's a joke. I make jokes.'

'And I pay my bets. I'll tell you what'—seeing she looked distressed—'I'll spend it in your shop. I've a hole in my socks. Do you sell socks?'

'Not the kind you would wear.'

'That's all you know. I'm wearing a pair just now that I bought in Fort William for ninepence—made of odds and ends of wool they knit hair shirts with. I daren't pull up my trousers when I sit down because they're striped like What's-his-name's coat—Esau, was it?'

'Joseph,' said Priscilla, shocked. 'Don't you sit under the Rev. Lamont?'

'Well, yes, if you mean he sits on me good and strong when ever we meet. All the same, I like old Lamont, though he keeps me in order. How is the shop doing?'

'I haven't really opened yet, but my sale began today. It's for two days, but I sold more than half today.'

'Good going.'

They had arrived at the door now, and he helped her out. Christy's greeting was not encouraging.

'Ye can try,' she said, 'but I ken fine, Dr John, ye'll never get it back in its right place. Eh, dear, I'll be lamed for life.'

'Not you,' said Dr John, getting hold of her hand. 'What set you climbing step-ladders with rotten treads? I thought you'd more sense.'

Before she knew what he was up to he had the thumb in place; then he bandaged it up, packed up his bag, and yet unaccountably lingered. He looked round the shop, asked questions, and gave advice. Then when there seemed absolutely nothing more to linger about he bade them good night.

Just as he was going he turned to Christy. 'I'll look in just to see the thumb's all right. You'll be here, I suppose?'

'Aye,' said Christy. 'I'll be here, but my thoomb'll dae fine. If it comes oot again I'll send for ye.'

He laughed to Priscilla. 'She's afraid I'll run her up a bill. It won't cost you anything more, Christy; it's to keep you from wasting Maitland's time or hieing away up to the hills to Jock the shepherd. Professional jealousy, in fact!'

'Haud awa wi' ye,' said Christy. 'Your tongue's ower

71

soople, and as for Redd Maitland, he'd better keep his distance and no be creepin' in here tae spy oot the place and betray an innocent lassie . . .'

Christy was off. Dr John turned, raised his arms as if to ward off blows, and fled.

Priscilla turned on Christy. 'You shouldn't have said that,' she scolded. 'He'll go and tell Mr Maitland. He was in the car when I stopped it, and the doctor's going to his house after he leaves here.'

'Aye, they're as thick as thieves; that's why I told Redd Maitland off . . .'

'But I didn't want you to. I can manage that Redd Maitland by myself,' she boasted. 'And you were very rude to the doctor, Christy. You ought to be respectful to doctors.'

'Hech! Many's the time I've clapped his ears for him, stealing apples out your aunty's gairden, but I'll say this for him: his father was a grand doctor and a grand man; if he takes after his father he'll do.'

'Does he live here? It's a small place for a doctor.'

'He lives in the auld hoose. It's been the Doctor's Hoose for generations, but both his father and mother are deid, and he hasnae a good hoosekeeper, poor laddie. It's time he had a wife.'

She ruminated a few minutes, deep in thought.

'Mebbe I was a bit hard on him. I'll need to mend my manners when he comes back.'

'I should think so too,' said Priscilla ruthlessly. 'And you're not to mention that man Maitland. I won't have it.'

Christy took this with such meekness Priscilla was surprised. There was as little of that virtue about Christy as about Priscilla herself. They had mercifully taken to each other, but when they clashed they clashed with a will; but neither minded that, Christy had been used to Aunt Purdie, who was another of the same breed, and Priscilla's high spirits had been kept under for so long—she had never dared to argue with the aunts or air her own opinions—that she thoroughly enjoyed feeling on equal ground and giving, so to speak, bang for bang. All hearty exchange of differences and open downrightness had long been refined out of the aunts, and they had tried hard to refine it out of Priscilla too, but the Purdie blood ran strong.

72

However, this time Christy meekly refrained from any counter-attack, and Priscilla thought she had got the better of her for once.

Little did she know her Christy. That deep one knew better than to let Priscilla have an inkling of her thoughts or the secret scheme that had suddenly entered her mind anent Dr John.

'Eh, what a fool I've been!' she was thinking. 'Dr John—the very lad for Priscilla. Her aunty was an auld maid and never thocht o' lads, but the lassie canna' aye be tied to a shop. Dr John's a fine lad, give him his due; he deserves better than that besom that's trying to get him. Priscilla would be the very wife for him—and I dinna trust that Redd Maitland; he could turn any lass round his finger-ends, that one, if he had a mind. I dinna think that thoomb of mine is feeling just recht. I'll need to have Dr John in again. He'll no be sweer to come back—him and his looking in to see Christy again. Christy, indeed! Howsomedever him and me'll soon understand yin anither!'

The next day the shop was less crowded, but there was a steady stream of customers, and towards evening the village children and mothers—word having been sent round by Christy in her own inimitable way that bargains were going and everything to be cleared out at rockbottom prices—gathered in a cluster like bees and bought up all that remained.

Priscilla, in the midst of clearing off pokes of sweeties put up by Christy and herself, saw the door open, and Dr John's head poke through. He surveyed the swarming mass, caught Priscilla's eyes, woefully shook his head, and disappeared.

At last it was all over. A few boys laden with some rubbish finally given away were pushed out of the shop by Christy, and the door locked and the blind drawn. She and Priscilla sank on to two upturned boxes absolutely done up, and surveyed the scene.

Except for boxes, papers, a few rotten apples and empty tins, and the remnants that strewed the floor, the shop was stripped bare.

'Isn't it lovely to see the place empty?' said Priscilla. 'But I feel like a bit of wreckage cast up on the shore after a tornado or a typhoon.'

'Well, I feel ravished with hunger mysel',' said Christy. 'Mercy on us! The chicken!'

Christy jumped up and fled. They were having, not a chicken, indeed—Christy kept the chickens for marketing—but a boiled fowl and cockie-leekie for their evening meal, as they had only been able to snatch a bite of bread and cheese at midday.

It was perhaps the happiest meal they had enjoyed together. They were both relaxed, tired and happy after their two harassed days. The sale had been a success. They were looking forward to the cleaning and scrubbing, the distempering and painting, of the next few days.

Christy had absolutely refused to have any workman called in for the inside work; she would distemper the walls and ceilings and paint the shelves herself. After that the joiner was to come in for a few odd jobs, the outside painting, and one or two of the more particular jobs.

Priscilla had worked out her colour scheme—very pale cream walls and bright blue paint. The cream walls might soil quickly, but they could be very easily given another 'lick over', as Christy put it, with distemper, and the bright blue paint was easily procured, as it was the kind used for painting carts and the joiner always had a stock; also it would look gay, and Priscilla was all for gaiety.

'How is the thumb?' she asked Christy later on.

'Well, it's stoondin' a bit,' lied Christy.

'I saw Dr John look in, but the place was humming like a hive. He was terrified, and flew off.'

'Eh, well, if he's no roon the morn I think I'll send him word; but like as not he'll be here.'

Sure enough, he called the next evening, when Christy, arrayed in a nightshirt of her late father's and a mutch of her mother's, was whitewashing the ceiling, while Priscilla, not to be outdone, had a large dusting-cloth tied round her head and a large sacking apron, called a 'brat', fastened underneath her arms, and was vigorously scrubbing such parts of the shop furniture as could be stowed away till the whitewashing and distempering were finished.

'This is what I call high jinks,' she had just announced to Christy, her face a mixture of sweat, dust, and drops of whitewash, when there was a sharp knock on the shop door.

They looked at each other, dismayed.

'Let's pretend we're "not at home",' said Priscilla. 'I'm sure my aunts . . .' And then she began to giggle, imagining her aunts' faces if they could see her.

A rap on the window came quickly after the knock.

'I know you're there,' said Dr John's voice. 'I can see you through the corner of the blind. Open the door.'

His brown eye could now be seen, glued against the window at the edge of the blind.

'For cheek and impidence . . .' began Christy. 'Eh, well, open the door, Preescilla. He's seen waur than this in his day, if I'm no far mista'en.'

She continued to slap the ceiling as Priscilla, vainly trying to get out of the brat, edged towards the door.

'It's not fair—you're the patient!' she indignantly *hissed* at Christy struggling with the brat, and pushing back the dusting-cloth from her hair.

Another knock made her cease her struggles and resignedly open the door.

'Keep us and save us! You're in a deil o' a hurry!' exclaimed Christy from aloft, as Dr John entered.

'I wanted to see you in all your glory,' he announced. 'I could only get a glimpse through the pane.' And then he put his hands in his pockets, leaned back against the counter, and roared with laughter.

Priscilla laughed with him. Christy solemnly dabbed the ceiling.

'Fools and bairns are easy pleased,' she remarked.

Dr John eased himself against the counter, half-sitting, his legs stretched across the floor.

'What are you doing on that rickety step-ladder?' he asked. 'Come down and let me see that thumb. How is it?'

'It's stoondin' fair awfu'.'

But she came down and allowed him to see it and bind it up again. Luckily it was the left hand.

Dr John, having finished with the hand, was not long in making himelf at home.

'Can I do anything?' he asked. 'I'm a dab hand at painting, paper-hanging, and carpentry. I can also use a screwdriver, hammer, and nails, and wield a scullery brush or broom.'

75

To Priscilla's surprise Christy did not meet this suggestion with a hail of sarcasm.

'Well, now you're here,' she said, 'ye might help Preescilla and me get that counter moved; it's gey and heavy.'

Once started he soon found other jobs, and in a twinkling they were all three as busy as bees and merry as grigs—at least, Dr John and Priscilla were merry as grigs, exchanging witticisms and sarcasms and teasing each other as though they had been acquainted for years.

They were both young and both rather repressed with the cares, individually, of a new shop and a new practice; an interval of irresonsibility and fun was most acceptable to both. Before they knew where they were Dr John had said he smelled supper and was dying of hunger.

Priscilla agreed that supper was the thing, and he helped her set the table, while Christy carved up the cold chicken and piled up the potatoes he had smelled baking in the oven.

'This is what I call a supper,' said he, as they spread large slabs of butter on the halves of baked potatoes. 'What's for pudding?'

'Rolypoly,' said Priscilla, 'made with leftover jams from the shop.'

'Oh, bully!' he exclaimed. 'Jam roly!' And while Christy dished it up he sang them a song he said he'd leaned in South Africa.

> 'O for a roly-poly
> Like mother used to make. . . .'

Altogether they had a royal evening, and on going away he told Christy—looking her straight in the eye—that that thumb of hers would need a little further attention.

She agreed so quickly that Priscilla was rather alarmed and innocently asked her if it was very painful, after he had gone.

'They doctors ken nothin' aboot banes,' said Christy. 'I dare say it'll take time or he gets it right. Jock the shepherd would hae slipped it into place in twa minutes.'

'Dr John didn't take two minutes,' said Priscilla indignantly, then added, 'but perhaps you'd better go and see Jock the shepherd.'

'Never change horses crossing the water,' said Christy, wisely shaking her head.

10

The Stable

After that the days passed quickly, and the shop-cleaning and decorating progressed with great speed.

Christy's thumb, with which she managed, nevertheless, to work with surprising agility, continued to 'stoond', and Dr John was in dressing it two or three times the week that followed. By that time he was on so friendly a footing in the house that the thumb retired from publicity into private life and was heard of no more.

Priscilla during the sale had become acquainted with most of the village people, and now was beginning to grow friendly with many of them and to have some inkling of the lives of the people round about her.

Bessie, the blacksmith's wife, with a horde of children, was a great friend, and Miss Pinn, the dressmaker, had made her some new blue overalls, and told her many tales as she fitted them on. She was a thin, tiny creature, with a touch of gentility, proud that her father had been a sea-captain and that she had a cousin a professor in Edinburgh University, and rather resented the village habit of using Christian names —she liked to be known as Miss Pinn. She lived on tea and bread and butter, and her little head with its large nose and bun at the back looked, Priscilla thought, rather like a teapot.

She had a mild sense of humour, and knew the history of every family in the village. She was also very discreet, however, and Priscilla got into the way of asking her for help when she was not very sure of her bearings in regard to the relationships and cross-relationships in the village. Christy knew everything too—indeed, more than everything—but Christy, if asked about anyone, was off into the third and fourth generations before you knew where you were, and muddled Priscilla more than ever. Miss Pinn's explanations were clear-cut and to the point.

It was she who gave Priscilla a clear story about Redd Maitland's upbringing by his uncle, who had insisted on putting him in the store, which Redd had always hated, being mad on horses and a country life. He had wanted to be a veterinary surgeon, and his uncle could easily have afforded it with his successful store in Lammerton and chain of smaller shops, but he had refused. After he had run away Redd had hired himself to a farmer, then as assistant to the District Veterinary Surgeon, who had later gone himself to try to persuade Old Maitland to pay Redd's college fees, but met with a violent refusal.

So Redd had started for himself by picking up and breaking in young and difficult horses, and gradually scraped together enough money to rent the old Mill Cottage and the long strath by the river, called the Long Haugh, where he was now breeding hunters and hacks, though sadly hampered by lack of money for extra stabling and help. He lived alone, and did practically everything himself with the help of an old groom.

Miss Pinn had got on to the subject by seeing Redd Maitland ride past her window while she was fitting Priscilla, who listened to everything, but said nothing, and, though Miss Pinn undoubtedly knew all about Aunt Purdie's vendetta with the Maitlands, she said nothing of that either. Miss Pinn, as already mentioned, was discreet.

On several occasions Priscilla had met Redd; it was impossible to avoid anyone in the small village community. Usually he was riding, but the first time he was leading a horse, and they had passed quite closely; his hand had moved to his hat, but she had cut him quite dead, since when he had passed without a glance her way.

She was pleased she had given him the direct snub, but vaguely dissatisfied that that seemed to be the end of it. Somehow she had inconsistently felt it was just the beginning. She wanted to give him another prick 'to have it out with him,' as she put it to herself in the night-watches, when his lean, hard face would rise clearly before her and those penetrating eyes disturb her. 'I'd like to tell him what I think of him,' she would say to herself, with a thrill of daring.

It was a little disconcerting that he had accepted her snub so casually and so thoroughly. He rode out of her way or unobtrusively disappeared if he caught sight of her, and it was remarkable how mysteriously he could disappear—it was more often his back than his face she saw, riding away.

However, she was too busy and absorbed with her shop to have much time for any other thoughts.

In a week it was finished, looking very clean and gay. The house was whitewashed, and she had it rewashed, and the doors and windows repainted in the bright deep blue. Inside the cream walls and blue paint pleased her too, and the old fireplaces in shop and storeroom were delightful with their high bowl-shaped bars, their wide hobs, and shining steel.

She was going to have a fire in the shop in winter, and keep the perishable provisions, such as butter, in the cool store room.

Christy made nothing of lighting fires, polishing grates, and scrubbing. She seemed to thrive on hard work, and was only happy when busy, which was all the time from five in the morning, till her early bedtime.

Now Priscilla began to be worried about her new stock, and was longing again for some expert advice about buying in, paying for her goods, judging quantities, and all the other problems of shopkeeping.

One night as she was poring over lists long after Christy had gone home to bed she heard two taps at the back door—Christy's signal.

'My mither's took bad,' Christy gasped, as soon as the door was open, 'and I canna' leave her to get some one to go for the doctor.'

'Run away back,' said Priscilla at once, for she knew that the old woman was alone in the house. 'I'll get him some-how.'

Christy sped back, and Priscilla ran to get her hat and jacket, and then flew down the garden. She had never been to the doctor's house, but she knew where it was, and that there was a short cut to it through her garden and field. At the bottom of the garden, which was a long, rambling bit of ground, there was a narrow plank bridge over the burn which led into a field, across which ran a footpath to a gate at the far end. This opened into a narrow lane, leading eventually to the river Blackwater and its green haughs. At the junction of this lane with another was the Doctor's House.

She was well into the field before she realised two things: that she ought to have brought her torch, and that it was beginning to rain. She was wearing only her knitted suit, but was in too great a hurry to go back. She might get wet, but the main thing was to get the doctor as quickly as possible—Christy had looked so terribly distressed.

She reached the lane and sped along it in the darkness. The Doctor's House was on the right, she knew, high up above the river and the haughs. She had seen it in the distance.

Her eyes had got used to the darkness now and she could make out the hedges on either side of her, but the rain had begun to come down heavily, and that impeded her vision. Still, she was sure she would see the gates which led into the garden surrounding the house.

But no gates appeared, and the lane was becoming rougher and rougher with deep ruts and big stones lying about, over which she stumbled. She was sure, too, that she was going downhill, and that didn't seem to be right. Yet she was certain she had seen no gates, and Christy had said there were white gates. The real name of the house was Whitegates, but no one ever called it anything but the 'Doctor's House.'

As she stumbled along the lane, which was getting steeper and steeper, she began to realise that she had made a mistake somewhere, and, finally, that she was completely lost. Other cart-loads led off from the High Lane, but she had been sure she had kept to her own road; now she was less certain. Should she return, or should she go on?

She was deliberating, standing with the rain pattering on the trees and swishing on the grass and muddy road, when a faint glimmer of light caught her attention. It must come from some house. Thankfully she hurried on towards it. Now she would at least find out where she was.

She came to a cobbled yard, and crossed it towards the light gleaming from a small window. It took her some time to find a door, but at last her fingers, moving over the rough stone wall, came on wood, and she gave a hesitating tap.

By this time she was so wet that she could not be wetter. The downpour coming from overhead splashed upward from the cobbles, and there was no shelter, so she could only just stand there and let the elements do their worst.

In a few moments the door opened, and she saw that it was a stable into which she now peered. Horses stood in a row; she could just see their gleaming hindquarters. A warm smell of mash came out, and the sound of champing and the rattle of chains.

It was feebly lit up by a stable lantern, standing on the sill of the small window that had guided her through the darkness.

'Who's there?'

She almost took to her heels and fled when she realised in a flash of dismay that it was Redd Maitland's voice!

Instantly she drew back, but his sharp eyes had recognised her even as he spoke.

'Come in.'

As she retreated farther into the darkness he put out a hand and drew her, not ungently, into the shelter of the stable, which seemed safe and warm and dry, coming in from the torrent of rain.

'What is the matter?'

So far she had not spoken. She was too taken aback by her malignant fate. Why should she have wandered here of all places? In her distress she made a quick turn and tried to run away again out into the rain and darkness. But his hand caught her again.

'I know you've come by mistake,' he said, 'but now you're here you must let me help you. What has happened? What are you doing out on such a night?'

'I've lost myself. I don't know where I am.'

'You are at the Mill House. Where did you want to go?' His voice was as cold and impersonal as ever.

'I want the doctor. I must find the doctor quickly—Christy's mother's is ill.'

'Dr John's away from home. He looked in here on his way to the Haughs.'

They stood silent a moment. He was looking down at her small, worried face, white and wet with rain, but she could not see his expression as his own was in the shadows.

'I must go to the Haughs.' She still called it 'Hoffs.' 'Please show me the way. I must get the doctor.'

He did not answer for a moment. He seemed to be considering.

'Can you ride?'

She shook her head.

'Then you'd better wait in my cottage till I go for the doctor. I'll send him on and come back for you.'

'Oh, no,' she said quickly, 'I couldn't do that.'

'There's no reason whatever why you shouldn't do that,' he said, almost angrily. 'You're soaked through. It's a long walk. It's dry in the cottage, and there's a fire. No one is there but a dog, and he'll look after you.'

'No,' she said. 'I can't do that. I *won't*.'

Nothing, she felt, would induce her to go into his house.

'Then'—he walked away and lifted down a saddle—'I'll have to put you up, and walk the mare to the Haughs.'

He had taken the yellow blanket from a horse as he spoke and thrown on a saddle. The beast looked round, its eyes flashing in the light of the lantern, and stamped a hoof. Priscilla, never having been within yards of a horse, was terrified.

'Oh, no,' she stammered weakly, as he tightened up the girths, but he took no notice, merely continued to saddle up.

She looked round the stable, and suddenly a sense of something homely and familiar about it welled up in her from long-ago farming ancestors. The whitewashed walls, the saddle pegs each with its saddle, the smell of leather, the tang of horses, the jingling of harness, the swish of tails, the sharp stamp of a hoof. She liked it. She wished she could stay there with the horses, and was about to ask him when he spoke again.

'Sit down,' he said, and turned to motion with his hands. 'There's a box there.'

She sank down, and watched him. His lean, hard face was lit up from the glow of the lantern, which he had set on the floor, his red hair darkened in the shadows. She saw the lines at either side of the thin, firm mouth, the fan of wrinkles at the corners of his eyes.

'He's as hard as flint,' she thought to herself. 'It's the

82

hardest face I ever saw. It's just bone and skin tanned like leather. There's no softness in it anywhere, and his eyes are small eyes with hot, fiery sparks like you get when you strike steel on flint. I don't like small, hard eyes, and I hate red hair.'

As she ruminated the mare threw up her head, and quivers of nervousness or impatience rippled under her glossy coat.

He turned his back on Priscilla, put an arm round the mare's neck, and, leaning his head against her, spoke in a low gentle voice, caressingly, reassuringly, and the mare, turning her head, rubbed it against him in absolute confidence and affection.

For a moment a swift and unaccountable emotion quivered through Priscilla, taking her by surprise. For a fraction of a second she found herself wishing that they two had not been enemies, though, indeed, the flash of feeling had scarcely formulated into a wish before she had recovered herself and driven it forth with a vehemence that seemed really more than was necessary for so fleeting a sensation.

'A Maitland!' she said to herself in scorn, and thought hard of the fat old man with his lard-like face and of her old auntie. 'I loathe the Maitlands. They are all hypocrites and snakes, and they want my shop—but they won't get it.'

But she had been shaken, and had to be very vehement indeed to reassure herself.

But it was Redd Maitland himself who brought her back quickly to what she considered realities.

He had saddled the mare, and, turning, led her out of the stall. He glanced at Priscilla, sitting very small and wet and forlorn on the upturned box, but there was nothing soft in his eyes, and his voice was another man's as he spoke with ruthless common sense.

'Do you think you could ride astride?'

'Astride!' She had never thought of that, and her voice was stunned.

'I have no sidesaddle. It would be easier for you and best for the mare,' he said briefly and coldly.

'But—I'm not—I haven't—I'm not *dressed* right,' she finished up severely, terrified that she was blushing.

'Good L . . .' he began, then stopped, and though he did not outwardly shrug his shoulders the impression was there all right. 'It's pitch dark!' he finished up. 'However, come along.'

He opened the stable door, but stopped her as she was about to step out into the rain.

'You've no coat,' he said. There was a note of stern accusation in his voice. 'You're soaked through.'

'It wasn't raining when I left.'

'It's been drizzling since four o'clock. Have you *no* sense?'

He led the mare out, spoke to her, and then, leaving her, he returned to the stable, and, going to a peg, took down a mackintosh.

'It's no use trying to put it on you,' he said, and for a moment she thought the ghost of a smile moved his close shut lips as he glanced down at her. 'I'd lose you altogether.' He was folding it longways, and now he wrapped it round her shoulders and drew it down about her.

'Keep your arms in,' he ordered, as she tried to move them. 'Hold it together from the inside.'

'But—how am I to get on?'

'Get on? I'll have to lift you on, of course.'

They were out now in the downpour, which had not abated in the least. He shut the stable door and turned to mount her, but Priscilla, to whom the horse now looked enormous and more terrifying than ever, shrank back involuntarily.

'He looks—so big. I think I'd rather walk,' she gasped.

'You're putting off time,' he said curtly. 'It's a rough road and would take you nearly an hour to walk. Do you want to miss the doctor?'

It was true. Though he had been quick and speedy in saddling the mare, and it had all taken much less time than it seems in the telling, five or ten minutes had passed, and she had none to lose. Christy would be distracted because the doctor had still not come.

'All right,' she said, stepping timidly forward.

He lifted her firmly but with surprising dexterity and set her on the saddle. She was shivering with apprehension, and would have slipped off again if he had not put an arm round her and held her on. Then he spoke to the mare, and they moved forward over the cobbled stones, but Priscilla could not sit still on the slippery saddle; she kept sliding sideways, and would have fallen off if he had not held her securely in place.

'I think I could do better without the coat,' she murmured feebly.

'Hold the coat with one hand, and grip the saddle with the other.'

She tried, but it was no use. Suddenly, as if impatient of her fumbling incompetence, he stopped the mare, put his foot in the dangling stirrup, seized the saddle, and flung himself up behind her.

11

'Hast Thou Found Me, O Mine Enemy?'

He had mounted so quickly and with such impatient force
that Priscilla would have fallen ignominiously across the
mare's neck had he not immediately gripped her round the
waist and drawn her firmly against him.

Immediately the mare, with confidence regained, gave up
her shivering and tossing and set off at a steady trot.

'You're no more use on a horse than a sack of potatoes!'
he exclaimed, his voice sounding hard and contemptuous.
'Sit still,' as she tried to move. 'We'll be there in a minute or
two.'

She kept as still as a mouse. She was no longer afraid of
the horse, which seemed a different creature now from the
terrifying monster on which she had been hoisted up. She
was afraid of the rider. He held her like a vice, but as impersonally as if she had indeed been the sack of potatoes to
which—to her resentful indignation—he had compared her.

But his hard hold was a little too strong for her slender body,
and after a few minutes she put her hand on his to slacken it
a little, which he did immediately.

'Am I hurting you?' he asked, and to her amazement there
was something of the same gentleness in his voice as when he
had soothed the frightened mare.

It took her so by surprise she could not answer for a moment. He bent his head, and she felt his hard, intensely
masculine face so near her own that if she had moved her
head her cheek would have touched his. She kept con-
strainedly still, but her heart began to beat wildly with a
strange fear that thrilled through her like an electric shock.

'Lean back,' he said in the same gentle, understanding
tones. 'Don't pull away like that, or I'll have to grip you
tighter to keep you from going over her neck.' And he drew

her firmly back against him so that she felt his rough jacket, soaked with rain against her cheek.

She tried to pull herself together, to be cool and matter of fact and stop the wild, terrifying beating of her heart.

'You are getting met,' she said in a prim, severe little voice.

'Whose fault is that?' He had drawn back, and his voice was as hard as ever again. 'Can't you look after yourself at all? Running out in the rain in a woollen rag and a pair of slippers. Girls like you should stay in the town where they belong with their grandmothers and aunts to look after them.'

Now was her chance to get rid of that deep, unsatisfied desire to have it out with him.

'I dare say it would suit the *Maitlands* if I stayed in town,' she said, very cold and distant.

'Not on your life!' said he. 'A soft bit of stuff like you is easier game than a wide-awake man like Murdo MacPherson —if that is what you are thinking of.'

Her amazement and indignation at his coming out into the open like this, instead of sneaking under her guard as she had been warned the Maitlands would do, almost took away her breath. She gave a gasp and pulled away from him.

'I'm not soft, and I'm as wide-awake as Murdo MacPherson . . .' she began, her voice full of anger and indignation, when she was suddenly jerked back against him as the mare leaped a wall she had not seen in the darkness.

An involuntary 'Oh!' escaped her, and she had gripped his arm before she knew what she was doing.

'Steady,' he said, drawing his arm tighter, but immediately slackening it again.

'Why did you do that?' she exclaimed indignantly.

He was silent for a moment, then said patiently:

'The gate is a long way round.'

There was a long silence after that. 'I know he thinks I'm a fool,' she thought, 'but I simply don't care what he thinks. He can't think I'm a bigger fool than I feel, and the horse thinks I'm a fool too and that's worse. Oh, how did I ever get myself into this awful situation?'

Her indignant thoughts rushed on. She was indignant with him, with herself, with the mare, with the weather, with

Christy, and even with Christy's innocent mother. They all, every one of them, seemed in league against her.

'What are you so afraid of?' He broke the long silence at last. 'I'm not going to let you drop.'

If anything could have incensed her more this did.

'I'm not afraid!' she exclaimed, trying to stiffen up straight.

'Yes, you are. You are shaking like an old ewe with the tremmles. Bless my soul, what is there to terrify you? The mare is as quiet as a lamb.'

'I'm *not* afraid of the mare.'

'Well, you're getting on. You've stopped calling her a horse anyhow, after I'd told you she's a mare. Her name's Jenny. you afraid of me, then?'

'No, I'm not. I'm not afraid of anybody or anything, but, if you want to know, I dislike you—I hate all the Maitlands, and I know you want my shop, but you're not going to get it.'

'Am I not?'

Was he daring to laugh at her? She glanced up, but his weatherbeaten face, which she could just see, was inscrutable.

'No, nor your uncle either. I know all about you both and your schemes,' she exclaimed.

'Those stables of yours would be very useful to me,' he said coolly.

Stables! She had never thought about stables, but she wasn't going to let him guess that.

'I know all about the stables and *everything*. You can't deceive me!'

'So I see.'

'So you needn't try. I'm a very determined person. The Maitlands never got the better of the Purdies, and they never will.'

'So put that in your pipe and smoke it!' he said, as if ending the sentence for her.

'I think you are insufferable.'

'It's more of a compliment than I pay you,' he remarked after a moment, with such icy indifference that she was left silenced. She knew what he meant. He didn't pay her the compliment of thinking about her at all. Tears of mortification sprang to her eyes, and she had to blink hard to get them away.

Suddenly he pulled her more tightly against him, and her heart began to beat so wildly that she was afraid he must feel it under his hand, but the next moment she felt more of a fool than ever.

'Sit steady,' he ordered curtly, as the mare took another jump and stood still.

Immediately he released her.

'Here we are,' he said, and, slipping off behind her, he lifted her down, but as he held her like a feather in the air he suddenly drew her nearer and put his face close to her cheek.

'Funny little enemy,' he whispered, then instantly set her down, gripped her arm, and marched her across the cobbles.

'This is the house. The doctor's car is still at the door. He'll take you home. Good night.'

He spoke the curt, short sentences with such perfunctory unconcern and indifference that even a 'Thank you', she felt, would have fallen on unheeding ears. It seemed, indeed, as if he had forgotten her already, as he swung off, flung himself on to the mare, and took the jump over the stackyard wall.

She heard the mare's galloping hoofs go thundering off as if they were both glad to be rid of her, and sternly quenched a feeling of loneliness that threatened to flow over her, standing waiting in the darkness for the door to open.

Then the handle turned, light flooded out, and she saw Dr John standing drawing on his gloves behind the woman who had opened the door.

'Good gracious! What are you doing here?' he exclaimed, as he saw her standing huddled up in the waterproof. 'I thought it was Maitland when I heard the horse. I didn't know you rode.'

Hastily she explained that Christy's mother was ill, and apologised to the woman, who was asking her to come in, and exclaiming at her soaked condition and at the rain, which was coming down again in torrents.

'I'll take her home,' said Dr John. 'That's the best place for her.' And with thanks and good-nights they got into the car, Priscilla not having said a word about how she reached the farm.

Nor did Dr John ask her any more about the horse he had heard, doubtless thinking it was some one for the farmhouse.

'I was told you were at the Martins',' she said, and let it go at that. Somehow she did not want to speak about Redd Maitland to anybody.

The doctor was his usual cheery self, and entertained her on the way back by good-natured fulminations against a doctors life—'only it has some compensations,' he said, as they rocked down the ill-made village street, turning and glancing at her with rather a rueful smile. 'Like tonight!' he finished up, as he changed gears and drew up the car.

He said no more on that subject, but contented himself with a meaning smile as he looked at her.

Then he became the doctor. Told her to get straight to bed with hot-water bottles and a hot drink, and said that he'd look her up in the morning to see that she was none the worse, and hurried off to his patient.

As soon as she was indoors Priscilla remembered the mackintosh! She was still enveloped in its folds, and the problem was how she was going to get rid of it.

She did not want anyone to know she had accepted help again from Redd Maitland.

Christy would insist on talking and talking and threshing the whole thing out, not once, but a dozen times, all interlaced with warnings about the Maitlands.

'I'm sick of those Maitlands!' she exclaimed aloud to the excited Barkis, who as usual was bounding round her as if she'd been gone for a month, or just rescued from the grave.

'Fair seek!' she repeated, imitating Christy. 'I wish I needn't see any one of them again—and now I've got that man's waterproof!'

Christy must have taken time to run in and replenish the fire, for it was blazing cheerfully. So she locked her doors, got into her warm dressing-gown, and heated herself some milk, quite determined she would not have a cold for the opening of her shop.

But somehow she did not feel like going to bed. She felt wide awake and excited, and her thoughts, as she sipped her milk, kept returning to Redd Maitland. She kept seeing his lean, weather-beaten face, and that up-standing crest of red hair.

'I know what he has,' she said to herself. 'He has dominating eyes. Yes, *dominating*—and I don't like small orange-brown eyes, anyhow. I do wish he didn't live so near. I'm always running into him. . . . A soft townsgirl indeed! I'll show him if I'm a soft townsgirl or not.'

Then she remembered that she had sworn to herself she would never speak to him again, and on that the problem of the mackintosh returned.

She might easily enough have made it up into a parcel and posted it, but she knew perfectly well that Mrs MacCleesh of the post-office knew everything about every one in the village, and would certainly have her curiosity roused if Priscilla went in and posted a parcel to Redd Maitland.

At last she gave it up, and to take her mind off the whole thing started on her lists again. Two travellers were coming on Monday, one for groceries and general stores, and the other for haberdashery and the drapery goods her aunt had stocked.

She got out the exercise-book, and went on with her lists of sugar, butter, jam, sauces, and all the stores of a village shop. It was fairly easy to make out the list of dry goods, as it did not matter so much if she got in more than she sold within a certain time, but butter and cheese and bacon and perishable goods worried her.

'Ask the travellers what your aunty got,' Christy had said, when confronted with questions about quantities, but Priscilla didn't want to expose her ignorance to strange travellers.

But worse than that was the dilemma about paying for them. The first stocking of the shop was coming to much more than she had bargained for, and though there was still money in the bank she felt that she must leave a sufficient sum to her credit and to be going on with.

She thought of her Aunt Flora's words about the foolishness of thinking she could run a shop with no experience, and sighed. Her Aunt Flora had had more than justfication for her doubts.

She was tired. She pushed the lists aside and began to think of her aunts. She had sent a postcard, 'Thank you for sending on the things,' and had signed it 'Janet Purdie.' She had written it in the first pride of resentment at their brief postcard, and now she wished she had written a letter. After all, they were old. They had been kind to her, and she had defied them and run away against all their wishes.

Suddenly she made up her mind to write again and say nothing about the postcards. She got out pen and ink, and started.

DEAR AUNT MAUD AND AUNT FLORA,

I know you are very angry with me, but I can't help loving you and feeling grateful for all you did for me, and grieving because you have cast me off and won't be even a little bit friendly. Of course, I know you won't be able to forgive me for a long time, but I do, do hope you will forgive me some time and come and see me.

This is quite a nice house. It is called the Clock House, and is very old, and there have been Purdies here for generations, and it is full of old things that would interest you—especially you, Aunt Maud, for you love antiques, and I'm sure you'd be interested in the furniture and china and glass that I haven't had time even to look at, though it all needs sorting and going over; besides, I haven't your expert knowledge, so there may be treasures I don't know enough to appreciate.

I have a pony and a little trap, and a lovely garden—at least, it will be lovely when the flowers are all out.

In Scotland it isn't so looked down on to keep a shop.

The Misses Selby at the Hall have asked me to go to lunch on Sunday, and then they are coming to have tea with me. Miss Prudence says she has always wanted to keep a shop, and will help me.

The doctor is a great friend, and comes often to tea or supper.

I have had a sale, and had the shop distempered and painted. It is pale primrose and bright blue, and I'm going to open it properly in a few days.

Miss Selby says she is going to come and help me, but of course that is just in fun.

She says she once met my Grandmother Delaine at Baxton, and exchanged a bull-terrier pup for a pom pup. They used to drink the waters together in the Pump Room. She was very fond of my Aunt Purdie. It is really quite different here from what you think.

But you were both quite right about difficulties. It is very difficult to know what to buy and spend too much money, especially on things that might spoil before you get them sold, but it is very interesting—really and truly it is; and no one despises you here for keeping a shop.

I wish you could see my house. It's not a little cottage with two rooms and sweetie bottles in the kitchen window. It's a real shop, only made out of two rooms of the old house—one for stores—and both have lovely old basket grates and hobs. I should love you to see it. It is whitewashed outside, with thick greeny-blue slates with house-leeks on them, and there's a big rose-tree growing all over the wall that has all to be taken down every year when the wall's whitewashed, and then nailed up again.

92

Please do not be so angry with me. I am very sorry I hurt you so much, and it's lonely not having anyone of one's own to write to.

Having finished this rather pathetic attempt to reassure them about her social status in Crumstane as a shopkeeper and to act as tempter through their love of antiques, she finished up with her dearest love and signed herself, 'Priscilla.'

Finally she stamped it, ready to post, and then her eye caught the extremely disagreeable mackintosh. She rolled it in a bundle, and hid it with as much care and as many signs of guilt as if she had stolen it, and went to bed.

It was not exactly the end of a perfect day. Of one thing, however, she had *definitely* (the italics are her own) made up her mind. Mackintosh or no mackintosh, she would not speak to that man again.

12

The Mackintosh

The next day was Sunday, and she met the ladies of the Hall and was driven in a barouche—at least, that was the only name she could think of for the ancient vehicle—by Andra, who had his green livery trousers on as well as the silver-buttoned coat, 'out of respect to his Maker,' as Miss Tibbie said in her sharp voice.

All four ladies were there, and she was introduced to Mrs MacWhan—Marion—the eldest, and Miss Leslie, the youngest of the sisters. Mrs MacWhan was rather more on her dignity than the others, but kind, and with a touch of humour of her own. Miss Leslie was very quiet and hardly spoke at all. She looked very delicate, and walked with a limp, but when she caught Priscilla's glance she smiled back very sweetly.

Miss Tibbie had a dry and acrid Scottish wit that rather frightened Priscilla at first, but she began to like her very much before she'd been an hour or two in her company.

She liked Miss Prudence best, and had made up her mind to take her at her word and ask her help about the shop, hoping she wouldn't mind talking shop on Sunday, but she had no chance as she discovered that Mr Lamont, the minister, always took lunch at the Hall on Sundays.

She liked Mr Lamont, a cadaverously thin bachelor of sixty or so with a frosty but humourous blue eye, and thoroughly enjoyed her visit, but there was no possibility of asking advice about her shop, as he offered to walk home with her and show her the Duck Poo,' a long, twisty little lake in the grounds, haunted by all kinds of duck and wild fowl, and on which all the village skated or curled when it froze hard enough in the winter. Then, he told Priscilla, all the children got a holiday from school to go skating and sliding—in fact, everybody took a holiday as a matter of course. Before the children were allowed on the ice the Misses Selby sent for the village policeman, who weighed sixteen stone. If he went through the ice they had to wait for another day!

'I warrant it's the only time he gets a real bath,' said Miss Tibbie drily, 'so a' things are mixed wi' mercy.'

They were all most amusing talkers, and kept her laughing all the time. They took her over the house, and told her about the Battle of Crumstane, and what Miss Prudence called the 'high jinks' over the Stone of Remembrance. They asked her to join the W.R.I. and the village dramatic society, and told her that on May Day she would have to get up at six and climb to the top of Battle Hill, as was the immemorial custom of the village.

They had also insisted on introducing the maypole—at least, Miss Tibbie said that Prudence had insisted on it— and on having a Queen of the May.

'You'll enjoy it,' said Miss Tibbie darkly. 'My sister Prudence insists on every one's enjoying it.'

'So we do enjoy it,' put in Teenie-in-the-Kitchen, as they all called the elderly woman who was serving them. 'It would ill become us no to enjoy oorsel's efter all the trouble Miss Prudence takes.'

'Teenie thinks that by a judicious use o' subtle flattery she'll be asked to be Queen o' the May hersel',' said Miss Tibbie at once, and Teenie led the laughter that irresistibly followed.

'Eh, Miss Tibbie,' she said, 'think shame o' yersel'—afore the meenister and all.'

'If you knew your place you wouldn't put your tongue in when the meenister is taking lunch with us,' said Mrs MacWhan severely, 'not to speak of our young visitor.'

'Deed you're right, mem,' said Teenie equably. 'The sproots are no whit they were,' she went on, passing the dish to Priscilla, 'but they're the best we can dae.'

Indeed, the 'sproots' and everything else were beautifully cooked and served on lovely old china and silver. She could not help contrasting the lunch with the food served at her aunts' table. These ladies were poor too, as she had been told, and were reduced to selling fruit and vegetables from the

95

garden, and Miss Prudence even wrote little stories for the papers, but they were not ashamed to work. Miss Prudence had reared the roast ducklings herself and helped to plant the sprouts, while, Priscilla gathered, Miss Tibbie did most of the cooking, and was proud of her pigs and the method of curing hams a Danish friend had taught her. Instead of an ultra-smart table-maid and a cheap slut of a cook, they had one servant, the delightful and efficient Teenie-in-the-Kitchen, and themselves put on aprons and helped with all the house-work.

She was glad when they asked her to come back again. She had enjoyed every minute of her visit, and felt very cheerful when she said good-bye to Mr Lamont and entered her own house—'my very own house,' as she called it to herself. She was dying to get at it and make it the lovely place she saw it could be, but first she must start the shop and make it pay; so she had a cup of tea, and then got out her lists again.

Christy's mother was still in bed, and Christy could only pop in and out to do necessary work, so she was alone.

She was disappointed at not having been able to consult the shrewd Miss Prudence, and sighed as she sat down to her task.

She was deep in it, with papers spread all round her, her cheeks flushed from worry, and her hair ruffled up from dis-tractedly pushing her fingers through it, when a knock came to the door. She thought it might be the doctor, who had said he would call, though she had concluded she would have missed him when up at the Hall; but Dr John was not so easily put off.

Quite glad of an interruption, she rushed out and opened the door—she was always pleased to see the cheery doctor.

But it was not Dr John who stood there—it was Redd Maitland.

'Oh!' she said, completely taken aback.

'Good evening. I've called for my mack,' he said briefly.

'I meant to return it tomorrow,' she said stiffly, turning away.

'Sorry. It's the only one I have, and I'm taking horses over to Kilpallet in the morning.'

'I'll get it,' she said, and looked at the hooks in the hall. Then she remembered deciding to hide it as she went to bed, and turned to run up the stairs.

She would not ask him to come in. She did not want him in the house. She wanted him just to go away. But her mind had been far from mackintoshes, concentrated on cheese and blacking and washing blue; then his knock came, and for the moment she could not think where she had put the coat.

In haste and confusion she looked in the wardrobe, throwing its contents about the floor, but it was not there; it must be in the downstairs cupboard.

Pattering down the stair, she saw the outline of his figure as he leaned against the lintel. She felt furious with herself that she had not been able calmly to take the mack from a hook in the passage, give it to him with a dignified word of thanks, and close the door; but Christy would have seen it on the hook, and asked questions. Oh, where had she put it!

He turned, as he heard her footsteps, evidently expecting to see his coat and no doubt wondering, she thought, why she had not just hung it in the hall.

'I thought I had put it in the wardrobe,' she said. 'It must be in the hall cupboard.'

But the hall cupboard went under the stair and was black dark. She fumbled among the assortment of things hanging there, growing more and more furious and distracted as she did not find it.

'I have my torch,' he said at last, coming forward. 'Perhaps it will help you.'

He took it out of his pocket and passed it to her, then turned away and stood with his back to the cupboard. From where he was he could look straight into the lighted room, with its table full of disordered papers, the exercise-book, and the pile of torn sheets scattered about all over the place.

In a few moments she discovered the coat and returned with it on her arm.

He took it, and put the torch in his pocket. Then he paused.

'In difficulties?' he asked, gazing at he flushed face and rumpled hair, and then shifting his eyes to the papers on the table.

'No,' she said stiffly, remembering her vow never to speak to him again, and crushing down a wild desire for help.

He turned instantly to go, but as he did so a quick catch of her breath betrayed her anxiety.

He swung round.

'What is troubling you?' he demanded roughly.

'Nothing. I can manage quite well.'

He took no notice of this feeble assurance.

'Is it the stock?'

'I don't want any help from you, Mr Maitland!'

He stood for a moment in silence, considering her with his small keen eyes; then, to her amazement—she could never fathom this hard, imperturbable man—he spoke quite courteously and kindly.

'Are you terribly taken up with staying here and running this shop of yours?' he asked gently.

Having expected a sharp retort and an instant departure, she was so nonplussed that she answered quickly and naturally.

'Of course I am. I love Crumstane, and I love my shop. I *must* make it pay, and nobody shall get it from me!' she answered fiercely.

He stood quite still, looking down at her frowningly, his eyebrows drawn above his hawk-like nose and fierce eyes, his red crest of hair sticking up, his mouth shut in a straight line. She noticed that some raindrops had caught in his hair and glistened in the lamplight.

'You should go home,' he said. 'Haven't you anyone to take care of you?'

That roused all her resentment again.

'I can take care of myself, thank you.'

'You mean you haven't!'

She thought of her aunts, and her eyes clouded and her cheeks coloured up. It was true they had cast her off, and she had nobody. She dropped her eyelids as she felt his penetrating gaze on her face.

'I don't need to be looked after. I can look after myself, and I'm going to make my shop a success.' She caught her breath. 'I *must* . . . and I know quite well what I'm up against too—*Maitlands*! Everything!'

'Why is your heart so set on this shop? Girls like you belong to the town and an easy life.' He spoke roughly again.

'That is my business, Mr Maitland.'

Again he took her by surprise by throwing his coat impatiently over the back of a chair and holding out his hand.

98

'Well, let me see those lists.'

There was no hint of having taken any offence in his voice, nor was there any disclaimer about the machinations of the Maitlands, nor any reassurance that he would not use the knowledge he might gain to her disadvantage. It was as if all that was, not so much beneath his notice, as absolutely outside it.

'He's as proud as Lucifer,' she thought to herself slowly, almost involuntarily gathering up the lists, 'but it seems that sort of unconscious pride that you can't deal with, that doesn't give you anything to get hold of and argue with.' Her mind went racing on, full of resentment on the one hand and relief on the other at the thought of help so close at hand if she cared to take it. 'After all, why shouldn't I *use* a Maitland—get all I can from him and then drop him like a hot potato? They used my aunt like that, didn't they?' she reassured herself. 'But I'm harder and more wide-awake than my aunt. I'll use them!'

She had gathered the smudged and blotted lists, and now rather hesitatingly and shamefacedly passed them to the open hand he held out. As his fingers closed they caught hers, and for a moment the same thrill of compelling fear caught her as it had done when he gripped her to jump the mare over the stone wall, and her wide, startled blue eyes caught his in the instant before he let her fingers go.

Something in them caused her to flush up again, but if he noticed it there was no telling, as he gave no sign of being interested in anything but the papers. He stood running his eyes over them, having, apparently, no difficulty in making out their crossed, blotted, and recrossed contents.

'Got a sheet of paper?' he asked, his voice curtly practical.

'Yes, I have a book here. I was going to copy them in neatly when I'd finished. What is bothering me most,' she went on quickly, 'is how to pay for them.'

'How do you mean? What exactly is the difficulty—lack of money?' came the quick, direct inquiry.

'I'm afraid I won't have enough money to pay for every thing at once. Will they trust me for a little?'

'When the travellers call you will order what you have on your lists. You need not pay for anything then. They will have the goods sent on with the invoice—the account. In a month, they will call again; if you pay your account then you will get the full discount allowed for ready money. If you cannot pay the first month you wait till the second; you will still get a little discount, but not so much. After the third month you will have to pay the full price. Do you understand? The sooner you pay the better, as you have less to pay, but there is no need to worry because you cannot pay when you give the order. You are not expected to pay before you receive the goods, and you have a little time for turnover—to make them into money. Is that clear? Is that what you wanted to know?'

He was the practical man of affairs now, as impersonal as if he'd been selling a horse.

'Oh, yes, thank you.' She could not keep the gratitude out of her voice, though she tried to be as impersonal as he was.

'You understand there are variations and details, but that's a foundation to go on. What else?' He clipped out the words, as if he had snipped them off with scissors.

'I wondered about charging—I mean, what is a fair profit —how much . . .' she was stammering, when he picked her up.

'You will soon get to know the usual selling prices, but, of course, you must have a general rule to go on of so much per cent that you ought to make as profit. You said you were good at arithmetic?'

'Yes, I am.'

'Well, twenty-five per cent, is a fair average profit, but, of course, there are many variations. For instance, on things such as the usual groceries, tea, sugar, and so on, with a quick and steady turnover—that sell quickly—you expect a smaller percentage of profit than on slower-selling goods, such as drapery and stationery. . . .' He went on, giving her a few clear and simple rules. While still speaking he picked up the lists again and let himself down to half sit on the edge of the table.

She was so interested and keen to learn that for the moment all her enmity was forgotten. All her mind was on business and on the shop. She was a quick and alert pupil, and he a clear-headed instructor, understanding at once her difficulties. No one looking at them would have guessed at the electric currents flowing underneath, or the tinder that a spark might set blazing.

13

Getting in the Stores

All went well for a while. He ran over her lists, correcting here, suggesting there, telling her not to order the same quantity of all the jams, as she would find raspberry and strawberry the favourites, and that half a dozen bottles of thick sauce would sell for one of thin.

He noticed that she had only ordered a large cheese, and told her to get in some boxes of portions wrapped in silver paper, as they sold well, though workmen still liked their slice of tangy American or Cheshire cheese with a raw onion for their 'elevenses'.

She had too many tinned soups and too few tinned fruits. Crumstane liked home-made broths, potato, pea, and barley soups, but she would find that fruit sold well in summer; the only tinned vegetable she would sell was peas, and it was no use whatever stocking brown sugar.

'That's for the Misses Selby.'

He glanced at her sharply.

'That's a private order,' he corrected. 'You are giving away information to the enemy.'

She flushed. Of course, Old Maitland would want to know if the ladies at the Hall were her customers since it meant so much.

Well, he could tell his uncle if he liked, or perhaps it did not matter; he could easily find out anyhow. She wished she knew what did matter. Again a half-formulated wish had to be quashed that this wasn't Redd Maitland, that they could have been friends.

'Of course, only because of the *shop*,' she assured herself. 'It would be such a help to the shop—otherwise I dislike him and never wish to see him again, and I think that a weatherbeaten face and red hair are downright ugly, however any . . .'

'Get a kit of butter at a time,' the cold, practical voice broke in on these decidedly personal wanderings, 'and weigh out pounds and half-pounds very carefully in private; if you do it in front of your customers at first you'll give over weight and lose your profit. The same with sugar, barley, and things that are not done up in packets—but not cheese, it dries too quickly; weigh it as you sell it, and charge a penny or two more or less—that's customary; and don't keep bacon until you can afford a slicer . . .'

'My aunt sold it.'

'Don't you touch it; you'd lose on it.'

'I'll think about it.'

She felt she must show her independence somewhere.

'Bacon is a man's job.'

'But if my customers expect it and are used to getting it?' ('I won't be downed,' she thought to herself.)

'They'll get it from the butcher's carts. Now, is that all? Is there anything else you are in difficulties about?'

He was rising as he spoke.

'No,' she said. 'I think I'll manage now—and thank you very much.'

'May I fill my pipe before going out?'

He had taken it with his pouch from his pocket, and stood waiting her leave.

'Yes—I'm sorry I forgot to ask you to smoke. I've never lived with men.'

'Haven't you?' If he felt any amusement at this declaration there was no sign of it. His face was as solemn as her own innocent countenance with its wide, serious eyes and inconsequent, perky ribbon. She shook her head.

'I've had no father or brothers or anything to live with—just aunts.'

'Um-m-m.' He was ramming tobacco into the bowl of his pipe. 'I thought as much.'

Instantly she was indignant.

'What do you mean?'

'I'm not going to tell you that.'

He was putting on his mackintosh now; he seemed to be hesitating about something, which surprised her, he was so far from hesitating about anything as a rule.

He shoved himself into the coat and buttoned it up, another thing she felt sure he never troubled to do.

Then he turned to go, stopped, and spoke.

'You should try to get Mysie Cree,' he said.

Mysie Cree! Instantly all her suspicions were reawakened, white-hot and fierce. Then it was all true about him that Christy and her aunt had said! He was hand in glove with his uncle, or, if not hand in glove, he was going to be; he was going to try to sneak in with him again and get his money, as Christy had guessed, and use her as a means to further his ends. The needles and thread had been his first excuse to worm himself in, and the mackintosh was the next, and now he was thinking she was so soft and unsuspicious he would try to get Mysie Cree in. That would be a big thing—to succeed where his uncle had failed—perhaps the two of them had planned it—put their heads together, perhaps. . . . For a moment thoughts and accusations rushed too swiftly through her mind for her to speak; anger shook her so that when she attempted to speak she stammered.

'Mysie Cree! Mysie Cree! How dare you? What do you think?' She was quite incoherent. 'Go away and never speak to me again. Never you come near my shop, or your uncle or his Mysie Cree either. I'll turn you out—any of you. You think you'll ruin me and get my shop, but you'll see. A soft girl—that's what you said I was—that's what you think, but I'll show you! I'll . . .'

At that moment, as she paused for breath, there came in the silence two taps at the back door. Christy's signal.

Utterly astonished and taken by surprise—Christy had said good-night and gone, and she always went to bed early —Priscilla was brought to a stop in mid-air! Her mouth dropped open, her face went scarlet. She glanced at the clock; time had flown; it was after ten. What would Christy think seeing her *closeted* with the enemy at ten o'clock at night, all her shop books and papers spread round? Christy didn't know about the mackintosh or last night's adventure. She would never understand; she would think—she would think . . . well, what might she not think?

In dismay, her eyes wide with consternation and fright, she stared towards the back kitchen. Could she pretend she was in bed? No, Christy must have seen the lighted window. What was she to do? What could she say?

'It's all right,' said a calm voice from beside the door into the passage. 'Good night.'

He was gone. She heard the front door softly open, and sped through the back kitchen to meet Christy at the back door.

'Ma mither's ta'en a fancy for some o' that cream o' chicken broth ye made on Setterday,' she said. 'Ye mind ye sent her a jugfu'. She says she's fair seek o' ma beef tea, and I kent there was a bowlfu' in the milk hoose and saw your light in the window, so I slipped ower . . . Eh, lassie, are ye still at they lists? It's time you were in your bed.'

Priscilla glanced round as they came in. Not a sign of Redd Maitland's presense was there, nor had she heard the front door close; he must have shut it very quietly. Relief mixed with the anger from which her cheeks were still burning; he was always getting her out of some mess, but she was not at all grateful.

She would have loved to tell Christy the whole story and join with her in loud and long imprecations against the Maitland villains, but her lips were sealed.

'I may tell Christy the whole story some time,' she said to herself, to ease her decidedly guilty conscience, 'but I can't go into all that just now.'

She rushed to the milk house to hide her confusion and get the broth. Christy's cooking was excellent so far as it went, but Priscilla had loved cooking at the domestic science class at school, and had been trying out some of the dishes she had learned to make. The cream of chicken had been a great success.

'How is your mother?' she asked. coming back. 'Can she not sleep?'

Christy went into some details of her mother's peculiarities, and then went off with the soup.

Priscilla gathered up her papers, still seething over Mysie Cree.

'Never again,' she said to herself. 'Never again will I speak to that man.'

Mysie Cree also shared her recriminations. 'Coming here,'

she reminded herself indignantly, 'to try and work herself in. I'll show them!'

But the next few days were so busy she never had time to think of the Maitlands or Mysie Cree. Travellers came and took her orders. She found them not at all what she had expected, but friendly souls who were anxious to help her, made suggestions, explained things, and offered advice which, even when she did not take it, helped her by odds and ends of information.

One elderly man she particularly liked, who came into the shop reading, and only pushed the book into his pocket when he saw she was ready for him. He was as shy as she was at first, but by the time they had laughed together over some of the names of his sweatmeats—Solomon's braces, tushie-laggies, allegreesh watches, and suchlike—they were fast friends, and he had offered to lend her the book he was reading. *The Life history of the Crawfish* was its title, but that made no difference—a book's a book.

Then the stores arrived in vans, and Christy and she had the time of their lives unpacking and arranging the goods. All the nice fresh packages thrilled their housewifely souls possibly even more than their shopkeeping minds, and they arranged and rearranged them as if their lives depended on the exact disposition of each packet of tea and every bottle of pickles.

They nearly came to blows, so to speak, over one shelf which Christy had fitted neatly with pink tins of salmon, which clashed, said Priscilla, with the orange labels on the bottles of sauce next to them.

'That's where your aunty kept the sawmon,' said Christy, which, she felt, ought really to have settled the matter, but she reckoned without Priscilla's *eye*.

'Those colours would offend my eye all the time,' said she, 'and that would worry me.'

'God send ye have no more to worry ye than that,' said Christy piously.

'That's what I mean,' countered Priscilla, to whom logic, as to most sensible women, was barren nonsense. 'I'll have plenty of worries without adding to them by clashing colours.'

Poor Christy! Her one idea was to put everything in the

exact place in which Miss Purdie had kept it; she racked her brains to remember, and then found that Priscilla had some quite different notion, and was just as obstinate as she was herself about having her own way.

However, their lively battles all ended in a good-natured truce or a frank capitulation on Christy's side.

'You're as thrawn as your aunty,' she would say. 'The Purdies are a' thrawn deils.'

While busy they had a call from Murdo MacPherson, a short, stout Scot with a slight cast in one eye which rather nonplussed Priscilla at first, as he never seemed to look straight at her. She had been rather afraid that Murdo would resent her having got the shop and property that would have been his, and had rather dreaded meeting him. She thought he might show his displeasure by ignoring her in the flesh and doing his best to frustrate her behind her back.

She was relieved when he called, and even more so at his first words.

'Well, Janety, my lass [a lot of the village people called her Janet or Janety], hoo are ye gettin' on? The wife's been at me for days to come and see you; she's no very spry on the legs hersel', but she wants you to come over to Byrebraes as soon as ye get settled in. Losh me, but you're young to rin a shop!'

'I'm nearly twenty,' said Priscilla. 'We're sort of cousins, aren't we? Oh, I do think it is kind of you to come and see me, and not mind about my taking the shop.'

'Mind! Bless my soul, I hae enough to daw wi' the pigs without a shop, and auld Janet wouldn't hear of it being sold. Na, na, my lassie, dinna get notions into your heid. Your aunty and me threshed it a' oot thegither. . . . Aye, she was a fine woman, your aunty, and nearly ruined hersel' to help me. It would ill become me to grudge her niece her bit property. And if thae Maitlands start bothering ye just ye come to me. I'll settle Auld Maitland's hash for him.'

'Oh, thank you very much,' said Priscilla. 'I know he wants my shop, but he's not going to get it.'

'The aild deil! He'll wurrum his way in if he gets a chance. Hae naething to dae wi' him.'

Murdo was a great talker, and before she knew where she was Priscilla was deep in lore about Middle Whites, Tamworth boars, Gloucester Old Spots, and Wessex Saddlebacks; she had lost her way long before he came to his own special cross, which was with Tamworths and Middle Whites, as far as she could make out while trying to take an intelligent interest in pigs, which she had never thought of before as anything *but* pigs, or bacon.

She was shrewd enough to gather, however, that he was a one-rut man, good-natured and kindly and a past-master at pig-breeding and -selling, but he had none of the cunning or brains of Old Maitland; his only method of dealing with the enemy would be to set his large round head between his broad shoulders and run at him with his stomach as a target.

But they got on like a house on fire, and she promised to go over to Sunday's dinner as often as she could—he invited her for every Sunday—and when he left he put a long list of goods into her hand that his wife had written out, and which he would call for the following week. He left a small ham and a large cake of 'Alison's baking', and departed with many 'good lucks' and good wishes.

Priscilla closed the door and turned with a smile to Christy, who had worked and talked with equal vigour during the whole of his visit.

'Oh, what a relief,' she said, 'that Cousin Murdo's like that! I do like him, only I'm sure I'll never be able to talk intelligently about Middle Spots and boars.'

'Set your mind at ease. Murdo MacPherson'll do all the talkin',' said Christy. 'Naebody expects a bit lassie like you to be upsides wi' a pig-dealer aboot pigs.'

There was, as usual, so much common sense in Christy's summing up that Priscilla straight away gave up the intricacies of pig-crossing and bothering her mind about Spotted Gloucesters and Middle Whites. This muddled but did not mar her future conversations with the farming community as she got mixed up and talked about Middle Whites when she meant clover, and wild whites when she meant pigs, and thus probably founded the game called pigs in clover.

14

Maudie Jones

The opening of the shop was a great event.

'We'll need to be up at the scriegh-o'-day.' Christy announced the night before, and sure enough she had Priscilla out of bed by six o'clock, though everything was ready to the last carefully weighed pound of butter and meticulously arranged bootlace.

Everything was scrubbed, painted, and polished till it shone. The shelves were filled with tins and bottles, with wools, toilet soaps, stationery, and bundles of haberdashery; newly opened boxes of oranges and apples stood on the floor, pounds and half-pounds of butter on the counter.

Priscilla had, of course, dressed the window herself, which was an old-fashioned bow like those ones seen in the illustrations of *Quality Street* or Jane Austen's novels. In it were rows of sweetie jars with gaily coloured sweets, and below them an assortment of her most attractive-looking stock.

She had a grand new weighing-machine of the latest type, but the old-fashioned till with wooden bowls in a drawer had to do her in the meantime.

Priscilla herself was scrubbed till she shone, and in her pale blue starched overall looked so excessively prim and workmanlike that Janet Purdie seemed the very name for her. Her ribbon was flat for once, and even her nose looked toned down and sedate. There was a tiny wrinkle of anxiety between her brows, for this was the real beginning of her shop-keeping. The sale had been more or less of a joke, but this was serious.

'My certes, but ye look the pairt!' said Miss Prudence, who, true to her word, was her first customer. She had to see and admire everything, both in the storeroom and the shop. 'My, but your Aunt Purdie would open her eyes!' she exclaimed. 'Janet's shop was aye a mixter-maxter. Many's the time I've helped her to hunt through the shelves and drawers for a set of knitting needles or a Seidlitz powder, but she aye had what was wanted. . . . Well, now, let's get down to business. Andra will call for the parcels.'

By the time Priscilla had taken down her list the shop was filling. Every one wanted to have a look in on the first day, and if it had been a criterion of what was to come she might have had no fears for the future, but she knew quite well that many of the visits were out of curiosity, and did not pin her hopes too much to the opening days.

Miss Pinn was among the first to come in, and bought sardines and tea and a stock of needles, threads, buttons, and tapes. She looked more like a teapost than ever, with a little round hat for the lid, and assured Priscilla she would buy all her 'little needfuls' from her.

'Not that my requirements are many,' she said, in her gentle little way, 'but every little helps.'

All her new-made friends turned up to buy something and wish her good luck. Mr Lamont brought a list from his housekeeper, and bought a writing pad for himself. Bessie arrived with her basket, and went off with it full. The farmer who had helped her in the bus the night she arrived looked in and bought a bottle of castor-oil for his dog. Even the bus girl came in for sweets, and the rest of the ladies from the Hall looked in through the day to wish her luck and buy some little thing.

Dr John, who had been out and in and had his finger in the pie about almost everything, had promised to look in and spend his five shillings, but late afternoon arrived without a sight of his cheerful blunt nose and pleasant face.

Christy had kept in the background, contenting herself with a peephole through the red curtains, but she seemed to have noticed every single customer from her remarks to Priscilla whenever she got a chance to speak to her.

Priscilla was just longing for a cup of tea, and, in a pause between customers, was about to slip into the kitchen to see if the kettle was boiling, when the door opened with a quick, sharp tingle, and a girl came in who, she felt at once, was a stranger to Crumstane. She was by way of being extremely smart in a jade-green suit, and wore a small jade hat with a

109

row of stiff 'permed' rings of fair hair standing above her forehead. She had pale blue eyes, a pretty complexion, rather spoiled with too much make-up, and her plucked eyebrows, revealing the fact that they had been very thick, gave her a rather skinned look. Still, she was pretty in a plump, rather shapeless way, and her full little mouth was charming, though a little petted-looking. The jade green was well chosen for her colouring, but just a little tight for her full figure.

She seemed rather in a hurry, and yet glanced round the shop as if looking for something to buy.

'Are you the new shopkeeper?' she asked.

'Yes,' said Priscilla briefly. She did not like the girl's tone.

'Oh!'

She was still standing pretending to look round the shop, but having a good stare at Priscilla.

'Is there anything I can get for you?' Priscilla asked.

She gave a short little titter.

'No, I don't think there is anything here I'd care to buy. I've lost my handkerchief and wondered if I could get one, but I see you just sell cheese and things.'

'I'm sorry,' said Priscilla, instantly sympathizing with this predicament, and thinking perhaps the girl had just been looking round for handkerchiefs. 'I don't stock real drapery, just what they call haberdashery—but I'll lend you a handkerchief.'

She had turned to race upstairs for one, when the girl stopped her.

'Oh, no,' she said, 'certainly not. Besides, I have no time. My *fiancé* is waiting in his car. Good afternoon.'

She had just reached the door when it opened, and Dr John put his head in.

'Oh, there you are, Maudie,' he said. 'I couldn't think where you'd disappeared to. Buying the shop?'

'No,' she tittered again. 'There isn't anything to buy. I've never been in a village shop before. Isn't it funny? Cheese and bootlaces and paraffin all mixed up together.'

She had turned her back on Priscilla and spoke as if she wasn't there.

'This is Miss Maud Jones,' said Dr John to Priscilla, putting a hand on the girl's arm and turning her round. 'Allow me to introduce you. This is Miss Priscilla Delaine, Maudie.'

'Oh, I thought her name was Janet Purdie—that's what it says above the shop.'

'That's the name of the firm,' said Dr John. 'One never alters the name of a long-established firm—does one, Priscilla?'

'My name is Janet Purdie too,' said Priscilla. 'I have taken my aunt's name.'

Priscilla had been ready to smile and hold out her hand, in spite of the girl's rudeness, but she continued to take no notice of Priscilla, notwithstanding Dr John's well-meant efforts.

'Let's go now,' she said to him, in the petted voice of a spoiled child. 'You seemed in a big enough hurry to get home before.'

'Oh, but I have a purchase to make,' said he. 'Have you any of that brown sugar left'—he turned to Priscilla—'or did your friends at the Hall take it all?'

Priscilla stared at him. Had he not declared only two nights ago that nothing would induce him to touch brown sugar, that it was dyed, and the dye came out in the wash, meaning his tea?

'Yes, they took it all,' she said, mystified. 'I thought . . .'

'Then I'll have lumps,' said he. 'A stone of lumps.'

'You mean a pound,' said Priscilla.

'Do I? Oh, well, you know best—a pound of lumps.'

'Of loaf sugar,' corrected Priscilla, getting down a packet. 'That will be fourpence.'

'Fourpence! Good Lord, I'll be ruined!'

He counted out the fourpence.

'There was something else,' he said, 'but I forget what it was. 'I'll have to look in again, seeing Miss Jones is in such a hurry to get home.'

He took her arm and hurried her out of the shop. Priscilla just heard a petted, 'But I don't want to go home. It was you . . .' as the door closed.

No sooner were they gone than Christy pushed open the kitchen door.

'There's impitence for ye!' said she.

'Who is she?' asked Priscilla, the name Maud Jones having conveyed nothing to her.

'Ye micht well ask. An ill lassie if ever there was one. That's

111

Maudie Jones, the vet's younger daughter. He mairrit twice, and that's the result of the second attempt. Her half-sister, puir lassie, is worth a dizzen o' the likes o' her. Her mither's just made a fule o' her. Come awa ben and get your tea, and I'll tell ye aboot Miss Maudie Jones.'

There was nothing that Christy liked better than a good gossip, and no sooner had they started tea than she was about to begin, when Priscilla asked a question that had been puzzling her.

'She said her *fiancé* was waiting for her in his car. Did she mean Dr John? Are they engaged?'

'She's no more engaged to Dr John, poor lad, than she is to Redd Maitland, though she'd eat her fingers off for Redd. Ye see, she got taken up wi' Redd when he was her father's assistant, and moved heaven and earth to get him, but he never as much as goamed her—he has mair sense—rogue though he be.

'Well, in a huff with Redd, she turned round and made up to Dr John, as like as not to make Redd jealous, and the next thing was she was saying she was engaged to the doctor, as bold as brass and calling him her *fiancé*, though she has neither ring nor anything else. Mind you, she wears one, but when my mither—he's been a great pet o' my mither's ever sin' he was a wee callant—asked him point-blank if he gave her the ring he said no. But no anither word can ye get oot o' him. Aye, he's no as cliver as Redd when it comes to wimmen. Nae doot he was sorry for Maudie and kind to her, and this is what he's got for it. But as to the hale truth, naebody kens that but theirsel's. He'll no speak about Maudie, but closes up like a whelk if ye speir at him.'

'But surely she couldn't say she was engaged if she wasn't.'

'That's all ye ken about Maudie Jones—ye heered her yoursel'. "Me fiancy's waitin' for me in his car."'

Christy's attempt to imitate Maudie's Pollokshields English sent Priscilla into a fit of giggles, but Christy, once in her stride, would be stopped by no giggles.

'Aye, she's heerd o' the doctor coming to see you, and came in to gie ye a claw. She doesn't want Dr John hersel' if she can get Redd. She'd throw him aside like an old shoe if Redd looked the side of the road she was on, but she'll see naebody else gets him if she can help it. Poor Lindy, her half-

112

sister—she's in the doctor's surgery—fair worships the ground he treads on, and Maudie makes fun of her afore folk—that's the kind o' little toad she is, and Lindy's that shy she wouldn't stand up to her own shadow.'

'And doesn't Dr John like Lindy?'

'Oh, aye, he thinks the warld o' Lindy. They were aye as thick as thieves the two o' them, and went to the skule taegither hand-in-hand. That's how he got her into his surgery, to get her away a bit from her stepmother and Maudie —they made a fair slave of her. But it's mair as brither, if ye tak me. No, there's nothing o' the sort there on Dr John's side, poor lassie!'

Christy paused, then went on insinuatingly:

'It would be a grand thing for the doctor if some nice lassie could get him oot o' that Maudie's clutches, for I sair misdoot me she may bring it off wi' the doctor if she canna get Redd. She'll work on his feelings and play the poor lassie in love wi' him. She's fit for onything. As a little bold frisk-ma-hoy in her teens, she used to laugh and say she'd be mairrit afore Lindy, and make her wear green garters at her wedding. Lindy's three year the aulder, ye ken.'

'Poor Lindy!'

'Aye, but it's Dr John I pity. Now if some nice lassie . . .'

But Priscilla saw where this was leading, and hastily changed the subject.

'Perhaps Miss Jones will marry Mr Redd Maitland, and then they won't spoil two houses, as you said about someone the other day.'

'Well, ye never ken. They say Scots love is a' scartin' and bitin' . . .'

This was not the disclaimer Priscilla had expected, but at that moment the shop bell tinkled, and she hastened off to her duties.

The next few days passed without incident. Customers came and went, and Priscilla began to find her feet and feel more at home in her little shop. She kept her books scrupulously correct and tidy. At first she made notes every day of what customers had asked for that she had not in stock, of what was selling well and what holding back, together with all sorts of odds and ends, but she soon found that she did not need this. She hung up a slate with a dangling pencil, and jotted down an occasional note, but as she began to get familiar with her stock and her customers she learned what it was to have the 'feel' of things, and by the time the month was up she knew there would be no more painful making up of lists. She just knew what she needed. A glance at her shelves was all the further help she required.

She had a good memory, and loved her work and the feeling of independence it gave her, and though the money was not exactly rolling in, she began to feel a little confident of being able to pay her way if things went on as they were doing. She had not heard from her aunts, but she knew them too well to expect a reply quickly.

Everything would have to be gone over and over again, thrashed out and repeated, before one of them gave the sign of weakening which neither of them would wish to give first.

So she waited, too busy to be impatient or very sad, except sometimes in the night, when she wakened remembering them. Meantime the spring came laughing on. Her garden, from being gay with sweeps of crocuses, like patches of colour in a sombre garment, sported daffodils that danced in the wind, and showed in damp corners the deep purple of scented violets. Later the wild cherries flowered round Crumstane till it was gay with clouds of blossom, and the first primroses arrived.

Occasionally she caught sight of Redd Maitland, riding sometimes stooped against the wind and rain that varied the northern spring, his horse's hoofs making sucking noises in the mud along the grassy verges of the road; sometimes with a group of hard-bitten men at the door of the little inn, taller but as keen and hard-bitten as any of them as they snapped out prices or remarks, surrounded by patient, muddy collies, in a masculine world of their own. After her first snub never by sign did he show her that he was aware of her. She even felt that it was a waste of time to hold her head high in the air and tighten her lips, since he never even seemed to see her.

'Why can't I be as unconscious as he is?' she asked herself, more than annoyed that her cheeks would colour up, that she would recognise him from afar and begin to feel self-conscious and awkward, when on his part he never, as Christy would have said, 'goamed' her.

That word had puzzled her a good deal, and Christy, to whom it was as simple as daylight, could not enlighten her.

'Do you mean "he never *noticed* her"?' she had asked about Maudie.

'Noticed?' repeated Christy disdainfully. 'That's nae kind o' a word. It's a deal mair than that. He never *goamed* her.'

And, indeed, 'noticed' seemed a light and bodyless word compared with Christy's meaty 'goamed'.

About Mysie Cree too Christy was rather mystifying. Priscilla never mentioned her stumble into Redd Maitland's stable or her ride on the mare, with the resultant call for the mackintosh, but she did say one day when they were discussing things:

'That Redd Maitland wanted to get Mysie Cree into my shop too. He's every bit as bad as his uncle.'

'Oh, well, Mysie's a nice lassie,' said Christy mildly, and left it at that. She was counting eggs as she spoke, and when she was finished went off on another tack altogether, a certain black hen coming in for all the denunciations that Priscilla had expected at the mention of Mysie.

She's that thrawn she'll neither lay nor fatten up for the pot,' she ended up.

'Well, she's only human,' said Priscilla, and they went on to another subject, both of them quite content with this solution of the black hen's stubborn attitude.

True to his word, Dr John came in that evening, and spent his five shillings on two of her best boxes of chocolates, which he then presented to Priscilla and Christy. He there-upon invited himself to supper in his own ingenuous fashion, and they had a hilarious evening together.

It was just when he was going that he made a remark that rather puzzled Priscilla.

'How goes the enemy?' he asked.

Priscilla, thinking he meant the time, glanced up at the clock.

'Oh, it's not that enemy I mean,' he said.

'Oh, Old Maitland,' said Priscilla. 'I've never seen him again, I think the old enemy must have given up wanting my shop.'

'From all I hear the other is the bigger one—for me, anyhow.'

115

Priscilla gazed at him.

'Do you mean Redd Maitland? I thought you were great friends.'

'So we are, but I'd punch his head for him if I thought . . .' He stopped, for Christy, who had gone into the pantry, returned.

'Oh, said Priscilla, with her nose in the air. 'He doesn't annoy me, if that's what you mean.'

'No,' said Dr John, 'that's not what I mean at all. *Au contraire*, as the sick Frenchman said when asked if he had had his breakfast.'

'Well, what could you expect o' folks that eat frogs and snails?' asked Christy, so aptly, in spite of the fact that she knew no French whatever, that they both laughed, and then he took his leave.

'What was he meanin' about Frenchmen?' asked Christy, as the door closed.

'I haven't an idea,' said Priscilla shortly. 'He talks a lot of nonsense.'

'Aye, his heid'll never fill his father's bonnet,' agreed Christy, pinning on her shawl.

'Now, what *did* he mean?' Priscilla asked herself, after she had gone. '*Au contraire* means "on the contrary." It sounded as if he'd been vexed if Redd Maitland were *not* annoying me.' She gave a snort. 'People shouldn't quote French if they don't understand it,' she remarked aloud.

Still, she could not help wondering what had made Dr John say that, or mention Redd Maitland at all. He had been so careful never to do so before.

15

Auld Maitland Again

'We've run out of strawberry jam and boxes of cheese,' said Priscilla to Christy, remembering Redd Maitland's advice to get plenty, which she had ignored. 'I'll need to order some more.'

It was market-day, and Christy was going into Lammerton with butter, eggs, dressed fowls, and other of their produce that did not sell in the shop. They sold a few dozens of eggs, but country people preferred salt butter for the most part, or had friends in the farming fraternity from whom they got it fresh. Christy did quite well with her stall in the butter-market, and was increasing Priscilla's store of poultry, geese, ducks, turkeys, and even guinea fowls. But this, of course, was a sideline. Her mainstay was the shop.

Ginger, the pony, was yoked to the tub, and waiting patiently at the door while Christy carried out her baskets and Priscilla made up her shopping list.

After Redd Maitland's remark about Mysie Cree she had been so doubtful about him that she had gone all over her lists again and ignored many bits of advice he had given her. 'I'll use my own common sense,' she had said to herself, making up her mind to be on her guard against him. Now she was finding out all his advice had been good, and she felt more muddled about him than ever. This rather increased her feelings of dudgeon than otherwise, for an open enemy who did everything against her would be easier to cope with than this one who actually helped her. 'Worming himself in,' as Christy warned her so often, 'the same as he did with your aunty.'

She had seen nothing more of Old Maitland, but she had seen Maudie Jones several times in the village.

'I wasn't going to *goam* her,' she told Christy, 'and I think she wasn't going to goam me, but we caught each other's eye and ended by sort of sniffing at each other.'

'You've put a spoke in her wheel, I hear,' said Christy, and she laughed to herself.

'Me? How do you mean?' asked Priscilla. 'How could I put a spoke in her wheel?'

'They tell me Dr John has been to her faither to ask him if he couldn't stop her saying he's her fiancy.'

'Well, if he did I have nothing to do with it. But how do you know?'

'So the folks say.'

'Just gossip! You know, you're a terrible old gossip, Christy, and I don't believe a word of it.'

'He mebbe telled Lindy Jones hissel',' Christy went on, quite unabashed. 'He tells Lindy everything. Only I'll say this for Lindy—she'd be the last to come over anything Dr John said to her.'

'Well, there you are!'

Priscilla felt she had got the last word, but Christy wasn't so easily downed.

'Hech! There's aye water where the stirkie's drooned,' she remarked, going off to bring in the 'powny.'

Things were quieter now in the shop after the first rush, but she was getting into what she thought of as 'a steady trade'.

She could count on several orders for groceries every week, and people had taken to running in for all their odds and ends of requirements even if they also patronised the vans that came round. She had the advantage that she was always there to set against their more or less regular visits to the door.

Christy did not usually get back until five on market-day, when they had a late tea, enriched, as a rule, by some delicacy Christy brought from the town.

She had a busy morning, with a rush, as usual, about one, as her shop was the village tuck-shop, where the children all came with their pennies. She loved that bit of her shopkeeping. The children were such pets, and she had already made friends with most of them. She had made home-made toffee and fudge once or twice which disappeared with such dispatch that she had suggested that she and Christy have a toffee evening and make toffee for them, which would be much more wholesome in any case than the highly coloured stuff they went in for.

For that, however, she would need something more than the small Calor gas grill, so she was waiting till they could have a new stove put in instead of the open fire they still used in the kitchen with its old-fashioned swee and resultant sooty pans and kettles.

It was the quiet time about three in the afternoon when she heard from the kitchen—where she was busy making a sweet for Christy's old mother, who was still bedridden, but enjoyed her food—the shop bell tinkle.

She lifted the pan of milk off the gas, and hurried in. To her surprise and dismay Old Maitland was standing in the middle of the floor leaning on his stick and gazing round the shelves.

'A very great improvement,' he said calmly. 'And how are ye doin'?'

Priscilla felt as nonplussed as ever when faced with her foe. He seemed so entirely unconscious of giving offence, and knew so well how to act the innocent old man. She felt he knew as well as she did how difficult it was for her not to be courteous to old age.

'Quite well, thank you,' she said shortly. 'Can I do anything for you?'

'Now na! Now na! Nae hurry. I've come to do something for you, but business can wait, sure-ly, till we've passed the time o' day.'

He let himself stiffly down into the chair she kept in the shop for appearance's sake more than anything else, and turned his moist eyes towards her.

'Ye'll no keep a pickle snuff by ye?'

'No,' she said. 'I'm sorry, but I have no licence for tobaccos.'

'No? Well, I could put you in the way of getting that, if so be you had a mind. Cigarettes, noo, cigarettes sell well—no that there's much of a profit on a packet of cigarettes'—he got out his snuff box and took a sniff—'it's quantity that counts there. But it brings folk about the place. They come in, and then they see something that takes their eye . . .'

She knew he was just talking for talking's sake, but she did

119

not know how to get rid of him. As a matter of fact, she had been thinking herself of stocking cigarettes, as she had so often been asked for them, but she was not going to take any advice or help from Old Maitland.

'Thank you,' she interrupted, when he made a pause, 'but I have only begun. I can think about that later on, perhaps.'

He gave her one of the sharp glances that passed so incongruously and quickly over his shallow-looking eyes.

'Aye, aye, time enough, time enough.'

'I'm rather busy,' said Priscilla, 'so if you could tell me what you want . . .'

She paused as she saw him glance with lifted eyebrows round the empty shop, devoid of other customers.

'I mean,' she said, 'I was busy in the kitchen.'

'One o' the first things a good shopkeeper learns, my lassie, is that the customer is sacred.' He gave her one of those slow, drooping half-winks that so embarrassed her, as she had no idea what to do about winks, and simply stared back in surprise. 'Everything must be set aside for the cusomer, and everything the customer says is right.' Again his eyelid drooped, though his face was almost as solemn as her own as she stared at him like a child watching for the 'little bird' to come out of the photographer's camera.

'But you are not a customer,' she found spirit to reply. 'You told me before you had plenty of shops of your own.'

'Aye, aye! But that's just where ye mak' yer mistake.' He felt in his pocket, and brought out a piece of paper, straightened it, and began fumbling slowly for his spectacles, all the time glancing round the shop and taking everything in.

'I aye like to do a good turn when I can,' he said. 'Aye, aye, ye'll find he's no such a bad chap, is Auld Maitland. So when ma guid-sister, Jane Farlane, gave me this order I said to her, "Janet Purdie's nearer hand than me. I'll just tak' it into Janet's for ye. Nae doot the lassie'll be glad o' a bit help."'

'Thank you, but . . .' began Priscilla, when he held up his hand.

'Giff-gaff makes good freens, as the sayin' is. Well, now . . .' He had got his spectacles on, and was examining the list while she stood wondering whether to refuse his order or what—he spoke so mildly and gently that it was very difficult

120

to be sharp and disagreeable in return. Besides, she wasn't hard enough in the grain to do it, and an order was an order.

'Get your pen and take them down,' he said. 'Put the prices down as ye go, and then add them up, and I'll pay ye. "Pay as ye go" has aye been Auld Maitland's motto.'

Almost mechanically she had drawn her pad towards her and lifted her pencil, still wondering if she should refuse to serve him or just take his order and get him away as quickly as she could.

She was wishing Christy were there to come and help her, but knew that he had deliberately chosen a time when Christy would be at the market. While she stood dithering, as Christy would have said, he began calmly to read out his list, and she started to take the items down.

It was a long list, the biggest she had had. One or two of the items were for things she did not stock, such as bacon.

'Aye,' he said. 'You'll be waiting till ye can buy a machine for the slicing. It's an awfu' job cutting it by hand when ye're no used to it—no job for a lassock like you. It takes a man to handle bacon onyway. Rolls and hams are gey heavy to lift. Weel, just tak' doon what ye haven't in stock. Ye can send them when ye get them.'

When she was finished he got out a case full of notes.

'I'll just pey ye for everything,' he said. 'Ye ken where Mrs Farlane bides?'

'Oh, yes, I know the farm.'

'Ye can give the parcel o' extras to the laddie to take hame after the skule. I warrent he's in often enough for goodies.'

When she had the list down he told her to add it up, and then put the paper in his pocket.

While she was busy she could feel his eyes passing and re-passing over the shelves and taking everything in. At the end he added one or two more items to her order. Then he paid the bill, and waited for her to do up the goods.

'The car's at the door,' he said. 'I'll just run them up.'

He shook hands as he was going away. 'And if I can dae anything for ye just let me know. Ye didn't come to me for your stock, but mebbe ye'll change your mind later on.'

'Is that why you gave me the order?' she said quickly, giving a half-smile in spite of herself.

He gave a little laugh in return. 'Eh, ye're a sharp lassie, I see. Well, mebbe it was. That van o' mine passes your door every week—it would suit us baith.'

He paused for her answer, and she wished she had not spoken.

'Eh, well, think it ower, think it ower,' he said, repeating himself as usual, and at last got stiffly and slowly along to the door and let himself out.

As soon as Christy came in Priscilla came out with the whole story, not even giving her time to get her baskets in and bed the pony.

'The auld hypocrite!' exclaimed Christy, taking out the long pin with which she still skewered her hat on to her bun of reddish hair. 'He's up to something.'

'He wants me to buy stock from him,' said Priscilla. 'That's what it is. But he's just wasting his time and his money.'

'Mebbe,' said Christy, bustling off to bring in her purchases and get the pony fed.

'What's giff-gaff?' asked Priscilla, after they had threshed it all over again during tea.

'Giff-gaff?' repeated Christy, who was always puzzled over putting good Scots into English. 'It kin o' means you gi'e something to me, and I'll gi'e ye something back—no payin' for a thing, ye ken, but giff-gaff—gieing something back. "Giff-gaff makes good freens", as we say hereaway.'

'Then that's it,' concluded Priscilla. 'That's just what he said, 'giff-gaff makes good friends"—but I'll never be friends with him, or giff-gaff with him either.'

'I should say not. Your aunty would turn in her grave if she thought ye as much as passed the time o' day with any o' they Maitlands.'

Priscilla thought rather guiltily that her aunt must have turned completely round more than once in her grave since her niece came to Crumstane. She remembered, then hastily tried to forget, a lean, weatherbeaten face, with deep reddish-brown eyes, and a whisper in the rain—'Funny little enemy. . . .'

16

The New Van

She was not long in finding out why Old Maitland had called.

It was Miss Prudence from the Hall who enlightened her. She had grown very friendly with the ladies at the Hall, and often went up to see them. They had all been in to have tea with her; they called her Priscilla, gave her advice both about the shop and the house, and enrolled her as a member of the Women's Institute; lent her books and magazines sent on to them by their wealthy friends, many of them from America, and told her all the news of the village from their own point of view.

She was now pretty well up in all the village relationships, histories, tales, and gossip. If she was told a Brown of Upaways was married to a Johnson of Yetts she had a fair idea of who they were and was getting used to a man being mentioned sometimes by his name and sometimes by the name of his farm—a custom that had puzzled her very much at first, when, for instance, Christy would say, 'I saw you had Carluke in the day,' which she would deny, having no idea who Carluke was, till after a heated argument she discovered it was the man she called Mr Johnson.

The ladies at the Hall had no great animus against Old Maitland, having bought toffee from his mother, and guddled trout with him in the burn, and watched with amusement his rise to be a multiple shopkeeper. They had patronised his shop when 'Janet Purdie' was closed, but made no bones about leaving him when Priscilla reopened the village shop, knowing very well he was rich and prosperous.

Miss Prudence had brought a bundle of magazines and a recipe for salad dressing, and stayed on to have tea.

'Have you seen the new van?' she asked.

'No,' said Priscilla. 'What new van?'

'It's a wonder Christy hasn't heard about it. But you'll see it tomorrow—it's Maitland's day for Crumstane. It's fitted up like a shop, the sides are let down, and you can see all the wares. I fear the novelty will attract the folks at first, but it will wear off, so don't worry if you see them crowding round like bees at a honey-pot.'

She went on to describe it more fully, having seen it at another village, but her very reassurances about it alarmed Priscilla, and as soon as Christy came in she began to tell her about it.

But Christy had also just heard about the new van, and had even fuller details.

'The auld deevil has everything we stock,' she said, 'and he's underselling you with everything, a penny here and two-pence there, the auld skinflint! Eh, dear, I sair misdoot me he'll get some o' your trade away from ye.'

'But I don't know how he can do it,' said Priscilla, with a little frown between her eyebrows. 'It isn't as if we had big profits.'

'It'll be the same as that new butcher Middlemass,' said Christy. 'When first he started his meat was that cheap everybody flocked to him, and then when he got his nose well in he put up the prices to the same as the ithers. It's just what ye ca' a ruse.'

When the van came to the village next day Christy was out among the first, not to buy, indeed—she would have turned it upside down into the ditch if she could—but to take in everything with an eagle eye and ask for or listen to prices.

She came home literally glaring with rage. It was a dead set at Priscilla. The brands she used were all there, marked below her prices, and although it was a grocer's van he had even added little sidelines that Priscilla had thought her own. Half of one side was devoted to sweets, and as he had timed it to arrive at the dinner hour, and arranged to give away little coloured paper kites, all the children flocked to the van, and then went racing back to their homes to beg for more pennies. You had to spend a penny to get a kite.

There was no doubt about it, it was a blow to Priscilla. She had almost made up her mind that Auld Maitland was going to leave her in peace and let bygone be bygones, as he had said.

Now she wondered if she should have gone to him for her stock and avoided making him into an open enemy. If he really had decided to make a dead set at her and undersell her in everything possible what was she to do? His purchases in her shop might well repay him. It had given him the opportunity for a good look round with his own sharp, calculating eyes, and the items on his list were no doubt things he had wanted to know about particularly.

Still, if she had refused to serve him he could have found out in other ways all, or practically all, he wanted to know.

Anyhow, she had no doubts now—this was open war. And another bit of news from Christy showed her how determined he was: he was trying to buy a house in the village. But it was the Clock House he really wanted, Christy told her; he had always coveted it. He had thought if he could take away her aunt's only means of livelihood she would have, in the long run, to sell her property. He had not succeeded with the old Janet Purdie, and now he was determined to try with her niece.

Priscilla and Christy were both sure it was he who had sent in the offer which the lawyer had told her about, as soon as Miss Purdie died and before he could know about her will.

They sat for a long time talking it over. Christy, as usual, was brilliant at invective, but not much use at practical schemes. Priscilla had always thought it was just her business he wanted. Things looked blacker when she heard of his coveting the house as well.

'Aye,' said Christy, 'he wants the place, but dinna you get thinkin' he no wants your bit business as well. It's his scheme to get the hale trade o' the kintraside into his hands. Then he'll hev no competition, and can charge what he likes. He's got Kilpallet and Wenlock and East Learmouth and Little Shiels—bought oot a' the wee shops—now he mun have Crumstane as well . . .'

'He won't get it,' said Priscilla. 'I'll fight him to the death.'

Which was all very well as a heartening boast, but she knew she was just an ignorant girl up against a keen and clever businessman. The village had been loyal to her aunt, but the old lady was one of themselves, known to them for

125

over sixty years. A young stranger from the South was a different matter altogether, even though she was Janet Purdie's niece.

She saw now that there had been more reasons than one for her aunt's wishing her to take her name.

Christy went off at last, but Priscilla sat for a long time wondering what to do, and counting over the friends who might give her help or advice.

There was Dr John, but Dr John was no businessman. She could count on his absolute loyalty and all the help he could give, but he was young and just making his way himself in his father's practice. There was Murdo, but Murdo's mind was all on pigs. There was young Mr Elder, the lawyer, who might give her some advice—she must go and see him. There was Mr Lamont, the minister, and lastly there were the ladies at the Hall. They had plenty of influence, but she felt a penny or twopence cheaper a pound would make a difference to them. But she would ask their advice too. When these were all gone over Redd Maitland's hard, weatherbeaten face rose before her. There, she knew, Old Maitland would have met a foreman worthy of his steel, but Redd Maitland was one of the enemy; he had helped his uncle before, and no doubt was helping him again.

In spite of the cheese and the jam, he must have betrayed her. How else, for instance, had Old Maitland known so well why she did not sell bacon? In giving his order he had mentioned it, and then given her in almost Redd's own words the reasons why he knew she did not stock it.

This and many other of his remarks returned to her as she sat thinking things over.

'Yes, he's clever,' she thought, referring to Redd. 'He got round my aunty, but he won't get round me, and in spite of his cleverness he gave himself away over Mysie Cree.'

Barkis knew quite well that something was wrong with his young mistress. It had taken some time to win Barkis entirely over; he had accepted Priscilla, but with reservations. There had been none of the utter devotion of the dog who has taken a master or mistress completely to heart, but latterly he had been coming round. He had never refused to leave the house with her now, as he had done at first, and the other day he had rushed at Dr John when he had seized

126

Priscilla round the waist to dance her down the kitchen when the wireless turned on a favourite dance tune, and snarled and snapped at his ankles till he let her go. Even when coaxed into acquiescence he had sat on his tail, ears and eyes alert for any sign of need for his help from his young mistress. That very day too he had refused to allow Christy to take Priscilla's old golf cape to put round her shoulders to run out in a shower. His growl when she touched it had had a warning note that she dared not defy till Priscilla came in and, picking it up, gave it to Christy herself.

Now he sat with his head on her knees, his brown eyes full of puzzled love, lifting his paw now and then for her to shake in reassurance that all was well.

'Yes, I know you'd help me, Barky, if you could,' she told him. Then she looked at the clock, and seeing how late it was, went off to bed, only to toss and turn and wonder where her profits would come from if she had to reduce all her prices.

She had worked herself up into such a state about the new van that she almost expected her shop to be deserted the next day, and was quite surprised and somewhat cheered to find things going on pretty much as usual. When this continued she took heart again.

'After all,' she thought to herself, 'it's true, as Miss Prudence said, the van only comes once or twice a week, and my shop is always here.'

Then she received another blow—in fact, two, one coming immediately after the other. So far none of her customers had mentioned the van to her, but on this Friday evening a woman whose name she did not know was making a few purchases, and when she came to pay paused before opening her purse.

'Ye'll have to be coming down in your prices, Miss Purdie,' she said. 'I can get these cheaper at the van.' And she went over a few items.

Priscilla was taken aback, though she had thought at first that this might happen.

'The van is trying to undersell me because Mr Maitland wants to do away with my shop and have no competition,' she said. 'Then he would put up their prices, and you would just have to pay what he asked, because there would be nowhere else to go.'

127

'We could aye go into Lammerton,' the woman countered.
'And pay the bus fares,' said Priscilla, smiling bravely, though
her heart was beating quickly.

'Well, you're not thinking of bringing down your prices,
then?' her customer asked. There were one or two people in
the shop who had paused in their chat with one another to
listen.

'I am thinking things over,' said Priscilla, noncommittally.

When she told Christy the story Christy, of course, wanted
to know who it was.

'I don't know,' said Priscilla, 'but she has a purple mark
on her cheek.'

'Fine I ken who that was,' said Christy. 'That was Jane
Farlane—Auld Maitland's guid-sister. And, what's more, I'll
tell ye something else—she was in to speir at ye, so that she
could tell that auld deevil what ye said.'

'Well, he won't be much wiser,' said Priscilla.

'But there's waur than that to tell ye,' said Christy now.
'Mysie Cree has been in to see hoo ma mither was keepin',
and she says she thinks there's talk of sending the van round
be Crumstane most days o' the week.'

'What!' exclaimed Priscilla, really thunderstruck at this new
blow of Old Maitland's.

'Aye, so she says.' Christy was so cast down that her usual
verve in reporting any kind of news was completely absent.
She spoke with a sort of dull hopelessness that immediately
communicated itself to Priscilla.

'Oh, Christy,' she said, 'what are we to do?'

'The deil's gone ower Jock Wabster sure enough,' said
Christy, who reserved this incomprehensible statement for
moments of deepest gloom. 'I sair dismay me we're goin' to
get orr kail through the reek.'

Neither of these ancient sayings conveying anything to
Priscilla but a sense of despair, she sat looking hopelessly at
Christy, who finished her tea and then said.

'I'm awa' ower to see Murdo MacPherson and get his
breath on it. It'll dea me guid to hear a guid, solid sweirin'
if it does nothin' else. We wimmenfolks are ower mealy-
moothed whiles. I like to hear a man sweir—when it comes
frae my ain heart.'

With which more or less admirable sentiment she went off,

after leaving instructions for Priscilla to bring in the 'powny'.

'Bringing in the powny' always seemed so easy when Christy did it. At his most obstreperous moments all she seemed to have to do was to take some corn in the tin baler out of the bin, rattle it at the gate, when he would come rushing up, and the halter was slipped over his head.

Priscilla was taking no chances. She took the halter and the tin of corn at once to the gate, and sure enough he came running up, but getting the halter over his head was another matter altogether, and, whereas he got but a sniff at the corn when Christy brought him in, the tin was empty and Priscilla's patience and temper were completely gone before she at last got him safely housed.

Then she remembered she should have taken him to the trough and let him have a drink of water, and had to unfasten him again, when he trotted off by himself to the trough.

At that moment she heard the bell ringing in the kitchen. She had bolted the shop door. When the house, however, had been turned into a shop a bell had been run through to the kitchen. There were no rules about shutting shop at a certain hour in those days, and it had proved very convenient after the new laws and regulations came in, for you could shut up the shop, but if anybody came and rang—well, they got what they wanted. Folks weren't so particular about laws in Crumstane.

Priscilla ran off, leaving Ginger to get his drink and go back to his stable, as he often did for Christy. The yard gates were closed, and he could neither get back to his field nor into the street. He was safe.

Her customer was Bessie, and as Bessie was a great talker it was twenty minutes or more before Priscilla got back to the stable to fasten up Ginger.

The first thing she noticed was this his stall was empty. Alarmed, she stood for a moment at the door glaring in. It was a big stable for six horses and with a loose box at the end, beside which stood the corn bin with its great, heavy lid.

She glanced round the yard, but he was not there. Then she heard an ominous champing, and rushed into the shadowy stable, whose dusty, cobwebbed windows let in but little light.

The sight that met her eyes filled her with horror. She had left the lid of the bin open when she took out the baler of corn, and there was Ginger, his front legs straddled, his head in the bin, munching corn for all he was worth!

Time after time Christy had warned her about always closing the heavy lid after taking out corn, warning her of the danger to the pony if he got at the grain.

'It wad be the death of him,' Christy had said. There were other things Christy said about his swelling up and bursting himself and various other lurid details. Appalled at her carelessness, terrified of the consequences, she rushed at Ginger and tried to get him away, but Ginger knew with whom he was dealing, and it was only when it seemed impossible that he could hold any more that, sweating and shaking, she at last got him away and fastened him up.

Then she took to her heels and flew. This was no time for nice distinctions or personal considerations—she was sure that Ginger was in the greatest danger. He might burst at any minute, for all she knew. The veterinary surgeon lived near Lammerton, and there was no telephone in Crumstane. Besides, she knew well enough that Redd Maitland did most of the horse-vetting round about Crumstane, where the people thought more of him than of the old veterinary surgeon when it was anything to do with horses or dogs.

She went down the garden like the wind, crossed the burn by the wooden bridge, and then cut across the fields; she had no time for the lanes with their twistings and turnings—a beeline was what was needed. Climbing over stone walls, pushing through hedges, taking leaps and strides over furrows, and toiling painfully through ploughed fields where she almost lost her thin shoes among the clods, she went headlong onward.

When at last she reached the Mill she made for the stable where she had run into Redd Maitland on the rainy night she was lost. But he was not there. To her left was the cottage where he lived, the mill lade flowed past it, and a little unfenced stone bridge crossed it to the door. 'It's almost like a moat, with a drawbridge to his castle,' she thought to herself, going slowly across it, for now that she was nearing his stronghold she began to feel almost as frightened as if Redd Maitland had really been a robber baron. 'And, what's more, he looks like one,' she said to herself, as this thought crossed her mind—'a wicked red robber baron, the scourge of the countryside!'

This brought her to the door, and she gave a timid knock with the horseshoe nailed against it for a knocker.

Her heart fell when there was no response. Through a window at the side she caught a glimpse of a room with firelight glinting on brass, and a table, covered with magazines and papers and bits of harness, on which a table-napkin was spread at one corner with a few dishes on it. Seeing this, she remembered that he lived alone and 'did' for himself. 'He doesn't like women,' Christy had said. 'Though, mind you, he's no saint there, neither,' she had added darkly, and Priscilla had not inquired further.

It was no use waiting. If he wasn't in himself there would be no one to answer the door.

She paused, wondering what to do next, where to find him. Then she remembered having seen him sometimes breaking horses on the long grassy haughs near the river. She recrossed the little bridge, and after some hunting found an opening out of the yard. Below her lay the haughs, and there she saw him with a horse on a long rope, running round him in circles.

As she ran down the steep bank he looked up and saw her slipping and sliding through the rocks and whins, and immediately came running towards her.

17

The Powny

As she took the last stretch of the slope at a run she suddenly discovered that it was much steeper than it had appeared above the whin-bushes, which were just bursting into
flower, and with a cry she went hurtling down, and, making
a run with the horse galloping after him, he was just in time
to catch her in his arms as she came pell-mell to the bottom.
He dropped the rope, and put his foot on it, and, holding his
arms wide, caught her—and not only caught her, but, lifting
her up, swung her round in a half-circle, partly from the
momentum of her own speed, and then with a laugh set her
on her feet again.

It was the first time she had ever heard him laugh, and the
gay, pealing sound surprised her. She almost laughed herself, as would have been her natural reaction to the absurd
ending of her descent—it was really such fun—but she suddenly remembered whose arms were holding her with
muscles as hard and tight as whipcord, and, pulling herself
together in mid-air, she managed to appear as stern as a
high-court judge when he set her down on her feet.

Seeing her immensely solemn face, his own returned to its
severe lines, losing its laughter as suddenly as if a sponge had
been passed over it.

'The pony! The pony!' she gasped, panting so much for
breath that she could hardly get the words out.

'The pony?' he asked. Then he added quite solemnly, '*Not
the shop.*'

She sent a sharp glance at him. Did he dare to laugh at her
shop?

'I thought the shop must be on fire,' he added. There was
not the ghost of a twinkle in his small keen eyes.

'No—it's the pony. He's eaten *all* the corn in the bin.
Christy's out. Will you come—please—at once?'

132

Her sentences still came out in gasps. He saw now that her hair was wet with sweat, beads stood on her forehead and round her mouth, and her face was crimson with the heat of her run.

'Yes,' he said. 'I'll come. Has Christy told you he'll burst? He won't.' His voice grew hard again. 'I hope you had sufficient sense not to give him anything to drink.'

'No, I didn't. I didn't give him anything—I just ran.'

'Did you shut the bin?'

His curt voice told her plainly enough that he did not expect even that much sense from her.

'Of course I shut the bin—at least—yes, I'm quite sure I shut the bin.'

'And the stable door?'

'Yes, and I fastened him up.'

'Then you needn't have raced as if you were in for a steeple-chase. Here, give me your hand.'

He had picked up the rope, and now he took her hand and went straight up the slope, dragging her after him, the horse scrambling up behind them.

'Wait there,' he said, when they reached the yard. 'You can sit on the mounting-stone.'

She was quite glad to sit down. Being hauled by one arm up a steep hill had not improved her breathing, which still came in pants.

He stabled the horse, and went quickly across the little bridge into his house.

She had a moment or two to wait, and looked round. It was a glorious day of late spring. A pear-tree in full blossom stood at one end of the Mill House, and dripped its white petals on the clear golden water of the dam, whose wooden sides were green with moss and fern. As she looked a king-fisher darted out and went like a flash of blue fire down to the river. Just beyond the cottage stood the mill, with its moss-grown wheel dripping with water. The wheel was still, but she knew from Christy that the mill was still used for grinding the coarser grains used as food for stock—some of their own grain came from the old mill.

The cobbled yard was very clean, every weed and grass tuft having been picked from between the stones—very different from her own neglected courtyard—and the brooms that had swept and swilled it stood upright against a wall, drying in the sun. The roofs of the out houses were patched and mended, the walls whitewashed till they gleamed, and the doors painted. They were all old, but only the mill stood hoary with age, while the creeper-clad mill house, with the lichened apple-trees behind it, also had an ancient, grey-green air beside the trim neatness of the cobbled yard and stables.

In the front of the house passed the mill lade, with its quaint little bridge and the few worn steps at one side, where a bright tin dipper caught the sunlight, ready evidently for use for the house supply of soft water. A few bunches of bright golden marigolds found room to grow beside the steps, and Priscilla saw that the lade running round the side of the house formed the boundary to the garden, with its gooseberry bushes, blossom-laden fruit-trees, and patches of vegetables and flowers.

It was a lovely scene, with the river behind it, and the old road winding down to the ford and the stepping stones crossing to the farther side.

'It *is* pretty,' she said to herself, 'and somehow like an old bit of England planted down in Scotland, only there should be curtains at those quaint windows, the doorstep ought to be whitened, and why didn't he paint his house door when he did the stables? The house lookes neglected, and the stables cared for . . .'

At that moment he came out with the pockets of his old jacket bulging out above his riding-breeches, weatherstained-hat on his head.

He went to the stable without speaking, and in a few moments came out with Jenny, saddled.

'Will you ride?' he asked her shortly.

'Oh, no, I'll walk,' said Priscilla. 'If you ride round by the lane I'll cross the fields.'

'You ought to learn to ride,' he said.

'I wish I could,' she returned, rather wistfully, 'but I've no horse.'

'That could be remedied. Like a lesson?'

She faltered. She would have loved to be able to ride, but she wasn't going to take lessons from him, though she knew that he had started a small riding school and fitted up a field for the purpose. Of course, she would have *paid* him if she had thought of it, which was quite different from accepting favours, but she wasn't going to have anything to do with Redd Maitland.

'Frightened?' he asked.

'No, I am not frightened.'

He glanced at her dress. She wore a short tweed skirt and yellow jumper.

As he stood frowning and impatient it seemed to dawn on him that she might be shy because she wasn't dressed for riding.

'You need breeches,' he said, and went on after a moment, 'Well, I have to take the mare—I'm going to Byrecleugh—but you could sit sideways. I'll hold you on.'

'Oh, no.' She stepped back quickly, remembering his mounting behind her the last time.

'I'll walk,' he said curtly. 'There's nothing to fuss about.'

'I'm not fussing. You ride; I'll go by the fields.'

She slipped off, ran across the cobbles, and climbed the wall by the steps at a gap. There she saw a footpath she had not noticed in her wild rush to the Old Mill. It seemed to lead in her direction, and she went off along it.

He stood looking at her for a moment; then, evidently giving it up, he mounted and rode off. She could see his bent figure as, having topped the rise, he took his way jogging along the lane.

When she reached home, tired and rather forlorn, he was busy in the stable, and took no notice of her when she went in, being occupied with Ginger. She stood leaning against the door, and in a few moments he came from the stall, rubbing his hands on an old piece of sackcloth.

'Haven't you learned yet how to fasten up a pony?' he asked shortly.

She started and stared up at him, frightened. Had Ginger got loose? Had he done more harm to himself?

'It's all right,' he said, looking down into her startled face. 'You had at least managed to secure him. But come here, and I'll show you how to do it properly.' She followed him into the stall, and he showed her the proper way to tie up the pony.

'Will he be all right?' she asked.

'Oh, yes. You mustn't give him anything to drink now . . .'

He went on giving her brief instructions, but his tone was friendlier.

Close together in the pony's stall, she felt somehow embarrassed by his nearness, which evidently he did not. He took her hands and deftly guided her fingers with his own in the knot he was showing her how to make, bending over her with his arms round her, but not touching her as he held her hands in his and passed them through and over the noose.

'Now do it yourself.'

He watched her hands, utterly impersonal, his brows down above his intent eyes, his bronzed face close to her own. She had hoped he would not see how they were shaking, but suddenly he shut them both in one of his own.

'You're tired,' he said, so gently that, for no reason at all, the tears sprang to her eyes.

Immediately he let her go, and, leaning up against the side of the stall, plunged both his hands in his pockets.

'Don't cry,' he said, but there was now no kindness in his voice; it was rather a command.

'I'm not crying.'

'All right. Can I go into your kitchen and wash my hands? I must go now.'

The request in the cold voice pulled her together, and made her feel deeply ashamed of having nearly broken down.

'Yes,' she said. 'I—I . . .' Then she walked away, and he followed her into the back kitchen, where he stood washing his hands, while she hastened off to get him a clean towel, holding her breath in case the queer gasping she was trying to control should escape and sound like a sob.

She lifted out a towel and suddenly put her face in it, pressing it against her mouth and eyes to keep back the flood of tears and steady her trembling mouth. She would not cry, she must not cry. She shook with the effort, but she kept back the sobs, swallowing them like lumps in her throat.

Then she heard him walk into the kitchen. He stood drying his hands on the rough towel Christy used and looking at her, his eyes under the frowning brows fierce and hard.

Suddenly he threw the towel aside, walked over to her, put his arms around her, and drew her swift and close, towel and all, against his rough coat smelling of leather and rain and peat.

'Be quiet, girleen,' he said, in a slow, deep voice. 'It's no use crying to me—you know that, don't you?'

She kept her teeth clenched in desperation, shaking her head, trying not to give way to the world-deep comfort of his close, sustaining grip. She knew that she had just to push back against his arms to be at once released, but for a moment she could not do it.

So he held her for a heart-beat. Then he stooped as if to kiss her, drew back, and let her go, steadying her on her feet.

'Now we'll be enemies again,' he said, and a faint smile moved the corners of his grim, close-shut mouth.

She could not trust herself to speak. Her knees shook so that she put out a hand to catch his arm to steady herself. He caught her wrists, and, pressing them against her sides, lifted her, and taking the floor in a stride, set her on the long settle.

'But before we resume our *rôles*,' he went on, as though this interruption were nothing, 'will you trust me for five minutes?'

She looked up. His face, caught in the firelight of the darkening kitchen, was inscrutable.

'I will about the pony,' she said after a moment, in a choky sort of voice.

'It's not about the pony. It's about your shop.'

'I don't know.'

He had been leaning down towards her; he straightened himself, put an elbow on the mantelshelf, and stood silent for a few minutes, looking at her.

'You're terribly keen on this shop of yours?'

'Yes, I am.'

'Still as keen as ever?'

She faltered a little; then spoke sharply. She had quite recovered herself again. The strictly impersonal attitude to which he had returned had helped her to pull herself together.

'Why are you and your uncle so keen to get my shop?' she asked.

He hesitated.

'My uncle would like your shop because it is in his district,' he said, 'and because Crumstane is his native village, and he feels he has failed until the shop he envied so long is his. He also wants your house with your land, because it is the

137

largest and best in the village, besides being the oldest and most associated with the history of Crumstane—the English King is supposed to have slept here the night before the Battle of Crumstane, you know. My uncle will leave no stone unturned to get it.'

He spoke as though he was merely informing her in an impersonal way of certain facts.

'And neither will you?'

'I dare say the stabling would come in handy,' he said coolly.

'And you would turn me out and ruin me and take the house and land of my ancestors from me so that you could have stabling for your horses!'

'You've only just come. Do you love the place so much?'

'My aunty . . .'

'Never mind your aunty. What about you? Wasn't life in Baxton happier for you? What does a townsgirl like you want with a little shop and the dull life of a village?'

'It's not dull.' She was up in arms at once. 'I love it. As soon as ever I saw Crumstane and the Clock House I loved them: I knew I'd come home. I've never been dull a moment. I love it, I love it all—everything about it, and you'll never get it from me—you or your uncle. I'll fight you both. You won't get it. You won't. You won't!'

She had half risen in her anger and excitement. Her red bow stood up like a cock's comb, her eyes flashed.

He felt in his pockets, took out his pipe and pouch, took a spill from the mantelpiece, then asked:

'Do you mind if I light my pipe?'

'Yes, light your pipe, and go away,' she said sullenly, the fire gone out of her since it fired no spark in him in return.

'Yes, I'm just going. . . . What are you going to do about the van?'

'That's my business.'

'Certainly—but it won't be your business for long if you don't get help.' He spoke sharply.

'Well, that's what you want, isn't it?' The tears sprang to her eyes again and shone in the firelight. '*You* don't want to help me.'

'No,' he said grimly and quickly. 'I don't want to help you. I don't want to have anything to do with you.'

'And I don't want to have anything to do with you.'

He put his pipe on the mantelpiece, turned, and bent towards her.

'No,' he said softly, and in quite a different tone. 'You and I must have nothing to do with each other, Priscilla.'

There was something so strange and full of meaning in his deep voice that she glanced up with her tear-filled eyes, and for a moment his own held hers. But only for a moment. Her lips quivered, and he straightened himself and took his pipe in silence off the chimneypiece.

'For God's sake don't cry,' he said, but though the words were grim and impatient there was something behind them that made the tears roll over.

He put his pipe in his pocket, looked at her, then pulled out his handkerchief and, bending down, wiped them away.

'Crying over that shop,' he said briskly.

'Yes,' she said quickly, glad of the excuse. 'Wouldn't you cry if somebody wanted your horses?'

He took up a box of matches and, striking one, lit up at last.

'Now,' he said, puffing briskly, 'let's get back to being enemies. You're the lamb, and I'm the wolf—and don't make any mistake about that; I'm the wolf all right. But just for a moment let's pretend—oh, whatever you like—that I'm an old sheep, say, and listen to me. You stick to your shop. Don't put down your prices; the van will just undersell you again, and you might as well stop when you are making some profit. The van is losing money, and that can't go on very long. It's a bluff. Stick it out—get some one to lend you some money if need be, and—are you listening?' He took his pipe out of his mouth, and fixed her with his small keen eyes, waiting.

'Yes.'

'*Get Mysie Cree in to help you.*'

'What?'

'*Get Mysie Cree in to help you.* Good night.'

He put his pipe back in his mouth, gripped it with his teeth, and, turning, picked up a case he had thrown down, rammed it in his pocket, and strode off.

She sat staring at him till he disappeared and the door banged after him.

18

Mysie Cree

'Mysie Cree!'

She had been listening convinced he had been helping her, as she had been convinced when he went over her lists. Now she was back in the old slough of doubt and bewilderment.

'I simply *can't* understand,' she said rather forlornly, and at that moment the door opened, and Christy came in.

'Was that Redd Maitland?' she asked, astounded.

'Yes, it was,' said Priscilla, and then the whole story of Ginger came out.

'Weel, ye did the best ye could,' said Christy. 'The powny's safe. But what did ye let him into the hoose for?'

'He asked if he could wash his hands.'

'Aye, thae Maitlands'll get in. They creep where they canna' gang.'

'You know, Christy, it's queer, but he sees to try to help me sometimes.'

'You have nothing a dae wi' him. It's a queer thing, but there's no lass in the kintraside but he could twist roon his fingers—and him as ugly as the deil hissel', and reid-headed into the bargain.'

'He won't twist me round his fingers,' boasted Priscilla. 'And you're red-headed yourself, Christy, if it comes to that.'

'Eh, weel, I was a bit o' a deil masel' when I was young. Mony's the time I got a beltin' frae ma faither. . . . What was he sayin' till ye?'

'Well, he told me not to lower my prices, because Old Maitland must be losing money with the van.'

'Aye, that cuts both ways, for if ye come doon he'll have to come doon still mair, and that wouldn't suit the auld rogue.'

'Yes . . . I see. . . .' She sat silent a while, turning this over. Then she said:

'And he told me to try and get Mysie Cree.'

But again all that Christy had to say to this was that Mysie was a nice lassie.

Priscilla began to notice now that her shop was definitely going back. People still came in, but, except for a faithful few like the Misses Selby at the Hall and, of course, Dr John, they bought less. She knew they were getting most of what they wanted from the van, which came round twice a week. The rumours that it was coming every day were not fulfilled, but twice a week was more than enough to ruin Priscilla's shop.

She put down the prices in desperation, but that did no good. The van undersold her again. She grew thin and pale with anxiety. She went to see Mr Elder, the lawyer, who shook his head and looked very sorry, and said he would think things over, but as a matter of fact the day of the small shop was done. Large dealers like Old Maitland could buy in quantities and so sell cheaper, and the old man had so many irons in the fire a loss here and there would not affect him so much.

All of which did not cheer Priscilla very much.

She began to lose heart, and, in spite of herself, the shop reflected her state of mind. It was no longer so spick and span with well-filled shelves, for she tried to economise by only buying what was necessary, and was afraid to strike out into anything new.

She was sad, too, about her aunts. She wrote every now and then, but got no reply. The house remained exactly as she had found it, for she had neither time nor money to make all the alterations she had visualised with such joy when first she saw it.

She had seen Redd Maitland a few times, and once saw him talking to Mysie Cree, which, strangely enough, did not upset her so much as when another time she looked up the inn yard to see him standing looking down on Maudie Jones, who was chattering and laughing as she gazed up into his face.

'I thought Christy said he never goamed her,' she said to herself, as she hurried on. It was a warm day in June, and she was depressed and tired. Old Mr Lamont's housekeeper had not come in for her usual order. She did not blame the old

141

minister; probably he knew nothing about it. Still, it hurt. She depended so much on her few regular customers.

Then she had had the idea of making a lot of jam and selling it, only to discover that all the village had made jam at the same time, and there it stood unsold on her shelves—a waste of sugar and energy. She could have wept as she thought of the new stove she had got in, the hours picking berries in the hot sun, and then the still hotter hours over the stove.

'You might have told me every one made jam,' she said to Christy.

'I telled ye your aunty never made it,' reproached Christy, which was true enough, but there were so many things Christy said her aunty had never done: her aunty had never kept books, her aunty had never shut the shop for half a day in the week, her aunty had never changed the shop window.

By the end of June Priscilla was in the depths of despair. She knew she could not go on as she was doing, yet she would not give up her shop. The lawyer, having thought things over, advised her to shut the shop and let the house. He had a good offer for it, he said, and advised her to get a job in Lammerton. Young Mr Elder even offered her one.

Then there was Dr John. He also advised her to shut the shop, and when she snapped back, 'and how am I going to live?' he said she could marry him.

It was not the first time he had hinted as much, but Priscilla didn't really want to marry Dr John, and she was determined to struggle on with her shop. She simply could not bear the idea of giving up her shop. She told him so.

'You are engaged to Maudie Jones, anyhow,' she had ended up. 'She says so.'

For Maudie had been in the shop once or twice to peer round and ask for things she knew Priscilla would not have, and get in some well-aimed but subtle shots.

'My *fiancé*, Dr Field, told me I ought to patronise you,' she said on her last visit, 'as everyone is leaving you. I'm so sorry, but your shop is so empty, isn't it? You haven't anything I need really.'

Priscilla was no match at the moment for Maudie, she was too downhearted, and she could not fight with poisoned weapons or lies; her sword was always clean, and she would not stoop to untruths.

'I did not know you were engaged to Dr Field,' she said, ignoring the cruel hits at her shop.

'Didn't you?' Maudie's large blue eyes were wide open and innocent. 'I thought everybody knew.'

'Does Dr John?' asked the goaded Priscilla, opening equally innocent eyes to their widest.

'What do you mean?'

'I mean he had never mentioned it.'

'Oh,' she asked, 'why should he?'

Then she had giggled in a sort of secret way as she made for the door.

'He told *me* all about you,' she said—'about you making Christy have him when she wanted the shepherd to put in her thumb, and going for him yourself in case she did. Of course, it was *awfully* good of you, and it was wicked of us to be so amused.'

And she went off, leaving Priscilla staring.

Ater that poor Dr John had got the cold shoulder for some time, so that his suggestion that Priscilla should marry him after giving up the shop was rather shy and tentative.

He had looked at Priscilla when she had brought in Maudie Jones.

'I wouldn't ask one girl to marry me if I were engaged to another,' he said.

'Well, she said so.'

'Maudie talks a lot of nonsense. She told me, for instance, you were very interested in Redd Maitland.'

Priscilla had flamed scarlet, so much so that Dr John stared at her, surprised. What Maudie had said was that Priscilla was trying to catch Redd Maitland, and, knowing his Maudie, he had just mentioned it as a joke, thinking Priscilla would laugh.

But Priscilla was furious, and poor Dr John had gone off with what Christy called 'a flea in his ear.'

In any case all these suggestions had left Priscilla cold. She had determined to make her shop a success; it was proving more difficult than she had thought, but she wasn't going to give in. She put on her thinking-cap and thought hard.

She went over all the advice every one had given, and reluctantly came to the conclusion that the only real help she had had was from her enemy, Redd Maitland.

She had not spoken to him since the pony ate the corn, but she knew he had been to the stables the next day, and, going out into the yard one day later, she had seen him standing with his hands in his pockets, his legs wide apart, and his cap drawn well over his eyes, more horsey-looking than ever, and glowering, as she put it to herself, at the clock over her gates from the other side of the street.

He had walked off as he saw her come out, and she had looked at the clock herself, but there was nothing peculiar about it—it still stood at ten minutes past two. The big, square cobbled yard was the same as ever, grass-grown and neglected, the stables, where so many coach horses and far-mers' nags had been crowded when the market had been held at Crumstane instead of Lammerton, empty except for Gin-ger her pony, the nettles hiding the old stone trough with its pump.

She knew from Christy how often her aunt had bemoaned the end of the coaching days and the Clock House Inn, and had felt sad herself at the departure of the glory. In some old entry books of the inn she had discovered that Sir Walter Scott and Dr John Brown and many another old Scottish and Border worthy had stayed in her house when a long-gone Janet Purdie had been the well-known hostess of The Clock.

It was about the end of June, and she was feeling very low, when one Thursday afternoon a knock came at her front door. It was the half-holiday, but she had been too downhearted to go up to the Hall, where she had a standing invitation for Thursday afternoons. Instead she was taking stock in expecta-tion of a traveller, and wondering how she was going to pay her bill; so she got down off the chair she was standing on rather impatiently. It had been one of those light, timid knocks with the knuckles of one hand that she connected with tramps and suchlike.

But when she opened the door it was no tramp who stood there—it was Mysie Cree.

'Oh,' said Priscilla, a little startled. 'Good afternoon.'

'I hope you'll excuse me, Miss Purdie,' said Mysie, 'but if you wouldn't mind I'd like to speak to you.'

Priscilla opened the door wider, and said, 'Come in,' in a not very inviting voice.

'It was Miss Prudence said she thought you wouldn't take it amiss if I came,' apologised Mysie, evidently feeling very shy and uncomfortable. 'I hope you don't mind.'

'Oh, no,' said Priscilla, her heart softening a little to the shy, plain little creature, who was so obviously ill at ease. 'Do come in.'

She took her into the kitchen, which continued to be Priscilla's living-room in spite of many plans for the two sunny sitting-rooms, which remained as Aunt Purdie had left them.

'Do take a seat,' she said, and Mysie sat down on the extreme edge of a kitchen chair, fingering the edge uncomfortably with her gloved hand. She was evidently dressed in her best for the occasion. Priscilla looked at her questioningly.

'You will wonder at me coming back, Miss Purdie, when you said before you did not want me, but the fact is I'm without a job. Mr Maitland has dismissed me, and I wondered . . . You see, I knew you wouldn't want me when I was with the Maitlands, but I've nothing to do with them now.' She paused, and then went on as Priscilla did not speak. 'It's difficult to get a job near at hand, and my mother is awful set against leaving home. You see, Miss Purdie, she's aye lived hereabouts, and it's hard on old folks to shift.'

'But,' said Priscilla. 'I couldn't afford an assistant, you see, even if I wanted one.'

'I'd come for very little,' said Mysie. 'You see, my mother makes enough with the laundering and knitting to get on, but I hate being idle, and if I just got my food and any little sum you could give me at first I feel I could help you to work up the shop, having been in the trade so long, first with my mother and then Mr Maitland. Oh, Miss Purdie, please give me a trial. Christy will tell you I'm honest and awfu' willing. You've aye had my sympathy, Miss Purdie. I mean, I knew you wouldn't want me that time I came, but I thought if I could get in ye might have got to know me and how things were with us, and kept me on. . . .'

She paused.

'Why are you leaving Mr Maitland?' asked Priscilla, trying not to let herself like Mysie or be sorry for her.

Mysie flushed. 'I wasn't satisfying him,' she said. 'We . . . fell out. He said me being lame and a bit stiff in my left side folks didn't like to see me in the shop, and he wanted to re-

145

duce my wages. He said he could get a young, active, nice-looking lass for less. . . . But the truth is, Miss Purdie, we haven't been getting on, though, of course, I am a bit lame.'

'Oh, but very little,' said Priscilla. 'Please don't think that is against you at all. I often wish now I had someone to help me, but I simply can't afford it. You see, I'm having rather a struggle at the moment.'

'Yes, I know—the van underselling you, and one thing and another.' Mysie leaned forward. 'Miss Purdie, I know I could help you. Would five shillings a week and my food be too much to begin with? Then you could pay me more if we succeed. I've lots of ideas. My! I should like to help you. Honest I should!' She leaned still further forward. 'I hate Auld Maitland too. He's no friend of mine or my mither's. Miss Purdie, do let me come and help. Two heads are better than one. We'd manage thegither.'

She had dropped a little from her prim English.

Something of the girl's faith affected Priscilla; for the first time she smiled a little.

'Miss Cree . . .' she began, leaning forward in her turn.

'Oh, call me Mysie,' said the other. 'I feel that strange if ye say Miss Cree.'

'Mysie,' said Priscilla, 'will you give me your word of honour that old Mr Maitland has nothing whatever to do with your coming here or asking me to have you in my shop?'

'Miss Purdie, I swear to you he hasn't. Him! He'd go crazy if he knew I was here. Miss Purdie, he offered me money to come that last time, but I said no. Then I thought mebbe I could get in, and you'd keep me on, and that I needn't tell him onything that would harm you, and so I said I'd come.'

'But—he wouldn't have dismissed you if he thought you would be free to come to me and help me—would he?'

'He thinks, like you, that you couldn't afford an assistant—he thinks you're just about done. I heard him laughing about it to a traveller.'

'Oh, he does, does he? We'll see about that!' Priscilla was up in arms. 'Mysie,' she said, 'let's have a cup of tea.'

19

The Owl's Nest

In a few minutes they were enjoying a cup of tea with some
of Christy's girdle scones. Priscilla found herself beginning
to like Mysie. She was plain and humble and shy, but she had
a self-confidence about her job that there was no mistaking.
It began to hearten Priscilla. By the second cup of tea Mysie
was well on the way to being accepted.

'I can't afford help. I can't afford anything,' said Priscilla,
sighing.

'That's because you need help,' said Mysie. 'Let me come
for a week or two for nothing, and then when things look up
we can talk about wages. I do wish you would trust me, Miss
Purdie. Won't you ask Christy about me? And Dr Field? And
Miss Prudence?'

'No,' said Priscilla. 'I trust you now—only, suppose I do
say yes, and you come, and still the shop doesn't pay? You'll
be wasting your time.'

'I'm willing to risk it, if you are, but, you see, I feel we
could do well. Your aunt did well, why shouldn't you and
me if we get together? The folks like you, and you are clever,
and it's your shop. I have the experience, but I've no shop.
See?'

Priscilla sat thinking for a few minutes, glancing at the plain,
honest face at the other side of the table. Then she suddenly
made up her mind.

'You are really and truly on my side against the Maitlands?'

'Eh, Miss Purdie, if you knew what my mother and me have
suffered from Auld Maitland you wouldn't ask that, but, sure
as death, I'm wi' you and against him.'

'All right, we'll trust each other, Mysie—shake hands!'

They shook hands across the table, and Priscilla, who never
did anything by halves, plunged in.

147

'I'll give you five shillings a week at first, just because I haven't any more, but as things look up we'll increase it. If you trust me about that I'll trust you about everything else. I say, can you stay now?'

'Rather,' said Mysie. 'I've nothing to do.'

'Well, I'm going over the stock and wondering what to get in. There's a traveller coming tomorrow.'

'We'll start straight away.' Mysie was taking off her hat. 'Have you an overall you can lend me? I've got my best frock on—or an apron of Christy's would do.'

In ten minutes they were deep in stock. With a sureness that Priscilla envied Mysie went over the depleted shelves, advising here, suggesting there. She had everything at her finger-ends, and when Priscilla demurred about lack of funds she went into ways and means with a master hand.

'You see,' she said, when Priscilla wondered at her knowledge, 'I've always thought that one day I'd like to have a shop of my own, so I learned all I could.'

When Christy looked in after the milking—she had been over at the Haughs to see her sister in the afternoon—she was absolutely taken by surprise to find the fire in the kitchen nearly out, and Priscilla and Mysie with their heads together over the books in the shop, lost to the world and to all but business.

'Keep us and save us!' she exclaimed. 'What are you doing here, Mysie?'

Mysie looked at Priscilla, suddenly shy and awkward. Priscilla was to find she was only easy and natural when at work in the shop. There she was mistress of her craft, knew it, and had no hesitations. Outside it she was diffident and humble.

'This is my new assistant,' said Priscilla. 'What do you think of that, Christy?'

'I think what I've aye thought. Mysie was the lass for you.'

'Well, you never said so.'

'I tellt ye Mysie was a nice lassie, but you were that set aboot her being in wi' Auld Maitland—no that I blame you. It was an ill day's work for us all when that auld hypocrite offered Mysie to us. Eh, he's as clever as the deil hissel.' As sure as death I believe he did it to set ye agin her.'

'Nobody knows the intricacies of that queer old man's brain,' said Priscilla, considering this new aspect. 'Don't let's

148

bother about his reasons. You get the supper, Christy, While we finish with the books. Mysie's staying.'

Over supper it was arranged that Mysie should walk over from Kirkpallet every morning and take over a good deal of the work in the shop, freeing Priscilla for the cooking and other jobs, which, in turn, freed Christy for the poultry and the garden. Both the house and the garden had been rather neglected, for Christy had turned very keen on poultry, and, indeed, Priscilla could hardly have kept on without the ready money she brought in. Now Christy was eager to provide shops as well as having the market stall.

Priscilla found everything different when Mysie came. It was such a relief to have someone to talk things over with—someone who was as keen as she was herself, but with plenty of experience behind her. She had been afraid alone to venture on new ideas, and Christy was always against anything Aunt Purdie had not done, which had a depressing effect on enthusiasms, but Mysie was quite different, immediately seizing on an idea and efficiently discussing all its outs and ins.

Before a week was over they had applied for a licence to sell tobacco, and were soon selling cigarettes galore, none of the vans carrying tobacco or cigarettes.

The empty shelves were filled up again, Mysie being insistent that nothing was better for trade than plenty of stock, even if it meant debt at first.

Gradually things began to pick up again. Keeping shop became a pleasure once more, with someone to share the worries and thresh out ways and means of overcoming them. They met each morning like generals on a battlefield, fresh with new schemes and ideas. Mysie bloomed out in the friendly atmosphere, and talked and laughed as much as Priscilla herself. There was always something to laugh over, even their troubles and mishaps, of which there were plenty. The cat, for instance, upset the ink over a bundle of wools, and, when banished, mice took the place by storm and spoiled pounds of rice and barley, so that they had to set traps everywhere, which were always going off by mistake, like guns.

When the weather grew hot they suddenly and simultaneously said, 'Ices!' one day, and, though it meant more outlay, they started selling ices in blocks and in little paper cups.

This was a great success. People stayed to eat their ices and gossip, and by and by ran in for a chat as much as an ice; then they would see something else to buy.

Mysie was convinced that sweets and chocolates should be their mainstay, instead of groceries, and enlarged Priscilla's small stock of goodies for the children with piles of chocolates and delicious mouthfuls of nutty mixtures wrapped in silver paper. Before long they had to get in the joiner to put up lines of extra shelves to display their sweets. These and the cigarettes brought in the lads and girls of the village, with whom the two girls joked and laughed and became very popular. Personality began to count, and against that the vans dropped their prices in vain.

Besides, the vans came in the daytime, and it was in the evenings, after working hours, that sweets and ices and cigarettes were bought.

Then another source of income opened to help Priscilla pay her way and get out of the debts that had given her such sleepless nights.

One evening just after Mysie had settled in Christy came into the shop after closing time, when Priscilla was busy with the books, and Mysie was tidying up.

Christy was looking so alarmingly warlike that Priscilla glanced at her in surprise.

'There's a *gentleman* to see you,' said she.

'Oh. Is it Dr John?' asked Priscilla. 'Tell him I'm busy, but he can come in if he'll just sit still and hold his tongue.'

'It's no Dr John.' Christy was as glum as a cod on a slab of ice.

'Then I'm too busy. Who is it, Christy?'

'It's himself—*Redd Maitland*!'

'Oh!'

'He says he wants to see ye on a matter o' business.'

Instantly Priscilla's heart missed a beat. Business! Her shop! Was some other blow coming to her shop, just when she was beginning to feel a little hopeful again?

'Shall I tell him to take hissel' off—him and his business!'

'Oh, no . . .' Priscilla hesitated. 'I think I'd better see what it is.'

150

Mysie had looked up, and was listening. Redd's name had never been mentioned between them.

'It's old Mr Maitland's nephew,' said Priscilla.

'Hech!' exclaimed Christy mysteriously. 'Fine Mysie kens wha' Redd Maitland is.'

To Priscilla's surprise Mysie flushed up scarlet, but said nothing. She turned round and became very busy over sorting out sheets of brown paper.

Priscilla, unbuttoning her overall and throwing it off, appeared small and belligerent-looking in a short navy skirt and scarlet jumper.

'Lead on, Macduff,' she said, in a would-be nonchalant air to Christy. 'What did you do with him?'

'He said he'd look round the stables till ye were ready. I niver asked him in, he's no a man for parlours—it would take a ten-acre field to haud him. Shall I come wi' ye?'

'No,' said Priscilla. 'You spoil my style. I can manage Mr Redd Maitland quite well by myself.'

With which boast, and trying to look as bold as her words, Priscilla marched out, her red bow already on end like the cock's comb it so much resembled.

She found him standing tapping his boot with his riding stock as he surveyed the rafters of one of the empty stables. He took off his cap and pushed it into his pocket as she came in.

'Good evening,' he said.

'Good evening,' said Priscilla, very stiff because she still did not know what to make of him—because, in spite of insisting to herself that he was hard and ugly and weatherbeaten and had red hair, he disturbed her so much that she had to pull herself together whenever she met him.

'I'm very busy,' she announced shortly.

'So am I,' he said, equally curt. 'May I look round your place?'

She was instantly alarmed. Was this something to do with Old Maitland wanting her property?

'Why?' she asked, her face growing instantly anxious and white.

'Particularly the stables,' he said. 'I'll explain later.'

This alarmed her still more. She remembered his saying that he could do with the stables. Did he want his uncle to

151

get her property so that he could have the use of the stables? In that instant she had the conviction that she could fight Old Maitland alone, but if it were them both—if Redd was in it—it was no use. A feeling of hopelessness came over her at the thought, but she still tried to keep her end up, to be defiant.

'They are my stables.'

'Yes, of course. May I look at them all? Have you the keys?'

'I don't want you to look at my stables.'

He stood looking down at her, a puzzled frown on his face.

'What have you got into your head now?' he asked curtly. 'Do you think I'm going to run away with them?'

She shook her head, the spirit dying out of her.

'I don't know.' She would have hated to know how forlorn her voice sounded, but she was in debt and terribly worried. The shop was still far from being, so to speak, on its legs again. Suppose she lost more money, suppose she kept losing money. . . .

'Come here,' he said. He took her arm in his hand, steady grip and led her out into the yard.

'Do you see all these empty stables, outhouses, lofts—all unoccupied, all going to ruin?'

'Yes.'

'Wouldn't it be better to let them if you could?'

'Oh, yes.'

'Yet when I come to look round them you want to refuse to allow me to see them.'

'You never said anything about letting.'

'Because I don't know yet if they'll be any use to me.' He spoke impatiently. 'I must see them first. I must calculate what would need to be done. I must find out if another entrance could be made. Then I could suggest renting them, not before. Now will you get the keys?'

She would have liked to say no, but suddenly it seemed too good an idea. Why had she never thought of renting them?

But, then, who was there in Crumstane to rent stables but himself? Never would she have *asked* him to rent them. She was too badly in need of money, however, to afford to be proud, and if he wanted another entrance besides the one in her yard she need never even see him perhaps.

152

'I'll get them,' she said. Then she put up her head and marched off, returning in a few seconds with a huge bunch of rusty keys. She was going off, leaving them with him, when he stopped her.

'You must come round with me,' he said. 'There will be things to discuss.'

Besides the stable with its six stalls and a loose box, where Ginger occupied one solitary stall, there were two others, dark and dirty with the accumulated dust of years. The windows were black with cobwebs, and piles of fallen plaster and lime lay about, but he went over them all, knocking at the wooden sides, swinging himself through holes over the mangers, and tramping about overhead.

'Come here,' he called to her, in the last stable. 'I want to show you something.' He had climbed into the loft and spoke from above.

'I can't get up there.'

'Yes, you can. I'll lift you through.'

He swung himself down again, raised her swiftly on to the manger, then, climbing after her, lifted her through the opening on the floor of the loft. When the way was clear he climbed in after her. The place was dimly lit, and cobwebs hung down in streamers from the great beams across the roof.

'Take care,' he said, as they started to cross the floor. 'Mind those beams.'

He was stooping himself, and, taking her hand, led her across the floor, almost ankle-deep in dust and plaster. At the gable end was a window space with a central rib of iron, but no glass. He stopped at a hole in the wall near it.

'You are interested in birds,' he said.

It was true, but how did he know it?

She had always been interested in birds, and now, fired by Miss Tibbie's enthusiasm, had started a notebook of her own on Crumstane birds and their haunts, to help Miss Tibbie, who was gathering material for a book on the subject.

'Oh, yes,' she whispered, peering into the shadows, not noticing in her intense absorption the nearness of his red head to her own dark one. She could just make out three white eggs.

'Know what they are?'

'Pigeons,' she guessed.

'No—quite cold.'

'They're not . . .' She paused. 'Owls.'

'Right,' he said. 'The barn owl.'

'Oh! In my stable, right in the middle of Crumstane! I must tell Miss Tibbie. She *will* be pleased. They're so rare now. Do you think we could bring her up here and show her them?'

'Yes, we'll manage it if you'd like to.'

'Oh, I should. Oh, isn't this fun? It's an adventure. Fancy *me* being able to tell Miss Tibbie where the barn owl nests in Crumstane!'

Turning her head quickly, she looked at him laughing; he smiled in return. For a moment they were friendly together, all enmity forgotten, and suddenly she was immensely happy. He lifted an egg gently with his long, hard, brown fingers, cupped one of her hands in his, and laid the egg in it.

'It's warm.'

'Yes—we must go. Mother Owl flew quietly away among the rafters as I came in, and she will be watching us.'

He led her back, but as they came near the opening she suddenly saw two round balls of fire gleaming from the darkest corner, and, quickly turning to tell him, caught the top of her head against the sharp edge of a beam with such force that she staggered back.

Instantly he caught her and drew her quickly against him.

'Are you hurt?'

Though dazed with the blow, she was not really hurt, but he did not release her for a moment, and she did not struggle. They stood there close together, silent for the space of a few heart-beats, his head bent over her, the air electric between them. Then he let her go, steadying her on her feet.

'You must bathe your head in cold water, or you'll develop a large bump,' he said, in a matter-of-fact voice that brought her to her senses. Then he swung himself quickly on to the manger and held out his arms for her.

She hesitated.

'Don't be afraid,' he said, gently and reassuringly. 'It's all right.'

She leaned down, and he lifted her expertly but quite impersonally to the ground, and set her on her feet. Then they looked at each other and suddenly laughed. Their faces were covered with cobwebs and dust, his red hair stood straight up on end, powdered with plaster, her ribbon was gone, and her usually smooth black locks were sticking out at all angles.

The laugh seemed to clear the air, which had been so tense and electric a moment before.

He gave her his handkerchief to rub her face, and then rubbed his own.

'Now for the rest of the stables,' he said. 'No use tidying up till we're through.'

20

The Quarrel

All went well as they went from the stable to outhouse, then round the yard and to the back of the out-buildings, to find where another entrance could be made.

'Why do you need another entrance?' she asked.

'Well, I thought it would be more convenient for you, as well as for me, but the cost will have to reduce the rent.' He stood frowning and gazing at the wall, evidently calculating ways and means. He looked as hard as nails, quite unconscious of her, summing up the costs, the pros and cons.

'Could you not use the front gates?'

He glanced at her, his agate eyes quick under the frowning brows. She noticed there were green specks in them.

'You wouldn't like the clatter of horses on the cobbles at all hours.'

'Yes, I do. I shouldn't mind that. I love the sound of horses, the clatter of their hoofs on the cobbles, the creaking of leather, the rattle of chains . . .'

'There aren't many chains on hunters and hacks,' he said briefly, but he had glanced at her with more interest for a moment. Then he walked off to the garden.

'What about that field of yours?'

'How do you mean?'

'Is it let?'

'No. We keep the pony and Christy's cow there.'

'Um-m-m.' He seemed to be considering this.

He examined the garden, looked at the tiny bridge, shaking his head occasionally, but silent except for a quick question or remark now and then as they went over garden and field.

'Your fences are in a bad state,' he told her.

'Are they?'

He pointed out gaps and weak places with his stock, standing towering above her, his small keen eyes shooting from point to point, firing quick, shot-like remarks that sounded like accusations to her. Then he glanced down and saw her small anxious face, frightened by these new cares and burdens.

'Don't look so woebegone,' he said Curtly. 'An afternoon's work will put that all right. I'll send up Simmons.'

She knew Simmons was his groom and man-of-all-work.

'Will it cost much?'

'It won't cost you anything if I take the field with the stables, which would suit me, as it links up with the mill. Do you see?' He pointed out with his stock, and she saw as he explained how conveniently the field lay between the mill and her stables.

'With a flat wooden bridge across the water I should not need to use your front gates, or very seldom, but I'd need a track through your garden. Would you mind?'

'No . . .' She hesitated. He was going too quickly for her; those eyes of his seemed to glance round and sum up everything in a few seconds. Simply letting the stables seemed easy, but here he was talking about fields and fences and roads through her garden, pointing out difficulties and clearing them away with that sharp decisiveness she could imagine him using among horse-dealers and such hard-bitten men.

Suddenly he seemed to come back to himself, and remember that she was just a girl.

'Never mind,' he said. 'I'll think it out for you.'

He took her arm and held it as they recrossed the narrow plank bridge, Redd going back to stamp on it and point out a rotting plank, but hurriedly adding that it was nothing; an hour's work would put that right.

As they walked up the garden he suddenly changed the subject.

'How is the shop getting on?' he asked.

'Quite well, thank you,' she answered stiffly.

He said no more till they were in the yard, where he went over to the troughs, examined the pumps, and so on.

'Any other outhouses you don't use?' he asked.

'Yes—in the old part of the house.'

She knew which was the key, and, going forward, unlocked the door, and he followed her in. Once inside he seemed very interested and curious about the old building, which was part of the original inn, and consisted of four rooms, two below and two above. They were all practically empty, except for a few bags of chicken meal and suchlike foods.

Priscilla was a little tired, and sat down on a bag of meal, while he looked at the rooms above, which were entered by a rough wooden staircase.

He came down and stood beside the old fireplace.

'I could do with them,' he said, and paused for a few minutes, his eyes going over the big beams and the places in the wall where plaster had fallen. Then he turned with one of his swift movements towards her.

'It's a pity to waste a place like this for keeping foodstuffs. It would make a good house for someone. What about Mysie and her mother? It's a long walk for her every morning.'

Instantly Priscilla remembered Mysie's scarlet flush when his name had been mentioned, and Christy's remark about their needing no introduction. Was this a plot? Was it all a plot between them—Mysie coming to the shop, and now this suggestion that she should occupy part of Priscilla's house, while he had the stables and would always be about the place?

Her cheeks flamed.

'Why do you want Mysie here?' she asked quickly.

He seemed utterly surprised at her tone. Then his deep-set eyes took on the reddish glow that she already knew meant that he was angered.

'What do you mean by saying that?'

His tone crushed her; she was frightened, and hated knowing that he could frighten her so easily.

'I mean—why do you want Mysie here?' she repeated rather feebly.

He stood looking at her for a few seconds, but his frown was more puzzled now than fierce.

'Want Mysie here?' he repeated questioningly. 'Now what in heaven's name do you mean by that?' He shrugged his shoulders. 'Is it impossible to talk simply to you? Mysie is lame, and has a long way to walk, even in summer. Their

158

cottage is old and damp for her mother, who suffers from rheumatism. It just struck me that here was a dry, well-built little house wasted to keep a few bags of chicken meal or feed for my horses. In it Mysie would be near her work—a godsend in winter—and near her mother. I can excuse your suspicion of me up to a certain point—you go beyond it.'

The last words came out with a snap.

Priscilla felt a little ashamed that she had never thought of that long tragic trudge for lame Mysie and knew nothing about the circumstances in which she lived with her mother, but she was too young not to resent being made to realise it.

'I don't want . . .' she began, and stopped.

'Well?' he shot out.

'I don't want *anything*—having strangers in my house and my stables let, and not knowing *anything* really,' she stammered.

He walked over to the window and stared out into the yard, his back towards her.

'Do you want to call it off?'

She hesitated. She knew it was all to her advantage to let the stables and outhouses now falling to ruin through disuse and neglect. No one else could conceivable want them but him, and she was too short of money to be proudly independent. Besides—her mind baulked at the fact—life did seem more full and exciting when he was about; she had been happier and more alive that afternoon than ever before.

'I've always lived so much with women,' she suddenly thought. 'I suppose men are more exciting. . . . Of course real men, not Mr Porter.'

'I don't know,' she said at last. Then she pulled herself together and tried to be very businesslike. 'It depends entirely on the rent,' she announced, in a severe little voice.

'The rent won't be much,' he said curtly. 'Not at first, anyhow, with all the expense of repairs and so on. Well, I'll make you an offer when I've gone into things. You can decide then.'

He turned half round, and she saw his dark profile against the window. His face looked more hawk-like than ever, with the red hair standing up like a brush above the hooked nose and gimlet eyes that caught hers as he swung farther round.

'Afraid to trust me?' She had been silent so long there was some excuse for the sardonic-sounding inquiry.

'I don't know,' she said, rather wearily. 'I wish you'd tell me if . . . if you are trying to get the better of me.'

He gave a short laugh.

'Do you think I usually tell people when I'm going to get the better of them?'

'It's my only way of fighting,' she said. 'I don't like fighting in the dark.'

'Well, let us fight in the open then,' he said quickly and fiercely. 'I don't want to help you. I don't want to have anything to do with you. I know all about your aunt's will, and, though she would not have believed it, and you cannot, I don't want your property. More than that, I don't want you to lose it, but from the moment I saw your soft little pixie-face I knew you were doomed unless somebody helped you. I as good as told you to go home to whatever warm nest such a callow fledgling belonged to, but you wouldn't go, you *would* have that damned shop—pardon my language, though it might do you good and relieve the situation if I gave you a good cursing; you might believe I was fighting in the open then—and though I didn't want to help you, there was nobody else. What's more, I knew you'd refuse my help. You'd have refused it in your self-confident pride if for nothing else, but you didn't trust me. I don't blame you; everything was spoilt for us both before ever we saw each other. Yes, my girl, though even now I could . . .'

He stopped abruptly.

But his onslaught had been too much for her; she was crying openly.

'Oh, go away!' she said, springing up from the meal poke on which she sat. 'Go away! Go away! I hate you!'

He strode across to her. 'Come here,' he said, and, putting his arms round her, he took out his dusty handkerchief and wiped her face.

'That's right,' he said. 'Hate me—that's what you must do. I'm helping you to, am I not?' He smiled a little with close-shut mouth.

'No, you're not,' she said forlornly.

'You're right,' he said, loosening his hold at once and lifting her back on to the open meal poke, where she sat crumpled up, not caring that she was getting all over meal, or that her eyes were wet and her nose red.

'How old are you?' he said abruptly.

'Nineteen—nearly twenty.'

'An infant—that's all you are to me, do you see? I want to stop you howling the same as I would any child. Now pull yourself together, put on your fighting gloves, and try to get as big a rent as you can out of a hard-bitten horse-dealer.'

He walked across the floor, felt in his pockets, and turned round.

'Do you mind if I light my pipe?'

'No,' she stammered resentfully. 'You're always asking me that.'

'Well, I must do something with my hands when you're about. . . . Now where were we? If you don't want to let this place as a house I'll take it, but you'll get a smaller rent from me than from Mrs Cree. Now for heaven's sake don't think I'm in love with Mysie Cree! I've no time or use for anything but horses—they're more sensible than women anyhow. Have you seen my cap?'

'It's in your pocket.' She was recovering herself; his hard common sense made her feel ashamed of the emotion that had shaken her, and also resentful that he had seen her with her face 'all begrutten', as Christy would have said. Christy had all the Borderer's impatience with tears.

He pulled out his cap, lifted it to put it on his head, then pushed it impatiently back into his pocket. He stood, feet apart, crop under his arm, hands in his pockets, the pipe evidently forgotten again, scowling at the corner where she sat on the meal poke among the shadows.

'What about that doctor?' he asked.

'Dr John?'

'Yes. Why don't you marry him?'

'I don't want to marry him.'

'John's good stuff'—his voice had softened a little—'and too good for—the fate that is catching him up. You go in and rescue him; the poor chap's a misery. I thought you and he were such friends? He needs a friend.'

'So we are friends, but that's different.'

He took no notice of this, but went on:

'He'd protect you from the Maitlands, and look after you.

Your precious shop would be safe from them—if you still wanted it.'

'I thought he was a friend of the Maitlands—of yours anyhow.'

'He'd skin me alive for a glance from you.'

'I have no intention of marrying Dr John, and anyhow . . .' She stopped.

'It's no business of mine?' he took her up. 'Well, I am concerned about him in spite of that. He needs rescuing, and there's nobody else but you who can do it. It's a pity to see a good man like that doomed to a . . .' He paused, evidently not liking to mention Maudie's name, or even the epithet at the tip of his tongue. Then he pulled out the crushed cap again, looked at it in surprise, as if he'd expected it to be a ferret or a horse's bit, and then repeated, 'You go in and rescue him—and tell Christy,' he ended up abruptly, 'not to give that beast Ginger so much corn, and that one of his shoes is loose, and his bridle needs a stitch. Good day!' And he marched off, yanking on the cap as he reached the door. In a few seconds she heard the mare's hoofs clattering on the stones of the yard as he galloped off.

21

Right of Way

The rent that Redd Maitland offered, though small, was more than Priscilla had expected. The offer came in a businesslike envelope, and was couched in short, businesslike terms.

He proposed to put the stables in repair, to erect a broader plank bridge across the stream to the field, and wire off a path at one end of the garden leading from the yard to the new bridge. This was easy, as it was through a neglected bit of the ground where the poultry had had a run before Christy had moved them all to a larger and better piece of wasteland at the foot of her own garden where it marched with Priscilla's, and where the ducks and the geese could have a part of the stream to themselves. Not that they stuck to this; they sailed up and down at will, causing Christy and Priscilla to go on many a hunt on the long summer evenings for straying ducklings and young geese.

Priscilla would have liked to have refused to rent the stables at one minute, and had to admit to herself the next that it was not only a splendid arrangement for her as well as for Redd Maitland, but that it gave her a thrill of excitement to think of seeing him about the place.

This she tried to hide from herself without a great deal of success, giving herself lectures in which a very severe and haughty Priscilla wiped the floor with a hang-dog Priscilla who did not even try to defend herself, but occasionally wept.

Christy and Mysie both noticed the signs of tears, and each expressed her concern in a widely different manner, Mysie being all sympathy and warm resentment that anything should make Priscilla sad, while Christy believed in the stoic's cure.

Not that either of them had ever mentioned Redd Maitland

between themselves or to Priscilla. The explanation they assumed was that it was her old aunties or the shop that worried her. Her aunts had still not written, and she had given up writing to them; for several weeks she had sent no word of her doings.

After several attempts, each a more strained effort to imitate his businesslike communication, she sent off an acceptance to Redd, and immediately the yard seemed to be filled with workmen mending, plastering, and cleaning up the place.

Nearly every day she would hear his brusque voice, giving his curt orders, pointing out what he wanted done, or swiftly commanding things to be undone again that did not meet with his approval. He never seemed to argue or waste time in complaining or nagging. If things were right, good; if not down they came, with him probably throwing off his coat and setting himself to expedite matters and get everything exactly as he wanted it.

Priscilla often saw him, but he merely nodded and went on with what he was doing, and pride made her keep out of his way as much as possible.

In a few weeks the place looked entirely different. He would have no half-and-half measures where his horses and stables were concerned. The stables and outhouses were mended and shiningly clean with newly painted doors and windows, the yard free from weeds, and the cobblestones scrubbed with hosepipe and brooms, the pumps repaired and painted, the troughs once again filled with clear water. A broad plank bridge had been built over the burn; a line of wire-netting separated a road through the garden down to the water, along which some quick-growing hedge had been planted; her fences had been mended, and her own little bridge made safe.

'I feel it's up to me to start on the house now,' Priscilla said to Christy. 'Everywhere else we are so smart.'

But Christy induced her to wait till the spring before starting on their outside painting and repairs. They had smartened up the front of the house, which faced the street, when they were doing the shop; the parts facing the yard and garden could wait, for Mysie and Priscilla needed every penny they could scrape together for the shop, which was now paying its way again.

Mysie's small wage had been doubled, and Priscilla hoped soon to be giving her what she called a real wage and a small percentage of the profits.

The ices and chocolates and cigarettes were going strong, and even the groceries were looking up, when Mysie had another idea. With the vans they had a great deal of competition in the grocery line, but there was practically none with haberdashery and stationery and suchlike, so she suggested using the storeroom for drapery, stationery, and fancy goods.

Mysie's mother was an expert knitter, and made quite a useful addition to her income by knitting shooting stockings, waistcoats, jerseys, and jumpers for the 'big houses' round about. The laundry work was getting too much for her, so they decided to try selling them in the shop, and if they were a success Mrs Cree would give all her time to knitting.

The joiner was in shelving and fitting out the storeroom one day when Priscilla remembered Redd Maitland's suggestion about the four rooms with an entrance from the yard, which he was now using as storerooms.

Christy and Mysie and she were at tea when she decided to mention it.

'Mr Maitland said when he was looking over the stables,' she began, 'that those four empty rooms would make a nice little house for some one if I let it.'

Instantly Christy was up in arms.

'That Redd Maitland is in far enough,' she said crossly. 'You'll see, he'll do you in the end; he's every bit as bad as his uncle.'

Mysie flushed up scarlet.

'He is not, Christy!' she exclaimed. 'He's not like his uncle. He's been awful kind to my mother and me.'

'I daursay,' returned Christy, 'but you've nothing he wants, or you'd see a different side of his face. It's Priscilla's shop and the Clock House they want, and her bit property. Look how he's wormed his way in already!'

'He has not wormed his way in,' returned Mysie hotly. 'He took the stables to help Priscilla—at least, I mean . . .' She stopped, her face getting more scarlet than ever as she saw Priscilla start and stare at her. 'I mean, he knew it would be a good thing for Priscilla—I mean . . .'

'What *do* you mean, Mysie?' asked Priscilla, flushing in her turn. 'Do you mean he rented my stables out of charity?'

'No, no, of course I don't'—Mysie was terribly flustered—'only he said—only he asked me . . .' She stopped again, feeling herself getting deeper into a mire of misunderstanding, as Priscilla and Christy glowered at her.

'Did he consult you about me and talk me over?' Priscilla burst out indignantly, while Christy exclaimed at the top of her voice:

'I aye thocht you were too far in with Redd Maitland, Mysie Cree, and that's what for I niver said to Priscilla mair than that you were a nice lassie when you and my mither wanted me to speak for you to her—no that I think any the waur o' ye for that. I ken you're a decent, honest lassie, and have nothing to thank the Maitlands for, but you're ower soft-hearted, and that Redd Maitland can twist any lass round his finger-ends. He's done his best to wheedle Priscilla . . .'

'He has not!' exclaimed Priscilla, almost shouting as she indignantly interrupted. 'Wheedle, indeed! He's been as rude to me as ever he could be. He called me a sheep and a bag of potatoes, and said I was soft and silly—he's simply insufferable. As if I'd let him wheedle me anyhow!'

The fat was in the fire! All three were at it: Mysie almost crying as she tried to stick up for Redd and at the same time deny that she had 'talked over' Priscilla with him; Christy, on the war-path, denouncing every Maitland among them, quoting Aunt Purdie and airing all her grievances about the shop being changed—she still could not bear anything being done that Aunt Purdie had not done—saying that Redd Maitland had 'got at' Mysie, and all the changes were due to him, which Mysie and Priscilla both hotly denied.

'Do you *like* Redd Maitland?' Priscilla at last demanded, turning on Mysie in her turn.

'Yes, I do!' Mysie was openly weeping now. 'I *do*. He's been a kind friend to my mother and me, and he's no more like his uncle than chalk's like cheese, and he *wants* to help.'

'We want no help from the Maitlands,' said Christy, the unreconcilable.

'I know,' said Mysie, drying her eyes. 'That's what makes it so hard.'

'We're no all as soft as you,' exclaimed Christy, 'an that's a fact.'

Mysie was silent, and Priscilla, recovering from her own indignation at the idea of having been 'wheedled' by Redd Maitland, suddenly felt sorry for her.

'It's all right, Mysie,' she said, taking her hand under the table and giving it a squeeze. 'Christy and I like you. It's just the Maitlands we are against.'

'Yes, I know,' hiccuped Mysie, 'but I can't bear you saying Redd Maitland is like his uncle. If it was Andra—him that's in the shop with his uncle now—you might talk: he's a little sneak if you like. But Redd Maitland helped Mother and me when Auld Maitland got our shop, and it was over your aunty he quarrelled with his uncle and left him . . .'

'You seem to ken a deal mair than ither folks about Redd Maitland,' interrupted Christy sarcastically, and Mysie was silent.

'Well, anyway,' said Priscilla, after a moment, 'what I was going to say was this: what about you and your mother taking those four rooms, Mysie? It would be convenient for us both.'

'Is that anither o' Redd Maitland's grand ideas?' asked Christy at once, and Priscilla and Mysie were silent, and the subject was allowed to drop for the moment.

A day or two later Priscilla was amazed to see Maudie Jones in her yard. She had just come out of the stables, and nodded to Priscilla in a condescending way, as she remarked:

'Redd's yard and stables look fine. I've just been seeing him about some riding lessons he's going to give me.'

Priscilla was too taken aback to say anything at the moment, though she seethed with indignation at Maudie's appropriation of her yard and stables as Redd's.

'I wish I'd never let them,' she thought to herself, as she stared haughtily at Maudie and returned indoors.

After that she saw her several times, but they were only fleeting glimpses, and though she was angry she felt that she could hardly make an objection to anyone coming to see Redd Maitland at the stables he was paying for.

It was partly the reason, however, for her curt refusal when one day Redd stopped her and asked her to come into the stable and see a saddle he had acquired.

She had noticed that Ginger had recently developed a much finer figure; not only was he less like a barrel round his middle, but he had been clipped and groomed till he shone and really looked a smart little fellow.

'It will just fit Ginger,' he said, referring to the saddle. 'Have you got a pair of breeches?'

'No,' said Priscilla shortly.

'Well, you'll need a pair; you're so light Ginger will carry you easily. You can learn on him, anyhow. Let me see . . . we could start on Monday.'

'Oh, I don't think I'll start just now,' said Priscilla stiffly.

'The sooner the better. You want to ride, don't you?'

'Yes, I did, but . . .'

'You're not frightened? You couldn't be frightened on Ginger!'

'No, I'm not frightened.'

'What is the matter, then?' He was glancing at her from under beetling brows.

'I won't waste your time.'

He continued to look at her in silence, saying nothing.

'And I'm very busy,' she went on uncertainly.

'If you don't want me to teach you,' he said at last, brushing all her excuses aside, 'Simmons could lead you round—but you'll get into bad ways. I'd like to see you have a good seat and ride well. I know you could; you have the makings of a horsewoman. Better let me start you off.'

'I'll see,' she said, and turned to go.

'Very well,' he said briefly. 'The saddle's in Ginger's stable if you require it.' And he walked off as she returned to the house and the shop to find Mysie on her knees before a heap of sugar lumps she had upset on to the floor.

'Oh, Mysie,' she exclaimed, 'what a waste!' glad to have something to relieve her irritation on.

Mysie was about as much upset as the sugar, and had to be comforted. When they had saved the most of it Priscilla swept the rest into a bag.

'Never mind, Mysie,' she said. 'It's an ill wind that blows nobody any good; I'll keep this for the horses, and then I won't feel I'm wasting it when I give them a lump.'

She was growing used to the animals now, and was very fond of them, especially Jenny, the mare of whom she had

168

been so terrified, and was getting into the habit of slipping into the stables and giving them a bite, an apple or a bit of sugar.

Since Mysie had come she had seen nothing of Old Maitland, but got a bit of news of her old enemy one day shortly after they had stocked the storeroom with drapery and fancy goods, including some of Mrs Cree's knitted jumpers, which, however, being more expensive, were hanging fire a little, as her usual customers from the big houses round about had not yet found their way to Priscilla's shop, and still went to her cottage to buy or give their orders—another reason why Priscilla was thinking it would be a good thing if she moved with Mysie to the house in the yard.

She had taken Bessie and another woman in to look round at the display of new goods, and then gone to help Mysie with an influx of buyers for ices.

When she came back the two had their heads together deep in gossip. She caught Old Maitland's name at once, and then Bessie turned to her and said:

'We're just talking of Auld Maitland and Andra. They tell me things is no goin' on weel there. That Andra's a rogue if ever there was one, and they say the auld man has found him oot cheatin' the till.'

'Aye, and the shock brought on a kind o' a stroke,' said the other woman. 'He'll be getting up in years now, will Auld Maitland.'

Priscilla made some remark and changed the subject. She did not like discussing the old man, except with Christy and a few friends, but she tried to be sorry about his misfortune in a Christian spirit, as she felt she ought to.

The Christian spirit was, she admitted, a little difficult, but not so difficult as when she tried to apply it to Maudie, whom she frankly detested, and who seemed to take a pleasure now in walking through the yard as if it belonged to her, and through the garden by the new road across the stream.

Christy met her once and told her there was no right of way through Priscilla's ground, but she immediately said she had Redd Maitland's permission to 'use the short cut to the mill.'

'Then he's a bigger fool that I thocht him,' said Christy, 'and he has no manner o' right forbye.'

She came in fuming once more about the Maitlands, and furious that Priscilla had let the stables.

'Did I no tell ye what it would be?' she asked. 'Let any Maitland get his foot within the door, and he has the hoose frae ower your heid afore ye know where ye are. We canna ca' the place oor ain. It was an ill day ye feu'd the stables till the likes o' him.'

'Well, it's done,' said Priscilla, in a disheartened voice.

'It's only Maudie Jones that comes in,' said Mysie soothingly, 'and she has cheek for anything. I'm sure Mr Maitland doesn't know about her haunting the place like she does.'

Priscilla was inclined to think too that Mysie was lying, but before long she had proof positive, as she thought, that that was not the case.

22

Priscilla Waters the Mare

The summer seemed to have flown past, and the days were already creeping in, when one afternoon Priscilla, in crossing the yard, thought she would give her favourite Jenny a piece or two of sugar. There was still some left from the large bag that had been emptied over the floor, and she had put a few pieces in her pocket.

Everything was quiet in the yard, but Jenny's stable door open at the top—it was one of those doors cut horizontally across the middle, the upper part of which can be opened, leaving the lower securely barred.

She went forward, and, leaning over the top, looked along to the father end, where Jenny had her stall.

She saw Jenny's hindquarters, and was about to unbolt the under door when some sudden feeling of tension in the quiet of the stable drew her glance to the shadows at the far end. Her eyes, grown used to the dimmer light beyond the sun-steeped yard, immediately made out two figures standing there in silence.

They were Redd Maitland and Maudie.

She was standing close to him, and had her hand on his arm in a very familiar way, while he, with his hands in his pockets was gazing down into her upturned face. There was something intimate in their position and their silence in the shadowy stable that suddenly drove the blood from her cheeks and sent her heart bounding. She drew quickly and silently back, and sped on noiseless feet to the house, where she found herself trembling so violently that her knees gave from under her, and she sank into a chair. 'What's the matter with me?' she asked herself, amazed. 'You'd think I'd had a shock.' She would not admit to herself that she had had a shock, but for all that she realised that her world had some-how tumbled about her.

She had never believed for a moment that there was, or could be, anything between Redd Maitland and Maudie Jones.

Maudie Jones! That hateful little piece, with her lying, im-pudent tongue, and that hint of a lightness of moral standards that made the humblest woman of the village regard her with contempt. 'Maudie Jones'—the very way in which her name was mentioned bespoke disdain.

Priscilla could understand Dr John better. Dr John was so kind-hearted and unsuspicious one could imagine her play-ing on his pity and getting away with it to a certain extent, though not, Priscilla was certain, to that of marrying her, as she boasted he wished to.

But Redd Maitland! That that hard-bitten, uncompromis-ing, and experienced individual should be philandering with Maudie Jones was unthinkable—well, not *philandering,* per-haps, Priscilla pulled herself together, but being sort of in-timate, talking to her secretly in a shadowy corner of the stables —it simply took her breath away. More than that, it made her feel stricken, wounded.

'It isn't that it really matters to me,' she kept assuring her-self, 'only I'm so surprised—shocked is the word, I suppose.'

That she was grieved and terribly hurt she would not allow, though she felt as though she had had a blow over the heart.

She heard Christy coming, and jumped up still surprised at the way her knees trembled under her, and terrified that Christy would notice anything, but Christy was full of her own concerns at the moment, one of her Christmas turkeys having gone off colour. They were delicate birds to rear, and she was always being told that they weren't worth their meat, but nothing would induce her to give up her turkeys.

By the time Priscilla had heard all about the turkey and that the bird was 'meanin' it' this time, by which Christy meant it was really seriously ill, she had pulled herself to-gether.

She went out into the yard again on her way to the garden to get the basket of plums she had previously started out for. She saw Jenny standing saddled near the stable door, with her reins thrown over a hook in the wall, and she remembered the sugar in her pocket. No one was about, and she went up to the mare, spoke to her, and gave her some sugar, which Jenny champed up, making a mess of her bit in the process, but as Priscilla moved away Jenny tried to follow, and seemed to be stretching out her neck to the trough of water close at hand.

'Do you want a drink?' said Priscilla, thinking perhaps the sugar had made her thirsty, and that anyhow the water would cleanse the frothy bit and remove the signs of her feast. She unhooked the reins and led the mare over to the trough, where she sucked up the water with great satisfaction while Priscilla stood holding her and looking on—she had no fear of the gentle Jenny now.

Suddenly she was arrested by a shout.

'What the hell are you doing there?'

Amazed, she turned to see Redd Maitland advancing furiously towards her, his brows down, his reddish eyes absolutely seeming to shoot out sparks of fury as he rushed to the mare, jerked the reins out of Priscilla's hands, drew the beast back so that she reared, and turned on Priscilla.

'Have you no sense at all? Or are you trying to frustrate me on purpose? Who but a born fool would set the mare to fill herself with water when she's saddled for riding? Are you completely senseless, or what? Understand this—you will leave my horses alone, or else I'll shut up the whole damned place and take them back to the mill.'

Terrified at the, to her, incomprehensible rage she had aroused, Priscilla shrank back against the stable door, white with apprehension. 'I—I—only gave her a drink,' she faltered. 'She seemed so thirsty.'

'If you've no more sense than to lead a mare to a trough to drink her fill before she goes on a journey you'd better keep away from my stables altogether! Here! Get out of my way till I get her stabled.'

Priscilla needed no second telling; she jumped out of the way as he poured his vials of wrath over her.

Half-way in he turned. 'You've been giving her sugar. Are all women liars as well as fools?'

'Oh, yes, I did, but . . .'

'You said you'd only given her water—only given her water, by heck! If I see you near my stables again I'll —I'll dip you

173

in the horse trough. What do you think I'm going to do now? Ride a lathered mare? To h . . .'

But Priscilla had fled before another onslaught. She had never before seen a man really furious with anger. She was like a bird caught in a typhoon and swept before it across the yard and into the shelter of the kitchen, where she fell into a chair and burst into shaking sobs. The second shock coming so soon after the first was too much for her.

Christy, busy in the back kitchen with her mash for the sick turkey, gave a shout of dismay as she rushed in which brought Mysie running from the shop, where she had been tidying up before going home.

It's that Redd Maitland!' shouted Christy. 'I heerd him cursing hell-fire, but I thocht it was one o' the men he was lettin' fly at. Wait till I get at him . . .'

She had the large wooden spurtle in her hand with which she stirred the mash, and was making for the door, when Prisilla jumped up and grabbed her skirt.

'Don't you dare!' she sobbed. 'Don't you dare say a word to him about me. Don't you dare go out—I won't have it. Don't you dare!'

Christy could as easily have swept Priscilla aside as she would have brushed a hen out of her way, but there was no mistaking the desperation in Priscilla's voice.

She paused but brought the spurtle full slap on the table, making the jars set out for the making of plum jam jump and rattle.

'Wait till I get at him!' she raged, and went off into one of her tirades about the Maitlands and how 'folks weren't safe in their beds' with the villains that now came about the place, while Mysie did her best to restore peace and stop Priscilla's sobbing.

'Christy,' Mysie said at last, 'your turkeys are out. They're all over the garden—you must have left their door open.'

Christy fled. The heavens might fall, but her turkeys had to be guarded as if they were delicate, high-born maidens.

'Thank goodness,' said Mysie, 'they really are out. What happened, Priscilla?'

Priscilla, still bewildered, tried to explain, now deeply resentful that an innocent, kindly action should have brought such a fiery onslaught upon her head.

'Well, you were a donkey,' said Mysie. 'Nobody would let a horse fill itself with water before a long ride. No wonder Redd was seething. He was taking the mare . . . Oh, well, never mind, but you've possibly lost him the chance of a good sale.'

'He's not going to sell Jenny!' Priscilla was appalled. Jenny was his favourite; she knew he adored Jenny.

'He may have to if he needs the money. The stables have cost him a lot to put in order.'

'You seem to know a lot about Redd Maitland,' said Priscilla, rather disgruntled at realising that Christy's oft-repeated accusation was quite true.

'Oh, well,' said Mysie easily, 'he can talk to me like a man, my being what I am, and then I know a bit about horses through my father being that keen about them. He did a bit of horse-copin' himself when he was alive, and used to take Redd to the horse fairs when he was a wee chap.'

'Well,' said Priscilla, with a final hiccup, 'he's a very rough man. No gentleman would have spoken like that to a lady.'

'Mebbe no,' said Mysie, 'but Redd's hot-tempered, and I expect there's lots more he would have said if you hadn't been a lady. Anyhow, he thinks you're just a bit lassie.'

'All the more reason to be careful of his language,' said Priscilla. 'It was *awful*! And anyhow I'm not a "bit lassie," I'm a grown-up woman, and expect to be treated with dignity and consideration.' Priscilla was mounting her high horse again. 'He told me he'd dip me in the horse trough.' Tears rolled down her cheeks at the remembrance of this indignity.

At this confession, delivered in a woebegone voice with no shadow of realisation of the funny side, Mysie could not forbear a giggle. 'Oh, he must have been getting over his fury then,' she said. 'He was laughing at you!'

'He was not!' raged Priscilla. *'He meant it.'*

'You don't mean to say you think Redd would really dip you in the horse trough?'

Mysie laughed again, but Priscilla was much too indignant even to smile.

'Yes, I do. He's fit for anything. He's'—she remembered her Delaine aunts' most sweeping condemnation—'an absolute outsider.'

'Well, maybe he is,' said Mysie equably. 'He's always outside, anyhow, among horses and men and rain and wind and weather—but if it wasn't for Redd you wouldn't be here.'

'What do you mean?' Priscilla had started up and was 'glowering' at Mysie, as Christy would have expressed it.

'Well . . .' she hesitated. 'Oh, dear,' she went on, 'Redd would be so mad at me if he knew I told on him, but I simply can't bear hearing you and Christy going on about him when I know all I do know, so if you tell him I'll just have to take the consequences. The very day after you came here Redd came to me and told me to come and help you. He threatened his uncle too—eh! what an opera!' Mysie could drop into broad Berwickshire when she liked. 'But Auld Maitland is that cunnin' he got in first, guessing he'd put you up against me. But Redd kept on, and he just made me leave, and said he'd see me though. He knew I hated being with that auld fox anyhow, so it was helping me too, for I'd aye felt I could make a shop pay if I got the chance. I just had the feeling, and Redd thought I could too.'

'I think,' said Priscilla, 'he wanted to help you. He has always hated me—yes, from the very first!'

'What for should he hate you? He was sorry for you. The same with the stables—he tried to get them let for you before he took them, but there's nobody hereabouts that wanted stables. He got Sir John Frobisher interested, but they were too far off.'

'You mean to say he's renting my stables for charity!' Priscilla had dried her eyes and was staring indignantly at poor Mysie.

'Redd Maitland has no money for that kind of charity,' said Mysie drily. 'He's that hard up he can't buy himself a new suit. Mother's patched his things till there's little else but patches. He needed the stables badly, but he thought you might get a better rent from Sir John. He's glad enough to have them at the nominal rent he pays you—but, you see, he didn't want to offer so little if you could do better.'

At that moment the shop bell rang, and Priscilla was left to digest all this as best she could.

'I expect Mysie's in love with Redd Maitland,' she said to herself at last. 'If he'd like me one little bit he could never have been so hateful and insufferable.' But she was a little

shaken in spite of herself, and sighed as she got up to go, remembering with a little heartache the few times when he had
been 'different', as she put it to herself.

That night she told Mysie she wanted her and her mother
to have the empty rooms in the yard. Mysie was delighted,
as her mother would be near her, and she had been wondering how she would manage when the snowy days of winter
came. They went over one day to see the place together, to
plan out what would be needed. The main thing was a kitchen range in one of the ground-floor rooms; otherwise a
little plaster and paint and papering would suffice, as they
were large dry rooms with sunny windows, 'a palace,' said
Mysie, to the little damp cottage for which they paid the same
rent as Priscilla was taking.

She would have cheerfully let Mysie have them for nothing,
but Mysie and her mother were of independent breed, and
would not hear of such a thing. Redd was never mentioned,
and Mysie had evidently no idea it had been his suggestion.

Priscilla stayed behind to measure the fireplace for a kitchen stove, and as she sat down on the meal poke in the corner for a final survey she remembered her first visit there with
Redd Maitland and how friendly they had been over the owl's
nest—she must go and see the owl's nest again. Miss Tibbie
had been over, and had seen not eggs but young birds; now
they would be fledged, but perhaps they still sheltered by day
in the old loft, as Redd, ordered to leave it as it was by Miss
Tibbie, had not used the place.

Suddenly she made up her mind to go and have a look. She
was going over to the Hall on Sunday, and could report to
Miss Tibbie, who would be sure to ask her if she had seen anything of the owls. She knew Redd was not about the place,
having seen him go off earlier with the groom who had come
for a couple of young hunters he had sold to Sir John Frobisher
for the coming season.

The stall below the entrance to the loft was empty, so she
climbed on the manger and pushed up the board over the
opening. When she put her head through she heard a slight
rustle, and then the large bird floated, in the still way of owls,
over her head to the deeper shadows beyond.

But it was difficult to scramble up through the hole without help, and she was just about to jump off the manger and

get the light ladder that she had seen hanging on hooks on the wall, when a slight noise drew her attention, and she shrank back, thinking for a moment that Redd must have returned, and terrified lest she had again done something to arouse his wrath.

But it was not Redd Maitland's tall figure that appeared. It was Maudie Jones. She was dressed in riding kit, and had under her arm the small saddle that Priscilla had seen hanging on a peg among the others and mentally designated Ginger's saddle, though nothing more had been said about her riding Ginger. Indeed, she had not spoken to Redd since the disaster of the watering-trough.

Maudie seemed rather startled for a moment when she saw Priscilla, but quickly recovered herself.

'Hullo!' she said airily. 'What on earth are you doing?'

'I'm looking round my stables,' retorted Priscilla, with as much dignity as she could muster, standing dusty and dishevelled on the manger.

'Oh—when the cat's away the mouse can play, I suppose?'

Priscilla reddened; she could never cope with Maudie's impudence.

'What do you want?' she asked her stiffly. 'Mr Maitland is not here.'

'Oh, I know where Redd is all right,' she giggled. 'I'm meeting him when he comes back—only don't tell Dr John, will you? He'd be furious, he's so jealous. Has Redd asked you about Ginger yet?'

'What about Ginger?'

'Oh, he was going to ask you to lend him to me to learn to ride. Of course, I'd pay you. He got this saddle specially for me.'

'What a funny thing to do,' said Priscilla, now thoroughly angry at the mention of Maudie riding her Ginger, 'getting a saddle for my pony without ever asking me if I would hire him out—which of course I would never do!'

'Oh, I expect he's still furious about you watering the mare,' she giggled. 'He could hardly believe even a shop-girl could be so silly. We did laugh when he told me, and I'd got him calmed down a bit. *I* thought you mightn't be keen about lending Ginger to me, but he seemed to think he could get anything he wanted out of you. Men *are* conceited, aren't they? Redd's a regular coxcomb.'

Priscilla looked at Maudie, who was laughing up at her, her round face full of mischief, her large ingenuous blue eyes gazing in seeming innocence at the victim of her malicious tongue. 'Perhaps she is attractive to men,' Priscilla thought rather drearily. 'She looks so plump and childish and innocent—but too plump,' she added, not without a shred of satisfaction, 'for riding breeches.'

'Mr Maitland has said nothing to me about lending Ginger to anyone,' she said, after a moment's pause. 'I wouldn't think of lending him to anyone. It's a pity, but your saddle will be quite wasted.'

'Oh, that's all right. Redd will manage something. You see, we thought I might ride one of Dad's horses, and the saddle would have come in for Pixie, but Dad's so nervous about me—the fond parent and his darling, you know—he won't let me even have Pixie—in fact, he would never let me learn to ride, but Redd's mad to teach me, so that's why we have to be so sly about things. You won't tell on us, will you?'

'Tell who? I don't know your father, and it's of no interest to me whether you ride or not.' Priscilla was climbing down from the manger now. She wanted to get away from Maudie's hateful presence; she could not bear her mixture of vulgarity and insincerity, and the pretence of intimate confidenced between two sly girls that her tones now implied.

She knew all about the old vet's two work-worn horses, or, rather, his horse and the shaggy white pony which occasionally carried him, with his feet nearly touching the ground, across the hills to outlying sheep farms, and could have laughed, if she's been in better humour, at its name Pixie, and the idea of its being mentioned in the same breath as her smart little Ginger.

'Well, I suppose I can just put back the saddle,' said Maudie, as Priscilla passed her. 'I expect Redd will be awful mad at me asking for Ginger before he'd got round you, but it can't be helped,' she sighed. 'Girls are always nicer to men than they are to other girls, aren't they? I am myself.'

'Oh, ride him if you wish to,' said Priscilla, instantly regretting the words, but, knowing that she herself would instantly have refused so ungracious an offer, never really expecting it would be accepted.

'Thanks awfully,' said Maudie, nonchalantly. 'I expect Redd will be able to give me a mount himself very soon.' And she swaggered off.

23

The Lantern

Dr John had been away on a holiday, a locum taking his place, and Priscilla had not seen him since he returned. She had wondered a little that he had not looked in, and was very pleased when, hearing a knock as she was busy doing some measuring in what was to be Mysie's new home, Dr John entered to her call of 'Come in.'

He looked rather tired, she thought, and did not seem to have gained much good from his holiday. She sat down on the meal poke while he took the step-ladder she had brought in to stand on at her measuring.

'Big changes here,' he said, after their first words of greeting.

'Yes,' said Priscilla. 'Mysie is going to live here with her mother.'

'Is she? Good. But that wasn't what I meant.'

'Oh, the stables. Yes—aren't we smart and tidy now? They make me feel ashamed of the house.'

'Hum-m. That wasn't quite what I meant either.'

He changed the subject, and began talking about his work, the ladies at the Hall, and various other subjects, but, though he laughed and joked and teased her a little about the shop, he seemed decidedly depressed and not at all the light-hearted Dr John he had always been.

'Is anything the matter?' she asked at last, when he had sat for some time, his hands round one knee, gazing at the fireplace.

'Plenty,' he said. Then, after a moment, 'I hear you and Redd are great friends nowadays.'

'You hear wrong, then. I have not spoken to Mr Maitland for *weeks*,' retorted Priscilla quickly, 'and I've no wish to speak to him.'

'Oh, Redd's all right,' said the doctor, visibly brightening. 'To tell you the truth, Priscilla, I was giving him a chance. You see, you made it plain enough you wouldn't have me, and it was finally knocked into my thick head that people were coupling our names together, and I was—well'—the doctor looked very uncomfortable—'spoiling another chap's chance —I mean, if you didn't want me it wasn't fair to you or— some other good chap—to let people think things were otherwise. . . .' He felt in his pockets for a cigarette, and brought out a crushed-looking packet. 'Excuse me smoking, but I'm getting all tied up in knots.'

'Is that what you are worrying about?'

'Well—a bit, and then there's Lindy.'

'Lindy?' Priscilla had almost forgotten who Lindy was.

'Yes, Lindy Jones, Maudie's half-sister. Lindy's my right hand, and she says she's leaving, and I feel there's something mysterious about it. I simply don't know what I'll do without Lindy. I wish you knew her. *You* might find out what's bitten her—I can't.'

Priscilla thought he seemed glad to get away from his rather muddled explanations about 'other chaps' and their chances, and was glad herself to get off that dangerous ground.

'I wish I knew Lindy too. Everybody seems to like her.'

'Lindy's tip-top.' He sat brooding a few minutes, playing with the cigarette packet, but not taking one. At last he put it in his pocket.

'Still no use, Priscilla?' he asked.

'What's no use?' she asked, to gain time, and because she hated so much hurting John.

He made a feeble attempt to laugh and keep things on a light note, which made her still more sorry, he was so obviously under the weather.

'You and me,' he said. 'You've still no use for the struggling country doctor? You know, a doctor ought to be married. People think he's only half a doctor if he isn't. He needs what they call a help-meet.'

His grin was unconvincing, but he managed it.

'What about Miss Jones?' asked Priscilla, anxious to keep herself out of the picture. She meant Maudie's sister Lindy, and was not thinking of Maudie at all at the moment. It was Maudie and Redd Maitland she thought of nowadays, not

182

Maudie and Dr John. In any case, she would have said Maudie Jones if speaking of her. But Dr John seemed quite oblivious that Lindy might be viewed in this light.

'Oh, Maudie is fixed up with Redd, isn't she? That's what made me feel the road was clear now. Surely you knew that?'

The room seemed suddenly to darken to Priscilla. Her spirit was quenched as if someone had puffed at the flame and blown it out.

'Are you sure?' she had asked before she knew what she was doing. Then she tried to cover up the nakedness of the inquiry by going on. 'I didn't know they were as friendly as all that—though of course, I've seen her about'—she had been going to add 'with him,' but her throat constricted at the words —'the stables,' she said.

Dr John looked at her curiously, and was silent for a moment.

'As far as I know it is correct,' he said. 'I have it on what one would naturally think unimpeachable authority. But it matters to me more than to you, doesn't it, Priscilla? I mean, I had a word with Christy, and from her accounts Redd Maitland is the villain of the piece, and you've told him where he gets off and so forth—but ...'

'Of course it doesn't matter to me,' interrupted Priscilla quickly.

'That's all right, then. I always felt you'd have nothing to do with me as long as Maudie kept on saying she was engaged to me. You see, I was rather silly about Maudie, Priscilla. I was sorry for her, and perhaps led her to think she meant more to me than she did, and then it was so difficult. . . . Well, I suppose I had made love to her a bit . . . Oh, hang it all? It's too difficult to explain. Won't you forgive me, Priscilla? I just got myself into a mess over that, but it's the truth that I never thought of marrying Maudie, or that she was taking a mild kiss or two—oh, look here, I can't go on with this ...'

He looked so terribly and yet so funnily distraught that Priscilla just had to take pity on him. She knew quite well it was not in his ethics to give a girl away, and that he couldn't explain unless he did.

'Well, I wish you wouldn't,' she said. 'I quite understand, and it doesn't matter anyhow.'

183

'You mean you don't care a button whether I'm free or not!'

'Oh, no, I do care. I like you so much, and I hated to see you unhappy—not that you look much happier now.'

'I'll be happy if you'll marry me.' He took the opening at once. 'Won't you think about it, Priscilla? Don't let's have other people doing all the marrying.'

She shook her head, her heart contracting with pain at his words.

'See, Priscilla, if there is anybody else just give me the word, and I swear I'll never bother you again.'

Again she shook her head. 'No, there isn't anybody else. I just don't want to marry.'

Her voice sounded so forlorn that he came and sat down on the next meal poke and put his arm round her.

'We both seem a bit lonely. Couldn't we comfort each other, Priscilla?'

Her lip trembled, and, turning, she put her face against his comfortable shoulder for a moment.

'You're very kind to me,' she said, thinking how another man had scolded and scowled at her. 'I wish I did like you more than just—just a brother.' The words ended in a little choke.

'That would do to begin with,' he said, and, turning, he kissed her lightly on her cheek. 'Shall we try being engaged? I wouldn't try to make you stick to it if you didn't want to, but I'd be there to help you. Don't say no just now'—as she shook her head again, not being able to speak for the lump in her throat—'just leave it as it is. I'll promise not to have too much hope, just a little. . . .'

She was so forlorn that she felt she didn't mind if he did have a little hope. Perhaps she might grow to love him some day when she felt less broken-spirited, he was such a dear.

'All right,' she said, drawing herself up and achieving a little smile, but when he tried to draw her near again she struggled up on to her feet, and he immediately desisted, and, taking her hands, pulled her up; then he put them together in his own and kissed them.

'I believe the sun's going to come out,' he said, smiling. 'Jolly old sun!'

'Mysie will be thinking I'm lost,' she said. 'I said I'd just be ten minutes.'

He drew out his watch.

'Gosh! It's high time I was back in the surgery. Good night, my darling. Shall I take you in?'

'No. I want to get my tape-measure and things. Good night . . . John.'

She had always called him Dr John. He laughed happily, gaily almost, and went off, turning at the door to say, 'Priscilla, sweet, I'll be over tomorrow.' Then he bent inward and whispered, 'Wouldn't it be fun to be married first—before those other two?' in a sort of half-mischievous, half-earnest tone.

Before she could say anything, or remonstrate at this taking of an ell where she had only given the hundredth part of an inch, he was gone. She heard his cheerful whistling as he crossed the yard, and then she began to search blindly for her tape-measure and pins with the tears running down her face.

'I won't cry—I won't cry,' she kept saying to herself, her lips drawn in a tight, straight line, her throat choking. 'Why should I cry? He's nothing to me. I'm only a little sorry that that horrid Maudie is going to marry him, because he must be nicer than he seems if it's true what Mysie said—especially as he was trying to help me even when he didn't like me.'

Then she thought of the evening she had seen him bending towards Maudie as she looked at him, and writhed inwardly.

'I don't care! I don't care!' she mumbled into the folds of some curtain material she had brought in from the shop, against which she pressed her mouth and eyes. 'He's nothing to me—nothing—nothing—nothing—nothing in all the world!'

With buried face and shaking shoulders she stood outlined against the darkening window, and did not notice the door open, but after a moment she had a feeling that some one was watching her, and, turning quickly round, saw Redd Maitland towering in the doorway, his red hair standing straight up, his fierce, small eyes shooting sparks from under glowering brows.

'What are you crying for?' The words were shot out full of accusation.

'I'm not crying.'

'You are crying. What the h—what in the name of goodness have you got to cry about?' The necessity for curbing his language in the presence of a girl was evidently a stumbling-block to his style. 'I came in here to congratulate you on being engaged to the best man I know, and here you are—howling!'

She turned on him, forgetting in her indignation the red nose and swollen eyelids she had been trying to hide.

'You've no right to congratulate me,' she accused him angrily. 'I'm not engaged. I won't be engaged—ever—to anybody!'

He knitted his brows, perplexed and unbelieving.

'Why are you denying it?' he asked. 'I saw you in the doctor's arms, and then he went whistling across the yard as if he'd found the key to heaven. I thought you'd both found the key.... What is it, Priscilla?'

The last words were in an entirely different tone, almost kind, indeed, though he still frowned, standing astride with his hands in his pockets and his brows drawn down as he gazed at her in angry concern. The darkness was creeping on, and he had brought in a stable lantern with him and set it on the window-sill. It's orange rays mixed with the glow of the reddening twilight and filled the room with a sort of unearthly witch light, the sort of light in which anything might happen.

'I haven't found the key.'

The words, sounding hopeless and forlorn, were out before she realised what she was saying. She had meant to tell him it was no business of his and order him off—but there it was! Instead of ordering him off, the words sounded full of appeal —it must have been the light.

Instantly he stepped forward and lifted her small, cold hands.

'Have you not?' he asked slowly. 'Neither have I, Priscilla.'

'Yes, you have.' She knew her voice was accusing, but she could not help it. 'You—you are engaged to Maudie.' She pulled away her hands. 'It's me that should congratulate you.'

Grammar had flown to the winds, and the congratulations sounded more like an accusation of blackmail and robbery, but Priscilla was past noticing such details.

He turned away and crossed the shadowy room, where he

186

stood, hands in pocket, feet apart, staring out of the window and framed against it in the dying light.

'I am not engaged to Miss Jones,' he said coolly. 'If it's of any interest to you, I'm not engaged to anybody.'

'Of course it's of no interest to me,' she started quickly.

He made no reply, and they stood there in silence, while the sky dimmed across the stable roofs, and the orange light of the lantern began to throw shadows across the floor.

At last he turned round.

'Come here,' he said.

'I won't come there'—she was nearly sobbing—'I won't be ordered about.'

'I wasn't ordering you. I suppose it was a sort of plea. I was hoping you wouldn't come. I was hoping you'd cheek me and send me off, and tell me you loved Dr John Field and were so happy you had no use for me. What about that?'

He spoke quickly and fiercely, scowling at her across the room.

'Well—go away, go away. I don't want you!'

'And leave you huddled up on a meal sack crying in the darkness? What do you think I'm made of—steel? Or ice?'

'Yes, I do—and I wouldn't be crying for you anyway.'

'Yes, you would'—his voice was fiercer than ever—'and I'd be crying for you, and what is the use of it all? Why the deuce can't you be happy with the doctor? I'd get along if I saw you happy, but your little pixie-face comes between me and every darned thing I do.'

He turned back precipitately to the window, where he stood with his back to her for a few moments, then he started to speak again.

'Yes, ever since you sat shivering in that bus like a little wet canary that had got out of its nice gilded cage you've been nothing but a nuisance—a nuisance, I tell you!'

He flung round again and stood regarding her.

'You are the roughest and unkindest and rudest man I ever knew!' she fired back, his hardness putting some starch into her again.

'That's good,' he said. 'That's the way to think of me. Heaven knows I've tried hard enough to be a bear to you.' He picked up the lantern as if to leave, paused, and hesitated.

'I dare say Maudie . . .' he began, then stopped as she gave a quick intake of breath.

'I can't leave you here,' he said. 'Come along. I'll take you to the door.'

She shook her head.

'No. I'll go in a few minutes.' Her voice sounded hopeless and forlorn, but she could not help it. Through the room a black wave of misery was rolling ready to engulf her. He might scold and browbeat her, but he kept it back as long as he was there. Once he was gone—and with that last hint about Maudie hanging in the air—it would roll over and engulf her.

He set the lantern on the floor and stepped forward, but as he did so his foot caught it, it rolled over, and went out, leaving them in the faint shadowy light of the moon, that had begun to rise. He let it roll away, and, stepping forward, put his arms round her and drew her close, putting his head down so that his cheek rested against hers.

'You never believe all the lies I tell—do you, Priscilla?'

'Yes, I do. Are you telling lies? Why do you tell lies?' she said chokingly, incoherently.

He straightened himself, and, holding her a little way from him, he bent his head so that the moonlight caught his eyes.

'I have to tell you lies, haven't I? I have to scold you and browbeat you out of my heart, and keep me out of yours, because it's no use, Priscilla—you mustn't let yourself think I'm anything but the scowling villain who wants your precious shop and your house and your ox and your ass and your— how does it go on?'

'My man-servant and maid-servant . . .'

'Oh, hell—not Christy! Can't I get out of that?'

He smiled down at her with tight lips.

'Laugh, Priscilla.' He drew her close again with one arm and stroked back her hair. 'Laugh!' he said desperately, giving her a little shake. 'I'll manage to go if you laugh.'

But instead of laughing she put her hand up quickly and held his for a moment against her cheek, and then she pushed herself away.

'Go—go to Maudie Jones,' she burst out childishly. 'You're engaged to her. I know it. Don't tell me any more lies!'

'No, I won't tell you any more lies. I'll see if the truth is any better cure. But you never believed that, did you?'

188

He had one arm round her, holding her lightly; he took her hand in his other, and lifted it against his breast.

'Yes, I did—yes, I did.' All her reserves were gone, her pride in the dust. 'You gave her my saddle,' she scolded, 'and you gave her my pony, and you said you would dip me in the trough, and you laughed at me with her. Yes, you did!' she reiterated, catching his eyes smiling down at her and the humorous lift of his mouth. 'You laughed at me when you were breaking my heart!' She paused, realising where this was leading her; then, 'About the pony,' she added. The words came out solemnly, but with such a sudden and comical jerk that there was no mistaking them for anything but an afterthought.

'Yes,' he said, very gently, 'about the pony.'

'And I saw you in the stable making love to her—yes, I did,' as his eyes still smiled down at her. 'I saw you—making love.'

'So you know all about how I make love?'

There was a dangerous edge to his voice, and she shied off at once.

'I mean—I mean . . .' She went off at a tangent. 'She said—she said you didn't like . . .' Again she paused.

'The pony,' he said solemnly.

She looked up into his face, trying to read in the dimness the meaning of that inscrutable smile, her underlip trembling.

'And now you're laughing at me!'

'Don't do that,' he said quickly. 'Don't reproach me—don't let your lip tremble. Scold me, Priscilla—scold me about the pony.'

'You said you would tell me the truth, but you don't, and I don't understand—I never do.'

'Don't you know the truth? Yes, I'll tell you the truth—which we both know already. There can never be anything between you and me, Priscilla, so the harder I am to you, and the more you dislike me, the better. Is that clear enough? You know your aunt's will, don't you? She spoked my wheel before ever I saw you—not that I blame her. I loved you from the moment I saw your little pixie-face, and I knew I could make you love me, so what was I to do? Spoil your life for you? Not I! If you hadn't been so keen on that shop of yours and the house and the whole blasted place I might have

tried to pick you up and carry you off and send all the old
women to blazes—that Christy of yours into the bargain—
but whenever I asked you about the shop you let me know
pretty quickly where I stood. How was I to do you out of all
you had? I've nothing to offer you in return, not even a coat
to lay your head against that isn't patched. No, my girl, the
king and the beggar maid may be all right, but when it comes
to the queen and the beggar man there's nothing doing—not
on your life!

'As for Maudie Jones, I thought I might give John a lift
there—draw her off him a bit, and give him a chance with
you. That day in the stable I saw you, and overdid it a bit
for your benefit, but I never offered her your pony or your
saddle—in fact, I forbade her to touch either. There's nobody
will get your things while they're in my stables. Oh, hell, I
suppose I shouldn't be saying all this, but if you will cry what
am I to do?'

He was becoming fierce again, and his grip on her arm was
so tight it was hurting her. She twisted her arm a little, and
he let it go, plunged his hands in his pockets, and stood regarding her with a deep wrinkle between his small, tempestuous eyes.

'Well?' he said at last, shooting out the word like an accusation.

'I'm tired,' she said, in a small, desolate voice. 'I think I'll
go home now.'

Stooping, he put one arm round her shoulders and the other
round her body, and drew her gently against him. The tears
came running over her face, and, standing on tiptoe, she
reached up and put her hands round his neck. He put his own
up and gently tried to unclasp them; then he gave it up, and
lifting her, strode over to the step-ladder, and, sitting on it
with one foot raised on a step to support her, held her close
with his cheek against her head, saying nothing.

She wanted to say she didn't mind about the shop or the
house, or anything, but the words in her Aunt Purdie's letter
about trusting her not to let the Maitlands get her place kept
ringing in her ears and closed her lips.

'My auntie . . .' she managed to say at last with a sob. 'I
promised her—I mean . . .'

'I know,' he said. He turned his face and kissed her cheek.

Then, standing up, he set her on her feet, got out his handkerchief, and, putting an arm round her neck, wiped away her tears, smiling down at her. Then his expression changed.

'Forget all this,' he said, in a brisk voice. 'The truth of the matter is you're such a small mouse of an enemy I've got to mop up your tears when I see them, and talk a lot of balderdash to you, but you're just a child to me—a child needing a bit of petting and comforting. Now cheer up! You don't care twopence about a rough horse-coper, and I know it. You were just a bit down in the dumps about *the pony*. I'll see nobody rides your pony, or as much as touches the saddle. You ought to ride him yourself. I'll get Simmons to give you a few lessons. Now where's that lantern?'

He put his handkerchief in his pocket, strode across the floor, picked up the lantern, and felt in his pocket for matches. The next moment a glow of orange light lit up his dark, saturnine face for a moment, showing it furrowed and ravaged.

Then he snapped the catch together, and swung the light towards the door.

'Off you run,' he said, in a brief, hard voice. 'I'll lock up here, and leave the key on the nail.'

She ran out and across the yard without pausing to say good-night.

24

Lindy

Priscilla was glad there was no one in the kitchen when she
went in. Mysie was in the shop. She could hear her asking
Bessie about each of her large family in turn, and knew she
was safe for a while, Bessie being a loquacious person, especially where her brood was concerned. Christy was out milking
and 'bedding the kye.' There was no one to see her 'begrutten'
face, as Christy would have called it.

She hurried to the cold-water tap by the window and
hurriedly bathed her eyes. As she did so she could make out
a car which was standing before Miss Pinn's door. Miss Pinn
was down with an influenza cold, and it did not take Priscilla much time to guess that it was Dr John's car.

Seeing it, her thoughts reverted to him and his proposal,
and she was immediately sorry, especially after what Redd
Maitland had said about him, that she had let him go with
some hope. She knew now that she could never marry Dr
John, whatever happened. 'I'll never marry anyone,' she said
to herself. 'Mysie and I will keep the shop, and be old maids
together.' And she had hurriedly to douche her eyes with more
cold water as they stung with tears at this prospect which
would have seemed so alluring to her only a few months
ago.

As she mopped her eyes on the towel she made a sudden
resolution. Miss Pinn and the doctor were great friends, and
he usually stayed and chatted a while in his kindly way to
cheer her up, knowing she was a lonely body, as people are
who think themselves just a little more genteel than the
commonalty.

'I'll write a note and slip it into his car,' Priscilla said to
herself, and, hastily combing back her wet hair, she ran to a

little bureau where she kept her accounts, and, sitting down, scribbled a hurried note.

DEAR, dear DR JOHN,

I am so sorry, but now I've had time to think it over a little I see I did wrong to say what I did and let you think there was hope. There isn't any really, dear John, because I didn't tell you quite the truth. Though I will never marry, there is some one else who makes it impossible for me to marry anybody else, but please don't think I'm engaged or ever will be, but just that I take back what I said, though I'm very, very sorry. This is really and truly my last word, and please forgive me.

Your affectionate friend,
PRISCILLA

Then she sat and thought for a moment, and finally scribbled a postscript: 'It was *Maudie* I meant this afternoon when I said "Miss Jones".'

She sealed it up quickly, because she felt if she read it she would want to rewrite it, and there was no time. Then she opened the back door quietly and looked up the street. The car was still there, and it was the doctor's right enough. She ran across to it, opened the door, and laid the note on the driver's seat. Then she hurried back to the house just in time to meet Mysie and Christy converging in the kitchen, Mysie from the shop and Christy from the byres.

'You've been crying,' exclaimed Mysie anxiously, before she had time to think, but for once Christy saved Priscilla from further questioning.

'It's nae mair peety,' said she, 'to see a woman cryin' than to see a goose go barefit,' expressing in this terse sentence the whole disapproving spirit of the Borders towards the subject of weeping.

'I'm not crying,' lied Priscilla manfully. 'I think I've got a cold.'

'And what do you expec'?' asked Christy. 'Bidin' in a cauld hoose for a' 'oors! Bed's the place for you, and a good stiff whisky. Off wi' ye!'

Gladly Priscilla fled, followed shortly by Christy with a hot bottle and a glass of Athole brose, her panacea for most ills, either of the body or mind.

'Sure as deith!' she said, going downstairs and encountering Mysie about to descend with a shovel full of hot cinders. 'Sure as deith that Redd Maitland's at the bottom of it!'

'Well,' said Mysie, firing up, but keeping to a whisper, 'Redd Maitland won't do her any harm. I just wish . . .' She paused.

'Aye, and what do you wish?'

'I wish that that old Janet Purdie you all crack up so much had had some sense and not put her foot in it and spoilt everything, and then they might have got married. Redd fair worships the ground she treads on.'

Mysie was fond of novelettes, and they sometimes affected her style. As she spoke she ducked back almost as if she expected Christy to box her ears, but to her amazement Christy said nothing. She marched off to the tap, where she rinsed the tumbler, and was drying it when Mysie returned.

'Is that what she's greetin' for?' she asked.

'I don't know. Redd Maitland could woo the stars out o' the sky if he set his mind to it, but he's aye been that hard on Priscilla.'

'Ye think he set himself to frighten her off?' suggested Christy, who, in her own way, was as sharp as a needle. 'And weel he may be. He kens all about the will, and that we want no Maitlands here. Thae stables was a mistake frae the beginnin'. I wonder at you encouraging her in that.'

'Well, he wanted to help her, and it's been a good thing for both. He hadn't room at the mill to branch out; now he's starting to get on, and he'll be able to pay her more. Still . . .'

There was a long silence.

'Aye di me!' sighed Christy at last. 'I sair misdoot me we're in for trouble.'

'Well, it won't be Redd Maitland's fault,' said Mysie, flushing up, 'and it won't be Priscilla's. There's no a man hereabouts can hold a candle to him. He's the king o' the lot.'

'Kings and bears oft worried their keepers,' said Christy, picking up her lantern and departing.

The Athole brose certainly cured the cold, but it did not make Priscilla sleep. She lay still staring at the light from the fire Mysie had kindled, but not crying any more.

'I suppose he thinks that too,' she said to herself, as the firelight died before the dawn—'that I'm just a goose going barefoot.'

Meanwhile things hadn't stood still with the doctor.

Ten minutes after Priscilla had returned to the Clock House

Miss Pinn's door opened, and he came out calling a cheery good night to the invalid.

He opened the car door, and immediately saw the white square lying on his seat. Sighing, because he thought it would be another call, and he was tired and longing to be home, he impatiently snapped on the inside light, slit open the envelope, then suddenly grew rigid as he read the letter inside. Slowly he tore it into tiny pieces, and absentmindedly (for he was on the local anti-litter committee) dropped them out of the window.

'So that's that!' he said to himself, darkening the car and turning the ignition key, and rather wondering to himself why he felt nothing but a deadly numbness and dreariness.

'I expect it's all these other worries,' he said to himself—'housekeeper leaving, Lindy threatening to go, Maudie hanging onto me like grim death till she settle things with Maitland. If he hasn't really taken her on—one can never be sure she's telling the truth, poor kid—I suppose I might as well do it. Nothing matters very much, and nobody else seems to be exactly anxious for my company.'

Poor Dr John was indeed in the depths. Steeped in gloom and self-pity, he drove glumly but rapidly through the village, but once in the country lane he began to slow down. Finally he stopped, felt in his pocket for the letter, remembered he had torn it up, and with an annoyed grunt drew out the usual crushed packet of cigarettes, put one absently into his mouth, and lit it.

Then he sat silently smoking for some time, his brow drawn into wrinkles, but, strangely enough, it wasn't so much Priscilla he was thinking of as her postscript.

Now what exactly was it she had written? And what in heaven's name did she mean by it?

The main part of her letter had not come as a great surprise; he knew Priscilla was not really in love with him, and though he had gone whistling away when he left her it had been more to keep his heart up than an expression of light-hearted joy.

Still, the letter had given him such a knock that he had read the postscript without taking it in. It had only now welled up as something important.

Something about Maudie . . .Ah! he had it. She had not

195

meant Maudie when she spoke of his marrying Miss Jones.
Then who the devil had she meant? There was only Maudie
and—Lindy!

Lindy! But he'd never thought of Lindy like that. Lindy
was his right-hand man, as much use to him in many ways
as any partner. She had suggested a partner when she said
she was thinking of leaving him, but he didn't want a partner,
even if he could afford one. Besides, he simply could not do
without Lindy. The place would be hell without her with those
awful housekeepers he seemed to get, and even if he married
he'd want to keep Lindy, of course. . . . What had bitten her,
anyhow, that she talked of leaving?

He threw away the half-smoked cigarette, started the car
again, and went slowly down the lane, wobbling along as if
his mind were on anything but the steering-wheel.

Once inside the garage he switched off the engine and the
lights, but he did not rise. He sat there in the darkness, thinking.

Time passed, but still he did not move. He sat in the car
staring at nothing, occasionally feeling in his pocket for a
ciagarette, and then evidently forgetting about it before he
found the packet.

At last he was aroused by a step in the garage behind him.

'I heard the car come in, and wondered if you had gone
out again on foot,' a voice said, as he switched on the feeble
lamp that lit the inside of the car.

He opened the far door.

'Come in, Lindy,' he said, 'and talk to me a minute. I need
cheering up.'

Though his voice attempted to be cheerful, she knew at
once that he was desperately unhappy. Lindy had loved him
since they guddled trout together, and he had stolen apples
for her on the way to school; but hope had long since departed.
Lindy looked for nothing for herself now. All she wanted was
to comfort him and help him, knowing he would never realise
either how much she loved him or how much he depended
upon her, telling her all his troubles and discussing with her all
his love affairs. Being a cheery, simple soul, he had had a good
many.

'Is it Maudie again?' she asked, getting in and sitting down
beside him.

'Well, not exactly, though I suppose now it might as well be Maudie as anyone else,' he answered, in black despondency.

'Oh, no! Not Maudie, John. What about Priscilla?'

'Turned me down.'

'Oh, poor John! I am sorry.'

'Are you really, Lindy?'

'Yes, I am. I like Priscilla. She is so genuine, isn't she? With all that young, comical charm, she is real through and through.'

'Like you, Lindy.'

'Yes, I'm real enough, though the charm was missed out—and she has such a taking little witch-face. Are you sure it's no good? You're such friends. Did you go the right way about it?' she asked severely.

'I don't know. How should I go about wooing a girl, Lindy—a girl I'm "such friends" with?'

Lindy crinkled the brows above her little freckled nose. 'Girls like attentions,' she said at last. 'They don't like just being asked to be married straight out. They like to be wooed and paid attentions. Did you ever give her any flowers, John? Girls adore being given flowers and little gifts. I don't mean expensive things; just little tiny things to show you are thinking of them, like hunting for a sprig of white heather for them, or . . . I think Priscilla would adore a puppy, John—one of Susan's litter. Miss Purdie's old dog would never be her very own, the same as a puppy. And they don't like men to be too humble either. Perhaps that was it with Priscilla. You really mustn't let girls wipe their boots on you, John.' She turned round, regarding him very seriously with anxious, clear brown eyes. 'I think you are too soft with them—look at Maudie!'

'Yes, Maudie has certainly wiped her boots on me!' said John, looking straight out before him. 'Pretty muddy they've been sometimes, too—poor kid. Go on, Lindy. Is it a mistake to be too friendly—sort of brother and sister business—with a girl when you find out later that perhaps she's the only girl for you? Do you think she could ever get over that and think of you in a sort of marrying way?'

'Oh, yes, if you didn't take her too suddenly—by surprise, you know. Perhaps that was it with Priscilla.'

Far from this comforting John, he seemed more plunged in gloom than ever. He sat glowering at the reflections in the glass before him, his shoulders hunched, his face perplexed and hopeless.

'I'd start wooing her all over again, John. There's nobody else, is there? Take her one of Susan's puppies tomorrow and pretend you've forgotten all about her refusal, and don't worry her about it—don't say a word. Just be awfully sweet to her. Perhaps it will all come right.'

'Hum-m-m,' was all his answer to that.

Her face was full of sorrow for him.

'Are you terribly broken-hearted, John?'

'I would be if it weren't for you, Lindy. You're not going to leave me in the lurch, are you?'

She sat silent for a few minutes. She knew she simply could not bear to stay on if he married Priscilla, or anybody—especially, of course, Maudie. But Maudie would never have given her the chance. She had said to her more than once, 'When I marry John *you'll* get booted out of there before you can turn round—no dear little girl friends in the surgery for yours truly.'

So she had taken time by the forelock, for she didn't want John to connect her going with his getting married. John must never suspect. It might hurt him a little, he was so kind-hearted.

So she prevaricated.

'I don't know,' she said. 'I sometimes think you'll really need to take a partner, the practice is growing so.'

'A partner be blowed! You're worth twenty partners to me.'

'Well, perhaps I'll stay a bit, but some day I'll have to go.'

She said it more sadly than she knew, and he turned quickly and glanced at the, to many people, rather plain little face, bound neatly round with thick plaits of fair hair.

'Would you mind very much, Lindy?'

Taken unawares, the quick tears stung her eyes, but he turned so quickly away and pretended to be looking for something that she was sure he couldn't have noticed.

'Of course I should mind,' she said, as casually as she could for a lump in her throat, 'but there's Father. He'd like me to help him now. He says he would pay me a good salary . . .'

'The devil he would!' broke in John. 'Here,' he said, taking out his handkerchief, 'is that what you're seeking for?'

198

She took it and dabbed her nose.

'I say, Lindy,' said he, after a few moments' silence, 'would you do something for me?'

'Of course, John. Is it to take Mrs Matthew's medicine over? I have it all ready.'

'No. Will you sit still and wait here for me three minutes? I want to do something.'

'All right. Is it the carburettor?'

But John did not answer. He had got out of the car and disappeared. She sat waiting, slightly puzzled, but glad of the opportunity to wipe her eyes without having to be surreptitious about it. She blinked them hard to make them look all right, and wished she could get into the way of carrying her powder case in her pocket.

Then she heard his returning footsteps, and leaned across his seat to open the door for him, but it was her door he came to and opened.

'Would you mind getting into the back seat, Lindy? I've something to show you, and the light's better there.'

Obediently she climbed into the back seat. John got in beside her, put his hand in his pocket, and extracted two rather weatherbeaten roses, which he laid on her knee.

'It was a bit difficult finding them in the dark,' said he, 'and the heather isn't out yet.'

Utterly mystified, Lindy sat gazing at the late roses; then as he spoke a slow pink began to mount in her cheeks.

'I'll get you a sprig of heather later—white, but'—he put his hand in his other pocket and drew out a squirming white bull-terrier pup, and was depositing it on the top of the roses, when she quickly rescued them—'here's a puppy,' said he. 'It's yours, Lindy.'

Holding the drooping roses in her fingers, and quickly putting a protecting hand over the puppy, Lindy gave him a quick, shy, bewildered glance.

'That's just a beginning,' he went on, turning a little doubtfully towards her. 'But, oh, Lindy, I thought there might be a chance for me when you told me the way to go about it—to get over all this brotherly-sisterly business. Oh, Lindy, I've been an awful fool not to know it was you all the time, but you are to blame as much as me. Only I'm terrified you'll never get over the sisterly business and look on me as anything but

199

a numbskull you have to help out of his troubles and warm his slippers for at the surgery fire. Don't speak yet, don't say no yet. You know you said there might be a chance with a girl if a man really started wooing her. Well, I'm going to start, but, oh, darling, it would be terribly sweet of you just to keep the roses and the pup—just to let me know it wasn't altogether hopeless.'

He paused, and Lindy, playing with a rose with rather shaky fingers, said, 'What isn't hopeless, John?'

'You—liking me.' He couldn't quite get the word 'loving' out. Poor John seemed to himself horribly unlovable at the moment. That was really too much to suggest.

'I do like you.'

He turned quickly at that and looked at her, but her lashes lay still on her cheeks as she looked demurely down at the rose. He put his arm half round her rather tentatively.

'I don't mean just liking. We've always liked each other, haven't we, Lindores?' Lindores was her real name, and he occasionally used it half tenderly, half teasingly. 'I mean, I want more than that. I want you . . .'

'No,' she broke in then, rather quickly and urgently. 'You don't really want me, John. You are just feeling down about Priscilla, but you will soon get over that. You know you do get over them, and if it is hopeless about her another one will turn up. I know you don't really want a plain little spinster like me. You'll find another nice, pretty one—you like pretty ones, you know.'

'You're as pretty as a primrose, and you're two years younger than me, little spinster. Do you think I ought to marry a widow? I've always thought how pretty you were, like one of those small princesses in fairy-tales—you know, with piles of pale, gold hair and little pointed faces—and I've been sitting here for hours and hours and hours thinking what a double-damned fool I was not to have made sure of you before any-body else got the chance—not to realise that I didn't want any girl in the world but you—all very well as *extras*, but you had to be there all the time or the bottom was clean knocked out of the world for me. I'll tell you what it was, Lindy; you were too near for me to see you. I sort of had you, darling, and never thought of what it would be like without you, but when Priscilla turned me down I found myself thinking, like the blighted ass I am, "Well, I'll tell Lindy. There's always Lindy to cheer me up," and suddenly, like a flash, it came to me that I mightn't always have you, that you'd spoken of going away, and the world went cold round me at the very thought, and I rushed off to find you, and then I thought, "But Lindy would never have me," and the more I sat and thought about it the blacker things got. I remembered the way I'd rushed to you about every silly girl that had ever looked at me—was there ever such a blasted fool born on the earth!—and I remembered how pretty and sweet you were, and thought of all the tall, handsome wooers—damn them!—that might come along, and I got deeper and deeper down into the depths, and then you came into the garage, and I was terrified of you—I'm terrified now. Won't you help me out, Lindy?'

She was sitting as stiff and prim as a little poker, staring at the puppy, now coiled up contentedly in her lap. She said nothing.

'Got to do it all by myself! Quite right—but, oh, Lindores, do say there's some hope for me. Just a scrap will do.'

'You haven't proposed yet,' said a small, set voice.

'By Jove! Neither I have—I was too frightened.' He began to perk up a little. 'Lindy, darling, will you marry me some time when I've wooed you and behaved less like a blighted ass and tried to make you love me?'

'No.' It came out very pointed and precise.

'What!' The arm that he had so tentatively slipped behind her came back, but before he had quite regained it there came a quick, soft demand.

'Now ask me again, John.'

John turned puzzled, but ready.

'All right, sweetheart. Didn't I do it right? Miss Lindores Jones, will you marry Dr John Field?'

The stiff little poker relaxed against the stiff arm.

'Yes, I will.' The arm suddenly became alive and drew her close. She snuggled up against him. 'Oh, John, I did want to boast that I'd had a proposal and refused, and I did want a *real* proposal.'

'Did you, you funny little darling? Let's have another then. Light of my life and star of my skies, will you marry me and be the moon of my delight? That was a good one, I think. Now you've had three proposals. Will that satisfy you? I'm ready for another, if you like, though why you want more than one beats me!'

'If you had Maudie for a sister you'd understand. Maudie's so pretty she gets about one a week . . .'

'Then you'll have two a week—will that do? Oh, Lindy, isn't it fun that it's you and me, and I'm courting you. Isn't that the right word? But I can't miss the fun either of telling you all about it, so tonight after supper I'll put you in the big chair and take the stool and say, "Lindy, the sweetest, most darling girl in the world is going to marry me, but she won't turn you out because we're all going to live here together, and every time I kiss her I'll kiss Lindy too"—and that reminds me—can I kiss you now? Nothing brotherly, mind—you have been warned. . . .'

But he didn't wait for an answer to that!

25

Miss Prudence Steps in

'I just stepped in for a packet of cornflour,' said Miss Prudence, a few days later, 'and to ask if you'd come up and have tea with us on Thursday—I mean, if you'd be sure to come. I've something to talk to you about.'

Priscilla looked at her a little doubtfully. She loved going up to the Hall, but wasn't quite sure she wanted to be talked to about anything; she felt too sore and sensitive at the moment, and Miss Prudence could be so very downright. She made a pretence of hunting the cornflour before she answered, wondering if she could find any excuse that would satisfy the old lady.

'The cornflour is on the right of the second shelf, where it always is,' said Miss Prudence, 'and don't try to think of an excuse, because we must have a crack. Come up early.'

She put the packet in the basket she was carrying, and changed the subject.

'Where is Mysie today?' she asked.

'They are moving in,' said Priscilla. 'We are all so pleased they've got a good day for the flitting.'

'Is that so? Well, you'll like old Mrs Cree, and all the "gentry" will be coming to your shop after the twelfth—they all want Jenny Cree's hand-knitted stockings and jumpers. You'll have to get her to show you how she dyes the wool with lichens and suchlike. Bless me! Is that the time? I'll have to hurry, because Teenie is making what she calls a "soofel" for lunch, and you know how quickly they collapse, and Teenie is very proud since Tibbie taught her to make a "soofel" from the cookery-book. Never shall I forget the day Old Jones the vet came to lunch, and Teenie made him a soufflé, because Tibbie had said the menfolk aye likit a savoury better than a sweet to finish up with. Well, Teenie made a fish soufflé, and he ladled sugar all over it, and said it was a "verra nice pudden".'

She went off, leaving Priscilla with a smile on her face.

'That child wants looking after. She ought to laugh more,' she said to herself. 'She's lost all her looks, and is as thin as a matchstick. I wonder what those aunts of hers are thinking about!'

She had no sooner gone than Christy came into the shop to help Priscilla, by her own way of it, but really to unburden herself of some of the gossip that was rife in the village at the moment.

Everyone in the village was delighted at the doctor's engagement to Lindy, and not at all backward in expressing their views. 'It seems,' he had said to Priscilla the day before, 'this was all nicely arranged for Lindy and me twenty years ago, and they've just been waiting for me to come to my senses.'

'Not before time,' said Priscilla severely.

'I think you ought to be hankering after me now I'm so popular,' the doctor announced, 'instead of taking it all so calmly. My self-love is wounded.'

'I'm glad to hear you've got some,' said Priscilla. 'Oh, John, it *is* nice to see you looking so happy—and Lindy too. She's as pretty as a picture.'

'I just wish I could see you looking happy too,' said John, suddenly serious. 'Nothing I can do?'

Priscilla laughed and shook her head.

'I know you want to think I'm looking unhappy and pining away for you,' she said, 'but it's no use. I'm as happy as can be—the shop is really succeeding now. We've been ordering our Christmas stores. Wait till you see them! We are going to have a real Christmas grotto in the storeroom, and on Christmas Eve Mysie's mother is going to be Santa Claus. We're simply bursting with plans!'

'That's the stuff,' exclaimed Dr John, and went off smiling, but outside the shop door he too shook his head.

'Priscilla is under the weather, poor kid, and my tonics are no good.'

Christy too was worried about Priscilla's thinness, and kept trying to feed her up, and cheer her with the village gossip.

'That's Mistress Cree,' she said, 'asking me about Maudie

204

Jones. Mysie says she's never set eyes on her since the doctor got himself engaged.'

'I haven't seen her either,' Priscilla remarked.

'That's no to say she hasna' been running aboot the stables huntin' Redd Maitland,' Christy snorted, 'but Simmons is all she got for her pains. Redd's no been nigh the place for days. They tell me she's going her ends aboot the doctor and Lindy, fair boilin' wi' rage she is, and set on Lindy like a Cromarty fishwife. Then went up to the doctor's hoose to ca' them baith doon—but Dr John soon set fire to her kilts. Now he's got Lindy the doctor's found his feet. He stood a lot from Maudie when it was hissel' 'at bore the brunt, but he's no having any of Maudie's impitence where Lindy's consarned—he sent her off with a flea in her ear. Hech, aye, she'll be madder than ever to get Redd Maitland noo, but she'll ha'e her work set there. Redd Maitland's no the big softie she found in Dr John.'

'I don't know. She's very pretty,' said Priscilla.

Christy looked hard at her for a moment, but said nothing more till she had pulled off the long rubber boots she wore to feed the stock in now the colder, wet weather was setting in. Then as she set them aside she remarked:

'Mebbe it would be a good thing if she did get him. It would settle the baith o' them and no spoil twa hooses.'

With that she lifted her pail for the pigs' mash and went off.

It was wet and miserable on Thursday afternoon when Priscilla set off for the Hall. The leaves lay thick underfoot along the avenue, and the little burn under the bridge was swollen and muddy as she stopped, as usual, to glance down over the parapet in the hope of seeing a kingfisher or the waterouzel that built its nest every year at the side of the little waterfall, but there was nothing to be seen but the sodden undergrowth and the swirling water.

As she straightened herself to go on she was surprised by a hail, and, looking round, was confronted by Maudie Jones.

'I thought it was you,' said Maudie. 'I suppose you have an afternoon off from the shop.'

'Yes,' said Priscilla, 'it's Thursday.'

'Going up to the Hall?'

'Yes.'

'Funny old trouts, aren't they? I do think it's kind of them, though, the way they ask everybody up there, riff-raff and all.'

'Yes, so do I,' said Priscilla. 'Have you been?'

Maudie stared at her, but there was nothing to be read from Priscilla's solemn face.

'Got over the shock of the engagement?' she asked.

'No,' said Priscilla, put on her mettle. 'I haven't got over the surprise yet. You see, you told me Dr John was your *fiancé*, and I believed you. Wasn't I a goose? But isn't it lovely? Every one says they've been expecting it for years, and the whole village is chortling, and the doctor looks so happy— he's simply bubbling over with joy—and Lindy's happy too.'

'Oh, she's welcome to my leavings,' said Maudie. 'Have you seen Redd Maitland recently?'

'Not that I've noticed,' said Priscilla, gripping her hands in her pockets and using all her force to keep her voice light. 'I suppose he's going about as usual, but I never see much of Mr Maitland.'

'Well—look out,' Maudie laughed. 'He's heard you are coming into money, and Redd's on his last legs for some money. I believe he'd rob the Bank of England for those horses of his—he told me he would—or marry an heiress even if she had a hump on her back. Well, ta-ta. I just thought I'd give you the tip.'

She turned and walked off, leaving Priscilla rather bewildered and more down than ever.

The rain was falling heavier now, and she was glad when she found herself in Miss Prudence's warm little parlour, being made a fuss of, with her feet in a pair of Miss Tibbie's slippers, while her own dried in the kitchen.

'Put your feet on the fender and get toasted,' said Miss Prudence, turning her own skirts above the knee to enjoy the glow, 'and tell me all the news. Has Mysie thought of anything yet to replace the ices in winter?'

'Hot pies,' said Priscilla, 'on Wednesday nights and Saturdays. The baker is to bring them, and we're to keep them hot in that old oven in the back kitchen in Mysie's house—you know, it was the oven for baking bread, and it's a very good one and will keep the pies beautifully hot.'

'Yes,' said Miss Prudence, always ready to plunge in with suggestions and to take an interest in the small details. 'And be sure to have mutton pies as well as beef, and you might vary them with a few hot sausage rolls—though they'll be apt to cool bringing them through the yard.'

Priscilla then told her about some antiques she had found. 'Bless my soul!' said Miss Prudence. 'That Clock House is full of surprises.' They then went on to discuss the attics and the chests and drawers that Priscilla had never thoroughly explored, till at last Miss Prudence gave a sigh.

'Well,' she said, 'you're not the only one with cupboards full of rubbish mixed with valuables. We were going over ours a few days ago, when I found a letter I'd thought I'd burnt, in an old Crown Derby teapot that had lost its spout. That's why I wanted to talk to you—but there's the tea bell. We'll come up here after tea, and I'll show it to you.'

Tea was the usual merry meal, for all the sisters were full of humour, and could tell the most delightful stories mimicking the dialect to perfection, even quiet, lame Leslie being gifted with a sense of fun.

Priscilla was interested but not very curious about the letter, which she could not think would have anything to do with her, and at first, indeed, it almost seemed as if Miss Prudence had forgotten about it, for once settled in the parlour again she began talking of Dr John's engagement.

'I used to think it was you and the doctor, Priscilla,' she said, after a few moments, looking quizzically at her with her bright brown eyes.

'Oh, no,' said Priscilla, so quickly and sincerely that there was no doubting the truth of her words. 'Dr John and I are great friends, and I'm awfully happy about him and Lindy.' Her face had brightened up as she spoke.

'Well,' said Miss Prudence, 'to tell the truth, so are we all. He was a fool not to fix it up with Lindy long ago, and to get himself into such a fix with that sister of hers. We were all sorry for him, and for a time it seemed as if you might be the solution, seeing he was so blind about Lindy, but . . .' She paused, and Priscilla looked up from the stool she had drawn close to the blaze. 'Redd Maitland's the man for you,' said she.

Priscilla went scarlet and turned away, a little resentfully.

'You mustn't mind me,' said Miss Prudence calmly, taking up a woollen vest she was knitting. 'This is just between ourselves. Redd's an old friend of mine, and though he's as dumb as a clapperless bell where you are concerned I ken fine which way the wind blows there—a blind man could see that Redd's fair taken leave of his wits about you. Don't you like him? He's a real favourite o' mine. Aye, he's a *man*, is Redd!'

Her voice was so kind that Priscilla's flash of resentment vanished. She knew Miss Prudence only wanted to help. She had the whole village under her wing, but never betrayed a trust. Nobody minded discussing their most intimate affairs with her, and no ice was too hard for her to break, or to melt with her warm-hearted interest.

'It wouldn't matter if I did like him,' said Priscilla, trying to smile and speak lightly—neither proceeding of the least use where Miss Prudence was concerned. 'Mr Maitland just tries to help me because he thinks I'm a helpless sort of nincompoop.'

'Well, I wouldn't put that past Redd either. He's as hard as brass wi' men and folk that can look after themselves, but under that he's terrified of hurtin' anything young or tender. Have ye ever seen him with our Leslie? He's the only man our Leslie's ever goamed since she had her accident, but Redd and she are as thick as thieves—old woman as she is. It fair makes me laugh to see the two o' them. It was Redd got her to ride again. He said she didn't get enough exercise, and he was quite right—she's that shy of meetin' folks because of her lameness. But he said nobody would know she was lame on a horse, and scoured the countryside for a gentle beast for her. . . . Well, well, it's no Leslie I meant to talk about, it's you. What's it all about, Priscilla? A lassie like you should have a mither or an old auntie to talk to about the menfolk and suchlike. I ken fine there's something . . .'

'Why did you never marry, Miss Prudence?' asked Priscilla suddenly. 'You never seem like—like . . .'

'An auld maid? Well, I'll just answer you as one of my forebears did a hundred year syne. "I wouldn't have the walkers, and the riders went by." '

'I expect it was one rider.'

'Aye, you're no far out there.'

'Well, I won't have the walkers either, and the rider's gone by.'

208

'That's what beats me. From what I know of the rider he's one o' the "Taking Men." It would have been more like him to swoop ye up and carry ye off. Na! Na! It's you that's shaking your head, Priscilla, or I'm far wrong.'

'It's not really, Miss Prudence. You see, Mr Maitland isn't a bit in love with me. He just tried to help me because he was sorry for me, but I annoy him really—and he annoys me too; there's no love lost between us.' And she managed a smile. 'But even if things hadn't been like that there's my auntie's will, and her letter. You know she hated the Maitlands—and so do I really, because of how they treated her, and anyhow I promised her never to have anything to do with them if I took the shop and house.'

'Promised her? How was that? You never saw her—not since you were a child.'

'No, taking the shop and the property was the promise. They came to me on condition I had nothing to do with the Maitlands.'

'Your Aunt Purdie was a gey silly body whiles,' announced forthright Miss Prudence, 'but don't tell me she was as silly as all that. It was Auld Maitland she had her knife in at. She liked Redd.'

'She did before he deceived her, and got her into debt with his uncle, and helped him about foreclosing the mortgage. Christy knows all about it. But, of course, after that . . .'

'Christy's tongue's longer than her heid,' put in Miss Prudence, but Priscilla went on:

'So, you see, we're enemies and never goam each other— at least, not if we can help it, only by accident.'

'So that's the way of it! Aye, he used to steal my plums by accident. Many's the good whack I've given him with my ashplant. He was a devil for plums as a callant, but he aye came back; ye'd think he liked a good hidin'. . . . Well, go on.'

'There's nothing more,' said Priscilla, rather drearily. 'He doesn't like me, so you mustn't think that. He said I was like a sack of potatoes'—Priscilla could never forget that deadly insult—'and so naturally I don't think *anything* of him except that he's the rudest, hatefulest man I ever knew . . .' Her eyes suddenly filled with tears, she blew her nose indignantly, and then, trying hard to be impressive, added stiffly, 'I apologise, if he is a friend of yours.'

209

'You're in love,' said Miss Prudence calmly. 'I thought as much.'

'No, I'm not—I'm not really, Miss Prudence. Please don't say that. I mustn't be, and I'm *not*.'

'Well, well, child, dry your eyes. We'll say you're not for the sake of peace. But now I begin to see wood through the trees. It's had me fair bamboozled. Redd puts on a face that would frighten the French if I as much as mention you, yet he's moved heaven and earth to help you over the shop and those stables, and has fallen out all over again with that uncle of his about you. Auld Maitland wants to make it up again with Redd now that his other nephew, Andra, has turned out a bad egg and is robbing his old uncle—who, say what you like, did his best according to his lights for his nephews. But will Redd? Not he! Put the fear of death on the auld man about you! And then there's yourself, pining away before our eyes— both of you eating your hearts out as far as I can see. So it's Janet Purdie, the silly auld maid, that's got between you!'

'If it wasn't everything else it would be Aunt Purdie,' Priscilla burst out. 'I promised Aunt Purdie when I took all she gave me to have nothing to do with the Maitlands, and that they'd *never* get her house and shop, and I'll *never* go back on her and betray her, and Redd—Mr Maitland, I mean —knows that too, and if he has helped me he has *no right* to, and I wish he'd stop. I wish everybody would stop bothering about me!'

Priscilla blew her nose so hard it looked like a red cherry when she'd done with it, while her eyes, to keep to the fruit motif, looked like boiled gooseberries.

'So that's the mouse in the meal poke,' said Miss Prudence, turning her knitting calmly. 'I jaloused as much, but wanted to make sure. Well, if you promised your aunty to have nothing to do with any Maitland in the countryside—and there's hordes o' them—that's your own look-out, but it strikes me that in the natural enthusiasm of youth to go the whole hog you've taken on a deal more than anybody asked you. I saw your aunt's letter, and as far as I can mind it was Auld Maitland that wasn't to get the shop or house'—she glanced up from her knitting with her quick glance—'wasn't that so?'

'Yes, but she said, "Have nothing to do with the Maitlands." '

210

'Aye, aye, mebbe she did, but I'm talking about the conditions on which you were to take the shop. It was Auld Maitland that was mentioned.'

'Yes—but . . .'

'You think you'll go one better than your aunty in discord and hatred and making enemies.'

'Oh, no, I don't mean that, but Christy says . . .'

'Christy's an old bag o' wind—and as fine a woman as ye'll find in the countryside, bless her heart!' said Miss Prudence. 'Christy knows about as much about it as you do yourself. The truth of the matter is that Redd trusted his uncle, like the young gomeril he was, and when he discovered too late that the old fox was using him as a cat's paw he went fair berserk and nigh frightened the old villain out of his wits. Then he flung out of the house without a penny in his pocket, went and told Murdo MacPherson he'd got to look after his aunt till he could do something about it himself, and then hired himself out as stableman with Elliot of Yoweslea till he got a job with Jones, the vet. Then he started picking up a young horse here and there on his own and training it. He's getting on now, but it's been a bitter struggle, with often hardly a bite or sup in the house—and now, if it hadn't been for you, miss, he might have made it up with his uncle, who might have put some money in the stables, but oh, no! Hoity-toity, instead of making it up, me lord has another row with the old rogue!'

Priscilla stared, but said nothing.

'Well, what have you to say to that?'

Priscilla sat, twisting her handkerchief.

'But my aunty didn't know,' she got out at last, 'so even if he did try to make it up it couldn't make any difference. Christy said the mortgage . . .' She stopped.

'You mustn't listen to all Christy's havers. I dare say she thinks a mortgage is some new kind of chimney-pot. Besides, there's wheels within wheels there too. Mrs Martin is Christy's sister, and she wanted the Mill House for her niece Susie Pike, who's married on a tailor body in Lanshiels, but Martin knew fine he'd never see a ha'porth of rent from that rascal, who'd let the place down besides, so he let it to Redd, and of course neither Christy nor Mrs Martin can forgive Redd for that. Have you got that letter from your aunt?'

'Yes, I'll always keep it.'

'Would you let me see it?'

'Yes, of course, Miss Prudence. Will you come back with me and see it—but it's even worse about the Maitlands than I said.'

'Yes, I'll come and see it, and in return we'll get back to the teapot.'

'The teapot?' Priscilla stared at Miss Prudence. Did she want to give her another tea?

'Have you forgotten? I told you about Tibbie finding a letter in the Crown Derby teapot without a spout. I was going to mend it, and found the letter inside with the spout. It's from your aunty. Now where did I put it?'

She went to her desk, and after some hunting produced a crumpled sheet of paper; then she put on her spectacles.

'It's no very clearly written, she was nigh her end, poor Janet. I'll just read it to you first.

'DEAR MISS PRUDENCE,
        'I'm near my end, and there's something on my mind I'd like to speak about if so be you could come and see me.
'It's about that niece of mine, Priscilla, that I told you about. I've left her everything on condition she comes here and keeps the place hersel'—you ken all about that.
'What's bothering me is Redd Maitland. He's been to see me, and we had it all out thegither. I aye liked Redd, deil though he be, and so I've forgi'en him, but I didn't tell him that, and I canna mind what I said in that letter, so would you come down and see me, for I haena the strength to write mair.
                                    'Yours respectfully,
                                            'JANET PURDIE.'

Miss Prudence took off her spectacles, wiped her eyes, and passed it to Priscilla.

'I went to see her, Priscilla, but she was too weak to talk then. But you see she did forgive him.'

Priscilla slowly folded up the letter and put it in her pocket.

'Poor Aunty!' she said, her throat tight. 'That makes me feel as if I'd never forgive them.'

'Well, "never's" a long word. I thought you ought to have the letter, anyway.'

'Just think how Aunty would have hated Maitlands to have her house and shop after all—they *never* will.'

She choked on that, and Miss Prudence stumped off to put on her thick brogues and old burberry to see her home.

But there a surprise awaited them that put all thoughts of the letter out of their heads for the meantime.

Christy met them at the door, looking for once scared out of her wits.

'The aunts is here,' she whispered hoarsely, 'sittin' yin agin the ither at the parlour fireside. I asked them intil the kitchen, but they fair freezed the marrow in ma banes. "Pray light the drawin'-room fire," said the long yin, "and acquaint us when oor niece has arrived." Dod, but they're ower fine leddies for me, Priscilla. I'm off. Ye can get some Sooth Country wurrum to sarve them. I'm no used to being spoke to as if I wasn't there.'

'Oh, Christy, you mustn't go—you must help me,' Priscilla gasped. 'They don't mean it. Oh, Miss Prudence, make Christy stay.' And with that she made a dash for the parlour—so suddenly raised to the dignity of a drawing-room.

26

The Aunts Once More

Seated one on each side of a chilly fireplace in which stood
a pot of dried reeds, sat, as Christy had said, the aunts.

They were dressed in their best. Between them stood an
ancient leather case with 'Ceylon' on a large label. On the
top was a carpet bag. Each carried a small black bag, and an
umbrella, which they still clutched. They looked like black
monuments of disapproval.

'Oh!' cried Priscilla, and rushed first at Aunt Maud and
then at Aunt Flora and hugged them. 'Oh, I am so glad to
see you! When did you come? Have you had tea? Are you
starving? Oh, Aunt Flora, you've got a new hat! And your
gloves aren't even off! Oh, I'm so sorry I wasn't here to throw
the doors wide and welcome you in and hug you till you were
dizzy with hugs. Have you had tea?'

'We have had nothing,' said Aunt Maud, in a sepulchral
voice. 'A most peculiar person asked us into the *kitchen*, and
then left us here without even bringing us a cup of tea. We
have been here an hour and twenty minutes.'

'You poor darlings! That was Christy—you terrified her.
She's the kindest dear in the world, you'll see! Only please
Aunty, don't treat her as if she were a servant—she's not. She
calls me "Prescilla", and she's been my greatest friend ever
since I came here. Please, Aunt Flora and Aunt Maud, *do*
understand, or she'll go away, and I simply can't do without
Christy. Now we'll have a fire and just a cup of tea before
supper—and I'll bring Miss Prudence in now to meet you.
She's chatting with Christy in the kitchen—Miss Prudence
Selby, you know, one of the ladies at the Hall. I've told you
all about them.'

'Don't talk so fast, child,' said Aunt Maud, visibly thaw-
ing under the hugs and the warm, loving welcome. 'I dare

say we put ourselves wrong with your Christy, but we thought she was the cow-woman or some outdoor worker. Surely she doesn't always go about the house like that!'

Priscilla had a vision of tall, gaunt Christy dressed in her own idea of what was suitable for 'milkin' the kye,' attending to her fowls, or bedding the 'powny' in wet weather—a short striped petticoat, reaching only to the knees, huge rubber boots, an old plaid, tied criss-cross around her, and a man's cap with a snout—and laughed.

'Of course not, Aunty! She must just have come in from her fowls. You'll see them tomorrow if it's fine—we make quite a lot of money with them. Now, darlings, I'm going to see about a fire . . .' She hesitated. 'I suppose you wouldn't come into the kitchen just for a few minutes to be warm, while Christy lights the fire? Miss Prudence is there.'

Both ladies rose.

'Certainly, Priscilla. We don't really mind the kitchen,' said Aunt Maud (Aunt Flora was keeping quiet as usual till she saw how the land lay), 'only we did not quite understand.'

'Poor lambs,' thought Priscilla to herself, 'they're quite out of their element, but they *are* ladies; they'll take their cue whenever they catch it.'

In the kitchen Miss Prudence was sitting with her brogues on the polished fender beside the glowing hearth, her skirt turned up over her knees, but the ladies all recognised one another as of the same breed, and from that moment things went swimmingly.

Priscilla introduced them, and then introduced Christy, who had quickly changed and looked a different being in her grey frock and large snowy apron, and whose pride having been appeased by the introduction and Aunt Maud's handsome apology for not knowing who she was, forgot her resentment, remembered that these were Priscilla's aunts, with a right and proper claim on her, and set herself to do what was 'menseful', so that no shadow of a slur should be cast on Priscilla's hospitality.

In no time she had a tray ready with the best tray-cloth, thin bread and butter, and steaming cups of tea, which she left them to enjoy while she rushed for Mrs Cree to come and help to make roaring fires in the parlour and best bedroom, carry up suitcases, make the beds, and put in bottles.

Then they set to in the back kitchen, and in two ticks had a couple of ducklings that had been dressed for market stuffed and roasting in the oven, an apple and bramble pie on the upper shelf, and vegetables steaming on the stove.

By this time Miss Prudence had been prevailed on to stay to supper, the best dinner service and silver hunted out and polished, and the aunts taken upstairs to unpack and change.

Supper was a gay meal, for the aunts thawed completely in the warm-hearted atmosphere, and as Miss Prudence knew Baxton and some of their friends the gossip flew back and forward with ever-increasing vigour.

They were all invited to tea at the Hall next day, and it was not until late that Miss Prudence—having sent young Tommy Dodds flying with a message to Andra—departed in state in the brougham.

After she was gone Miss Maud said to Priscilla, 'We have not told you yet why we came so suddenly and unannounced, Priscilla, but that can wait now till tomorrow. We did not mean to upset you, child, and had arranged to stay at the hotel.'

'Oh, but, Aunt—as if I'd have allowed you!' exclaimed Priscilla, keeping back a gasp at the mention of the 'hotel'. Dicky Bird's little public-house was not exactly a hotel as Baxton understood the word.

'Poor lambs,' she said to Christy, having said good night and shut them safely in the large double-bedded spare room that had once been the pride of the Clock coaching-house, 'they are in the "hotel", if they only knew it. Oh, Christy, I'm so happy! Aren't they pets? I never appreciated them and having some one of my own till I lost them. You'll like them, won't you, in spite of them being all stiff and bombaziney when they first came?'

'Oh, they're gentry and toonswomen, ye can see that,' said Christy magnanimously, 'and mebbe we neither of us took each other in at first. They'll no be used to seeing folks working. They'll come to when they've been to the Ha' a few times and seen Miss Prudence and Miss Tibbie diggin' the gairden and feedin' the pigs. Meggie Cree is comin' in to help while they're here. She'll be glad to do you a good turn in return for lettin' them have the Yard Hoose—my, but it's a cosy place! A fair palace to them, and Meggie Cree has mense;

she'll no tak' everything and gi'e nothing. . . . Now awa' to your bed, there's a good lassie, and dinna' fret. We'll see to your aunties.'

Priscilla slept better than she'd done for weeks. She was actually happy, rather to her own surprise. 'It *is* lovely having the aunts,' she said to herself, 'and knowing Aunt Purdie forgave Redd—even if it makes no difference.'

Then she remembered Miss Prudence's parting words.

'I showed Redd Maitland that letter, and told him I was going to show it to you.'

'Of course that doesn't make any difference either,' she said to herself sleepily.

She was quite surprised herself when she woke up next morning in a rage. It took some time to define what she was so cross about. Then it came—she must have been dreaming. 'I won't have them trying to push me on to Redd Maitland!' she exclaimed to herself. 'That's what they're doing, and he'll know it, and he'll think that I . . .' She paused. 'But I'll let him see!' she finished up fiercely.

The aunts had their breakfast in bed, and then descended to the parlour, where they brought out their knitting, and let Priscilla know they would like to have a talk with her when she was free from her shop and household duties.

'Oh, I'm free now,' said Priscilla. 'We're never very busy in the mornings, because the children have to be got ready for school, and then there's the dinner to make for twelve o'clock. I'll just get my knitting too—I'm knitting a woolly vest for Mrs Martin's baby.'

'We meant to write to you first,' said Miss Flora, 'and then Maud said we'd come and surprise you and see for ourselves how things were.'

'No camouflaging,' said Aunt Maud.

'Yes, I understand,' said Priscilla, 'and I'm glad you did. It was such a lovely surprise.'

'We have another surprise for you,' said Aunt Maud. 'That is really why we just decided we must come and see for ourselves how things were—and how we could be of use.'

'Oh . . .' began Priscilla, looking puzzled and letting her knitting drop to her lap. She had been going to say she did not need help now, but stopped in time; they might feel hurt.

'I suppose you have not heard of Mr Porter's death,' Aunt Maud said very solemnly.

'Oh, no! Is he dead? I *am* sorry.'

Priscilla tried to feel really sorry, but it was difficult to feel anything about Mr Porter.

He left us five thousand pounds,' said Miss Maud, so heavily it might have been a tombstone he'd left them.

'Oh, I *am* glad!' burst out Priscilla, without any difficulty at all. She was overjoyed. Five thousand pounds were really so much nicer for her aunts than Mr Porter for herself. She wished he could have thought of it before.

'Yes, a very handsome gift,' said Miss Maud. 'Of course, he was an old friend and had no relatives to speak of—still . . . of course we regard it as a *trust*.'

'What sort of trust?' asked Priscilla, drawing down her brows.

'You see, my dear . . .' began Miss Flora, when Miss Maud interrupted her, I will explain it, Flora.'

'Do be quick, then, Maud. I want Priscilla to know.'

'Yes, as a trust,' said Miss Maud. 'We quite understood that Mr Porter, who was very fond of you, Priscilla, would have liked to leave the money to you, but delicacy forbade, so he left it to us, knowing that we should pass it on to you.'

'Oh, no!' gasped Priscilla. 'You were his friends. I hardly knew Mr Porter. Of course he meant it for you.'

'You can scarcely say you hardly knew a man who had asked you to be his wife, Priscilla,' said Miss Flora, quite shocked at this levity.

'Well, I mean . . .' began Priscilla.

'We know perfectly well what you mean,' Miss Maud interrupted, 'but that does not alter the fact that Mr Porter was very fond of you, very fond indeed—and always so apologetic, poor man, at having asked you to marry him . . .'

'The greatest compliment a man could pay a woman,' Miss Flora interposed solemnly, quite sure she was making a freshly minted and original remark.

'So,' went on Miss Maud, 'we regard the money as held in trust for you. We shall, of course, not touch the capital and the income must go to assist you with the upkeep of your property—and, of course, your shop,' she added magnanimously. 'So we came off at once to see how things really were, and how we could best use the money to your advantage. We were just afraid you might have seen about his death and his will in the papers.'

'Oh, no,' said Priscilla. 'I never see the Baxton papers.'

'His death was in the *Times*,' said Miss Maud stiffly.

'Oh, the *Times*. It wouldn't get here till the day after—but of course, Aunt Maud and Aunt Flora, the money was meant for you. Of course I won't touch it. Oh, I am so glad for you! Just think what a difference it will make!'

'Indeed, no . . .' the argument went on, till Priscilla, with two to one against her, was silenced, but unconvinced. The Misses Delaine, once they had made up their minds, were a difficult problem to tackle. At last Priscilla gave it up, kissed them both, and said they were the dearest aunts in all the world, and left it at that for the present.

The next days were full of excitements, surprises, and activities. Luckily Mysie and Mrs Cree had got settled into their new house. Mysie could give all her time to the shop, and her active little mother help in the house, for all Priscilla's time was taken up with the aunts.

She had thought they would like the house, but had been a little doubtful over their reaction to the fact that it had been no 'country house', but just a large inn or coaching house. To her surprise they were delighted with its history, and never tired of hunting through the old books and discovering who had stayed there. As they went back hundreds of years there was plenty to employ them in the evenings, and their days were spent going over the house.

To their amazement they discovered that Priscilla had only made the briefest survey of her possession and never even opened many old chests, drawers, and cupboards.

'I've had so much to do and so many worries over the shop,' Priscilla excused herself, 'that I just had to leave the house to itself, except to keep it fairly clean and tidy.'

Nothing could really have pleased the two old ladies better. They were both intensely interested in antiques, and experts in their own way on the subject.

They went into raptures over old furniture, rescued innumerable pieces from the huge attic, lecturing Priscilla on Sheraton and Chippendale, and even putting on gloves and polishing them up till they shone again. They washed china

219

and cleaned silver. With the loan of Christy's aprons over their silk frocks they meticulously soaped and scrubbed the old ornaments stowed away, black with the dust of years, on cupboard shelves.

They made havoc of every room, ruthlessly turning out—mostly in their mind's eye, for everything could not be done at once—the modern stuff, the brass beds and 'three-piece' sets that had doubtless been the apples of Aunt Purdie's eye, and making plans for refurnishing with what was left of the ancient pieces and those rescued from loft and attic. As every room was crammed full of old and new jumbled up together, they foresaw weeks and weeks of delightful work, and were quite evidently regretting the fact that they would have to go home and leave all this entertaining employment.

Regardless of Priscilla's fainter and fainter refusals, they also planned the spending of the income from their legacy on repairing and doing up the whole house and garden. Occasionally the shop was mentioned, but they had no interest in the shop. Only what they considered their duty made them make tentative inquiries about how it was doing and if Priscilla needed anything for it.

They went to tea at the Hall, and immediately struck up a firm friendship with the four ladies. They gossiped and played bridge, discussed antiques and knitting patterns and embroideries. They brought fresh interests and news of the town to the old country ladies, and in return were initiated into the interests of the countryside. The days flew past, and in the meantime Priscilla saw nothing, or practically nothing, of Redd Maitland. Once or twice she saw him hurrying through the yard, and one afternoon she saw him talking to Maudie Jones.

Maudie winked impudently and waved a gauntleted hand to Priscilla. She was dressed for riding, and, Priscilla had to confess with a sore heart, looked very pretty with her curls bunched under the felt hat, even if she was too plump to look well in breeches. She had her hand on Redd's arm, and slipped it more closely through as she saw Priscilla. Redd was standing, feet apart, as stiff as a poker, and made no sign of having seen Priscilla, who turned away at once and began chattering to Aunt Flora, with whom she had been round the garden discussing plans for the spring.

27

The Taj Mahal

'They tell me,' began Christy one morning, a day or two after the aunts had arrived, 'you've come into a fortune.'

'Well, they've told you wrong,' said Priscilla rather crossly. 'I haven't come into any fortune at all—not a penny.'

Mysie, who was in the kitchen counting out eggs for the shop, looked up quickly at Priscilla, her eyebrows raised.

'Every one has that story,' she said.

'Mebbe it's a lee, and mebbe they've something for it,' said Christy. 'There's aye water where the stirkie's drooned—they may have got it that your aunties are rich with all this talk of improvements. Sure we did weel enough without improvements when your Aunt Purdie was alive—and all that good furniture to be hoyed oot. Seventeen pounds ten she paid for that sittee and two chairs in imitation morocco; it fair made the parlour a different place. She'd turn in her grave hearin' them talkin' o' turnin' it oot and bringin' doon that auld rubbish frae the loft, and no longer than yestreen Miss Flora says to me, "That old spice press in the back kitchen would look nice in the hall in the place of the umbrella stand"—that good umbrella stand! Two pound it cost at the pork butcher's sale at Lammerton—a fair prize your Aunt Purdie said it was, worth five pounds if it was worth a penny. I'm no sayin' but what your aunties are weiss-like women in the main, but when it comes to furniture and the likes o' that they're fair away wi' t. Look at that overmantel wi' the looking-glasses and green plush shelves and the big blue vases with pink roses—hand-ented, the man said they were—bought no longer than two ear syne at the May fair . . .'

Christy was off, and might have gone on—or off and on— ll day if Mysie hadn't pulled her up.

'Old things are the fashion now,' she said. 'A visitor at the Towers offered Mother five pounds for two old jugs, but she wouldn't sell them because they were Granny Bruce's. But I can tell you who's spreading the story about Priscilla's fortune—it's that Maudie Jones. She told Redd Maitland he would be throwing *her* over now he had an heiress on his doorstep—that's the truth, for I heard her say it. Taunting him, she was saying the whole village expected he'd be licking Priscilla's boots now she'd got money. "It will be a great laugh for them if they're right", she said. "I wonder who'll laugh loudest."

'And what did me lord say to that?' asked Christy, pausing in her work to hear the answer.

But Mysie turned very prim.

'I didn't hear; I was just passing them in the yard. I think Maudie spoke loud so that I would hear what she was saying.'

'Swearin', was he?' said Christy. 'Well, I'll no' say I'd like to repeat Redd Maitland's swears myself, but if I'd been there, Mysie Cree, I'd have let Maudie Jones have the rough side o' my tongue—speaking like that about Priscilla.'

'I wouldn't demean myself speaking to that piece,' said Mysie, going off with the eggs.

But their talk had made Priscilla more unhappy than ever, especially as Christy echoed her own thoughts when, picking up the empty egg basket, she exclaimed:

'Aye, she's a clever one, is Maudie Jones. It's a good thing ye dinna like Redd Maitland—she'd spoke any lass's whee before ever she got a chance There was Jeannie White an' young Todd—for sheer mischief she told him Jeannie had laughed and imitated him dancin'—puir lad, he dances like a bear on twa legs—but he fancied hissel' at it, till Maudie showed him how Jeannie had mocked him, and he's never goamed her sin' syne. Well, I'll need to see aboot thae mongrels o' ducks Miss Tibbie sent ye.'

And she went off, intensely interested in the runner ducks, though she called them mongrels, and was always finding fault because they were slimmer than the Aylesburys.

'I won't have people thinking I've got money,' Priscilla said to herself, wondering how Maudie had found out about the aunts' legacy—or if she was just guessing, or telling lies. But was strange that she had spoken of money to Priscilla befor her aunts had arrived—or, at least, on the very day they came, and before she, Priscilla, knew herself of their legacy.

Anyhow, she made up her mind to nip that tale in the bud, and went straight to Mysie to ask her to deny it, as it wasn't true, and repeated the injunction to Christy when she came in.

Then, as luck would have it, that same evening after tea she saw Redd mounting one of the young hunters he was training, at the stable door. He had his foot in the stirrup, but took it out and pulled off his cap as Priscilla came towards him, and stood looking very stiff an unapproachable.

'Mr Maitland,' she said, braving his frown, but determined to scotch Maudie's story, 'Mysie told me she heard Miss Jones telling you I had come into a fortune. I don't want people to think that is true, because there isn't any truth in it at all—nobody has left me any money.'

'I'm sorry,' he said, 'but it doesn't concern me.' Then, seeing her flush, 'I'm just sorry it's not true for your own sake. Otherwise . . .' He shrugged his shoulders, and, putting his foot in the stirrup, mounted, then sat looking down at her as he gathered up the reins.

'But I want you to deny it if anybody says that.' She looked up at him, her eyes unconsciously full of a despairing appeal utterly at variance with her precise words. 'You see, it would be so bad for the shop.'

Some feeling seemed suddenly to master him as he gazed frowningly down on the small pale face and anguished eyes contradicting so innocently the sedate and sober words.

There was a pause. Then with a sort of desperate effort to be very unconcerned, she went on, 'And I shouldn't like you to think, to think'—the last words rushed out—'that money or anything would ever matter to me if—if . . .' She stopped.

His hands tightened on the reins till the knuckles stood out white; then suddenly he flung himself off the horse, which stood between Priscilla and the yard, sheltering her from view. He put his arm round her shoulders, caught her chin in the cup of his hand, and raised her head.

'If what?' he asked, looking grimly down at her. He saw the nerve beating in her cheek by the side of her mouth, but she veered off frightened at the look in his eyes, and more of those meaningless words came, words so utterly alien to the pleading in her eyes.

'I don't want the customers to think I have money,' she said primly, 'when it isn't true.'

'The *customers* shan't think that, Priscilla,' he said, one corner of his mouth jerking a little upward.

There was a moment's silence, and then he asked again:

'If what, Priscilla? It's no use . . .'

He stopped suddenly at a sound across the yard, and jerked upward. The kitchen door had opened, and Miss Flora appeared, tripping into the yard. He quickly put his foot in the stirrup and his hand on the saddle.

'How many aunts have you got anyway?' he growled.

'Two,' she said, moving away.

'Two? There must be two hundred the way . . .' But Miss Flora was almost on them, calling to Priscilla as though she did not notice the horseman, who, without a glance at her, sent the mare forward and rode off.

Miss Flora watched him go with puzzled but quite innocent eyes.

'If he had stopped a moment I should have spoken,' she said graciously. 'Who is he?'

But Priscilla did not want to mention his name to her aunts.

'He just came for one of the horses,' she said. 'Come and see Ginger, Aunt Flora. He's my very own, not one of the stud. You've never seen him yet. This is where he lives.' And, talking fast about Ginger, she took her aunt along to his quarters, trying to keep her mind on ponies and aunts and not to let it go vainly and anguishingly puzzling over what Redd had meant when he said, 'It's no use. . . .'

On the following Sunday they had been invited to lunch and tea at the Hall, but when the day came Priscilla hoped as she gazed out at the teeming rain, that her aunts would decide it was too wet to go.

The Misses Delaine, however, were made of sterner stuff. They had decided to go to church and then on to the Hall and had no intention of allowing any downpour to stop them. In any case they always went to church on Sundays, and though a Scottish kirk hardly met their High-Church ideas of worship, it was the next best thing.

By this time Christy had taken both of the elderly ladies under her capacious wing. Christy considered that they were on the whole, well-meaning, but 'thowless', and therefore needed some 'weiss-like' body to look after them. So Christy looked after them, listened to all their peculiar ideas as a nurse might have listened to a child's prattling, but saw to it that their beds were exactly as they liked them—sheets loose for Miss Flora, tucked tight for Miss Maud—that any preferences they expressed about food were noted—though, indeed, being long used to ill-cooked and half-cold meals, they were in a continual state of gratified admiration of Christy's good but simple cooking—that they remembered their umbrellas and goloshes, and were carefully shooed the other way when she thought the street might be a bit rough round Dickie Bird's public-house on market days.

'I dare say they never heerd a swear-word in their lives,' she confided to Mrs Cree, 'or collided wi' a drunk.' So she carefully 'convoyed' them, to use her own word, into safety when they set out on their 'little excursions' at such times as sheeps, pigs, and cattle might be overflowing the village, while the drovers refreshed themselves at the inn.

At the Hall Mr Lamont proved a great asset at lunch, seeming quite in his element with seven ladies (eight, counting Teenie) to entertain.

Then they all gathered round the fire in the big drawing-room, and stories were the order of the day. When Tibbie took them all off to see a waistcoat that King Charles had worn when he stayed with some ancestor of theirs on his visit to the Borders, Miss Prudence beckoned to Priscilla to stay behind.

'I wanted to tell you that Dr John and Lindy are coming to tea. I asked John at church this morning, but he didn't know if Lindy could come. Teenie's just told me they are coming.'

'How nice!' said Priscilla, rather wondering that Miss Prudence had thought it necessary to keep her back to tell her this.

'But that's not all,' said the old lady, with a twinkle in her eye. 'Some one else is coming.'

Priscilla started and looked at her.

'Redd Maitland,' said Miss Prudence.

'Oh!' gasped Priscilla. 'You *shouldn't* have asked him, Miss Prudence.'

'Ask him! Nobody asked him. He never waited for an invitation or a "with your leave" or "by your leave." He said he was coming.'

'But does he know . . .' She paused.

'I don't know what he knows. If he knows you are here it wasn't from me he got it. I never know where that Teenie's long tongue may land her,' scolded Miss Prudence, still with that wicked twinkle in her eye.

'I think I'll go home,' murmured Priscilla.

''Deed, then, you'll do no such thing. What are you afraid of? Six auld ladies and a meenister should be too much even for his lordship Redd Maitland. We'll keep him in order.'

'Oh, but I don't mean that—I don't mean anything. I just mean I think I'd rather go home.' Priscilla was certainly rather incoherent, but Miss Prudence did not seem to notice it.

'There's the tea bell,' she said. 'Don't look so scared.'

'But the aunt's don't know him. They've never met him. They just know about Aunt Purdie, and I told them I hated the Maitlands too, and said I'd never *speak* to a Maitland. It might be embarrassing for them, and then he's so—so . . .'

'Stuff and nonsense! He can behave like a gentleman even if he's an uninvited guest'—Miss Prudence paused, with a faraway expression on her face for a moment—'though what Redd Maitland wants coming to tea with a posse of old women beats me! Well, let's go down.'

She took Priscilla's arm as though she might make a dash for the door although wearing Miss Tibbie's blue velvet bedroom slippers, which, as usual, had been called into requisition when she arrived in wet and muddy shoes, for Priscilla absolutely refused to wear goloshes in spite of aunts or ladies at the Hall. She said the name put her off them—as well it might!

The ladies all met in the hall, and entered the dining-room, where a real country tea was set out.

As they went in Priscilla saw Redd and Dr John speaking and laughing together, but to her surprise it seemed to be Dr John who was congratulating Redd about something. Marion introduced them all, but said nothing about the engagement, either thinking every one knew or not considering it necessary.

In spite of Priscilla's doubts and fears it turned out a merry

226

meal. Dr John at once set himself with his usual kindness to entertain the ladies, and soon had Aunt Flora almost giggling, and even Aunt Maud wreathed in gracious smiles. They hardly seemed to take in Redd at all. Probably the name of Maitland really meant very little to them in spite of Priscilla's diatribes, and, in any case, they looked on Aunt Purdie and what they called her 'whims' as hardly being worth serious consideration —especially after they'd seen the sort of furniture and ornaments she admired.

For the most part Redd sat very silent and reserved. He looked, as usual, excessively clean and scrubbed, and excessively shabby, his patched coat threadbare with brushing, his freshly laundered shirt carefully trimmed with scissors round the edges of the cuffs at his bony wrists. But hard work and scrubbing with strong carbolic soaps had not been able to spoil the fine shape of his hands. Priscilla saw Aunt Maud glance at them as he rather shyly passed her dishes and looked after her where she sat next him.

Once when Miss Leslie innocently said something about being surprised to see him at afternoon tea among the ladies he gave Priscilla a quick sardonic glance from beneath his eyebrows, partly amused, partly savage.

'Now,' said Mrs MacWhan (Marion was a widow) brightly, when they had finished, 'I think you should show Lindy these pictures we were speaking of, John.'

'And we shall have to be thinking of going,' said Aunt Maud, knowing that the Misses Selby were fully occupied on Sunday evenings, and that an early departure after tea on that day was always expected.

'Andra will run you down—it's still raining,' said Miss Prudence. 'I'll just order the carriage, but there's no hurry. Andra aye takes his time. We'll have a chat in the drawing-room until he comes round.'

Marion led the way, the aunts followed; Priscilla came after Miss Prudence, and last came Redd just behind her.

Just as they were passing the door into the little conservatory off the hall she felt a grip on her arm.

'I'm going to show Miss Priscilla . . .' he began, when Miss Prudence with a broad twinkle turned round and said in a loud voice:

'Oh, yes, the Taj Mahal! Priscilla said she didn't know what

227

the Taj Mahal was—time she learnt! I was just going to show it to her myself. You'll find us in the drawing-room when you've seen it.'

Redd opened the conservatory door, and the ladies went chattering on to the drawing-room.

28

The Pigeon-hide

Once inside the conservatory with the door safely shut on the ladies, Redd gave a sigh, or it might have been a gasp, like a nearly drowned man coming up to the surface. Then he glanced quickly round, gave a grunt of impatience, and then, his eye falling on a huge sort of knitted woollen antimacassar in reds, purples, and bright greens hanging over an old basketwork sofa, he seized it, wrapped it round Priscilla without a word, opened another door into the garden, grasped her arm, and rushed her out.

'Come on,' he said peremptorily, 'or they'll be after us.'

Out of doors the rain was drizzling down from a grey sky in a steady, hopeless downpour, but he did not seem even to notice that it was wet—possibly he thought it was a slight mist. He put his hand on her arm, closed the door behind them, and ran her full speed down the sopping garden path.

'Where are we going?' she panted at last.

'To find somewhere where I can talk to you without being cluttered up with a lot of cheeping old ladies. By the Lord Harry! No less than six of them clustering round you!'

He stopped at a potting shed in the far corner beside the rhubarb and the hot-beds, tried the door, and swore fiercely under his breath when he found it locked. Then his sharp eyes swept the garden and the belt of trees beyond.

'Ah!' he exclaimed, grabbed her arm again, and rushed her through a door in the wall into the spinney beyond.

There it was a little sheltered, but the ground under the larches and the slender fir-trees was spongy with soaked moss and leaves, while every here and there were boggy patches of marsh that sucked at her useless velvet slippers, but willy-nilly on she was rushed through the trees.

'Oh!' she cried out suddenly. 'My slippers!'

He paused and glanced down at her feet. On one was a wet and muddy stocking, on the other a mushy-looking object that might once have been a pale blue velvet bedroom slipper.

'What the hell . . .' he began, then his eye caught a blue scrap in the mud behind them.

'Where are your shoes?'

'Drying at Teenie's kitchen fire. Those are Miss Tibbie's best bedroom slippers,' she exclaimed indignantly. 'Look what you've done!'

'Can't you put something sensible on your feet?' he scolded back. 'You seem to live in rags of slippers. Stand there and keep your foot up. Lean on the tree.'

He left her propped against a fir, standing like a crane on one leg with the other foot pulled up to her knee, while he returned and retrieved the slipper, and then knelt in the wet moss to draw it on. 'Oh, you're getting wet. You'll be soaked,' she remonstrated.

'Wet?' He glanced up at her with a comically puzzled frown, then followed her eyes to the ground. 'Good Lord, girl, do you think I'm made of sugar?'

'Steady yourself on my shoulder,' he went on, tugging at the soaked slipper, but wriggle her toes as she might the wet velvet would not slip over her stockinged foot. He tugged and tugged, but it was no use. At last he gave it up, shoved the slipper into his pocket, stood up, and, lifting her as if she was indeed the sack of potatoes to which he had so ignominiously compared her, threw her over his shoulder, and clasped her round her knees.

'Be quiet,' was all he said to her gasped remonstrances. Not that they were very effective in any way. Far away down in some unexplored corners of her being Priscilla was exulting over something, she didn't quite know what—the rain and the mud and the dripping branches! The aunts and Sunday evening service at which she would be late! The blue velvet slippers —Old Maitlands and Aunt Purdies and village shops—everything!

He had taken a stride or two between the trees, and now with a shock she saw his wet brown fist take hold of a queer, ladder-like object that descended swayingly from the top of one of the larger fir-trees. The next moment he was ascending it as unconcernedly as a squirrel, paying no heed to her cry and gasp of dismay.

'Keep still or I'll drop you,' he commanded.

Over his shoulder she saw far beneath her the floor of the wood with the heavy drops from the trees splashing on to the dead leaves or seeping into the moss.

'It's all right,' he said gently, as they mounted higher and higher and she involuntarily gripped his shoulder. 'Don't be afraid. I'm not going to drop you. You'll be safe and dry in a moment in the pigeon-hide.'

As he spoke he stepped onto a wooden platform built into the top branches of the trees and roughly thatched with heather—a 'hide' for pigeon-shooters, where they watched for the birds coming in to roost in the evenings.

He lowered her to the shaky floor, where a bundle of heather made a seat. Then he felt the soaked antimacassar, and, unwrapping its green and crimson folds, threw it into a corner. Standing up, he took off his own thick jacket and slipped it round her. It felt warm and dry, but he apologised for it as he sat down beside her in his shirt-sleeves.

'I'm afraid the shawl is spoiled as well,' he said.

'It's not a *shawl*!' she exclaimed, too horrified to laugh. 'It's Miss Prudence's best antimacassar that her grandmother crocheted with her own hand's.'

'By Hexham! I'm in for it all round!' he laughed. Then he turned a little towards her, lifted one of her hands, looked at it, and then laid it back on her knees.

'Well!' he sighed. 'I'll have peace for, say twenty minutes.' He looked at his watch. 'It takes Andra half an hour to yoke a horse.'

'How could you bring me up here?' she interrupted. 'What would my aunties say if they saw me?'

'They won't see you. After manœuvring for days on end to see you alone; after being hunted from pillar to post by peering old ladies—do they think I'm a horse-thief after your horses, by the way?—after telling as many lies as would set up the devil himself for a month of Sundays; after crawling on my knees for an invitation to a woman's tea-party, while Miss Prudence snorted and laughed—do you think I'm going to be interrupted now? Not on your life!' He plunged his hands into his pockets.

231

'But I didn't know you wanted to see me.'

'Didn't you? Then you ought, after telling me you didn't mind about money and shops—and aunts and . . .'

'Oh, but my aunties are darlings,' she said, quickly and inconsequently. 'I love them.'

'Oh, yes, *pets*!' He repeated grimly this favourite word of hers, then went off at a tangent, 'But a man doesn't want a horde of women either shoving a girl into his arms or gathering like a swarm of bees round her to keep him off!'

'I don't want to be shoved into your arms!' Her lips began to tremble. 'I wouldn't be! I didn't want to come here. I want to go home now.'

'That's just it!' he exclaimed. 'I knew that once Miss Prudence started doing my courting I was done for—if I hadn't done for myself already.'

He had drawn his hands out of his pockets and picked up a bit of heather, which he was turning gloomily round and round in his fingers.

'And those two at your house—only two, are there? Do they ever let you out of their sight for a minute? And now you talk of going home! Have you any conception, my girl, what I've been through to get hold of you for ten minutes?'

'What did you want to see me for? You always just scold me,' she said rather spiritlessly. 'And anyhow it isn't any use.'

He sat for a moment gazing out into the tree-tops with lowered brows. His red hair was covered with a mist of fine drops, and his bony, aquiline face still wet with the rain. At last he brought his eyes back from the distance and looked round at her.

'Where shall I begin?' he asked smiling the slightly tender, sardonic smile that always sent her heart off beating wildly.

She shook her head, a lump rising in her throat.

He put out an arm as if to put it round her, but she drew herself quickly away, still aching over those words about being pushed into his arms.

'Miss Prudence told me about the letter,' he went on, turning the sprig of heather round and round in his fingers, 'and said she was going to tell you, and that I was more than one sort of fool and a savage and a robber of—and a robber into the bargain. I've been haunting those stables, stalked by Maudie, who wanted to rub it in about your fortune, ever since your Aunt—Flora, do you call her?—came out to warn me off that day, but they were always about you. But I thought we ought to have it out together, just you and I, without any aunts or old ladies interfering, Priscilla, so I got myself invited to tea when Miss Prudence said you were coming, and trusted to luck to abduct you—and here we are! Are we to have it out, Priscilla?'

Again he lifted his arm, then, remembering his former re-buff, dropped it and took her hand in his instead, holding it out on his open palm and looking at it as if it were something strange and new.

'I don't know,' murmured Priscilla, looking too at her own hand as it lay in his. Her voice was low and hopeless. 'Miss Prudence showed me the letter too, and said Aunt Purdie had forgiven you—but it doesn't make any difference, because—because . . .' Her voice faltered into silence.

'No,' he said, suddenly gripping her fingers and laying back her hand on her knees. He clasped his own together, and, looking straight before him, went on fiercely, 'It does not make any difference, because the main thing, my girl, is not the house or the shop or the blasted money or any damned aunt or old woman in the world. The main thing is—do you love me, Pris-cilla?'

There was no hint of tenderness in his roughened voice, it was more like an accusing demand for the truth than any tender inquiry. His far-seeing eyes—she knew he could watch a vixen at play with her cubs on a distant hillside where she could see nothing—were fixed seemingly on some object far out of sight, but as he spoke he reached out and, taking her hand, gripped her fingers reassuringly in his.

'You don't want me to,' she said at last, hardly above a whisper. 'You said you were just kind to me because I was a *baby*.'

'Yes, we've told each other plenty of lies. Now let us have the truth.' He still looked away as though he would not allow his eyes to use their compelling force. She must find the truth for herself.

They were both silent. The rain now drummed on the thatch in a heavier shower, and gathered in drops on all the needles of the fir-trees. A little brown owl moved in the darker corner of the hide, but Priscilla did not hear it, and, Redd's alert ears telling him what it was, he let it pass. Then suddenly a wood-pigeon with a great clatter of wings shot out of the top of a near-by fir-tree, and, shattering the silence, flew off across the wood. It startled Priscilla so much that she gave a little cry, turning towards him in her sudden dismay.

Instantly his arm went round her, and he drew her close. 'Just a wood-pigeon, my darling.'

The word of endearment in his deep voice broke through all her shyness, and, speaking quickly as if she were afraid of her words, she said, as her head came against his shoulder:

'Yes, I do. Yes, I could—I mean, if you want me to, but you won't let me, and you seem sometimes as if you wanted to lash me off—to make me hate you. How can I like you like that? How can I know?'

Half scolding, half sobbing, the incoherent words tumbled out.

'I'll tell you how you can know,' he took her up quickly and fiercely. 'Would you let the whole infernal mix-up go to blazes and come to me? Would you turn your back on the whole pack of old women and marry me without a yea or a nay from anybody? Would you give up your property and your expectations, whatever they are, and that damned shop you're so keen on, and be as poor as a church-mouse with me? You are free to choose, aren't you? If you don't keep your aunt's shop and property Old Maitland does not get them. They'd go to that old idiot Murdo MacPherson, and he'd stick to them like a leech, and his family after him Would you let him have them, or do they still come first with you? Tell me that!'

Never was there a more tempestuous wooing, but as he spoke a sudden beam of light radiated the world for Priscilla. Of course! What a fool she had been never to think of that solution! Never, never had it dawned on her till that moment that she was free if she liked to pass on her heritage to Murdo, whom her aunt had liked, who would have got everything if she had not written that letter reminding the old lady of her existence.

She thrilled to the fierce, bitter words, like a peregrine to the call of the storm, and a shiver of elation ran down her spine. What did he think, indeed? That she, Priscilla, was afraid of hardship? That she liked a soft existence and a cosy

234

nest better than being really alive and on with a hard struggle? She'd show him, she would! ...

But her spirit was braver than her heart at the moment. After this triumphant but silent declaration to the world at large, and himself in particular, she looked at the stern face, staring out into the rain, the eagle nose, small fierce eyes, set chin, and the up-standing red hair, and her courage dwindled.

'You tell me first,' she whispered.

He turned his head and looked down at her, his hands holding her firmly, the rest of his body as still as stone.

'Tell you what, my darling?'

Only his voice was soft and gentle; his face was inflexible. She hesitated. Then:

'About loving me.' The whisper was lower than ever.

He tightened his arm round her and drew her to his side.

'No. How old are you? Twenty? And I'm just on thirty. What have you got? Everything. You are young and lovely, and surrounded by adoring aunts and old ladies. You have your property and your comforts and your beloved shop. What could you want with an old leather-jacket like me? No money, no fine house, just a cottage of four rooms. Think well. I'm not going to tempt you with love-making or putting everything in a rosy light of unreality. If you realise what it all means, and are willing to leap over the world that lies between us, I'll catch you safe at the other side—never fear about that. But—I can't tempt you, Priscilla, or smother the pill round with jam. I've nothing to offer, and you have everything to lose—that's as plain as a pikestaff. Now shall I take you home?'

She shook her head.

He drew her closer.

'Think—it means Murdo MacPherson taking your house and your shop—that precious shop of yours—your aunts casting you off, probably. It means being poor ...'

She pushed him off, jumped up, and ran to the other side of the hide. A great bunch of heather lay between them.

'Catch me!' she said. 'I'm going to leap right over the world!' And with that she sprang over the heather. He had just time to shoot up to his feet when her little flying figure bounced against him, making him put one foot backward to steady himself as he wrapped her tight in his arms.

235

'That's my girl,' he said. 'It's all right, Priscilla, I'll take care of you. Don't be afraid.'

'It's you that's afraid—you won't even love me or help me. I've had to throw myself into your arms, and I'm not sure yet . . .'

'Not sure?' His genuinely puzzled face was in the shadows as he stood holding her, his shoulders bent under the low roof, his head brushing the thatch. 'Not sure of what, my darling?'

'That you—*like me too*. You've never told me, and you've never asked me to marry you, and you've never . . .'

'Never?' He was smiling down at her in a way that melted her whole heart, with closed lips, tilted a little at the corners, and inscrutable, tender eyes. Then he slowly bent and kissed her, pressing his hard mouth against hers as he tilted her head in the crook of his arm.

'Sure now?' he asked.

She put an arm round his neck and turned her head inward against his shoulder, and she laid his cheek against hers. The little owl in the corner blinked at them; the wind rose, and the rain swished through the opening, wetting him as he stood with his back to it, keeping her sheltered.

'Will you marry me? Will you marry me today? Shall I lift you on my horse and gallop off with you over the edge of the world?'

'Yes,' said she.

'That's my girl—but I've got to look after you better than that. We'll ride off in a dream—but no one will know but you and I. We must go back. Not afraid, are you? I'll be there.'

'I wouldn't be afraid of tigers and wolves and lions if you were there, but . . .'

'Yes—but?'

'I'm afraid of my aunties!'

He laughed, gave her a little shake, swung round with her in his arms, and then set her on her feet and drew out his watch.

'By Hexham! I must get you home, or the whole ladies' seminary will be out hunting the woods to the view halloo.'

He took her hands, liften them, opened them, and put a kiss on each palm, then closed her fingers.

'Those are to keep and give back to me next time I manage

to get you alone.' He cupped her face in his hands. 'Ever been made love to before, Priscilla?'

She glanced up into the fiery yellow-brown eyes questioning hers.

'Just Mr Porter,' she said demurely.

'To the devil with Mr Porter! Have you?'

She shook her head, and he broke into one of his slow smiles.

'I didn't need to ask you that. I'm only teasing you, you little innocent, and warning you I don't make love like Mr Porter. Well, come on home before I run off with you.' He lifted her off her feet and swung down the ladder with her. At the foot he remembered the blue velvet slipper in his pocket, set her up on a tree stump, and pulled it on humming to himself:

> She has kilted her coats of green satin,
>   She has kilted them up to the knee,
> She has kilted her coats of green satin,
>   And she's ower the Border wi' me.

'When are you coming over the Border with me?' he questioned softly.

'I don't know. We'll have to be engaged properly and tell the aunts.'

'Christopher Columbus! All right, little coward. Don't look so scared. I'll tackle fifty aunts. But if they say no, Leezie Lindsay, what then?'

'Have you a very fast horse?' she inquired primly.

With a sudden laugh he picked her up, gave her a last hard hug, then taking her hand rushed through the wood and up the rainy garden. As they entered the conservatory, and he retrieved his coat, she suddenly exclaimed in a voice of awe:

'The antimacassar!'

They both stood dismayed, and then they both laughed.

'I'll get it,' he said, 'and give it to Teenie to dry. Teenie's a friend of mine.' He had taken out his handkerchief and was drying her face and smoothing back her hair with it, picking off the bits of heather caught from the thatch.

'Now,' he said, 'we're for it!'

'Oh, don't tell them now, please,' she whispered, suddenly grown shy. 'Please don't—let me.'

237

'Why? Sure you'd rather?'

'Yes, I would—and the aunts would think I ought . . .' Then in an agonised whisper as he put his hand on the door, 'Redd—quick—what is a Taj Mahal?'

'That's it, little ignoramus.' And he pointed to a marble model of a temple standing under a glass shade. 'An Indian rajah built it for his love. It's a tomb.'

'Oh,' gasped Priscilla, 'a tomb! I thought it was a stuffed bird!'

29

Scenes

Andra drove the three ladies home, in a mixed state of high dudgeon at being kept waiting and high satisfaction because Miss Prudence had bestowed a knowing wink upon him behind their backs.

'Up to her mischief again!' he exclaimed delightedly to himself. 'Eh, what a lassie! Noo what's she been efter this time?'

To Andra Miss Prudence was still more or less the mischievous snipe of a girl who had got him into all kinds of pranks when he first came to the Hall as a round-faced freckled bumpkin of fourteen. Nobody was allowed to find fault with her but himself.

Miss Prudence had risen nobly to the occasion, keeping the conversation going in the drawing-room, and remarking that the young folks were all off, she understood, to see the bull-terrier puppy Dr John had brought up for Leslie, a sister to the one Lindy had.

Luckily John and Lindy had appeared just before Redd and Priscilla, and Miss Prudence with a straight look at John had inquired after the pup and asked if the others were following.

'Sure,' said John, who could also be trusted to rise. 'Redd thinks Miss Leslie's pup will have to have one ear seen to . . .' and at that moment the other two walked in.

On the departure of Priscilla and the aunts her sins found Miss Prudence out, but did not dismay her.

'Many's the lee I've told,' she confessed comfortably. 'I was never one for spoiling other folks' ships for fear of getting a ha'porth of tar on my own skirts,' with which surprising edition of the old saying she completely routed them, since they all fell upon her to correct it, and then quarrelled among themselves about the true version.

Priscilla had made up her mind that she must break the news very gently and gradually to the aunts, who did not approve of surprises, and were as innocent as doves about the under-currents going at Crumstane. They had never met either John or Redd before that afternoon, and were still ignorant of John's engagement to Lindy, though they seemed to have gathered some idea that engagements were in the air.

They were so hearty and yet so mysterious in their praises of John, however, that Priscilla began to fear that they'd got hold of the wrong pig by the tail, as Christy would have said, and was about to put things right when Andra drew up with a flourish at the gates of the Clock House, and it was not till later in the evening that she got a chance, as they were met by Christy bursting with the news that Auld Maitland had called to 'pay his respects' to the aunts. He had waited a while, and then gone off to the kirk.

'I hope you gave him a cup of tea,' said Miss Maud, whose ideas of Auld Maitland always remained vague.

'Tea!' exclaimed Christy. 'I'd as soon give him a dose o' pushion! Na, na, there's no Maitland will get bite or sup in this hoose as lang as I'm here to keep an eye on things. It's mair mischief he's up tae, I'll be bound, the auld deil!'

She went croaking about like an old raven for the rest of the evening, much to Priscilla's dismay, as she did not want Christy to start pouring tales into the ears of the aunts at this stage of her affairs. So far Christy had been too subdued by Aunt Maud's reticence on family affairs to really get going on a good gossip.

Priscilla was still wondering how to introduce tactfully a hint about Redd, when, as they sat chatting by the parlour fire, Aunt Maud completely took the wind out of her sails and swept all her careful preparations for tactful treatment of a difficult subject overboard.

'While you were out, Priscilla, looking at the puppies with the doctor,' said Miss Maud innocently, 'we were discussing things with Mrs MacWhan. She's a very sensible woman, and she thinks with your Aunt Flora and I that it would be a good thing to knock a hole through that wall in the storeroom into the Crees' little house. It would be much more satisfactory for Miss Cree than having always to come through the yard and the house, and it would cut off the shop entirely from the

240

house—the space where the glass-panelled door opens from your kitchen would make a nice large cupboard if it were bricked up.'

Priscilla sat staring aghast at this proposal to knock holes in the wall and pull to pieces the property which, she now considered, belonged to Murdo MacPherson.

Taking her speechlessness for amazed admiration at her cleverness at grasping architectural possibilities, Aunt Maud went calmly on:

'And Mrs MacWhan tells me it would be a great mistake to wait till the spring for our little improvements, as the workmen and artisans are so very busy at this season. The early winter is their quiet time, and we should get everything done in *weeks* that it would take them *months* to do in the spring, so I think . . .'

'But, Aunt Maud,' gasped Priscilla, 'you mustn't!'

'Why not, my dear? Your Aunt Flora and I have decided that Mr Porter's money must be spent in your cause, as he clearly meant it for you. Now the house and shop . . .'

'Oh, no, you mustn't,' Priscilla suddenly electrified both herself and her aunts by declaring. 'I'm giving up the house and the shop. You must put it into *horse-copering,* because I'm going to marry a *horse-coper!*'

So much for Priscilla's wonderful tact!

'Horse-copering!' gasped Miss Maud, as if she were picking up a frog by one leg and examining it. 'What does the child mean, Flora?'

But Miss Flora was absolutely out of her depths, being drowned under waves of awful disapproval at the very sound of the word. 'Horse-copering,' she repeated feebly. 'It sounds like—like *tinkers.'*

'Not even respectable,' gasped Miss Maud. 'Really, Priscilla, where did you pick up such a vulgar term?'

Then she suddenly remembered the last part of Priscilla's speech about marrying.

'Surely,' she asked faintly, 'that young man John is not a *horse* doctor?'

'Oh, no,' said Priscilla, feeling quite gay now the ice was broken. 'That's Dr John. He's going to marry Lindy. I'm going to marry the man with the red hair.'

241

'What!' exclaimed the two aunts at once, both seeming to shrink visibly with horrified dismay. *'Priscilla!'*

'That wild, horsey-looking man in breeches,' gasped Miss Maud.

'Heavens, child,' gasped Miss Flora, 'he looks as if he might *beat* his wife!'

'Yes, doesn't he?' said Priscilla jauntily, more jauntily perhaps than she felt. After all, he had said he would dip her in the horse trough!

Just then Christy announced that supper was ready. They were all relieved, Priscilla because the truth was out, the aunts because they felt sure that this was all light-headed nonsense Priscilla was talking. A meal would do her good and steady her.

Their consternation when they discovered that not only was Priscilla going to marry a horse-dealer, but that she intended giving up the property left to her by the despised Aunt Purdie, was quite pathetic. By this time they had fallen in love not only with the house and its contents, but with Crumstane and the neighbouring families, especially the ladies at the Hall. They even wept, and refused to meet the terrible Redd Maitland.

Christy went up like a paraffin barrel set on fire, burned herself out, and then to Priscilla's amazement began to take her part against the aunts, for Christy was sharp-eyed and saw that Priscilla in spite of her brave front was 'pining', as she put it, and Christy genuinely loved Priscilla.

One day she put on the extraordinary object she called her best hat—it had been passed on to her perhaps ten years before by Mrs MacWhan, and consisted of the entire skin and feathers of a bird the late Major MacWhan had shot in India. On Christy's head it looked partly like an old hen on its nest, and partly like a cat on the prowl. Christy would not have cared if it looked like a tiger ready to spring—it was a good hat. She put on the hat, then, and disappeared on a mysterious errand known only to herself.

On the same afternoon Priscilla had also put on her best hat—not a patch on Christy's!—and gone to Mr Elder, the lawyer, to acquaint him with her decision to relinquish the inheritance.

She went rather sadly. She too had grown to love the Clock

House, but she had only to think of Redd and the little Mill Cottage with its mill lade curving round the garden, its little bridge to the front door and the water-steps with the flowers in the crannies to cheer herself up.

The aunts were, therefore, left alone when two visitors paid a call.

The first was Old Maitland, who, while regretting the absence of Priscilla, at once began to ingratiate himself with the ladies, telling them how he had tried to help Priscilla and even offered her Mysie, but 'young folks would be young folks,' and there you were!

However, he had heard some rumours—he winked at Miss Maud, who stared in return as if he were some kind of Chinese exhibit—and if so be that they were true he would welcome Priscilla into the family, and, what's more, would receive his nephew back into favour if he would come back to the business, and in case they did not rise to what that meant, he assured them that he was 'a warm man' several times and had no one of his own.

Very politely they listened, offered him a cup of tea, and opened their eyes a little when he offered to buy some of the old 'rubbish' in the house—he had heard they were making a clearance, and quite right too. When, however, he discovered that Miss Maud knew a great deal better than he did which was the 'rubbish', and had been offered the highly varnished umbrella-stand and ornate overmantel, he drew in his horns.

'We'll see, we'll see,' he said. 'Ye see, it's a maitter o' sentiment wi' me. Aye, aye, the auld days—there's nothin' like them. That tea-set now—many's the time my auld mother and me had oor teas oot o' it when the auld lady was alive—that's the late Janet's mither. I'd give a ten-pun note to have them—for auld syne's sake, ye ken.'

'Those are Green Worcester,' said Miss Maud drily, and left it at that, while he got himself away with many apologies for intruding, and a warm invitation all round to come over and see 'Auld Maitland', who wasn't such a bad chap, though he and Janet Purdie had had their wee differences.

'Oily old hypocrite,' remarked Aunt Maud as the door closed—and Redd's chances of any approval after his uncle's visit went down to zero.

243

'We must really take Priscilla away,' said Miss Flora. 'I don't think she's seen him since Sunday, but it's difficult to watch her all the time.'

In this she was mistaken, however, having bargained without Redd. He had seen Priscilla more than once, and had heard all about the aunts' horror and opposition, with which he had a certain amount of sympathy when he heard Priscilla's report.

'I told the aunts you were a horse-coper,' said she.

'Holy Moses!' He leaned back, and, after the first dismayed gasp, went into chuckles and rumbled of laughter.

'Well, that's what Christy said you were, and I *like* you to be a horse-coper.'

'You bet I'm a horse-coper then, my darling,' said he, very soberly.

But later, when he lifted her from the manger, where he had set her to talk to her, and held her close for another good-bye:

'You are still laughing at me,' she reproached him. 'I can feel you shaking with laughter.'

'Can you, darling?' he said, hastily swinging her away. 'Yes, I'm still laughing at you.'

But his face looked so little like laughing she was not so sure.

The aunts had scarcely settled themselves down to their knitting and a discussion of Old Maitland, when there was another *rat-tat,* and Miss Flora went to the door.

Her rather short-sighted eyes did not at first recognise the figure on the doorstep; then she caught the gleam of his red hair, and was fixed by a pair of keen, undaunted eyes.

'Good afternoon,' he said. 'I am Redd Maitland. May I come in?'

'Oh!' stammered poor Miss Flora, wondering what Maud would say. 'Oh, yes, I think so.'

He strode silently after her into the parlour, where Miss Maud, on seeing him, rose majestically and laid aside her knitting.

'Priscilla is out, I'm afraid,' said Miss Flora, nervously stooping to pick up Maud's ball of wool, which had rolled across the floor, but he was there before her, swooped up the ball, and, winding the wool round it with his long, lean fingers, laid it on the knitting.

'I know,' he answered Miss Flora. 'That is why I came.' He gave a quick, sardonic smile. 'Priscilla is afraid of us meeting.'

His eyes went to Miss Maud, and the two of them crossed swords, looking straight at each other.

'Why have you come here?' she asked.

'Because I am going to marry Priscilla, and I thought we'd better have it out together. Would you tell me your objections?'

The sentences came out staccato and short. He had his cap and riding stock under his arm, and had evidently just dismounted. They had heard the clatter of hoofs on the cobblestones a moment before.

'Certainly,' said Miss Maud, who could never help relishing an adversary who stood up to her. Then, unlike Miss Flora, who shrank from its frightening strength, she secretly enjoyed the sense of masculine power that had swept through the close room with him as he entered like a wind from the moors.

'Certainly,' she repeated, bracing herself for the encounter. 'In the first place, if you will excuse my saying so, you are not a gentleman, and I expect my niece to marry a man of breeding who will treat her with the consideration she has been used to. In the second place, you have, I believe, no money, and expect your wife to be also your general servant. I do not cavil at that, but in those circumstances you ought to marry a working woman, not a tenderly nurtured child. In the third place, I hear you have a very bad temper, and have already threatened to ill-use her. I think that is sufficient, Mr Maitland. You can go now.'

'I am not going,' said Redd, whose only reaction to these insults was a tightening of the muscles of his face and an alteration in the colour, which instead of a reddish brown had turned the shade of old ivory. 'I must answer your accusations. In the first place, I am of better breeding than you are yourselves. There have been Redd Maitlands of Stanes for over six hundred years. I trace my descent back in the direct line to twelve-sixty-six. My mother's people were the Wolves of Badenoch. My people have made history; the only history the Delaines have made, that I know of, is to have given, as linen drapers, a name to a dress material. Priscilla will change her badge of cotton for an eagle's feather.'

His eyes shot out sparks of anger and disdain, and Miss Maud stepped back before the onslaught.

'In the second place,' he went on, stepping forward so that he still towered above her, 'I am poor, but I have enough money to keep my wife above the necessity of scrubbing floors or cleaning my boots, as you seem to think I should ask Priscilla to do, and I have a stud of horses that will in time be second to none in the country.' He paused as he saw a slight sarcastic smile lift Miss Maud's long upper lip, took out a worn leather case, and extracted a paper. 'As Priscilla's guardian, I admit your right to what proof I can give.' He passed the paper, and she saw it was the offer to Mr Redd Maitland of three hundred and twenty-five guineas for a young hunter. It was signed by a name that made Miss Maud start and lift her brows. 'There is the cheque!' He passed it, then, as she returned the papers, slowly strapped them back into his case, and put it into his pocket. 'As for number three . . .' He smiled his close-lipped smile, standing silent and looking down at Miss Maud till she glanced up at him, when an answering smile suddenly dawned on her face. 'You don't believe that,' he said emphatically.

'We'll let number three go,' she agreed, and there was another interval of silence.

'Well, you can boast loudly enough, young man,' she said at last, tartly.

'Yes,' he said, 'I can boast when necessary, and I can forgive insults when Priscilla's aunt offers them—or'—he shrugged his shoulders—'any woman, for the matter of that—and I can make my own way, and look after my own girl, and—I intend to marry Priscilla.'

'You know, Maud, I like this young man,' suddenly came in Miss Flora's voice from behind them, interrupting him.

'He seems to have won his spurs,' drily acknowledged Miss Maud. 'And now I think after this unseemly row and exchange of insults a cup of tea would calm us down. Sit down, young man. I can't see you properly up there—and ring for Mrs Cree to bring in the tea. And now'—she turned to Redd—'the necessity for boasting is ended will you please tell m

246

exactly who you are and what you propose to do about Priscilla?'

That was how Priscilla found them when she came in and halted white-faced and frightened in the doorway of the parlour.

'Come in,' said Aunt Maud, 'and tell me if you really want to marry this ferocious young man, or if he has put the fear of death into you if you refuse. *I'm* not afraid of him, if you need rescuing.'

'Oh, Aunt Maud!' said Priscilla, and ran and hugged first Maud and then Flora. 'Oh, I'm so happy!' Then she stood stock-still and stared at a figure coming up the street. 'Oh, but what will Christy say?'

'A good deal, I dare say,' said Miss Maud drily.

Redd rose.

'Shall I tackle Christy?' he asked Priscilla. 'I'm not going to have her worrying you.'

'Not in her best hat,' laughed Priscilla, in a shaky voice to cover her nervousness. 'Christy is so thorny and superior in her best hat, and she said she'd never get over this.'

The words were hardly out of her mouth when Christy, forgetting, as she acknowledged later herself, 'a' her manners,' burst into the room, a basket in each hand from which protruded a pig's snout in one and a string of black puddings in the other.

'They've killed ower at Merton,' she said, explaining the baskets, 'and, eh, Priscilla, everything's a' right. Murdo says it never entered his mind to sue ye for the property.'

'You didn't go to Mr MacPherson and ask him not to?' gasped Priscilla.

'And wherefore should I no? The likes o' him disna need your bit hoose and shoppie—but I never needed to press him; he's ower ta'en up wi' his pigs. "Haud yer tongue and dinna talk havers," said he to me. "Thae lawyers only want to get the money for theirsel's. Afore we were done there'd be nothing left, and what pit it into yer heid I was gaun to sue the bit lassie? Ye surely think I've little adae." Then he took me oot to see his new Tamworth boar—but gi'e me Middle Whites every time ...'

'But he wouldn't have needed to sue me,' interrupted Priscilla, 'only, you see, I've been to see Mr Elder, and both Mr

Elder the elder and Mr Elder the younger say I can't give up the Clock House or the shop because the law won't let me, because they are mine whoever I marry as long as I don't sell them to Old Maitland, and that Redd is never mentioned, and he's only a nephew, and has nothing whatever to do with his uncle, and anyhow there's no *word* of Old Maitland getting them, so what am I fussing about . . .' She stopped, out of breath after this rather confused outpour, and Redd rose and said good-bye, very plainly indicating this was none of his business, and they had better thrash it out together.

When he had gone Priscilla turned on Christy indignantly suspecting her of some deep scheme of her own.

'It doesn't make any *difference* about the house, Christy, so you needn't think you are stopping me marrying Redd by making me have to keep the house and shop. Aunt Purdie would have understood. She forgave Redd. She liked Redd and knew it was all a mistake about him helping his uncle!'

'Fine I ken ye'll gaun yer ain gait,' stormed Christy now the Indian fowl cocked in battle formation over one eye 'You've made yer bed, and ye'll lie on it . . .' She stopped as Priscilla's knees suddenly gave way and she fell into a chair turned her back on them, and, putting her arms across the back, broke into heaving sobs.

At once Christy ran across, and, kneeling, put her arm round her.

'There now! There now! Dinna ye greet, ma wee croodlin doo. Auld Christy's nobbut blustering like a wind that maun blaw itsel' oot. Redd's a fine upstandin' lad, and him and m will make up oor differences to please ye. I never thocht as il o' Redd as I said, but I had to keep the Purdie end up. Dr your een, like a good lassie.'

'Will you come to my wedding?' demanded Priscilla from the folds of her handkerchief.

' 'Deed will I—and dance the cock-a-bendy. Will that su ye?'

'We'll all dance the cock-a-bendy at your wedding,' sai Aunt Flora, adding her portion of comfort without th vaguest idea of what the cock-a-bendy was.

'Well!' said Miss Maud sensibly. 'We've had plenty scenes for one day. Go and take off your things, Priscilla, an then come down and help me to make a list. We'll need t

248

give a small dinner-party and announce the engagement properly.'

Aunt Maud was starting to enjoy herself.

'I saw it was no use going against a determined man like that,' she excused herself to Flora later in the privacy of their room. 'Priscilla should have introduced him properly without all that horse-copering nonsense. I saw at once he was well-bred, if a little startling, and that we'd been making a mistake. I must say I do like a man that *is* a man.'

'Well, he'll be a change for Priscilla from us old ladies,' said Miss Flora, with a sigh and a laugh mixed up.

At that moment Christy knocked and came in with the hot water.

'We were just remarking,' said Miss Flora, thinking it as well to let Christy know that the ban had been lifted from Redd, 'that now Mr Maitland and Priscilla are engaged we'll have to give a small party to announce it.'

' 'Deed aye,' said Christy, as though she knew all about it, 'a pairty would let the folks see ye weren't hangin' back. When's the weddin' to be?'

'Oh, there's nothing settled yet. We were just saying it would be a great change for Priscilla from being with her old aunts . . .'

'Weel, a change o' deils is lichtsome,' said Christy, and departed.

They looked at each other with raised eyebrows—and then laughed.

They were coming on.

30

The Taking Men

So after all Priscilla did not have to give up the Clock House and the shop. To satisfy themselves the Misses Delaine went and interviewed the lawyers themselves, and came home having made a new friend in Mr Elder—the elder. It appeared he collected snuff-boxes, a sort of side-line of Aunt Maud's, and took her and Aunt Flora to see the ancient one still in use in the Lammerton Council Chamber, and then into Old Maitland's shop to see the one that had belonged to Redd's forebears and had a king's signature scratched on the inside, and which Old Maitland still had in daily use.

Miss Maud took the opportunity to make some inquiries of Mr Elder about the old man. 'He seems a wily old fox,' said she, 'and very different from his nephew.'

'Yes, he is,' said Mr Elder. 'He'd wile money out of a stone, but he had done his best for his nephews. Redd left him in high dudgeon, but the old man has tried to help him secretly—not with any success, I admit—and though that rascal, his sister's son, cheats him right and left, and he knows it, he keeps him on, so that he won't get into mischief with strangers. As we say hereabouts, even the deil's no sae ill as he called. I'd never trust him an inch about money matters, but if ever I wanted help for a Maitland I'd know where to go. Once your niece marries Redd she's safe—the clannish spirit, I suppose. He'd never do her an ill turn once she bore the name.'

'Well, I'm glad to hear that,' said Miss Maud, 'for he gave me the feeling that none of us would be a match for him if he really set himself against us. I sometimes wonder how old Miss Purdie and Priscilla ever got the better of him.'

'Well, there you are—Redd's the answer to that. As soon as Redd caught him putting out his horns he made him draw

them in again. "Maitland warred Maitland never", as the saying goes, and that doesn't exactly mean they never fought
each other—far from it—but that they never *cheated* each
other.'

Mr Elder then took the ladies to his house and gave them
a bachelor tea, and they came home quite satisfied that Priscilla's heritage was safe, and that she could keep it with an
easy mind.

The next difficulty was what to do about the house and
shop.

Redd said that he was going to live at the Mill House till
he could afford a bigger place, and that if Priscilla married
him she was going to live there too, and *he* was going to keep
her, and not a penny of anybody else's money would he
touch.

'And what is she to do with it?' asked Miss Maud indignantly, thinking of Mr Porter's legacy as well as Aunt
Purdie's.

'She can keep it for your great-nephews and -nieces,' said
Redd, looking her straight in the eye. Miss Flora blushed, but
Aunt Maud was made of sterner stuff.

'Quite a good idea,' said she, 'but I'd like Priscilla to have
some comforts.'

'I'm putting in hot water and a bathroom,' said Redd
patiently, 'and having an electric-light plant—there's a grand
fall of water just going to waste from the mill lade. Simmons's eldest girl is coming as a maid, and I've engaged a lad
to be Priscilla's own groom-gardener and odd-job man. I have
a nice little filly picked out for her. We'll have out own cow,
pig, poultry, geese, ducks, and so on, but Simmons's wife looks
after them. Is there anything else you can suggest? I want
Priscilla to have everything I can give her. What I cannot give
her now she will have as I can afford it, but I'll give them myself. Neither her Aunt Purdie's nor Mr Porter's money is
going to keep my wife.'

'Hoity-toity!' said Aunt Maud, and then they both laughed.
The two were beginning to understand and respect each
other.

As for Aunt Flora, she secretly kept to herself a sort of terrified fascination for her nephew to be.

'I think that is all very satisfactory,' went on Aunt Maud, 'but what is to be done about the Clock House?'

'Why don't you and Miss Flora come and live in it yourselves, and spend the money improving it?' asked Redd.

This brilliant idea immediately appealed to them, and from that moment the house was a buzz of plans and excitements.

They liked Crumstane, and were very fond of Priscilla. They adored the house and its contents, and could not bear the thought of anyone else taking charge of them. They had struck up a great friendship with the ladies at the Hall, Dr John, and even Mr Lamont. They renewed their youth at the thought of redecorations, turning out attics and arranging and polishing old furniture and selecting pieces suitable for the cottage. The china and silver would, of course, all go to Priscilla. They had plenty of their own to come from Baxton.

Miss Maud's idea of breaking through the wall between the Crees' house and the shop was to be carried out, and Mysie was to run the shop, but as a partner with Priscilla.

During these weeks before the wedding Redd saw so little of Priscilla alone that he asked her how many of the old ladies were coming with them on their honeymoon.

He had caught her coming from the garden, and rushed her into the harness-room, where a wintry sun caught her red ribbon as he set her on the deep window-sill and told her that he had almost forgotten what she was like, and that they would have to be introduced on their wedding-day, and he'd have to start wooing her all over again, after which nonsense he drew her nearer still and whispered, 'But I'll love that. It will be such fun to woo you, Priscilla, you're such a little thornbush!'

'Well, you did have chances, but you never did!' Priscilla's English was not always Wordsworthian.

'Never did what, my darling?'

'Be nice to me or try to make me l—like you. I had to like you all by myself. You never helped me—you just scolded.'

'Did I?' He seemed genuinely surprised, and then after a fiercer frown than ever went on, 'But how could I try to help you, my little sweet? How could a scarred old leather-jacket like me dream of making you like me? Look at my beak of a nose and my grizzled hair—one of the first things you

252

told me was that you hated red hair—and my ugly lined face, and then think of your slender girl's body and small soft witch-face. No, don't think of all that, or you'll maybe run away, and what should I do then?'

'Come and catch me again. Oh, but I couldn't lose you either, Redd. Hold me tight—as tight as ever you can!'

He laughed softly, drawing her so tight that she had to cry out.

'As tight as I can! All your little ribs would crack if I weren't terribly careful. I wish there was more of you to hold. When am I going to see you again?'

'You're seeing me now.'

'Am I? I don't call snatching a moment . . . Oh, Lord, there's an aunt calling again. Have you got those kisses safe? I've never got them back. Don't you lose them.' He opened her palms and kissed them again. 'There's another two—that's four to give back to me—and here's one to take.' And he bent back her head into his elbow and kissed her long and deliberately, with Aunt Flora clucking and calling just outside the door like an anxious, feathery old hen. Then, swearing softly under his breath such mild expletives as he thought fit for her ears, he swung Priscilla to the door, just as the old lady was about to poke in her innocent old head.

'Oh, there you are, Priscilla! Didn't you hear me calling? Miss Pinn wants to try on that frock . . .'

But there were not many of even such short interludes as this. Not only were the aunts old-fashioned in their notions of propriety, but there was so much to do, as Redd was determined they must be married before Christmas—because he'd bought her present, he said—and December was nearly in.

The cottage was ready all but the finishing touches, which Priscilla wanted to do herself, and she was dying to try the new little cooker, hand up the curtains, switch the electric lights off and on, and play with all the gadgets Redd had put on, for there was so much power that with lights everywhere in cupboards and outhouses and of course in the stables there was still enough to spare.

'And *no* electric light bills,' she assured Aunt Maud, who was shaking her head over them. 'The water goes on making *for ever*. Redd says so.'

'I wish we didn't need to have a honeymoon,' she told

Redd. 'I'm just dying to try the cooker and the Ideal boiler, and to wash in the soft water out of the lade, and there are all those bulbs and flowers to put in for the spring. A honeymoon is just a waste of time!'

'I believe you are just marrying me for the cottage,' he grumbled. 'I saw you looking at it with an envious eye that very first day when you sat in the sun on the mounting-stone.'

'Well, it's so lovely with the mill-wheel and the moss and the little bridge over the moat, and the ferns dipping into the water, and the thrush in the old pear-tree, and . . .'

'Just what I said.' He stood smiling down at her. 'I don't seem to come in anywhere.'

'But you'll be there, always everywhere, won't you? I wouldn't want anything without you too—not even the thrush singing in the pear-tree . . .'

There was only one answer to that, interrupted as usual.

'Quick! There's Aunty—go and sit over there—quick!' And Aunt Maud's head came in at the door.

'Dear me, I've been looking everywhere for you, Priscilla. Miss Pinn . . .'

In the end there was a double wedding, for Dr John and Lindy decided to be married on the same day, and the Misses Selby insisted on holding the reception at the Hall, as they were dying to open up and use the great old rooms which had stood shrouded for so long in holland covers.

It was no use pleading for a quiet wedding, so everyone was there. Old Maitland, looking like a bridegroom himself in his smart trousers and frock-coat and a pink geranium in his buttonhole, Mr Elder the elder, and Mr Elder the younger, the former most attentive to Aunt Flora, looking plump and pretty in her flowered silk.

Christy had a new dress of so bright a blue it fairly dazzled the eye, and a new hat with a blue feather—chic wasn't the word! She was smiling grimly but happily, having assured Priscilla that she had quite forgiven Redd for her sake.

'When all's said and done,' she had announced, 'Redd Maitland's a man to ride the water wi'.' Than which no greater praise could be given on the Borders. 'Aye, his forbears were Taking Men, and he's anither o' that ilk—the red-headed deil that he is.'

Priscilla knew that the 'Taking Men' was the old name for the Border reivers and raiders of whom it was sung:

> Let them take who have the power,
> And let them keep who can.

'But Redd isn't *taking* me, Christy. I'm giving him myself.'

'Aye, that's as may be. I aye knew that if Redd wanted you he'd get you; nobody would stop him but hissel'—no but what he'll treat ye like a wee queen and love ye truly. Redd can look after his ain. *He'll* no time his jewel.'

And she went off rattling the milk pails loudly unless anyone should think she was giving way to sentiment.

Maudie, tossing her head and vainly trying to hide her chagrin at being her sister's bridesmaid instead of being able to crow over her about dancing in green stockings, was the only one that didn't look happy, but nobody was troubling much about Maudie. Even the best men seemed both to prefer plain, shy little Mysie, whom Priscilla had insisted should be her bridesmaid, and who looked too happy to be really plain that day.

When it was all over one car went out of the village to the north, and the other to the south.

Once the northward-bound car was well out of the place Redd turned from the wheel with a half-smile.

'Your Aunt Flora looked as if she still thought I might beat you.'

'She does think so. I think that's really why they've taken the Clock House.'

He was silent for a few moments as the road twisted and turned over a mountain torrent.

'Well, perhaps now,' he said, his eyebrows frowning as he peered through the windscreen, 'I'll get a chance to make love to you. Most men make a start before they get married, but I'll have to begin where I left off at the top of a tree! By Hexham! Did ever another man have to run off with six old ladies after him and mount with his girl over his shoulder up a ladder into a pigeon-hide to get a chance to propose to her!'

He put his foot down on the accelerator and raced along as if he thought the six old ladies had picked up their petticoats and were tearing down the road after them. Priscilla laughed, and put her cheek against his shoulder as he slowed down.

'Where are we going for our honeymoon?' she asked meekly, this point never having been settled.

'Where there are no old ladies,' he said grimly, 'and where I can beat you without twelve hundred aunts looking on!'

Priscilla seemed undismayed. 'I wish we were riding away,' she whispered, 'like that night you rode with me in the rain.

He drew up the car and stopped. Just then a flake of snow fluttered down from the grey sky, and before it had melted on the bonnet the air was full of softly falling flakes.

'Priscilla,' he whispered, putting an arm round her and drawing her close, Let's go home. I hate cars, and I hate hotels.'

'Oh, Redd, so do I.'

'It's going to be a storm. We'll be as lost to them down there as anywhere, and I'll take you riding in the snow. You can switch all the electric lights off and on, and try your new stove —I'll light it for you. The pantry and cupboards are stocked; there are chickens and eggs and geese and ducks. We'll have a roast chicken for supper, shall we?'

'Oh, I'd love it—and potatoes and bread sauce, and I'll put up the curtains and draw them over the windows, and we'll listen to the wind driving the snow over the moors.'

'And I'll have time at last to make love to my little sweet.'

He backed the car, turned it round, and, tucking one of her hands tightly between his arm and his side, went hurtling back through the blowing snow while she leaned against him with her cheek on his arm.

If you would like a complete list of Arrow books please send a postcard to P.O. Box 29, Douglas, Isle of Man, Great Britain.